Joel Sacks

CITY OF CARDS

Produced by:

FriesenPress

Suite 300 – 852 Fort Street
Victoria, BC, Canada V8W 1H8

www.friesenpress.com

Distributed to the trade by The Ingram Book Company

To the memory of my father Saul who loved to regale me with stories of his time in the O.S.S. during World War Two.

Much thanks to Ken & Kristin Navarro, Beth Farber and of course my lifelong partner Ann for their support and feedback. A special thanks to Jeff Bieber (no relation to Justin) without whose ideas and criticism this book would never have been written.

PROLOGUE

November 2001

S ayid Hassan loved thunderstorms. He loved the brilliant streaks of lightning, the struggle of trees arching against the wind, the sudden drop in temperature and the occasional punctuation of pelting hail. He especially loved them at night, when the hypnotic wall of sound from rain hitting the roof would lull him to sleep. He was so taken with that sound that he swore someday he would build a house with a fountain on the roof just to hear it every time he went to bed. But the biggest impression these storms had on him came from the booming thunderclaps that resonated in his chest, although he couldn't imagine a machine able to replicate that. His earliest recollection of sleeping through a thunderstorm came at age eight while attending summer camp in the mountains of western Massachusetts. He couldn't recall ever hearing thunder as a young child living in a middle class suburb of Cairo, but after his parents moved to Boston and he'd witnessed firsthand nature's awesome display, he always relished the experience.

Curled under layers of blankets as he drifted in and out of sleep, the muffled rumbles off in the distance transported him back to the Berkshires of his youth. Outside his tent, others could be heard scurrying for the protection of the caves from what was about to be unleashed, but not him. He would wait for the wind to ruffle the canvas, for the rain, gentle at first before erupting into torrents of water and lastly, for the white flashes followed by those great explosions of sound. As the rumbles grew louder and the fog of sleep started to lift, he remembered where he was – not in the bucolic woods of the New England mountains, but in the barren hills of eastern Afghanistan – and he knew. In the pit of his stomach he knew. The growing crescendo of thuds outside his tent were not the result of super-heated air from lightning, but from high explosive bombs dropped from American B-52 war planes some six miles above in the blackness of the night sky.

Sayid willed himself awake, threw a blanket over his shoulders, crawled outside his tent and like the other fighters around him, ran for the safety of the cave. Along the way he saw a couple of men dousing fires and others searching for their weapons, but most like he, simply scampered for shelter. Once inside the cave, he tried to calm his racing heart by sitting down beside a small fire and taking slow, measured breaths. He wasn't sure why the cave didn't fill with smoke from the fire – perhaps there was a natural chimney – but he was thankful for the warmth. With only a thin blanket for a coat, it was better to die of asphyxiation than from freezing. He looked at the other fighters huddled around the flames. To call them soldiers would be an overstatement. They ran the gamut from young teenage boys to wizened old men who looked to be in their eighties but were probably much younger. Some were religious jihadists or part of the Taliban, but many seemed to owe their allegiance to local warlords or smugglers of jewels, currency, hardwoods and of course Afghanistan's biggest and most profitable exports, opium and heroin. A few spoke Arabic but most only Pashtu or Dari, of which Sayid knew but a smattering words.

Sayid was living in a world that a year earlier he could never have imagined. He sat by the pathetic flames warding off frostbite from his fingers, trying to come to terms with how he'd arrived at this place, at this point in time. The men and boys surrounding him had only the slightest clues, gleaned from fuzzy images seen on a television in some village or from photos in a newspaper, of what life was like in societies not mired in the Middle Ages. Their prejudices against modernity had been learned since birth from parents, elders and mullahs, so in a way, they couldn't be blamed. With one exception, Sayid had received more formal education by age ten than anyone else in that cave had in their lifetime. He held advanced degrees from some of the most famous universities in the world and had lived in great cities of the West like Boston, London and Paris. But from his outward appearance, you couldn't tell any of that. His clothing was as tattered, his hair as unkempt, and his face as dirty and unshaven as any of the others.

For the hundredth time in recent days, he wondered if this wasn't the biggest mistake he could have made. And for the hundredth time, the answer was the same – perhaps. He held citizenship in two countries, Egypt, the land of his birth, and America where he became a naturalized citizen at age fourteen. He hadn't started down this path expecting to be in a shooting war with his adopted country. It was the rulers of his native land and their Saudi supporters he wanted gone. America had opened up paths to choices and opportunities in life limited only by his talents and work ethic, and for that he was thankful. For most men of his generation who'd grown up in this part of the world, the concept of meritocracy was as foreign as the pilots flying the jets above. These men's success in life relied primarily on their familial connections. And as for women, well not even their bloodlines would afford them much in the way of choosing for themselves what kind of life they'd lead. Yet American citizenship did not bring with it any sense of belonging. He never felt truly accepted in society, although he spoke English without a trace of a foreign accent and with his light complexion, he could easily pass as being of European descent. He never changed his name or adopted a nickname and he never shied away from his family background, which inevitably kept him from feeling like a full member of the body politic. This quasi-alienation probably explained why he had chosen to live in Europe as an adult, although he discovered that things weren't all that much different on that side of the Atlantic. He was well on his way to building a successful career as an economist but even a respected job with a large income could not free him from a sense of isolation and the feeling that his life lacked purpose. Hence the questions, and hence no answers.

The bombs stopped falling. Sayid felt sensation return to his fingertips, which meant no frostbite. He had survived. He rose to his feet and sought out the only other person in camp that he conversed with, Ibrahim Fuad. Ibrahim was the de facto leader of this group. Like Sayid, he was Egyptian by birth but had spent most of his adult life in Saudi Arabia, first as a student and later a professor of history at King Abdulaziz University in Jeddah. He was a young assistant professor teaching his first class in 1979 when by chance he had as one of his students the son of a wealthy Saudi businessman with close ties to the royal family. The student's name was Osama bin Laden. Ibrahim often remarked that, as a student, bin Laden was so reticent to speak in class that he was sure that Osama would end up as a bookkeeper closeted in some office building owned by his father. So much for predictions.

Sayid spotted Ibrahim quietly speaking with two Taliban fighters who had just returned from the cave where Osama was holed up. When Ibrahim finished with the fighters, he motioned to Sayid to come over. "What is happening?"

"We should speak in English so as not to alarm the others," Ibrahim told him. "There is an American brigade about seven kilometers away. They have stopped for the night but will probably be here by mid-morning once the sun comes up."

"How large a brigade?"

Ibrahim rubbed his eyes. "Not sure how many soldiers. But there are twenty or so armored vehicles and tanks. Plus we can assume they will be backed up with air support from jets and helicopter gunships."

Sayid heard the strain in Ibrahim's voice. He knew the situation was bad and for the first time contemplated the real possibility of capture by the Americans or death. As he looked at the others in the cave, he realized that the latter held no dread for them. Quite the contrary, for these boys and men, death in the service of jihad was something to be cherished. For him, the gift of paradise for martyrdom was not something he particularly aspired to achieve.

"So what are we to do?"

Ibrahim had already started to walk away and didn't answer. He shouted to the men to run out of the cave and retrieve as many light weapons as they could, but to leave behind any heavier arms that could not be easily carried. Immediately the youngest boys obeyed. He turned back to Sayid.

"There is a plan. We are going to agree to a cease-fire with the Americans. We will turn over our weapons, at least some of them. That will buy us time to escape."

"Escape? To where?"

"Pakistan. There are routes through these hills that the smugglers use and, God willing, we'll evade the Americans. They won't attack us in Pakistan. There we will regroup."

Just as Ibrahim finished, a deafening explosion only meters outside the cave entrance knocked them both to the ground. The force of the blast blew out the campfire and the cave quickly filled with smoke and dust. The scene was chaotic and, for an instant, Sayid was unsure whether he had been seriously hurt or for that matter, whether he was even alive. Two additional blasts from slightly farther away convinced him that he was still very much of this world.

"Are you okay?" Ibrahim asked him.

"I think so. And you?"

Ibrahim again did not reply but turned on his flashlight and stood to survey the situation. The air was slow to clear and the beam from the flashlight cast eerie shadows on the ground. Groans from the injured echoed through the cave. Sayid made his way outside to clear his throat. His eyes were stinging and teary and he couldn't clearly see the ground in front of him. He stumbled over what he at first thought was a tree branch but reaching down to toss it away, realized was a severed arm. He recoiled in shock and quickly dropped the limb before pulling out his own flashlight to see what surrounded him. A few feet away he spotted a body. He ran over to it and recognized the clothing as that of Mohammed, a fourteen-year-old Taliban fighter.

"Mohammed," he shouted at the body but there was no response. "Mohammed, are you all right?" he repeated in Arabic and turned the body over. He tried but could not find a pulse. Sayid pulled the blanket off his shoulders and gently covered the corpse.

"Sayid, we have to move," Ibrahim said but Sayid remained kneeling over the body. "Sayid! Daybreak is only an hour off and the Americans will be here soon after."

Sayid sat down on the ground beside the dead boy. "What's the point? We can't escape."

"The Taliban will stay and hold them off. It will give us time to go over the hills and into Pakistan." Sayid didn't move. "If we stay, we will be caught. We know too much." Still Sayid remained motionless. Ibrahim pulled his AK-47 off his shoulder and aimed at him. "Sayid. Get up now."

Sayid turned his head slowly up towards Ibrahim. "What are you going to do? Shoot me?"

"I have no desire to kill you. You know I like you. But I can't risk having you captured. The Americans will soon enough figure out who you are, and you and I both know that you will not withstand their torture. It's nothing to be ashamed of. Few men could withstand it."

Ibrahim's voice was void of emotion and Sayid did not doubt that he would pull the trigger. He slowly got to his feet. "This whole experience can only be described as Kafkaesque."

"What did you say?"

"Kafkaesque. You know, Franz Kafka? The author?" Even in the darkness, he could tell by Ibrahim's blank expression that he had no idea who Kafka was, and Ibrahim, a one-time college professor, was by far the most educated person around, other than himself. "Doesn't matter. The Americans don't torture. I will stay and fight."

Ibrahim took a sip of water from a canteen and handed it to Sayid.

"Your years of living in America taught you nothing of their army. Perhaps the students you went to college with wouldn't kill you but I can tell you from personal experience, their military and CIA will do anything if they think you know something."

Sayid remained unconvinced, but was too spent to argue. He took a sip of water before handing the canteen back to Ibrahim, then simply nodded. He returned to what remained of his tent, found his backpack and rifle, slung them over his shoulder and prepared for the trek that lay ahead. Ibrahim introduced him to a local smuggler also named Mohammed who would serve as their guide through the mountain passes. This Mohammed, like his dead namesake, spoke some Arabic but no English. A half dozen other men from countries spread across the Middle East and North Africa joined them for the attempted escape.

By the time the sun broke over the mountain peaks in the east, they had managed to cover nearly five kilometers. With luck, they would cross the border into Pakistan in a day or two. No one spoke as they traveled, which was fine with Sayid. He was still trying to process all that he had experienced in the previous hours. Around noon they stopped to rest and have some food. Sayid was too tired to eat. He stretched out on the ground, used his backpack as a pillow and covered his head with his jacket to block out the sun. He had just nodded off when he felt a boot kick at his feet. He looked out from beneath the jacket and there stood Ibrahim, cutting off hunks of lamb from a shank bone. "Eat," he commanded. "You need your strength."

"I can't remember the last time I slept for more than an hour. I'm not hungry." He pulled the jacket back over his face. "How much farther till we cross the border?" His voice was muffled by the coat, but intelligible enough.

"Tomorrow night. Friday morning at the latest, providing we don't run into more of your countrymen." Ibrahim pulled the jacket off Sayid's face and flung a piece of lamb on his chest. "You'll get sick if you don't eat. The locals have a tradition when travelling. They leave those who take ill under a tree by a stream to die. You want us to leave you here?"

Sayid picked the meat off his shirt and took a bite. "I don't see any trees or streams around."

"The other option is to just put you out of your misery and shoot you," Ibrahim laughed.

"Where are we anyway?"

Ibrahim cut another piece of lamb and handed it to Sayid. "The people call this Spin Ghar. It means White Mountains in Pashtu."

"Doesn't remind me of New Hampshire."

"Why should it?"

"They have their own White Mountains, but covered with trees. In the fall, the colors the leaves turn are spectacular. People come from far away just to see it. Hotels and inns are booked for months, sometimes years, in advance."

Ibrahim spat out a piece of gristle, which ended up in his beard.

"Typical Americans. They like their vacations and their other comforts. Look at what we're going through. They can't conceive of the sacrifices we are willing to endure in the name of Allah. That is our strength. That is why we will prevail. The fact that so many of our fighters are willing to die for our cause scares them to death."

Just then, the percussive low-pitched thumps of high-explosive ordinance in the distance could be heard. Mohammed, their guide, ran towards them pointing at several high-flying jet fighters above. The group quickly gathered their rifles and other belongings and followed Mohammed along a small footpath until they reached an area beneath a rocky outcrop. Seconds later an explosion tore open the ground where just moments before they had stopped to rest.

"I'm glad our strategy of scaring the Americans is working so well," Sayid said sarcastically to Ibrahim.

"I didn't see where that one came from, did you?"

Sayid shook his head. "They can drop their bombs from many kilometers away and be long gone before they detonate. Besides spending on vacations, Americans spend a hell of a lot of money on their military, and they love their technology."

Mohammed whispered something in Ibrahim's ear to which Ibrahim nodded.

"It's too risky to travel now," he told Sayid. "Mohammed says there's a cave on the other side of this hill where we can wait until night. Let's go."

The rock-strewn paths along which they walked were filled with places where one false step could find you falling a hundred feet or more to your death. Traveling at night sounded suicidal to Sayid, but what other choice was there? He followed well behind the rest of the fighters. At least a cave would be dark and perhaps he could sleep. By the time he arrived at the cave, Mohammed had already started a fire near the entrance and was boiling water for tea. Ibrahim gathered the other fighters a little deeper inside and instructed them to sit in a circle as he explained what the plan was. Not caring to hear it again, Sayid found a spot a well back from the cave entrance where it was darker, and stretched out on the ground. He watched as Ibrahim, who must have sensed that the Americans' overwhelming firepower was affecting his fighters' morale, began to lecture. It was something that his years as a professor made him particularly well suited for. He began by saying that since the time of Alexander the Great, western powers have met with only defeat in Afghanistan. *Alexander the Great?* Sayid thought to himself. *These men wouldn't know Alexander the Great from Alexander Graham Bell or Alexander's Rag Time Band. Ibrahim forgets who he's speaking to.* Sayid rolled over on his side and tried to ignore Ibrahim's voice but the walls of the cave only amplified his words.

Ibrahim went on to recount how in the 1880s, the Afghans under Ayub Kahn defeated the British at Maiwand, and of course, how the muhajideen drove out the Soviets. *At least he's getting closer to this century and telling them something they can relate to. The older ones probably have firsthand memories of the Soviets.* Ibrahim reminded his audience that bin Laden himself gave up a life of wealth and comfort in Saudi Arabia to fight for years alongside other Muslims in that struggle, and that fighting for the truth as revealed by the Prophet was the only route to salvation. Just as he'd done in delivering the Afghans from the Russians, Allah would surely deliver them victory over the Americans. Ibrahim reached into his pocket and pulled out frayed and yellowing clippings that he'd saved from various newspapers containing pictures of the crumbling World Trade Center towers and the Pentagon on fire.

What Ibrahim failed to mention in his little speech was that the defeat of the Russians would probably not have happened without the advanced weapons supplied by the United States. While he didn't deny the bravery and skill of these al-Qaeda fighters, Sayid knew that from the long bows of Henry V at Agincourt to the atomic bomb at Hiroshima, military technology often determined the outcome of war. Sure, al-Qaeda could recruit men to fly a plane into a building, but they could never build the jet in the first place. As long as the Western nations were willing to empty their treasuries on their military, their vastly superior weaponry would prevail and the Middle East despots, Sayid's real enemies, would maintain their grip on power. At least bin Laden had got it partially right when he went after the Twin Towers, although Sayid was convinced that was just coincidental. The World Trade Center, by its name alone, symbolized the underpinnings of America's strength, which is to say, its economic power. With a weakened economy, the U.S. and her allies couldn't afford to maintain their global military superiority. A severe economic downtown in the West would have the side effect of reducing the oil revenues that kept the Saudi royals in power, and without the flow of money from the Saudis and the Americans, Mubarek in Egypt would be hard pressed to maintain his rule. But it would take something far more significant than bringing down a couple of skyscrapers to wreck an eleven trillion dollar economy, something that was way beyond the capabilities of al-Qaeda.

Sayid turned back towards the men and saw how they gawked in admiration at the photos of 9/11, like adolescent boys drooling over a Playboy centerfold. It was only then that he realized that the fighters who were fleeing to Pakistan with him and Ibrahim were all about the same age, late teens or early twenties. Whether or not it had been voluntary, the old and young had stayed behind to take on the Americans. Sayid knew that the greatest obstacle to overthrowing the regional despots was the fact that while these fighters spent their days learning how to make improvised explosive devices and reading the Koran, their counterparts in the West were in universities studying medicine, physics, engineering and economics. Ibrahim of all people should know that, he thought. If Ibrahim really wanted to recapture Islam's glorious past, the model for that society could not be found in the repressive totalitarian rule of the Taliban but in the grand Islamic-led societies of places like Moorish Spain, where art, architecture, math and science flourished at a time when Christendom was staggering through the Dark Ages. That version of Islamic rule promoted tolerance and respect for men and women as well as for other religions, allowing Muslims, Jews and Christians to live harmoniously together. And most of all, they valued education.

He thought back to his own days as a student at the Massachusetts Institute of Technology. Those undergraduate years were among the happiest he could remember, surrounded by other intellectually elite and highly motivated students who enjoyed taking on the mental challenges of classwork while coping with the responsibilities and emotions of being on their own. In one way his MIT classmates were like every other student on the cusp of adulthood, convinced that their generation had the insight and intelligence to avoid the mistakes of previous generations and remake the world as something better. Being in a highly selective environment of the best and brightest only heightened this conceit. He thought of the classes he'd taken, the friends whom over the years he'd lost track of, and those few professors who influenced his choice of profession. If only he'd stayed in that profession, he'd not be lying on a bed of rocks, tired, cold, hungry and on the run from an enemy he couldn't even see. He recalled that first undergraduate economics course he'd taken. Suddenly, he sat up as though he had just been stung by a scorpion. "That might work," he said aloud to no one in particular.

Ibrahim noticed and came over. "Are you all right?"

A sly grin came over Sayid's face as he glanced up at Ibrahim. "It just might work," he repeated.

"What might work?"

"It's a bit of a long shot, but I may know a way of defeating the Americans. It can't be done through suicide bombers or crashing jets into buildings. It will take some time, maybe years, and it depends on two bedrocks of American society, greed and hubris. There are a lot of reasons why it won't succeed, but from what I've read of George Bush's philosophy of government, it just might work."

"That's quite a statement."

"I understand your skepticism."

"Remember my young friend, victory will come to us through the righteousness of our cause and the courage of our soldiers. While you were living a life of comfort in Paris, our leaders were in places like this cave fighting and dying in holy wars. They have experience that you do not."

"I did not mean to insult or diminish any of what has been accomplished. But you must admit that the success of 9/11 had as much to do with the U.S. underestimating our capabilities as it did with the performance of the men who carried it out. There is a phrase their politicians love to toss around – American Exceptionalism they call it, and the population seems to accept it as fact. They now know that we can launch asymmetrical attacks on them and so they will adjust accordingly. What they'd never expect, never believe possible for an organization like al-Qaeda to have the resources and skill to pull off, would be an attack on their economy sophisticated enough to cripple it to the point that they could no longer pursue their military policies."

"The leadership still believes that we will defeat their army."

Owing to fatigue, fear, and the reality of the situation, Sayid snapped. "What planet are they living on?" he shouted. "Look around you! We are no more than a fleeing rag-tag group of men, forced to travel at night like rats because we're rightly too scared to travel by day. If the leadership truly believes a military victory is possible, then they're guilty of the same mistake the Americans made about us."

"And what is that?"

"As I said, underestimating the capability of your enemy." Sayid sensed by Ibrahim's reaction that maybe he was starting to get through to him, and he quickly began to map out in his head the broad outline of what would be needed to put his plan in place. At a minimum, it would require a large financial investment and al-Qaeda, for all the looseness of such a shadowy organization, never seemed to lack for funds.

"If I were to put together a plan, could you get me a meeting with whomever it is that would need to approve it?"

"What types of resources are you looking for?"

"Really all I need is funding."

"How much?"

"I won't know for sure until I've done more research."

"Can you give me an estimate?"

Sayid closed his eyes and did some quick math in his head. "Fifty million, maybe more, maybe less. That's just a stab at a number."

"Dollars?" Sayid nodded affirmatively. Ibrahim let out a slow breath. "That's quite a big stab. An amount that large would need approval of senior leadership, and it will be a months before we are settled enough to get everyone together."

"That's okay. I can use the time for research and write up a business plan. Can you get me the meeting?"

"Bring me your plan. I'll show it around to a few people and if they think it's something to consider, you'll have your meeting. Now get some sleep. We will be moving out as soon as it's dark. Praise be Allah."

Ibrahim walked back to where the rest of the fighters were preparing for prayers. Sayid tried to go back to sleep but his mind was racing. The mournful chants of the men praying left Sayid pondering the extent to which Allah, if there were such an omnipotent being, would intercede in his plan, and if so, on whose behalf.

ONE

Cambridge, Massachusetts, 1992

For many of the quarter million or so college students living in the metropolitan Boston area, the spring of 1992 was an exciting time. The anticipation of warmer weather after a long and dreary winter was augmented by the upcoming presidential primary contests. For this segment of the population, far more politically engaged than the American populace as a whole, politics were often the topic of casual conversation and the occasional heated debate. Although the incumbent president, George H. W. Bush, was the presumed Republican nominee, the Democratic challenger was far from certain. Most were attracted to candidates who could be classified as liberal, or at least iconoclastic. The darling of many was the intellectual former Massachusetts senator, Paul Tsongas, who seemed poised to win the first-in-the-nation primary in neighboring New Hampshire. Others were supporting better-known names like Tom Harkin or Jerry Brown. And then there was the governor of Arkansas who was getting a lot of play in the national media. When the conversation turned to him, most remarked on how he lacked experience or name recognition – and Arkansas? He might as well have been from Armenia, leaving most students to pay little attention to Bill Clinton.

Jacob Himmelfarb wasn't paying attention to any of the candidates. Jake, as everyone called him, was far too preoccupied with the upcoming men's college basketball championships and with sex, not unusual interests for a man his age. The irony was that Jake had little direct involvement in either. He was decidedly un-athletic, to the point that he was cut from his high school junior varsity basketball team, a somewhat dubious if no less remarkable feat considering that no one had ever achieved it before or since. His dismissal from the squad probably had more to do with Jake's non-stop commentary on the coach's game-time strategy than his abilities on the court, although his lack of skill on the hardwood was certainly a factor. As for sex, being a student at the predominantly male Massachusetts Institute of Technology afforded little opportunity for meeting available young women. Those he did rarely elicited any sexual desire, which for a twenty-year-old straight male, says something. When friends back home asked him about the dating situation, his standard response was that MIT co-eds were on campus to prove Newton's third law of motion – that every action has an equal but opposite reaction. Whereas girls at other colleges often aroused a boy's libido, his actual term was "give you a hard-on," the reaction that MIT women caused was a "soft-off."

Jake was in his junior year at MIT. A math major from Brooklyn, he lacked patience for classwork, especially those courses requiring copious amounts of reading and writing. This made the fact that he had made it through nearly three years at such a rigorous university with a GPA just below 4.0 all the more surprising. He had been judicious in his course selections, choosing as many classes as possible that dealt in quantifiable subject matter and where the final grades would be determined on exams rather than class participation or in-depth research papers. His luck ran out that spring semester when he had exhausted all of the high-level math courses and needed some humanities credits if he was to graduate on time. He chose an economics course because, of all the courses available that could go towards fulfilling this requirement, he assumed it would be the most math-based with a minimal amount of writing, and hopefully, no term paper. He was wrong.

Jake knew nothing of Adam Scott Meecham, the professor of a course with the seemingly benign title of "Economics for Engineers and Scientists." Had he bothered to read the course description in the catalog, he would have seen that A. S. Meecham was a Nobel Laureate in economics and he might have thought twice before enrolling. He arrived at the first class ten minutes early in order to take a seat in the last row near the exit. The room was typical of the smaller MIT classrooms, with about twenty desks lined up in rows and one large desk in the front facing out. He always arrived early to the first class in order to check out the other students. His purpose was twofold. First, he wanted to get a sense of what his competition was in case the professor was one who graded on the curve. Second, he always took note of the female students just in case there was that one co-ed who might be the exception that proves the rule. As students began to filter in and take seats, he quickly resigned himself to the fact that this group was much like the other classes he had taken, overly male, overly Asian, and underly attractive.

Jake sensed he was in trouble when Meecham walked in and handed out a syllabus. There were to be no exams and the final grade would be based solely on a term project, which meant writing a research paper. No sooner had he finished reading the syllabus than he began thumbing through the catalog of courses searching for an alternative class to transfer into. As he was dog-earing pages with possible substitutes, Meecham wrote on the blackboard: "*Science is a wonderful thing if one does not have to earn one's living at it. – A. Einstein.*"

"Unfortunately, most of you sitting here will, at some point, have to earn a living, and it behooves you to have some knowledge of how to go about it. Knowing what forces drive commerce may come in handy."

Meecham spoke deliberately with a refined British accent, the kind of voice that convinces the listener that whatever is being said must be profound and true, even if it is mundane and concocted. He went on to explain that their project would entail developing a business plan for a new enterprise and then writing an analysis of how certain basic macro-economic principles factored into the plan. Jake heard none of this, nor Meecham's instructions about how the class would be organized into small groups to work on projects together. Meecham went on to say that as he had done in previous years, he was going to arbitrarily assign students to groups. Since there were eighteen students enrolled, he decided that there would be six groups of three students each.

Meecham pulled a class roster from his briefcase and began reading names in alphabetical order. Jake assumed that the professor was taking attendance, which he found a bit insulting at this stage of his education, but it was the first day. Meecham read the first three names and Jake was befuddled when the students whose names had been called rose from their chairs and took new seats next to each other. Jake whispered to the boy sitting next to him and asked what was happening. He was informed that they were being assigned to their groups. Groups? For what? Jake looked at the kid, a nerd even by MIT standards, with thick glasses and a shirt pocket full of pens and knew for sure that there was no way he was staying in this class if he was going to have to spend extra time with people like him.

Meecham continued calling out names. "Hassan." A tall skinny kid in the front row replied, "Here" and stood up. "Himmelfarb." Jake froze. Should he acknowledge his name, or sit quietly and sneak out of the room when Meecham's back was turned? "Mr. Himmelfarb?" Meecham asked louder, before bellowing out his name a third time. Jake slowly rose from his seat. "You are Mr. Himmelfarb, I take it." Jake nodded sheepishly. "Come, come, Mr. Himmelfarb and meet your new business partner, Mr. Hassan." Jake started to say how he had a scheduling conflict and was unfortunately going to have to drop the class when Meecham called out the next name "Miss Jang." Jake could see only the back of the slender girl who got up from a chair in the first row. He assumed by the name and her long silken-straight black hair that flowed all the way down to the small of her back that she was Chinese. He hadn't noticed her enter the classroom, but he pictured a buck-toothed girl with acne and glasses with Coke-bottle lenses. She picked up her backpack, pivoted towards Jake and flashed him a quick smile. He nearly gasped as he stumbled into the desk in front of him. She was one of the most exquisitely beautiful women he had ever seen on campus, with large, dark almond-shaped eyes, a perfect nose, the complexion of a porcelain doll and lips he could only dream of coming into contact with.

"You were saying something Mr. Himmelfarb?" Meecham asked.

"Um, no, uh yes, uh … where should I sit?"

"I trust your writing style is more articulate than your verbal abilities would seem to indicate." Meecham continued reading out names.

Jake took a seat between his new colleagues. He did his best not to stare at the girl seated to his right, but it wasn't easy. Whenever he sensed that his ogling was becoming obvious, he made it a point to look at his other project partner seated to his left. Questions kept running through his mind – what was she like, did she have a boyfriend, would she find him attractive, was the guy to his left competition, and so on. Meecham finished assigning students to their groups and began to deliver his opening lecture. Hassan opened a new spiral-bound notebook and scribbled circles on a page with a ballpoint pen to get the ink flowing. Jang reached into her backpack and took out one of those new portable computers, an Apple Powerbook 100. Jake was impressed. He knew a few kids that had laptops, but most of the computers that students owned were of the desktop variety. Jake couldn't afford to own any computer, so he was relegated to using the ones in various computer labs scattered across campus. "That's really cool," he said to Jang. Not the greatest of pickup lines, but at least it had the qualities of spontaneity and appropriateness.

"Thanks. I really don't know how to use it yet, but it was something my father insisted I have. God help me if I lose it, 'cause my father will kill me."

"Yeah, they're pretty pricy."

"I know, and to be honest, I can write faster than I can type."

"Then why use the computer?"

"My writing, fast as it is, is often illegible. I guess that's because I'm left-handed and was taught to write using my right hand. At least with this, I can read what I write."

"So you're a southpaw."

"A what?"

"Southpaw. Lefty." He could see she was confused. "In baseball, they call left-handed pitchers southpaws."

"Why?"

It was something he'd never really considered before. In sports in general, and baseball in particular, traditions are simply not questioned. Perhaps that's what makes sports so enduring and ingrained in society. "I'm not really sure. Maybe it's because most baseball fields run along an east-west axis, so when a pitcher stands on the mound, his left arm faces south."

"I see. So righties are called northpaws?" Again something he'd never thought about. His first instinct was to laugh derisively, but he stifled himself so as not to seem condescending. He tried to think of a response, it was after all, a logical assumption, but he said nothing.

"Shouldn't you take out something to take notes with?" she finally asked.

Taking notes was something Jake never did and he especially saw no need to do so now since he had two others to rely on for that. But again appearances meant something, so he took out a notebook and prepared to write. Unlike the others, Jake used the rest of the class time not to listen to

Meecham's lecture, but to scour pages he had cut out from that morning's Boston Globe, New York Times and Daily News sports sections. He wasn't interested in the outcomes from the previous night's games, he already knew those results. What he was looking for were reports of any injuries and the morning lines on upcoming professional and college basketball games. For as long as he could remember, Jake had been fascinated by the subject of probability. Being endowed with a mind that could easily and quickly solve complex mathematical equations, he had developed a talent for setting odds on sporting events. Even more importantly, he recognized when others, in his opinion, had mis-set those odds. His uncle Lenny, a somewhat degenerate gambler, had been lucky enough to pick up on Jake's talent when Jake was only twelve. At least once a week, he'd call Jake for advice before calling his bookie. Jake was right far more often than he was wrong, and for the last year and half, he'd been supplementing his income by having his uncle place bets for him. Had his mother known what her younger brother was having her son do, she might have committed fratricide. Jake's other source of income came from playing poker in several regular games held mostly at fraternity houses around Cambridge. He was not nearly as successful at cards, but that stemmed more from the fact that poker requires as much ability in reading your opponents' state of mind as on determining the probability of a winning hand.

"My name is Mia." Jake was still reading about basketball and unaware that Meecham had finished his lecture and class was over. He looked up from his notebook and saw Jang's hand extended toward him.

"I'm Jake Himmelfarb." He took her hand and stared into her eyes. He couldn't help but smile.

"I'm Sayid Hassan."

Jang had to struggle to release her hand from Jake's grip. Jake's failure to respond to Sayid was not intended as a slight, it was just that his mind was obsessing on Mia, and the fact that the Chicago Bulls were only four-point favorites over the Knicks, which he knew was a steal.

"Oh, hi," he said finally. Sayid Hassan, no doubt an Arab, Jake concluded. Jake's opinion of Arabs had been shaped by years of listening to his parents' and other relatives' unabashed support of Israel and that country's endless conflicts with her Arab neighbors. He didn't fully share their Zionist zeal for Israel's welfare or their fear of Arabs. It wasn't for lack of understanding the history. A dozen years in a Jewish day school had seen to that. It was just that for as long as he could remember, he'd been hearing tales of how this family member had barely escaped the Nazis in Poland, or how that second cousin never made it out of Auschwitz. And the stories always ended with the obligatory "never again." But the Holocaust happened long before his birth. As Jake saw it, the relatives who'd perished might just as well never have existed, and as for the survivors who actually faced the Nazis, they never, ever spoke of their experiences. Of course it would never happen again, the world was a far different place from what it was in 1940. And as for Israel, of course it would prevail over the Arabs, if for no other reason than that Israelis are that much smarter than their neighbors, or so his thinking went. His only concern now was that this Sayid kid might harbor some ill will toward Jews in general, which could translate to him in particular.

Before leaving the classroom, Jake, Mia and Sayid agreed to meet later that afternoon at a luncheonette just off campus. Mia and Sayid had wanted to meet right then, but Jake explained that he needed to contact his uncle first. Immediately he regretted his honesty and he covered his story by saying that it was Lenny's birthday, and he always called his uncle on his birthday.

"That's so sweet" Mia said with a heartfelt smile. Jake returned the smile, and not lost on him was the irony that his mild prevarication seemed to have impressed her.

Jake was the last to arrive at the eatery. Mia and Sayid had taken seats across from each other at a booth and Jake faced his first decision, where to sit. Sitting next to Mia had the advantage of close physical contact, with the possible accidental brushing of arms and legs. As bad as his instincts were when it came to women, Jake chose to sit next to Sayid, which in his mind made it look like he was playing it cool, even hard to get. It also made staring at Mia appear more natural, not as though he was salaciously picturing what she looked like without clothes on, which of course, he was. Sayid and Mia were both sipping coffee when a waitress asked Jake what he'd like.

"I'll take a Coke, and a menu."

"Pepsi okay?" the waitress asked.

"No. I'll just have water." The waitress rolled her eyes and walked away. Jake tapped out a short drum roll on the tabletop. "So, either of you guys have any ideas for a great new business that'll get us 'A's?"

"We were kicking around some concepts," Sayid said. "I was thinking about setting up some sort of business that would build IBM compatible PCs outside of the U.S. where labor is cheaper."

Jake shook his head. "I don't like it. The cost of shipping would probably off-set any labor savings."

"However, these cheap computers could be sold around the world to less affluent societies, so shipping would actually be cheaper."

Jake laughed. "That it'll never work, and for a number of reasons. These less affluent societies," Jake raised his hands to motion air quotes around those last words, "wouldn't be able to afford even the cheapest computer. And even if they could, let's be honest, they don't have the education to be able to use them. And lastly, you need a well-trained, highly intelligent work force to build something as high-tech as a computer. That just aint gonna happen in any third-world country." Immediately he regretted what he said, not because he didn't believe it to be true, but because he was afraid that he might have offended Mia.

"Maybe, but what's your idea?" Sayid asked.

This was a problem, because Jake had no ideas. He glanced over at Mia who was busy typing on her laptop and seemed to be ignoring the boys. "Have you ever used the UUNET? Imagine if you could easily connect your computer to a lot of other computers and have access to all sorts of information, such as databases and the like."

"The world wide web," Mia blurted out from behind her laptop screen.

"What?" asked Jake.

Mia pulled down the top of her screen so she could see the faces of her classmates sitting across the table. "Last semester I heard a lecture by Tim Berners-Lee about a concept he came up with while working in Switzerland. I didn't understand it all, but the gist of it was that he foresees the day when anyone with computer access can tie into a large network of computers and access files on various servers."

"Not likely," said Sayid. "First off, you've got incompatibility issues. MS-DOS, Apple O/S, Unix, and so forth. And how would computers tie into the network?"

"Berners-Lee said they'd solved the compatibility issue by coming up with a standard protocol for encoding files – hyper something or other. He said people could use modems to tie into the network over phone lines."

Sayid shook his head. "I've used modems to access bulletin boards. They're slow and really finicky if there is any noise on the phone lines."

Jake was pleased with the direction of the conversation because it seemed as though he and Mia were on the same page with Sayid being the contrarian.

"Yeah, but if you could solve those problems, imagine the possibilities. You could get your news, see what's playing at the movies, read reviews of restaurants and shows," he said.

"But how do you make money?" asked Sayid. "Remember, we are supposed to be developing a business."

"Maybe you could sell things," said Mia. "You know, like L. L. Bean and those other catalog stores. You could have your catalog available on people's computers. You could collect the money by credit card."

Jake perked up. "You could open up a computer casino. Allow people to bet on sports, maybe even develop a program that lets them play games like craps and blackjack."

Sayid and Mia instantaneously responded in unison with "What?"

Jake knew he was in trouble as Mia skeptically shook her head. "I think that would be against the law."

"No, not if it was done by legitimate casinos, like in Vegas or Atlantic City or Foxwoods down in Connecticut."

"I don't think Meecham would be impressed with the idea of a computer casino," she replied.

Jake thought about it for a moment. "Probably not, but I think your catalog idea is a good one. What next?"

Mia closed her laptop and stowed it in a backpack. "Why don't you both come back to my place? It's only a few blocks from here and we can draw up an outline and present it on Thursday." The boys both nodded, and Mia signaled to the waitress for the check.

"Excuse me for a minute, I've got to visit the lady's room."

"She's very nice," Jake said after she left.

"She's a knock-out," Sayid responded.

"That's rather sexist, don't you think?"

"Oh come on now, don't you think she's gorgeous? Her face, those high cheekbones, those eyes, and that body. Don't tell me you hadn't noticed."

Jake took a long sip of water. "I noticed all right. I'm kinda surprised you did too."

"Why are you surprised?"

"I don't know, maybe because of where you come from."

"I come from Medford."

"I meant with your name, where your family came from."

"I'm Egyptian, not gay."

"No, no. I thought that maybe your cultural background prevented you from noticing things like women." Jake knew the more he said, the worse things sounded and while he wasn't looking for a friend in Sayid, he didn't want to antagonize him either.

"Don't you guys keep all the women covered up from head to toe?"

Sayid began to snicker. "You've never been to Egypt, I'm guessing. Maybe in Saudi Arabia the women are all covered, but Egypt is different. Anyway, I've been living in America since I was four, and I'm not blind."

Jake didn't reply. Despite Sayid's potential as a rival for Mia, he was beginning to like him. "I'm sorry if I sound stupid. Pretty girls have that effect on me, and to be honest, I have a hard enough time getting dates and any competition doesn't help."

Sayid laughed loud enough to draw the attention of those seated at the nearby tables.

"You needn't worry about me. I could never date her. My father would inevitably find out, and then he'd kill me. Well, not literally kill me, but he'd cut me off, stop paying for school and living expenses."

"Because she's not Egyptian?"

"Because she's not a Muslim." Jake nodded in agreement. "You understand?"

"Yeah, I understand. If I brought Mia home to my parents, they'd have a similar reaction because she's not Jewish, only it would be my mother who'd take action. I can picture the scene. We'd show up at their apartment. They'd invite us into the living room. My mother, being extra courteous, would bring in some coffee and rugullah on a tray, offer some to Mia, take a look at my father, then go back into the kitchen and stick her head into the oven."

"What?"

"Stick her head in the oven so that the gas would kill her. At least that what she always says she'll do, not to me directly, but when she's talking with her friends at Mah Jong. Of course, what she keeps forgetting is that the oven is electric, not gas, but that wouldn't deter her."

"Hold on, hold on. What is ruggulah? And what is Mah Jong?"

"Ruggulah are small pastries usually filled with nuts and fruit. Quite good actually. And Mah Jong is a Chinese tile game that's played by old Jewish women."

"What do Chinese women play?"

"I have no idea, probably canasta. Maybe Mah Jong too."

"If they do, then Mia and your mother have something in common."

"Perhaps, but she's been planning my wedding to Debbie Moshman since I was born. Debbie's mother and my mother have known each other for forty years."

"What's she like?"

"Debbie's mom?"

"No, Debbie."

"Oh, she's all right. Maybe a little on the chubby side, but very zoftig." Jake held out his two hands in a cupped fashion in front of his chest and Sayid nodded indicating he understood. "She laughs a lot and likes to drink and have a good time."

"So what's the problem?"

"Debbie is not the sharpest tool in the shed, if you get my drift. She attended community college in Long Island for a year, but had to drop out. Last I heard she was working as a receptionist in her father's dental office."

"So the two of us are saddled by the religious and cultural limitations of our parents," lamented Sayid.

Mia returned to the table. "Did the check come?"

"I've got it," said Jake.

"How much do I owe?" she asked.

"My treat," said Jake.

"But you didn't order anything," she said.

"I insist."

"Thank you. That's nice."

"I'll meet you outside," Jake said as he glanced at the bill and reached for his wallet.

"Sayid, wait a second, I've got a question for you." Jake waited until Mia was out of earshot. "You got ten bucks I could borrow?" Sayid shook his head, reached into his pocket and handed Jake the cash. "Thanks. I'll pay you back tomorrow."

"Don't worry about it. Like Mia said, you didn't eat anything anyway. Are you still intending on pursuing her?"

"I'm gonna try."

"But your mother?"

"She's in Brooklyn. That's two hundred miles from here. What she doesn't know won't hurt her."

"Good luck. My father would find out somehow. But then again, he lives only twenty minutes away."

Jake left the money on the table. "My mother will find out as well. She always does," he whispered to himself. "Besides, she probably already has a boyfriend."

Mia lived in a two-story wood frame house not far from campus. As they neared it, Jake noticed a blondish haired boy sitting on the steps that led up to a small front porch.

"Oh shit," Mia said. "Wait here guys, this will take just a minute." Jake strained to hear their conversation while he and Sayid kept a respectful distance. The boy appeared upset at whatever Mia was saying to him, and after a few minutes, he walked away.

"Sorry about that," she said when Jake and Sayid came over to her.

"Who was that?" Sayid asked.

"Him? Oh, he's my boyfriend." Jake glanced skyward and wondered whether his mother had somehow managed to make sure that the one cute non-Jewish girl at MIT already had a boyfriend. "Well he *was* my boyfriend."

"Was?" Jake's interest was suddenly piqued.

"Yeah. I broke up with him last night."

"He seemed upset," Sayid said.

"I guess. It's a shame because Tyler's a nice guy. I hate hurting him."

Jake didn't hesitate to offer advice. "Listen, if he's not right for you, you're both better off moving on."

"The thing is, maybe he is right for me. It's just that my parents were giving me hard time about my seeing him." Mia pulled her keys out of her pocketbook and unlocked two deadbolts on the front door. "In case you didn't notice, he's not Chinese."

"Jeez, I can't believe it." Jake did his best to sound shocked. "In this day and age, how can people be so prejudiced?"

"Yeah," Sayid chimed in. "I've never heard of such a thing."

"Well, that's the way it is with ethnics, or at least in the Chinese community. Come on in."

The house where Mia lived was neatly, although sparsely furnished. She invited them to sit in the living room while she went to the kitchen and began to boil water for coffee and tea. Sayid took a seat on the couch while Jake walked around the room, noting the titles of the books that, along with a few photographs, filled a shelf against the wall. He picked up a framed picture of a slightly younger Mia standing arm-in-arm with another girl who could have been her twin atop the Great Wall. He was amazed that there was another girl as pretty as Mia somewhere out there, not that it would do him any good, except in his imagination. Mia returned.

"You've been to China," he said to her.

Mia walked over. "Several times." She gingerly took the photo from Jake and slowly ran her fingers over the face of the other girl.

"Your sister?"

"Toni. She's sixteen months older. That picture was taken two months before Tiananmen Square. She was studying in Bejing."

"Where's she now?"

She placed the picture gently back on the shelf. "I don't know. We haven't heard from her since before the massacre."

"But that was like three years ago."

"I know." There was an awkward moment of silence. Jake recognized that he had hit upon an obvious source of pain, but he didn't know what he could say that wouldn't sound patronizing, or worse.

"Shall we get back to the project?" she finally said.

"Oh no," Sayid said looking at his watch. Jake had all but forgotten that he was in the room. "I'm sorry, I have a class to get to. Look, whatever the two of you decide is fine with me. Just give me a call tonight and fill me in."

Jake watched as Mia showed Sayid to the door. He couldn't take his eyes off her body, an enticing combination of athleticism and curvaceous softness. Based on what he'd seen with regard to her ex-boyfriend, he knew as betting man that the odds did not favor a romantic relationship. Yet he couldn't remember ever experiencing such a sudden, deep infatuation before. It would be worth the attempt, even if failure were the overwhelmingly likely outcome.

She came back to where he sat on the couch. "Have some tea?"

"Ah, no. I'm not much of a tea drinker."

"Can I get you something else? Coffee, soda, water, juice? I'm sorry I haven't any beer or wine. I usually keep some on hand, though I don't drink."

A little straight-laced, he thought, which further diminished his prospects, but it was his increasing nervousness around her that was really hurting his cause and he knew it.

"No, I'm fine really."

"Care for a smoke?"

That offer surprised him. It was incongruous that a girl who didn't drink would smoke. "No thanks. I don't smoke."

"Mind if I do?"

"No, it's your place. Go right ahead." She walked over to the bookshelf and opened a small box made of polished teak and ivory. From it she took out a small glass pipe, lighter and a small baggie from which she withdrew a pinch of marijuana and filled the bowl of the pipe. She lit up, took a long drag and returned to where Jake was sitting.

"Oh, I thought you were going to smoke a cigarette. I didn't know you meant pot."

She burst into laughter as smoke poured from her mouth. "God no, cigarettes are disgusting."

"But you don't drink."

"It's a physical thing. The alcohol affects me in weird ways. I turn bright red and often get a horrible headache. It's like an allergic reaction, the histamine or something." She took another hit off the pipe.

"Sure you don't want some?" she asked while still managing to hold the smoke in her lungs.

Jake shrugged. "Maybe just a little." He took the pipe from her hand. "Aren't you afraid about the others, or do your roommates smoke as well?" he asked before inhaling.

"What roommates?" Jake took a hit and immediately broke into convulsive coughing.

"I should have warned you, it's a little harsh, but it's pretty good shit." Mia took the pipe back from Jake, took another hit and again handed it back to him. "I don't have any roommates."

Jake was careful this time to inhale a much smaller amount. Briefly he held in the smoke before exhaling. "You mean you live here all alone? It's a pretty big place. How can you afford the rent by yourself?"

"I don't pay rent. My father bought this house last year. For what he pays in mortgage payments, less the tax deductions, it costs less than renting. When I'm through with school, he'll either sell the place at a profit or if I stay in the area I can continue to live here. I don't understand the economics of it all, but he says the way the tax laws work, he takes what most people consider an expense of college and turns it into an asset."

The effects of the pot suddenly hit Jake like a wave crashing on the shore of his cerebral cortex. "Your father's a pretty clever guy. I'd like to meet him."

"Hah. No you wouldn't. He's one of the most humorless people I know. Five minutes with him and you'll realize why there's a stereotype of Asian-American parents who push their progeny to overachieve. Anyway, aren't you getting hungry? I'm famished. The pizza place down the block is pretty good, especially when you're high."

Jake sat there half immobilized by the intoxicating combination of the marijuana and Mia's eyes. It was all he could do to nod his head in agreement and he followed her out the door and into the chilled early evening air of Cambridge.

Three days later, the three students prepared to present their concept for an Internet-based business to Dr. Meecham. In the intervening time, the group had long discussions over the phone to finalize their plan. In the end they decided to let Jake act as spokesman since he was the one who had first hit upon the idea. He hadn't seen Mia since they'd gone to dinner but she had been in his thoughts virtually non-stop, verging on an obsession. He didn't remember much about the dinner. He couldn't even recall what kind of pizza they'd eaten but he did remember they laughed a lot. No doubt the marijuana was mostly responsible for that since Jake wasn't known for his wit. He had wanted to ask Mia about the dinner but feared that her recollections might have been less favorable than his. It was better to live with a fantasy than to risk a disappointing reality.

The group strode confidently up to Meecham's office, the door to which was partially open. Jake knocked on it to announce their arrival. The professor sat behind a large oak desk covered with papers, folders and books. He barely acknowledged their presence and didn't look up from whatever he was reading. Only a brief wave of his left hand let them know they could come in. There were no chairs so they stood silently waiting for him to speak.

"Is it bigger than a bread box?" he finally said in an ominously deep voice that imparted a sense of impatience, if not outright disdain.

"Uh, excuse me?" Jake responded.

Meecham still didn't look up. "Since none of you seemed eager to tell me about your concept, I assumed you wanted to play twenty-questions and have me guess."

Jake looked at Mia and Sayid who both wore the same mixed expressions of embarrassment and trepidation.

"No, I wasn't sure if you were done reading and ready to listen," Jake said.

Meecham glanced up at the group, not looking pleased. "Mr...." he pulled out his appointment book.

"Himmelfarb," Jake said.

"Yes. Mr. Himmelfarb, in case you were not aware, reaching the level of a tenured professor at this institution requires that you demonstrate certain abilities. I, for example, had to prove that I could do more than one task simultaneously by standing before the board of trustees and reciting a Shakespeare sonnet while juggling three oranges."

"You're kidding," Jake exclaimed.

"Yes."

"Oh."

Meecham's sarcastic barbs cut at Jake's ego and he realized he needed to proceed in a more cautious manner. Even so, Meecham stopped him before he'd spoken for twenty seconds.

"Is this an Internet business?" he asked. Jake nodded. "You are the fourth group today to come in here with that idea. I'll tell you what I told the last two, think of something else."

"But we've already spent a lot of time planning this," Mia burst out with.

"Well then," Meecham glanced down at his appointment book. "Ms. Jang, I suggest you spend a little more, only use it in a more constructive manner. Am I wrong in assuming that you came up with more than one concept during all of your long deliberations?"

"Of course we did," Jake quickly replied.

"Good. Tell me one of them."

Jake could see that his partners were becoming more than a little irritated by Meecham's dismissive attitude. Or perhaps they were just panicked. He, on the other hand, found it stimulating. Before him sat a man of great intellect who clearly did not suffer fools and who challenged Jake's own intellectual prowess. It was now a contest, and Jake loved contests, although his reactions would have to be fast and well thought out if he were to earn Meecham's respect.

"How about this. Students all over this city are faced with housing problems if they cannot or do not want to live in dorms. For the vast majority, this means renting either an apartment or a room in a house. Tax laws favor owners over renters."

Meecham interrupted, "The hardest thing in the world to understand is income tax."

Jake stood there without a clue as to what the professor's point was. Meacham didn't look up from what he was reading. "An Einstein quote. Continue."

Jake took a deep breath. "What if instead of renting, students could have those payments accrue towards mortgage payments?"

"And how would you do that?"

"A corporation would own the properties, that is, they would be capitalized and take out the mortgages on the properties. They would collect the rents from the students, but instead of just being landlords, those rents would actually count as investments in the property, and by extension, the corporation. As equity grew in the property, both through the paying down of principle and the natural increase of real estate values, the students would be gaining assets."

Meecham stopped reading, clasped his hands behind his head and leaned back in his chair.

"Interesting. I suppose at some point the property could be sold and each of the renters would receive a payment from the profits on the sale based on how much they paid in."

Jake knew he was on a roll and didn't hesitate to challenge Meecham.

"The problem with a sale, as Einstein could tell you, is that it would create a capital gains tax liability for the students. A better solution would be that as the value of the property rose, you refinance the mortgage to take out the equity. That equity can then be distributed tax-free to the student investors because there was no sale of an asset but simply a loan was made."

Meecham pushed further back in his chair, to the point that Jake feared he would tip over. He suddenly sprang forward. "Okay, go with it. It will require more research into the tax implications, as well as the downside risks if the market destabilizes."

"Thank you," Jake said and as he, Mia and Sayid turned to leave, he had a sense of victory.

"One last thing. Mr. Himmelfarb, you're obviously a very clever fellow. Don't mistake cleverness for wisdom. And make sure you close the door when you leave."

As soon as they were out in the hallway, Mia grabbed Jake's arm. "That was amazing. How did you come up with that?"

"Yeah, I thought we were dead," added Sayid.

He smiled at Mia. "Actually, you gave me the idea, or at least your father did. I've been thinking about how he purchased your place and did a little research into the real estate world."

Sayid slapped Jake's back. "Well it paid off. I guess we all need to do some research into it. Listen, I've got to be somewhere in ten minutes. Let's all talk on the phone. How about seven-ish?"

"Seven works for me," said Jake.

"Me too. See ya." Mia said then turned to Jake. "You never called me."

"What are you talking about? We've done a lot of talking on the phone."

"That was always about this project. I thought after dinner the other night, you said you'd call. I took that to mean more than just to talk about the stupid project."

"I have to be honest. I was so high I don't remember what I said. And again, being honest, I wasn't sure how you felt. I mean, I had a great time, too good a time perhaps. I mean, oh shit, I'm usually not this tongue-tied. I'd love to go out with you, but I know that your father wouldn't approve."

"Were you planning on asking him to join us?"

"No, of course not. Um, so you would go out with me?"

"If I'm free, I might."

"When are you free?"

"After seven tonight."

"Great. Where do you want to go? Dinner? A movie?"

"How about you come by my place before Sayid calls. Afterwards, I'll make dinner. I bet you've never had real Chinese food."

"Of course I have. I'm from New York. We have the best Chinese restaurants in America."

"Really? Have you ever had Xin Li Zhi Wan?"

"Gin Lee what? Maybe. Not sure."

"You'd remember if you had. It's snake." His eyes bulged and he felt just a tad queasy at the thought of eating snake. "Relax, I'm kidding. Not about the dish, it really is snake. But I was thinking more along the lines of garlic chicken." She gave him a quick kiss on the cheek. "See you tonight."

He watched as she walked away and again imagined what she looked like underneath that blouse and skin-tight jeans. He was clearly having a very good day. He knew that as a gambler, when you're on a hot streak, you ride it as long as you can. Somewhere in the deep recesses of his consciousness, he also knew that the laws of probability always prevail and that all good streaks eventually end.

TWO

As the spring semester wore on with each day marked by the sun rising a little earlier and setting a little later, Jake found himself in unfamiliar territory. He had never had what could be called a steady girlfriend before – more a series of casual dalliances usually lasting a few weeks and then dying off from their own lack of inertia. He didn't know how to classify his relationship with Mia. Their time together fell into two categories – there was time spent working on their economics project, which nearly always included Sayid, and time when they were alone, often getting high, going out to dinner, catching a movie, or just lying around Mia's house watching television or listening to music. Jake was reluctant to move the relationship to a more intimate phase, but it wasn't for lack of desire. He justified his hesitancy as owing to his lack of experience and knowledge of Chinese culture. Offending her sensibilities was the last thing he wanted to do. Yet deep down he knew the real reason had more to do with his own insecurities, and that as long as he didn't push the matter, she couldn't reject him, which at least left him his fantasies.

After more than a month, Mia grew tired of waiting. It had been a long day of work on the project and after Sayid left, the two smoked some potent pot. Mia commented on how "grungy" she felt, it having been an unusually muggy and warm day for March. She stated matter-of-factly that she was going up upstairs to take a shower and she left Jake sprawled out semi-conscious on the couch. Minutes later, although Jake's perception of time made him think it was more like an hour, he heard a blood-curdling scream, so shrill that at first he thought it must have come from an animal in the alley behind the house. Mia shouted his name and he realized that she was the source of the scream. He stumbled to his feet, stubbed his toe against a table, muttered some expletive, and made his way upstairs to the bathroom. Finding the door slightly ajar he froze, not sure if she had actually called for him or if, in his semi-coherent state, he had imagined it.

"Jake, are you there?" she finally shouted loud enough to be heard above the din of the shower.

"Yeah, need something?"

"I saw a mouse run across the floor."

"What?" he shouted back.

"I saw a mouse, or maybe rat. Get rid of it."

He slowly entered the bathroom with his eyes closed. He needn't have bothered since by now the room was fogged up. "Where is it?" She answered with another scream. He opened his eyes and saw Mia standing in the tub and pointing out from behind the shower curtain.

"It's behind you."

The rodent scurried across the floor at his feet. He managed to direct it towards the slightly opened window where, using a towel, he swatted it out. "There. He's gone."

"You didn't kill it, did you?"

"I thought that's what you wanted."

"I just wanted it gone. For as long as I can remember, I've been deathly afraid of mice and rats."

"Maybe you should get a cat."

"Maybe I should. Thanks." He nodded and started to leave. "Wait, this shower feels fantastic. Wouldn't you like to try it?"

Jake was either too clueless or too stoned to catch the implication of her offer.

"Yeah, thanks. Let me know when you're done." He glanced back long enough to see her seductive but exasperated expression.

"Why wait?"

She might as well have tossed a bucket of ice water over his head.

"Really?" he blurted out. Mia nodded in a slow, enticing manner. Jake never shed his clothes so fast, and he couldn't hide the physical evidence that he was already aroused. He stepped into the tub and stood there, eyeing her from head to toe. He had visualized her nude body so many times in the past weeks that seeing it for real was an odd mix of the familiar, yet still very new. It occurred to him that the last time he had been in a shower with someone else was probably when he was four years old with his younger brother. This was definitely better.

"You like?" she asked.

"You have no idea."

She laughed and pulled him under the flowing water. She shampooed his hair and washed his body, much as he had imagined that geishas do, never mind that Mia was of Chinese not Japanese descent. He then returned the favor and found it erotic beyond even his own lurid imagination. They stepped out of the shower, dried off, and she took his hand and led him to her bed. All that Jake would remember about that night was how he just kept going, like one of those Eveready Energizer Battery Bunnies in the TV commercials. And he wanted to go on all night, but after the third time, all of the libidinous energy that had been building since the first time he'd seen her in Meecham's class was spent.

Following that night, Jake was ready to commit to an exclusive relationship, which was made easier by the fact that he had no other women, or even the prospect of other women in his life. Mia made it clear in a considerate and sensitive way that she wanted to keep things on a more casual level. She especially did not want Sayid to know about them, arguing that it might make working on their project uncomfortable. He could have reacted to her point of view in a hurt, even resentful manner, but the opportunity of being with her, even if limited, led him to accept her position.

Despite this adult and sophisticated take on their relationship, a sharp pang of jealousy and insecurity hit him a week later. He had gone to Mia's house expecting to meet with her and Sayid. At first he thought he'd gotten the time wrong since no one was around when he arrived. He was about to leave a note on her door when his classmates showed up. They were clad in running shorts and sleeveless T-shirts, and were breathless and covered in sweat. Even in that condition, she still had a siren's allure. Sayid, with his long, lanky frame and surprisingly muscular biceps, exuded a virile magnetism of his own, which troubled Jake. "Where have you been? I've been waiting here for like half an hour."

"Sorry. It was so nice out today that we went for a run," she replied panting.

"It's my fault," said Sayid bending over at the waist and trying to catch his breath. "I suggested we do an extra mile."

Jake looked at Mia who scrunched her mouth in a corkscrew kind of smile, which he interpreted to mean that she didn't want to get into any sort of discussion about the personal dynamic of the three of them.

"Don't worry about it," he finally said, "let's go in and get to work."

"Yes, let's," she quickly added, "but first I need a quick shower." She unlocked the door, let them inside and made her way straight to the upstairs bathroom.

"So, how long have you and Mia been running together?" Jake asked.

"A few weeks," Sayid answered before walking into the kitchen and pouring a tall glass of water.

Jake followed right behind. "How did that start?"

Sayid took a long drink. "She saw me one day jogging down by the Charles and stopped me. Asked me if I run regularly, which I do, then suggested that we do it together. You should join us."

"Maybe I will." He could hear the shower from the upstairs bath and his mind quickly flashed back to their night together. He decided to change the subject and began talking about how he'd been researching interest rates on mortgages and historic real estate property values.

"Sayid, don't you want to shower?" Mia shouted from above, and Jake felt as though he wanted to throw up.

"Sure. I'll be right up."

Jake wanted to say something to stop him, but nothing plausible came to mind. He took a seat at the kitchen table and imagined the worst of what the two of them were doing up there. After five minutes, he could stand it no longer and he scribbled a note making up some story as to why he had to leave and headed for the front door. "Where you going?" Mia said walking down the stairs as she dried her hair with a towel.

"Um, I just remembered something I have to do."

"Right now?"

"Uh, no, I guess it can wait. I wasn't sure how long it would be before the two of you came down, uh, so..."

"Jake," she whispered, "what did you think was going on up there?"

"I don't know."

"Do you think I invite every man I meet to take a shower with me? Do you take me for some kind of slut who was fucking Sayid in the tub?"

"No, of course not." It was obvious how angry she was with him. "I don't know. I'm an idiot about these things and I can imagine all sorts of stupidity. It's just that since last week I can't stop thinking about you, about us. Yet whenever I've tried to get together with you, you've been busy."

"Do you think I'm avoiding you? It's been what, six frigging days. I *have* been busy."

"Look, let's just forget we ever had this conversation. Like I said, I'm an idiot."

"Yes you are." Her expression softened. "And by the way, I'm not busy tonight." She took his hand and gave him a quick kiss.

"How fast can we dump Sayid?" he whispered in her ear.

She stepped back from him. "We have to get some work done or we're all going to flunk this class. But," she paused, "in an hour I could make up an excuse that I'm not feeling well. After you both leave, come back." He started to move in to kiss her but Sayid was heard coming down the steps and she quickly pushed him away.

"So where are we?" Sayid asked while he finished buttoning up his shirt.

"Let's go into the kitchen," she said.

Jake took out a pad of paper from his backpack and began to read. "Back in '81, mortgage rates averaged about 13.5% for a fixed-rate loan, and a point and a quarter less for an adjustable. Today they're at 8.5% for a thirty-year loan, and under six for an adjustable. This is more in line with historical rates. When rates fall, home prices go up because buyers can afford to pay more for a house since what they are most concerned with are their monthly payments."

"Slow down, I'm trying to get this all," said Mia who had just finished booting up her computer.

"What does this mean?" asked Sayid.

"If you go back, say over the past thirty years, we are still above the average, which means that interest rates could fall even more."

"Then our company should be buying up properties now," said Mia.

"That's one way to look at it. The problem is that the company would require massive capital in order to get loans and then have the expenses of marketing to students to create the cash-flow needed to make the payments."

Sayid walked over to the sink and poured another glass of water. "Have you calculated a budget?"

"I started to, but didn't have enough data on the some of the ancillary costs."

Mia stopped typing and looked over her laptop screen. "Guys, we are running out of time. We have two weeks before we have to be in Meecham's office with our initial draft business plan. Any suggestions?"

Sayid finished drinking his water. "Maybe we should change our premise. Maybe we should be looking at the financing side of this."

"How does that help?" Mia asked. "Being a mortgage lender isn't exactly an original idea."

Sayid returned to the table. "Jake says the problem is one of obtaining mortgages to buy the properties. Banks won't lend money unless you can prove you don't need it."

"Not so much that you don't need it, as that you can pay it back," Jake said.

"Whatever. You still need to raise money before you can borrow it. What if we became the lenders specializing in student-occupied housing with an equity advantage?"

Mia shook her head. "I don't know. It seems as if we're getting off on a tangent that is different from what we originally told Meecham. Changing our premise means that all the work we've done these past weeks is wasted." She looked straight into Sayid's eyes. "What do you think Jake. Don't you agree? After all this was mostly your idea." Jake didn't respond, but was uncharacteristically busy writing in his notebook. "Jake?" She turned towards him.

"I think Sayid is right," he said.

"What?"

"We should go into the financing end, only expanding it beyond the student market."

"And how would you do that?" she asked.

"I've also been looking at historic interest rates," Sayid said. "Those high-interest loans from a few years ago, well those people are already well qualified to re-finance. Even without their planning, the value of their homes has risen. They could actually take out new mortgages at a lower monthly cost and cash out the increased equity. If we packaged a bunch of them together, that would be an asset that could then be sold to investors or other banks. As a matter of fact, you could divide the value of the loans among several investors. And because the risk would be spread among a lot of mortgages, it would be a very safe investment, for which you could charge a premium."

Mia slammed her computer shut. "You've lost me. I'm not sure I understand any of what you just said."

"I think I do," said Jake. "And if rates stay level or even continue to fall, housing prices will continue to rise, and people will continue taking out new loans so they can cash in on the equity."

Mia closed her eyes began rubbing her temples.

"Something wrong?" Sayid asked.

"It's nothing, just a headache."

"We should go," Jake blurted out.

"No" she said, much to Jake's surprise.

"Can I get you an aspirin or something?" Sayid asked.

"I already took some Tylenol, but it's not helping. I'm afraid it may be a migraine coming on. I'm sorry. Maybe you should go. The only thing that helps is if I lie down in a dark, quiet room."

"Let's leave her, Sayid. We're nearly done anyway."

"Are you sure you'll be all right?"

"I'll be fine, Sayid. Thanks for asking."

Sayid stood up to leave. "Okay then. I'll see you tomorrow night."

"Right," she said. "It's at eight?"

"Eight," he confirmed.

"What's at eight?" Jake quickly asked.

"Mia and I are playing duplicate at the MIT bridge club's Wednesday night game."

"What's duplicate?"

"It's bridge," she said.

"You two play bridge?" They both nodded.

Sayid slung his backpack over his shoulder. "Yep. You play?" Jake shook his head. "Yeah, not many kids our age do anymore, which was why I was surprised to find out that was one more thing me and Mia had in common."

"One *more* thing?"

"You know, along with the running. Anyway, I've been playing at the club since I was a freshman but my regular partner is out of town, so I asked Mia to be my partner. We should go now." Jake followed Sayid out the door. They walked together for a few blocks discussing their new business concept. "I'm not sure Mia is too happy with us," Sayid said.

"She'll be fine." Jake started to thumb through his backpack. "Shit. I left my notebook in her kitchen. I gotta go back and get it. We'll talk tomorrow." He started to walk away, turning back several times in Sayid's direction until he saw Sayid board a bus. He then ran the remaining distance back to Mia's house. He knocked on the door, but there was no answer and finding that the door was unlocked, he let himself in. Mia was sprawled out on the couch in the darkened living room, a wet towel draped across her forehead and covering her eyes.

"You act very well," he said.

"I wasn't acting. I really do have a headache."

"Oh." He didn't bother to disguise the disappointment in his voice. "Do you want me to go?"

"No. Stay."

"So tell me about bridge."

"What do you want to know?"

"How did you start playing?"

"My parents both played. They taught my sister and me but as Sayid said, most people our age don't play. Like him, I was surprised when he said he did."

"Is it hard to learn?" he asked.

"I guess. I mean it's not hard to learn how to play. It's similar to hearts but with bidding and trump, which I think intimidates a lot of people."

"I know how to play hearts."

"Can you keep track of cards that have been played?"

"Of course," he said, as if anyone could.

She lifted the towel off her eyes. "Oh really?"

"Got a deck?"

"Over there on the shelf."

He found the deck, shuffled the cards quickly and handed them to her.

"Show me the cards, one at a time, but not the last one."

Mia sat up, took the deck and gave it another quick shuffle. She flipped the cards, slowly at first, but with increasing speed as she went through the deck. She got to the last card and looked at Jake. "Well?"

"I have to confess, I wasn't paying as close attention as I should have, so I'm not sure."

"I thought so," she said.

"I mean, I know it's a four, and a black four, just not sure if it's clubs or spades. I'll guess spades." She flipped over the card. Four of clubs. "Damn," he muttered.

"That's still impressive."

"I learned card counting from my uncle. It's helpful if you're going to play blackjack at a casino. Just don't let them catch on that you're counting. I think anyone can do it."

"Not so. Anyway there is more to bridge than just counting cards. It's rather like… like … how can I put this in terms you'd understand? It's not unlike sex."

Jake leaned in close. "Tell me more."

"First there's the bidding. This is the flirtatious phase when you try and feel out the person sitting across the table with various proposals to see if there's any interest in a relationship. At the same time, your opponents may be doing the same thing, or even trying to sabotage your conversation with your partner by throwing in spurious bids. Whichever side bids the highest gets the contract, which establishes how many tricks they have to win and what suit, if any, is trump. If you get the contract, you should have a pretty good idea of what cards your partner has, but then again, so do your opponents."

"How do you know that?"

"There are bidding systems, codes if you will, that describe to your partner what your holding, even to the point of how many aces or kings you've got. "

"Sounds like cheating."

"No, because most of these conventions as they're called are pretty standard, and to top things off, when you play in a formal duplicate game, you have to divulge to your opponents exactly which conventions you are using. So the first thing you do when you pick up your hand is count the points in it."

"Points?"

"Yes. It tells you whether or not you can bid, and if so, what to bid." She dealt out all of the cards into four piles, told Jake to pick up two of the piles and sort the cards into suits as she did the same with the other two. She then laid the four hands open faced on the table.

"Let's start with this hand." She picked up one of the piles. "This is a really bad hand. It only has one point, the jack of hearts. Jacks get one point, queens two, kings three and aces four. As with sex, the female is superior to males with names that sound like Jack."

"Very funny, but the king tops the queen."

"Don't flatter yourself into thinking you're a king. Besides, aces have a single spot in the middle, which an astute mind would take note of the likeness to the female body. But we digress. In addition to points for high cards, you can count points for distribution. If you have none in a suit, called a void, that's worth three points. A single card, cleverly known as a singleton, gets two and a doubleton gets one. Distribution is important because you can trump suits only if you are out of that suit when it's played. So if spades are trump and I'm out of diamonds and a diamond is played, I can play a spade and win the trick. Tell me, how many points are in the hand in front of you?"

He counted the face cards and distribution. "Seventeen."

She gave him a look that said, *are you sure?* "What? I've got two aces, two kings and a queen. That's sixteen. I also have only two spades so I get a point in distribution for the doubleton."

"You're forgetting the analogy. Just like sex, things aren't always as they appear. One of your kings is the king of spades, which is also your doubleton. I'd be leery about counting it both as a king and a doubleton, since having so little protection, it may not be able to take a trick."

"But it would as long as I keep the five of spades for protection. If the ace were played, I'd play the five."

"Perhaps, but depending upon which other hand held the ace, that might not be possible."

"Hey, I know enough about card playing to know that I wouldn't be so stupid as to lead the five."

"You'll see once you've played some."

"How do you win?" he asked.

"If your side bids the highest, you get the contract and if you make it, you get points. If you are the defenders, you win by preventing the other side from fulfilling their contract. The higher the contract, the more points you get, plus the points change by suit. Suits go in order, with clubs, diamonds, hearts then spades in ascending order. Clubs and diamonds are called minor suits and are worth twenty points each and hearts and spades are worth thirty points each and are called..." she paused for a second. "They are called... anyone... Bueller... Bueller..."

He got the *Ferris Bueller's Day Off* reference. "Major?"

"Your parents will be glad to know they have not wasted sixty-thousand dollars on your MIT education. Continuing with today's lesson, if I bid one club, which is the lowest bid you can make, and no one else bids, I win the bidding. It means that I am saying that my side can win seven of the thirteen tricks, as long as clubs are trump. So when you make a bid of one, it means you think you will win one more than half of the thirteen tricks."

"What is the highest bid – seven spades?"

"Close. Seven no-trump, which, as the name implies, means you play the hand with no suit being trump and have to win every trick. After the contract is agreed upon, the person who first bid the suit that is trump is called the declarer. His partner is the dummy, who lays down his cards on the table. The other two are the defenders who will try and stop the declarer from making the contract."

"So only three people actually play the hand. Sounds boring."

"Maybe for the dummy, but when you're the declarer you get to pretty much control the line of play, unless the defense can quickly grab their tricks. And since everyone can see the dummy's cards, everyone knows exactly where half of the cards in the deck are at any one time. The trick is figuring out who is holding what in the other two hands."

"In the end though, success still comes down to the cards you're dealt, which is why I don't see how they can have tournaments that are more than just luck."

"Au contraire, chéri. The cards have nothing to do with who wins, because in duplicate, you are not being scored against your opponents at the table, you are being scored against every other group of partners that will play the same cards that you will. You see, the cards are dealt only once at the beginning of the night, and then kept in order so that after you play four rounds, you move to the next table and face a different partnership. The table seating follows the compass, North, South, East and West, so if you and your partner are North-South, you are scored against how all the other North-Souths did on each hand.

"I'm beginning to see some of the appeal of this game," he said. "The problem I have with it is that it doesn't have the psychological component of say poker, and there's no money involved."

"To begin with, I haven't even scratched the surface of bridge. It's far more complex than just the bidding. The play of the hand, whether trying to make your contract or prevent the contract from being made, forces you to come up with a plan of attack instantly, and to make allowances when things don't go as you'd expect. It often comes down to judging your opponent's abilities and mindset. Like sex, when you succeed, there is no greater stroke to the ego. As for the money, although the bridge world is far smaller, perhaps because the game can be so daunting, there are those that play for very high stakes. I've heard tell of games for as much as a dollar a point."

"Doesn't seem like a lot to me. I won three hundred bucks playing poker at the Tri-Delta house two nights ago."

"Yeah, but did you get anything stroked?" she laughed. "I've played in friendly games, not for money mind you, where the winners at the end have been ahead by ten thousand points or more. By the way, did I mention my headache's gone away?"

Jake, in typical fashion, didn't digest the implications of that last statement. The thought of such a large payoff had him mesmerized. She finally took the cards and away from him and said there were things more fun they could be doing on the couch than playing out bridge hands. Afterwards, they went out for dinner at a place just off Harvard Square. On the way back they stopped, at Jake's insistence, at a bookstore where Jake bought every book he could find on bridge. The next evening, Jake showed up at the weekly game at the MIT bridge club. He wasn't there to play, just to observe and learn. Still harboring a lingering insecurity, he spent as much time observing the way Mia interacted with Sayid as he did on the card playing.

With Meecham's mid-April deadline fast approaching, the three met every day and managed to piece together a business plan based on mortgage financing. A few days after turning in their project, they again appeared in Meecham's office to hear his reaction, and most importantly, to find out their preliminary grade. Meecham, as before, sat behind his desk leafing through their plan when they walked in. He instructed them to take a seat. Jake was glad to see the addition of chairs to the office.

"Do you have any questions?" Mia finally asked.

Meecham peered over the top of the paper and slowly shook his head no. He then flung the paper on his desk toward her. "Open it up if you're interested in your grade."

She reached across the desk turned to the last page. C minus. Her shoulders slumped as she showed the grade to Sayid then Jake. "What was the problem?" she asked.

Meecham let out a small sigh.

"Where to begin? This bears little resemblance to what you originally proposed. Didn't any of you remember the purpose of this project? The idea was to demonstrate some of the basic principles of economics. This paper does little of that."

"It presents a new concept for structuring mortgage financing," Sayid said. "I thought the idea was to come up with a new business model, and by researching the subject and creating a business plan, economic principles would be revealed."

"Your idea isn't new. In your research, didn't the term collateralized debt obligation ever show up?" Sayid turned to his partners, both of whom wore blank expressions on their faces. "Does the name Imperial Savings Association ring a bell? How about Drexel Burnham Lambert?"

"Milken. The junk bond king," Jake piped up.

"Correct you are, Mr. Himmelfarb. Drexel, you may recall, went belly-up two years ago, and a company that could trace its lineage for over a hundred and fifty years and had grown to being the fifth largest investment bank was gone. But before they went under, Drexel put together CDOs for Imperial, which within three years became insolvent and was taken over by the RTC. All you've done is to resurrect the CDO."

Sayid started to read through Meecham's comments, which were liberally scrawled in the margins of their paper. "The basic concept is sound," he said. "Mortgages historically have had a very low foreclosure rate. In addition, the underlying investment is backed by a tangible asset – the property. Logically then, it should be very safe."

Meecham reached into his desk and, to Jake's surprise, took out a deck of cards and began building a house with them.

"My nephew loves to do this. He can do it for hours, constructing buildings seven stories high." Jake's sense was that this professor was losing his marbles. "Mr. Hassan, if the world always behaved in a logical manner, there would be little need for economists. Everything would just flow organically, save for the randomizations introduced by nature via storms, drought and disease, and even those can be anticipated and planned for. The problem is that humans do not act like computers. Do you know what Einstein said regarding stupidity?"

"I'm sure you're going to tell us," Jake said under his breath.

"Impertinence, Mr. Himmelfarb, is not one of your better qualities. Uncle Albert said that only the universe and stupidity were infinite, and he wasn't sure about the universe. We do not base our actions on logic but are wired by eons of evolution to respond to fear. Fear is what caused some ancient hominid roaming the African savanna to respond quickly to the threat posed by a hungry lion, escape becoming dinner and live long enough to reproduce offspring which would eventually evolve into you. Greed is nothing more than fear on amphetamines. The illogical need to acquire wealth and possessions far in excess of what one needs for survival and comfort is nothing more than the result of fear trumping reason. If mortgages were to be financed through your model, it would be difficult, if not impossible, to assess the true value of the underlying individual loans which could lead to less than scrupulous mortgage bankers making loans not properly underwritten."

"But as I said, mortgages have historically been very sound," Sayid argued. "The foreclosure rates haven't been more than one percent in the past fifty years. One could expect with virtual certainty that the overwhelming bulk of these loans would be safe and secure."

Meecham continued building his card house.

"Countless civilizations have been tossed on the dung heap of history, borne by the hubris of leaders who were certain of their expectations. When it comes to expectations, the only certainty is that the unexpected will lead to uncertainty." Jake glanced at his watch. "Are we keeping you from something Mr. Himmelfarb?" Jake shook his head. "Good. I believe you are a math major, which means you have some facility with equations. What is the most famous equation you can name?"

Jake's mind went blank. He couldn't imagine what Meecham was getting at, but since he always was quoting Einstein, he blurted out $E = MC^2$.

"Very good. A simple and elegant expression of how matter and energy are really one and the same. I have my own version to explain how much of economics works: G equals F I squared, where G is greed, F is fear and I times I is ignorance times irrationality." Meecham slowly and carefully removed his hands from two cards completing the third level of his pyramidal card house. "There. Nice, isn't it?"

"Lovely," Jake said sarcastically.

Meecham stared at him for a moment before removing one of the cards at the bottom of the pyramid, causing the quick collapse of his structure. "Now you know why they call shaky investment schemes a house of cards. It would take a surprisingly small number of loans to go bad and ripple through the economy causing home prices to fall, especially if, as you posit in your paper, a large number of loans were of the adjustable type and people were encouraged to refinance often and take out equity. What you have created isn't the blueprint of a house of cards, but an apartment building, and a high-rise one at that."

Jake looked at the flat pile of cards. Two had fallen right in front of him face down and he couldn't resist looking. The queen of clubs and the ace of spades – a perfect blackjack hand he thought until he noticed that in front of Meecham were two cards with one face up, the ace of diamonds. Were he at a casino, he'd be tempted to take what they call the insurance offered by the house on that hand since it guaranteed a payoff, albeit a smaller one than if he risked not taking the insurance and won.

"What if you could lay off the risk?"

Meecham's eyes locked onto Jake's and they stared intently at each other for what seemed to Jake like an eternity.

"Explain, Mr. Himmelfarb."

"Suppose you could sell off some of the risk to a third party, like bookies do when they've taken on too much action on one side of the line."

Meecham continued looking straight at Jake, as though Mia and Sayid were not even in the room.

"Sell to whom? Another bank? Their capital and reserve requirements might not allow it. Besides, they may have their own lending portfolio problems and want to sell to you."

"CDSs," Mia said.

"Miss Jang, I'd almost forgotten you were with us. Do you two gentlemen know what she is referring to?" They both shook their heads. "Credit default swaps, or CDSs are a way to shift risk to a third party, like taking out insurance, or to use Mr. Himmelfarb's more colorful analogy, like a bookie laying off some of his bets to another bookie. They are generally used by financial institutions wanting to insure that their portfolio of government and munici-pal bonds are safe. There are two problems with your CDS idea. First off, gov-ernment bonds are far safer and easier to value than a mish-mash of individual mortgages packaged together. Secondly, the logical buyer of CDSs would be insurance companies and, thank God, U.S. banking laws prohibit insurers from engaging in that type of business. Were it not for those safeguards, I dare say that your apartment building of cards would soon grow into a city. Good try though, Ms. Jang."

The three students sat dejectedly in silence.

"Any other questions?" Meecham asked. Mia and Sayid stood up and started for the door. Jake remained seated and stared at the scattered cards on the desktop. He couldn't resist leaning over and flipping the other card below Meecham's ace. It was a nine, which meant that had it been a real hand of blackjack in a casino, he would have done better risking it all by refusing the insurance.

"Something the matter Mr. Himmelfarb?"

Jake was momentarily embarrassed by what he'd done and he quickly began picking up the rest of the cards.

"No, I just wanted to help." He continued picking up the cards and noticed a copy of the New York Times resting on the desk. It was open to the daily bridge column and he saw that the diagram of the hand had a number of the cards circled.

"You play bridge?"

"I have been known to on occasion."

"Are you any good?"

"I'm a Life Master."

Meecham's response meant nothing to Jake.

"So are Mia and Sayid." Had Jake bothered to look back at his partners, he would have seen the expressions of shock on their faces.

"You feel confident in your abilities?"

"What are you getting at, Mr. Himmelfarb?"

"Well, you say you're a Life Master but are you a betting man?"

"What did you have in mind?"

"How about you and whoever you want for a partner go up against Mia and Sayid in bridge. If they win, you give us an A for this class."

"And if I win, what do I get?"

"You can give us all Fs."

"Mr. Himmelfarb, it is already within my purview to fail you all, and I am not in the habit of giving out grades based on wagers."

"Okay," Jake said as he stood. "Didn't mean to offend you. I just thought you might be up for a challenge, but I guess not."

Jake walked to the door where Mia and Sayid stood dumbfounded at what had just transpired between him and Meecham. Just as he was about to close the door to Meecham's office, the professor's baritone voice boomed out.

"A week from Thursday, eight-thirty at the Harvard Faculty Club. There's a monthly game I play in with my regular partner, Professor Harold Andrews, of the English department over there."

"We'll be there," Jake said.

"One thing you may be interested to know is that Hal is a Grand Life Master."

"Good for him," Jake said and he closed the door.

As soon as they were in the hallway Mia punched Jake in the arm. "Are you crazy!"

"What have we got to lose?"

"Last time I checked, a C minus beats an F on your report card," she replied.

"Nah, don't worry, I've seen you guys play. I have confidence in you two."

Mia stormed off. "I thought she'd be happy for the chance at an A," Jake said.

"Achieving Life Master status isn't easy. My father has been playing in tournaments for years and hasn't reached it. But do you know how many people are Grand Life Masters? Like a handful, maybe ten or fewer I'm guessing. They are the best players in the world. I'm telling you, it is time to worry." Sayid patted Jake on the back and walked away.

Thursday a week later arrived faster than Jake could believe. He had spent the intervening time reading all the books on bridge he'd purchased and acting as the self-appointed morale booster whenever Mia and Sayid met to go over strategy. Jake arrived at the Harvard Club twenty minutes early but was unable to enter to the building until Meecham showed up and vouched for him. "Are your classmates going to make an appearance?" Meecham asked.

"Don't worry, they'll be here." But with five minutes to go before the scheduled start, Jake was far more concerned than he let on to. With less than two minutes to go, Sayid came running in the door. He was briefly stopped by a security guard until he showed his student ID.

"Where have you been, and where's Mia?"

"She's not coming," Sayid said breathlessly.

"What?"

"Her mother's taken sick. She may have had a heart attack or something."

"Shit. Let's go tell Meecham." They tried to get to their professor but he was already seated at a table looking at the first deal of the night, and rules strictly forbade conversation with players once play began.

"We're fucked," said Sayid, at which point the director, a kindly looking grey-haired lady whom Jake guessed to be in her seventies and whose job it was to act as the grand referee of the game, approached them and asked for their names. "I'm Sayid Hassan."

"Oh yes, you are starting at table nine playing east-west. Where's your partner?"

"I'm here," Jake said impulsively.

"You are Mia Jang?"

"No. Mia's been called away on a family emergency."

"Oh dear. What is your name?"

"I'm Jacob Himmelfarb."

The director made a notation in her records. "And do you have a ranking?"

"Grand Life Wizard," he said, which elicited a confused look from the woman.

"Grand Life Master, he means," said Sayid.

"Oh really? You must be one of the youngest in the world."

"Yes, he's quite a joker when it comes to these things, and he's very humble, doesn't like to show off, you know. Come on Jake, let's find our seats." Sayid pulled Jake away. "What the hell are you doing? I thought you didn't know how to play bridge."

"Mia's been teaching me."

"Great. As I said, we're fucked."

They took their seats and Sayid even managed to smile at their first opponents of the night. When asked to produce his convention card, Jake froze.

"Here they are," Sayid said as he handed each opponent a copy.

"There's nothing on here," complained a hunched-over little man with thinning white hair and black plastic framed glasses sitting to Jake's left.

Probably a professor in the law school thought Jake.

"Oh, we don't play any conventions."

"None? Can't be. In the thirty-five years that I've been playing in this game, no one has ever given me a blank card. I don't believe this allowed. Director! Director!" he began to shout.

"Not a problem. I'll put something down." Sayid took the sheets back and quickly entered a few common conventions. "Better?"

The old man snarled. "You'd just damn well better follow what you wrote here. I don't know what it is with the kids they let in. They act like they know nothing and waste our G D time."

Jake made a quick visual survey of the room, and couldn't find anyone other than Sayid and himself under age thirty. As a matter of fact, he didn't think anyone else was under fifty, with some looking as though they could have booked passage on the Mayflower. This was of some comfort since a slight age bias that he unconsciously harbored led him to conclude that many of these "geezers" had lost a few brain cells. He was, to a small degree, right. Fortunately, he and Sayid faced much of the weaker competition early on, which allowed Jake to gain some confidence. After they had played at several tables, Sayid complimented Jake on how well he was doing and that perhaps they had an extremely remote chance to best Meecham.

"How will we know?" Jake asked.

"We won't until all of the hands have been played and the scores are turned in and the standings calculated. Usually doesn't take long if the scorer is any good."

"Speaking of Meecham, when will we get to play him?" asked Jake.

"Judging by the way we've been moving so far, I'm guessing he'll be our last opponent."

"Figures. Do you think he planned it that way?"

"Is the Pope Catholic?"

Jake felt stupid for even asking the question, but the next round of deals was about to get underway and he couldn't afford the luxury of a slightly bruised ego distracting his concentration. After about an hour of play, Jake looked up and saw Mia standing in back of the room by the refreshments table. He caught her eye and mouthed the words "Your mother?" several times until she understood. She gave him a thumbs-up sign, but the distraction had cost him and Sayid, as Jake failed to follow suit when he should have. The director was called over and she explained the penalty. "I'm surprised that a Grand Life Master would make such a mistake, but I guess we're all human."

"I haven't played in a long time. I guess I'm a little rusty," Jake explained.

"You're a Grand Life Master?" one of the opponents seated at the table asked.

"The director is a very nice old lady. I like her a lot. I think she just has me confused with someone else."

At last, after over two and a half hours and what seemed like endless hands, Jake and Sayid reached the final table of the night. Meecham and his partner, Harold Andrews were already seated. Jacob had spent some of the last few days doing research on Andrews, and came to realize that when Meecham said they'd been partners for twenty years, he wasn't just referring to bridge. On the first of the four hands to be played, Sayid made a mental mistake on defense when he failed to lead a diamond back to Jake. It wasn't a major gaffe, but Sayid could tell that Jake knew he'd made an error. Immediately after the hand had been played, Sayid apologized which Jake quickly dismissed as no big deal. Jake had played cards long enough to know that mistakes such as this were often the result of intimidation from the opponent and the worst thing that Sayid could do was to ruminate over his error. Jake's response was meant to calm his partner and it had the desired effect when on the next hand, Sayid was the declarer and made a difficult contract.

The third hand was a simple contract that Andrews as the declarer, quickly played out and made. That left the final hand, and although no one could know it at the time, the Meecham/Andrews team was slightly ahead of the second place team, with Jake and Sayid not far behind in third. For the final hand of each four-hand set, each team is termed vulnerable, meaning that the point values on the scorecard are raised to roughly double what they would otherwise be. Meecham was the dealer and he opened with a one-club bid. Jake, sitting to his left, slowly unfolded his hand and had to use his best poker face to conceal his disappointment. He held only one face card, the king of clubs, and that suit had only one other card, the six of clubs, to protect the king. Using the standard point system for evaluating hands for bidding purposes, his hand was worth only four points, and as he remembered from the first time Mia had explained the game, even that might be stretching it. Jake passed. Andrews responded with a bid of one heart and Sayid also passed. The bidding then quickly progressed to the point where Andrews bid six clubs, a small slam worth extra points if they made it. Meecham took a long time staring at his cards, and Jake knew why. If Meecham passed they would play the contract at six clubs, and although they would almost surely make it, most of the other tables that had already played this hand would also have played it at the same contract. If Meecham were to get the top score and the most points, he would have to play it at a higher contract. The bidding had revealed that Meecham and Andrews probably had between them 32 to 34 points, not usually enough to make a contract of seven, which would have been a grand slam. However, the bidding had revealed that they held all four aces between both hands, and even though they also had a lot of clubs, a different contract might be worth more.

"Six no," Meecham boldly proclaimed.

Jake looked at his hand one more time, hoping that maybe he had missed a card somewhere along the way, but he hadn't.

"Pass," he said quietly, followed quickly by a pass from Andrews.

Jake, having already assumed that Sayid would pass, began assessing which card to lead against the six no-trump contract.

"Double" said Sayid, doubling the risk/reward of the hand.

Meecham looked at Sayid, who sheepishly smiled back at the professor.

"Re-double," Meecham said, which essentially quadrupled the points, after which everyone passed.

So the contract was to be played at six no-trump, vulnerable and re-doubled, as high as a single deal could be worth without going to a grand slam. Jake again looked at his paltry hand for a card to lead. Something in the back of his mind told him to look at the convention sheet that Sayid had filled out earlier. He saw the word Lightner written in the "Special Doubles" box, which somehow he remembered meant that Sayid's double bid was intended as a signal to him for what suit he should lead. In this case, against a no-trump hand played at the slam level, it told Jake that he should lead the first suit bid by the dummy, who in this case was Andrews.

"Can I have a review of the bidding?" asked Jake.

By now, most of the other tables had finished for the night and a small group of players gathered at a respectful distance to observe what was commonly agreed upon by most club members as the best team of players in Andrews and Meecham. Meecham recounted the bidding which Sayid and Andrews concurred with, reminding Jake that Andrews' first suit bid was hearts. Jake started to play the seven of hearts from his hand but froze. He looked first at Sayid, whose outwardly calm countenance was belied by the sweat on his forehead. He then glanced at Mia who he knew had been watching this table for a while and undoubtedly had seen this hand played several times. If she was trying to give him a signal it was impossible to discern since her eyes were closed and her face tilted up at the ceiling as if plaintively calling on divine intervention.

"Any day now, Mr. Himmelfarb. I was hoping to get home before dawn," uttered Meecham.

In the next instant, Jake did something that at the time seemed insignificant, but in reality, would change the course of his life. Recalling the moment years later, Jake said it was as though an invisible hand were guiding him. He put back the heart and impulsively laid down his six of clubs! He looked at Sayid whose jaw seemed to clench, then at Mia whose face was now buried in her hands trying to conceal her disappointment. It wasn't just that he had missed Sayid's request for the heart lead, but she had to have known that Jake had led away from his king leaving it unprotected. It seemed a fundamental playing error that not even a novice would make.

Andrews laid down his dummy hand on the table and it was Meecham who now sat for some time before playing a card. The dummy had five clubs led by the ace, queen, jack, as well as five hearts with the ace and queen. Meecham now knew that between his hand and the dummy's, the only face cards his side lacked were the king of clubs and the king and jack of hearts. He also knew that with the five clubs he held in his own hand, Jake and Sayid had only three clubs between them. There were no losing tricks in spades and diamonds, but there was a problem. Based on his double, Meecham assumed that Sayid held the missing high hearts. If Jake held the king of clubs, it would be trapped by the dummy's ace. But Meecham reasoned that Jake couldn't hold the club king because no one would lead away from it, therefore Sayid had to be holding both kings. Meecham played the ace of clubs from the board, hoping that Sayid's king was a singleton and the ace would take it.

When Sayid played the three of clubs, Meecham was still confident he could make his contract by using what is known as an endplay. The concept is simple enough – draw down all of the other suits until Sayid is left with only hearts and his club king, then lead a club letting Sayid take the trick. Sayid would then be forced to lead a heart from his king-jack into the dummy's ace-queen, assuring that they would not lose a heart trick. Meecham played the next eight tricks fast and everything went as he had planned. There were now only four tricks left. In his hand Meecham held four clubs and on the board were the queen and jack of clubs, and the ace and queen of hearts. Meecham, sure that Sayid held three hearts and the club king, smiled at Jake as he led a club from his hand. Jake smiled back and held out his king of clubs. Meecham was stunned.

"That can't be."

"Afraid so," said Jake who won the trick and led a heart. Meecham couldn't avoid losing the last heart to Sayid. The final tally was down one, which translated into a score of 400 for Jake and Sayid. Had Meecham made his contract, he would have scored over 2,100 points. The net result on the final scoring for the night was that Meecham and Andrews fell to third place with Jake and Sayid coming in second.

As everyone stood around the refreshments table waiting for the final scores to be posted, a man who appeared to be in his mid-forties came up to Jake and introduced himself as Arthur Morrison.

"That was some gutsy play of yours at the end."

"Not really. I figured sitting behind the dummy my king was dead anyway, and we needed two tricks. My only hope was to bluff. Maybe that comes from too much poker playing."

"Remind me not to play poker with you, not that I play poker. So how long have you been playing bridge?"

"This is my first time."

"What?"

"It's true," said Mia, "I'm his teacher."

"Well young lady, you've done one hell of a teaching job, and you've made me the winner tonight. I've been playing here for years and this is only the third time that Andrews hasn't been on the winning team. I've never come in first before. What do you do?"

"I'm a junior at MIT," said Jake. "We're all undergrads there."

Morrison reached into his wallet, took out three business cards and handed one to each of them.

"If any of you are ever interested in a job, give me a call."

Jake looked at the card. First Pilgrim Equity Partners, Arthur Morrison, Chairman. The office address was 2 World Trade Center in Manhattan.

"I don't have any experience in finance, I'm just a math major."

"You're bright, energetic and willing to take risk. We'll teach you the rest. I've got a boat load of people with MBAs from Harvard and Wharton and any of them will tell you, if they're being honest, that what they learned in school was basically useless. Everything they know they learned on the job."

Meecham approached the group from behind Morrison.

"Arthur. Haven't seen you in a while. How is life among the jackals?"

They didn't shake hands. "Adam, you're looking good. Are these your students? Always happy to see that the socialists are still around to corrupt our youth. It gives me something to fight for."

"Remember Arthur, even though you exist in a world of the 'haves,' the 'have-nots' make up a far larger group."

"All I know is that I beat you and Hal tonight. That will be solace enough. Jacob, it was nice to meet you, and remember what I said." Morrison walked away. Jake was already regretting that he was responsible for Morrison's victory even though it meant Meecham's defeat.

"Interesting opening lead, Mr. Himmelfarb. Was it planned or just dumb luck?"

"Truth be told, I'm not sure."

"No need to be disingenuous, Mr. Himmelfarb. It was brilliantly unexpected."

"The certainty of unexpected uncertainties," Jake replied.

"Right you are. By the way, what was Morrison saying to you?"

"Oh, something about a job. I wasn't really paying attention."

"Be warned, Arthur Morrison is not above playing fast and loose with the rules. People can end up sitting behind bars if they are not careful."

"I wasn't planning on working for him, but you speak as though you know him."

"Twenty odd years ago, he was where you stand today, a student taking the same class as you do now. I flunked him then and would do the same today."

Mia leaned forward and wiped some crumbs off Jake's shirt. "Which begs the question, what is our grade?"

"Here, see for yourself. This is the original copy of your business plan. I always give my students a photocopy of their papers first and judge their reactions and defenses. This copy has your real grade, which was marked ten minutes after you left my office last week. As I said, I'm not in the habit of giving out grades based on wagers."

Sayid open the paper and looked at the large "A" circled on the last page. "So, it was a good idea after all."

"Oh heavens no, Mr. Hassan. It's a terrible idea that would eventually lead to heaven knows what. But, you did demonstrate the basics of many economic principles, which after all was the purpose of the assignment. Well, it's getting late. Have a good summer, and you should all consider taking another economics course. You'd be good at it."

The three students left the Harvard Club and headed straight to the nearest bar where Jake intended on celebrating long into the night. After Mia and Sayid both ordered soft drinks, he realized that he'd be drinking alone.

"I know why Mia doesn't drink," he said to Sayid, "but why don't you? No fake ID?"

"Force of habit, I guess. Muslims are supposed to shun alcohol, although I'm not really religious."

"I know the feeling. Though I don't keep kosher, I still can't eat pork."

"Of course not," Sayid said. "Who would eat a pig?"

"I love pork. I eat it all the time," said Mia.

"That's different," said Jake. "You eat pork in Chinese restaurants."

"And?" she said.

"Pork in Chinese restaurants is okay for Jews."

"That makes absolutely no sense." She reached into her purse and took out a joint.

"Regardless, I don't think this falls under anyone's dietary laws." Jake quickly downed his beer and the three headed out into the balmy spring night. They walked through Harvard Square, sharing the marijuana, and laughing uncontrollably when recalling the events of earlier that night, especially when the director thought that Jake was a Grand Life Master. It was the last time the three would be together for a long time.

After the semester ended, Mia informed Jake that she had been admitted to Johns Hopkins Medical School and was foregoing her senior year. As the summer wore on and Mia left for Baltimore, Jake grew despondent and depressed. Two weeks into the fall semester of his senior year, Jake, to the shock and dismay of his parents, dropped out of college and moved to Manhattan to take a job with First Pilgrim Equity. Sayid stayed at MIT for an extra year and graduated with a dual major in civil engineering and economics.

He then earned an MBA from Harvard before he left for England to pursue a doctorate from the London School of Economics.

In the fall of 1996, four years after he left Cambridge to work in Manhattan, Jake spotted a picture of his old professor in the New York Times. He read the first lines of the accompanying article. "Adam Scott Meecham, Nobel Laureate and Professor of Economics at the Massachusetts Institute of Technology died in his sleep after a brief illness. At his side was his longtime companion, Harold Andrews."

THREE

Beijing, February 1999

Mia sat in her room on the twenty-second floor of the Hotel Kunlun, sipping coffee and eating a breakfast consisting of an overly dry croissant topped with what passed for strawberry jam, but tasted more like fruit punch with the consistency of Jell-O. She stared out at the leaden-gray late winter skies that hung low over Beijing's Chao Yang district. In the distance she counted at least twenty construction cranes marking the sites of new high-rise buildings in various stages of completion that would soon remake the capital's skyline. Beijing had already changed dramatically from her last visit a decade earlier. The government had clearly made an effort to expunge Tiananmen Square from both the Chinese and world's memory.

Mia had changed too. After earning her medical degree from Hopkins, she started a two-year residency in San Francisco where she took an interest in genetics. She found patient care not to her liking, preferring instead the hours spent doing research in a lab, often on a solitary basis. She had gone into medicine at the strong urging, she would say insistence, of her father, a man who managed his family in much the same manner as he ran his small pharmaceutical company, which is to say that he was not one who tolerated those who disagreed with him. The last time she had defied him turned out badly. In her first year of residency, she became engaged to a radiologist from India. Mia's father strongly disapproved, but she didn't care. She was twenty-five years old at the time, self-sufficient and with a solid career path ahead. She no longer needed her father's approval to make decisions about her life. Raj Desai was charming and attentive to her needs, unlike many of the unmarried male doctors she knew who were enamored by their own self-perceived abilities. Mia and Raj were married in a small private ceremony that neither of Mia's parents attended.

Two months later, Mia's mother collapsed from an aortic aneurism and died. While back in Massachusetts attending her funeral, Mia received a call from Raj informing her that he was going back to Delhi to be with his Indian wife. Mia, already reeling from the death of her mother, was devastated. It wasn't so much the hurt of losing Raj as the pain caused by the embarrassment of the situation and her own poor judgment. Her father arranged the annulment and was surprisingly sensitive in not harping on the fact that he had opposed the marriage from the outset. She didn't know whether this empathy was the result of her father's own state of mind following the loss of her mother or whether she had simply been wrong all these years when it came to his nature. Whatever the reason, from then on she no longer felt the need to prove her independence and dismiss his advice out-of-hand.

She decided to leave her residency after meeting with a close friend of her father named Fred Lee, an entrepreneur who was starting a biotech firm in Silicon Valley. It was a nearly perfect situation for her. The company, Micro Bio-Genetics, Inc., referred to by its initials MBG, specialized in the developing but unproven field of gene therapy. With a workforce of only nine employees, she was getting in on the ground floor, and if the company failed, at least her father had approved. Lastly, the company's location was ideal. She had taken a strong liking to northern California in general and the city of San Francisco in particular.

If she had it to do over, she would have majored in one of her two real passions, art history or cooking. She spent all her free time either sampling the best of San Francisco's restaurants or on short trips to Napa for tastings and cooking classes at various wineries. She had managed to overcome her allergies to alcohol, at least when it came to wine. When not developing her culinary skills, she could often be found at one of city's art museums or small galleries. She was fond of the Asian Art Museum, with exhibitions that evoked a heritage that her parents had striven hard to maintain against the lure of assimilation. That struggle formed most of the conflicts she and her sister had had with their parents, especially during their teenage years. But her favorite spot was the San Francisco Museum of Modern Art, and in particular, the art of the abstract expressionists, where she sometimes spent hours losing herself. While only a teenager, unable to reconcile her parents' Sino-chauvinism with their devout Christianity, she announced she was an atheist. Her declaration led to a number of arguments regarding religion. They were able to reach a compromise of sorts when she started referring to herself as a Buddhist, which at least had Chinese roots. Now as an adult, she found Buddhist philosophy reflected in the subtlety and harmony of space and color in a Marc Rothko or Barnett Newman painting. Yet she was consumed with the raw energy and frenetic motion of the canvasses of Willem De Kooning and Jane Frank, or the bold starkness of Robert Motherwell or Franz Kline that evoked the chaos, pathos and unexplainable absurdity that she saw as humanity's condition at the end of the twentieth century.

In the less than two years since she'd started at MBG, the company had exploded to over three hundred employees. Mia was now the executive vice president in charge of strategic planning, and with the announcement that MBG had been given preliminary approval to begin limited trials of a new therapy for diabetes, the company went public. After the I.P.O., Lee informed Mia that she was now, at least on paper, worth about twelve million dollars. He then dispatched her to Beijing to enter into discussions with the Chinese government about establishing a manufacturing site there.

She finished her coffee and checked her watch. Nine-ten she muttered, meaning she had almost two hours before her scheduled meeting with Li Xuan, a deputy minister for foreign industrial development. Arranging this meeting had taken up much of her time for the three days that she'd been in China. Despite the lip service paid by the Communist Party regarding equality for women, her experiences had proven that, even more so than back home, men held the reins of power and it was almost impossible for a woman to be taken seriously. As if she needed any reminders, the Kunlun Hotel provided them. Built a decade earlier as a five-star hotel to attract Western commerce, the facility must have been some bureaucrat's concept of what businessmen want. There was a room with a dozen billiard tables, a cigar bar, and a rotating circular restaurant and bar on the roof that always seemed populated by enough high-class hookers to satisfy all the CEOs of the Fortune Five-Hundred. There was even a men-only spa that offered fifteen different types of massages, but no women's spa. So while at the hotel, she preferred staying in her room and it was clear that the hotel management was more than happy to oblige.

At ten-thirty promptly, a man wearing a military uniform appeared at her door and explained in rudimentary English that he would drive her to the meeting with the deputy minister. Mia assumed that the Chinese would send someone to keep tabs on her, she was just surprised at the lack of sophistication the government showed by not even bothering to dress her "guide" in civilian clothes. She walked into Li's office and was politely greeted by a woman who introduced herself as the translator and then introduced the deputy minister. Mia extended her hand to Li's and greeted him in Chinese. "Your Mandarin is quite good Dr. Jang," Li replied in English.

"Though I suspect, not as good as your English," Mia said, forcing a polite smile.

"I attended the University of Chicago."

"I am impressed. Do you think the translator is really necessary?"

Li nodded, dismissed the translator and offered Mia a cup of tea. They spent the next ten minutes alternating between English and Mandarin, exchanging pleasantries and hitting on topics as important as the differences in the weather in Beijing and San Francisco. Mia used the time to study the man. From the limited amount of research that she had done, she knew him to be in his early forties, a Party member and bureaucrat. Although he was fit looking and sported a full head of thick black hair, he looked older, especially around his eyes. Perhaps that was the result of the Marlboros that he chain smoked as they conversed. But the longer they spoke, the more she realized he wasn't the party apparatchik she had anticipated, but rather a civil servant trying to live out a comfortable life with his wife and son whose pictures hung on the wall below that of Mao's. And there was something she detected in the corners of his mouth as he talked that made her feel that Li was more complicated than the initial impression he tried to portray.

"I apologize it has taken so long to meet," he said. "We usually do not meet with junior staff members at this level."

Since her assistant Jeff had already met Li six weeks earlier, Mia knew he was lying, which did not surprise her based upon the cultural sexism she'd already seen at the hotel. She was savvy enough to let it slide.

"So why did you agree to take this meeting?"

"I have a letter from your president, Mr. Lee, assuring me that you have full authority to negotiate on his behalf. You know, I was wondering if maybe your company's president was a distant relative." Mia let out a shrill laugh.

"Oh, I know it is not likely, the spelling is different, but that could simply be the result of a phonetic translation, and there are millions of Li's. Yet it is possible."

"Not likely is right," she said trying to regain her composure. "You see, Fred is a descendent of Robert E. Lee. He can trace his ancestors back to the American Revolution. He's as white as Wonder Bread, if you get my meaning."

"Yes, I remember Wonder Bread from my time in America."

They spent the next hour or so discussing MBG's needs and how China fit into their plans. Their meeting ended with Li arranging a tour for Mia of various sites in and around Beijing that might be suitable for MBG's use. "Have you plans for dinner?" he asked as she was leaving.

"No. I've been eating most of my meals at the hotel, which I know is a waste of an opportunity, but the two meals I've had at restaurants thus far have been disappointing. The food was clearly prepared for foreign tourists' palates. I was hoping for something more authentic, something that my grandmother might recognize."

"I will have my driver pick you up tonight, shall we say eight?"

Mia, surprised at the offer, quickly nodded.

"Good. You like duck?" She nodded again. "I will show you the best duck in Beijing."

Exactly at eight, the same uniformed driver who had picked her up that morning knocked on her door, promptness being one advantage of a regimented society. Li took her to a small restaurant in one of the city's working class neighborhoods, a place that could only be described as a hole in the wall, and there were, quite literally, holes in the walls. The restaurant looked as though it had last been remodeled during the Ming Dynasty. There were no menus, just a chalkboard on one of the walls with Chinese characters, only some of which she could decipher. Li took the liberty of ordering for them both, starting with a duck soup, followed by an appetizer of pickled duck feet, a duck and pork stir-fry, and then the main course, two ducks carved at the table. It seemed that no part of the bird was wasted yet each course had its own distinctive flavorings. Even dessert, a type of rice pudding was made with, as one might guess, duck fat. Mia savored each flavor, and on more than one occasion, closed her eyes and let out a long, soft murmur that sounded nearly sexual in delight.

"It is nice to see a Westerner who can appreciate our cooking," Li said.

"I've never had duck like this. Thank you for taking me here." When the bill arrived, she quickly reached into her purse and took out an American Express card. Li brushed her hand away.

"No, no. You are a guest in my country. And I'm pretty sure this place does not take credit cards." He took the check from her hand and signed it – all that was necessary for a man with his position in the government. He had his driver take them on a tour of Beijing at night. The economic activity, even in local neighborhoods not usually seen by foreigners, was impressive. China's deviation from Marxism was having an immense impact on society, which explained why all of the economic forecasts of their future growth she'd been reading were so bullish. The evening ended with a drink at the Hotel Kunlun's rotating rooftop bar. As Li pointed out various historic sites which, it being nighttime were impossible to discern, his charm and occasional dry sense of humor grew on her.

The following morning, much to her surprise, Li appeared at her hotel sans driver-bodyguard-government watchdog. He showed her three industrial parks in various stages of completion and drove her to two additional tracts of land slated for future development.

"We can have space ready for you in two months if necessary."

"Frankly, it's not so much the space as the workforce that I'm concerned about. We do highly technical work requiring very skilled labor, most needing at minimum, a college degree."

"That will not be a problem. We have millions of college-educated workers, including thousands, if not tens of thousands, who have studied abroad. And like me, many have studied in the U.S. Tell us exactly what you need and we will supply the candidates for you to choose from. Would you like to see another research park?"

"No, what you've shown me so far is more than enough."

"I have blocked out the whole day for you, so is there anything else you would like to see?"

She was not expecting the offer, but realized that with Li's credentials, she would have access to sites most tourists, including native Chinese visitors, never get to see. "I have never really explored the Forbidden City."

"Done. We will stop first for lunch, then have the afternoon to explore."

As much as she was in awe of the splendors that Li showed her, she was even more impressed by the depth of his knowledge of the art and history, sometimes even correcting professional museum guides when they misstated facts. Li was far more animated and, at the same time, relaxed than he had been the previous day in his office. She could easily relate to the excitement in his voice when he described a painting or sculpture. When the private tour ended in Tiananmen Square, Li's demeanor changed. He identified the location, although she already knew where they were, and stood silently.

"Is everything okay?" she finally asked.

He nodded slowly. "You have not asked me about Tiananmen. Were you told not to?"

"Nobody told me what to say."

"I'm surprised. Most Westerners I meet have been well prepared in what they should and should not discuss."

"I am a guest in your country. It would be the height of poor manners to insult your host." In truth, the subject of Tiananmen had never been far from her thoughts. As soon as Fred Lee told her she would be going to Beijing, she had been thinking about how she might meet with some locals, perhaps even dissidents, to ask about what had happened a decade earlier. A relatively high-ranking government official was the last person she would have thought to ask. After Tiananmen, Toni was never heard from again. It took four years before her father received an official report of her sister's death, which was said to have been the result of an automobile accident in faraway Sichuan province. The Chinese blamed the delay on an inept local police department, an excuse no one in her family believed. All they knew for sure was that Toni had been in Tiananmen Square at some point during the freedom demonstrations.

Her heart began to race. She wasn't sure what Li's reaction would be or how much she'd believe anything he said, but there might never be another opportunity to bring the subject up.

"What really happened, if I may ask?" she said haltingly.

Li stood silently for a minute before letting out a small sigh.

"They were so, so wrong."

She didn't know whether he was referring to the government or the protestors, but she said nothing.

"I had been here early that last day. The students were in an exhilarated state. They were sure they were going to prevail, that the government would yield. You see that lamppost over there?" He pointed to his right. "That is the spot where I saw my younger brother for the last time. By the next morning, he and many more were dead. Most of those students' parents were government officials, with some, like my own father, very high up."

Mia could see his eyes glisten and she began moving towards him. As she started to put her arms around him, he quickly stepped away. "I know in the West, public showings of affection are common, but we do not do that here."

"I know that. It was stupid and inconsiderate. Please forgive me."

"Apology is not necessary." He looked at his watch. "It is getting late. I should get you back to your hotel since you have an early flight tomorrow."

They sat in silence for most of the drive back to the Kunlun. As they neared the hotel, she had one question that begged asking. "We have something in common. I lost a sister in China."

"Yes I know," he said.

That surprised her. "You do?" He nodded. "Of course you do. You probably know more about me than my boss does."

"It is part of my job."

"Then you know they say she died in Sichuan in a car wreck." She took a deep breath. "Is that what really happened?"

"That is what the report says."

"But do you believe it's true?" He pulled up to the hotel and stopped in front of the main entrance. "Well?" she repeated.

"Dr. Jang…"

"Mia" she interrupted.

"Okay, Mia, have a good flight back. We will talk about the next step after you've discussed this with Mr. Fred Lee." He reached out his hand to hers. They shook once, but she wouldn't let go. "I will call you next week," he said.

She slowly released his hand and stepped out of the car, but leaned back toward him before closing the door.

"I look forward to it. Thank you for all your hospitality. I had a wonderful time today." He smiled and nodded. She gently closed the car door. She remained outside the hotel until his car disappeared among the buses, bicycles and pedestrians of Xinyuan South Road.

The flight back to San Francisco was over twelve hours of torturous boredom. Mia alternated between reading magazines ranging from Forbes to Gourmet, doing work on her computer, and trying to sleep, but she kept replaying what Li had told her over and over in her mind. She was still in somewhat of a state of disbelief that the conversation had taken place.

The first thing she did upon returning to work was to sort through the hundreds of emails received while she was away. Most she mindlessly deleted without reading them, based on the sender or subject line. Near the end of the list was an email from Li. She felt a brief flutter of nervous anticipation before opening the message. It was mostly a pro-forma outline of what they had discussed regarding MBG's needs and how a deal might be structured. It was the last paragraph, however, that she read over several times. Clearly written in a different style than the rest of the message, Li informed her that he was being moved to a different position in the government, and that all future dealings with MBG would be handled by a new person yet to be named. Mia focused on the word "moved." Had anyone had been listening in on their conversations, and if so, what exactly did "moved" mean?

FOUR

Cairo

In twenty minutes Sayid's taxi had managed to move less than a block. Congestion was the norm for streets around the Khan el-Khalili souq, but this was worse than usual for nine in the morning, with car horns beeping, donkeys braying and pedestrians and drivers shouting curses at each other. Sayid sat in the cab reading a day-old copy of the Wall Street Journal, oblivious to the chaos outside. Being trapped in the car so to speak, he had the time to read the articles rather than just take a cursory scan of headlines as he usually did. It was the third paragraph of an article buried on page six about international business agreements, an article he would usually have skipped, that caught his eye.

    Mico Bio-Genetics, Inc. has announced an agree-
    ment in principle with the government of China
    for construction of a new research and manufac-
    turing facility outside Beijing. Dr. Mia Jang,
    Executive Vice-President and head of strategic
    planning for MBG says that the new facility

should be ready sometime in the first quarter
of 2000. Dr. Jang added that MBG's early trials
on a group of new gene therapy treatments were
very promising.

Mia Jang. There was a name he hadn't thought of in years. He assumed the name in the article had to be his old classmate. "Good for her," he whispered as he tore the article from the paper and put it in his pocket. Sayid had been working in Cairo since April, a stretch of nearly six months that was two months longer than originally planned. He didn't mind the extension. Cairo was his birthplace and he knew he had relatives that still lived there, although he hadn't bothered to look them up. The French consulting firm Argonne/ DeVeux for whom he'd worked since earning his doctorate paid all of his expenses, and the corporate philosophy was to spare no expense. He knew Argonne's largesse had little to do with concern for the welfare of its employees, but stemmed more from the fact that their contracts were usually written on a cost-plus basis, with the plus being a percentage of the costs. Thus it was to Argonne's advantage to incur higher costs since this resulted in higher profits. Sayid couldn't understand why any client would agree to such arrangement, but that wasn't his concern. If the Egyptian Ministry of Transportation was willing to pay for his suite at the newly opened Four Seasons Hotel, who was he to object?

The taxi crept along at an achingly slow pace. Sayid glanced at his watch and took out his daily planner to check the time of his meeting.

"Are we going to get there by ten?" he asked the driver in Arabic.

The cabbie, a short, stocky mustachioed man just lifted his shoulders as if to say, "Who knows?"

"Do you know what is going on?"

The driver mentioned something about demonstrations regarding the government's announced intention to raise the price of state-subsidized bread by twenty percent.

"If they do, there will be riots," the cabbie added.

"This is ridiculous. I can walk faster than this." Sayid took out his wallet, threw what he knew was a sufficient amount of money on the front seat and got out of the cab. It took him a moment to get his bearings before deciding which way to go. The temperature, unusually high for late October, was climbing rapidly as the morning wore on. Thankfully with this client, casual attire was the norm. Had he been wearing a suit and tie, he would have been soaked in perspiration long before he reached the ministry.

Sayid thought he was pretty familiar with the area and decided on taking a circuitous route through alleys and small streets that were less likely to be crowded. As he left one of the alleys, he found himself on a street filled with men, many of whom were dressed in traditional white clothing, sitting down and blocking traffic. His first thought was that they must be praying, a common sight five times a day in a Muslim country. But he quickly realized that it wasn't the right time of day and he had heard no muezzin's call. At once, apparently by command, the men all rose up and began walking down the street towards a group of policemen dressed in riot gear with helmets, shields and rubber batons.

When the protestors came within ten meters of the police, all hell broke loose. The policemen parted and a truck topped with a water cannon opened up on the crowd. The demonstrators in the first few rows were thrown off their feet by the force of water. This was quickly followed by policemen swinging batons and cuffing the men on the ground behind their backs with plastic restraints. Sayid knew it was time to get away and he turned back down the alley he had just come from. Some of the protestors trying to flee followed him, but it was too late. The police had already sealed off the neighborhood and from the other end of the alley they came charging towards them. The protestors behind Sayid quickly turned back, but he, assuming he had nothing to fear, remained in place. He started to take out his wallet for identification when a baton crushed into his side. He immediately bent over from the blow and tried to catch his breath, but a second whack across his back landed him on the pavement. He screamed, first in English then Arabic, vainly trying to explain that he was not part of the protest.

The weight of a policeman's boot on his shoulders pressed Sayid's chest against the cement roadway, making it nearly impossible to speak. His hands were tied behind his back. He arched his neck to try and get a better view. About a foot in front of his face he spotted his wallet lying open on the ground. The policeman's foot came off as another cop pulled him to his feet. He shouted about his wallet but the police didn't care. He and a dozen or so other men were packed into the back of a police van and the door was slammed shut and locked. They sat there, sweltering in the oven-like conditions for what must have been an hour before the van started moving and they were driven away.

Sayid guessed that the holding cell he was put in was designed for ten prisoners, but at least double that were packed in there. Whenever possible, he protested to his jailors that they had made a mistake. He was not a rioter and in fact, was doing work for the government. His pleas fell on deaf ears. For all they knew, he was no different than the hundreds of others arrested that day and his claim of innocence sounded no more valid than similar claims they'd heard before. He resigned himself to the reality that until he spoke with someone in authority, he would have to endure the confinement. The side of his chest ached from where he had been hit, and breathing was difficult and often painful. He knew enough of human anatomy to speculate that he might have a cracked rib. He found an unoccupied corner of the cell and eased himself onto the bare concrete floor.

Hours passed before any jailors came by. Looking around the cell, it was clear that many of the other men had suffered far worse beatings than he had, as revealed by their white clothes now liberally spotted with burnt umber patches of dried blood. The air was filled with moans from the injured echoing off the brick walls. He leaned back trying to get into a more comfortable position and closed his eyes. If he fell asleep, maybe he'd awake to find that this nightmare had in fact been just that.

"Are you okay?" a voice asked in Arabic.

Sayid slowly opened his eyes and looked up at a portly middle-aged man with a full beard sporting a blue embroidered taqiyah cap on his head. The man bent down and offered him a drink of water from a glass.

"Thank you," he said softly in Arabic.

"You don't look like you belong here." This time the man spoke in English.

"I don't. How did you know I spoke English?"

"I didn't for sure, but your clothes gave me a clue. You won't find any others here wearing shirts with a Ralph Lauren Polo logo."

"You know about Western fashion?"

"My name is Ibrahim Fuad. At one time I was a professor at the American University here. Before that, I taught in Saudi Arabia."

"What do you do now?"

"Now? Now I teach the people," he said pointing to the others in the cell.

"And you make a living at this?"

Ibrahim sat himself down beside Sayid.

"Depends upon your definition of living. Do I take money from these people? No. By the time they've paid for their food, meager clothing, rent, electricity and the rest, there's nothing left. But spreading knowledge and wisdom to them is my definition of a living."

"So how do *you* eat, pay rent, buy clothes, and so forth?"

"The Brotherhood takes care of my needs."

Sayid shifted his position to try to get more comfortable and put a little space between him and this teacher. "By brotherhood, I assume you mean the Muslim Brotherhood." Ibrahim nodded. "Well," Sayid grimaced as he slowly rose to his feet, "thank you again for the water, but I'm not really interested in the Brotherhood. First off, I'm an American citizen, second, I work with the Egyptian government, third, I'm not found of terrorist organizations, and lastly, I don't follow Islam."

Ibrahim remained sitting on the floor and started to laugh.

"What is your name?"

"Sayid"

"Not an American name."

"I was born in Cairo."

"I thought so. Well Sayid, you *are* Egyptian, the government that you work with has beaten you and thrown you in here, the others here are not terrorists, and you are far too young."

"Too young?"

"Too young to have seen enough of life to know what you do and do not believe in."

"I'm old enough to know that I don't plan on spending the rest of my life in Egypt. I'll be going back to Paris or London or the U.S. soon enough."

Ibrahim laughed again and started to get to his feet. Sayid reflexively helped him up.

"Thank you," he said brushing off dirt from his shirt, "but before you return to the West, you're going to have to get out of here."

"That will happen as soon as I speak with someone in charge."

Ibrahim just shook his head. He leaned in close to Sayid and whispered in his ear.

"Good luck. You may be in here for quite some time before you find that someone. Let's just hope that when you do, he believes you before he begins to question you. The standard procedure in these matters is to, as they say, 'convince' you first of the importance of telling the truth before they ask any questions."

Sayid's brow furrowed. "You don't seem concerned for your own welfare. Aren't you worried that I'll give them your name as a Brotherhood member?"

Ibrahim shrugged his shoulders. "I'd hope that you'd remember who beat you and who comforted you, and act as Allah would expect." He started to walk away, but paused a moment and placed a hand on Sayid's shoulder.

"Don't worry about me. If you tell them my background, you are telling them nothing that they do not already know."

"Then why are you so calm?"

"Simple really. The great weakness of a corrupt government is that the people who do their bidding are easily corrupted. Unlike you, I'll be sleeping tonight in my own bed. Good luck," and he went on to the next prisoner to offer water.

When they finally came to take him, Sayid was no longer so eager to be led away. He was glad to be getting out of the cell, yet Ibrahim's warning had him somewhat disconcerted. Two guards stood on either side of him holding each arm and escorted him down a shabby hallway with paint peeling everywhere. They stopped at a small room that had a couple of chairs and wooden table. The guards placed Sayid in one of the chairs then stood silently behind him until there was a knock on the door causing one of the guards to order Sayid to stand up for the colonel. In walked a disheveled officer who said something to one of the guards before he took the seat across the table from Sayid, opened a file and began reading.

Sayid sat down. "Sir. There's been a mistake," he said in Arabic. No sooner had the words been uttered than one of the guards slapped him across his face knocking him off of the chair. The corner of his mouth felt like it had exploded. His tongue tasted the trickle of blood just beginning to flow from his upper lip. His chest, which had been feeling better, once more started to throb.

"Shit," he blurted in English.

The colonel across the table didn't bother to look up from his papers.

"This will be easier if you just answer my questions. It says here your name is Hassan. Is that correct?"

"Sayid Hassan, yes. I'm an American. I was…" and another slap from the other guard landed across the other side of his face.

"Hassan, as I said, just answer the questions. Why were you taking part in the protest?"

"I wasn't. I didn't even know that one was going on. I was just trying to get to the transportation ministry. If you'll call there, they will tell you. Ask for Mohammed Muqtahd. He can vouch for me."

The officer sighed. "You don't look like you were on your way to a government meeting. How come you have no ID?"

"I lost it." The colonel's eyes squinted and his mouth turned down into a contemptuous frown. "I took it out to show the police, but they clubbed me and my wallet fell to the ground."

The colonel's gaze dropped down to the papers.

"How long have you been a part of the Brotherhood?"

"What are you talking about? I'm not a member of the Brotherhood."

The officer looked up at him for a moment before he nodded to the guards. In a flash, the guards lifted Sayid by his armpits and flung him face down on the table. His trousers were ripped down to his ankles and one of the guards lashed him with a rubber baton across his bare buttocks.

"How long?" the officer calmly repeated.

"I tell you I'm no member," he pleaded. His eyes began to water. The colonel's face hovered over Sayid's. Sayid plaintively stared back into his eyes. He felt faint and thought he would pass out. As one guard grabbed a hank of his hair and pulled back his head, the other reamed the end of a baton up his rectum. The pain that shot through his body made him forget his aching ribs. Speech was now beyond his ability and he tried to communicate to his tormentors by furiously shaking his head. They flipped him over on his back. One guard and the colonel held him down by his shoulders. Sayid's heart was pounding and he was covered in sweat.

"You worthless piece of shit. What happens to you people after you leave here and go to America? What do they teach you? To come back here, take a wife and then try to overthrow the government? You know what's really a shame? You will probably get out of here in sixty days and go back to your wife, or do you have more than one? Do they instruct you to have many children and raise them to strap on bombs and kill innocent Egyptians?" Sayid started to pant in short, spasmodic breaths. The interrogator seemed mad beyond all reason. The thought crossed his mind that perhaps this police colonel had suffered some personal loss and had decided to take out his vengeance on him.

"Well Hassan, at least you are one traitor who will not be making little terrorists." With that the officer nodded at the other guard not restraining Sayid. That guard pulled a six-inch knife from his belt and held it out for all to see before moving closer and placing the edge of the blade under Sayid's scrotum.

"Oh Jesus," he screamed. "Oh God. Fuck. No! Please, I beg you. No. Don't. Jesus. What do you want? I'll tell you whatever I know. Please." His voice cracked. "Please," and he broke down sobbing.

The colonel eased off of his shoulder and signaled to the guards to step back.

"Pull up your pants and sit down."

Sayid tried to compose himself but couldn't completely stop crying or contain his shaking.

"Get him a glass of water." Sayid took several deep breaths before accepting the glass from one of the guards. "So Hassan, are you ready to continue?"

"I'm telling the truth," he began, his voice shaky and cracking. "I was there in the street just trying to get to a meeting at the transportation ministry, not to protest anything. I'm not in the Brotherhood. I have American citizenship. I live outside Paris. I'm in Egypt only for work. What else can I tell you?"

"It's almost four. You've been here most of the day in that cell with others, some of them I assure you are terrorists even if it should turn out that you are not. Have you spoken with any of them?"

"Just one."

"And what did he say to you?"

Sayid now faced a decision – reveal to the colonel that Ibrahim was a member of the Muslim Brotherhood, or not. Exposing Ibrahim might gain favor with the colonel, but at what cost to his psyche? He didn't worry about how Allah might view his actions; being fairly sure of God's non-existence makes it easy not to worry about that being's opinions. But he did believe in two concepts inured by a decade and a half of formal education; the American ethos of justice augmented by the British sense of honor. Betraying Ibrahim ran counter to both. Yet there was also the possibility that his captors had been watching all the time he had been in the cell, even listening in on his conversation, and the colonel was now testing him. Still, if they hadn't been watching, then informing the colonel that the one person he'd spoken with was an enemy of the state might raise new suspicions regarding himself. It was a quandary that overloaded his decision-making ability. Ibrahim had more or less given him his permission when he told him that the police already knew of his background, and anyway, Ibrahim wasn't worried about his own safety. He wasn't sure what to say, he just knew that his lip was swelling, his ribs were sore and his ass felt as though it was on fire.

"Mr. Hassan, what did the other prisoner say to you?"

"Not much. He gave me some water and I think he said his name was Fuad or something."

"Nothing else?" Sayid just slowly shook his head. The colonel looked up at the guards.

"Take him back." Sayid stood and prepared to leave with the guards. "And when you're done with that, get me the transportation ministry on the phone."

"Thank God," Sayid whispered, and then did something which when he later thought about, he found embarrassingly inconceivable. He reached out and offered to shake the colonel's hand. Hesitantly, the colonel accepted his offer. "What made you believe me?"

"You called out to Jesus. Jihadists don't invoke the Christian god."

Sayid shook his head in disbelief that an expression he cried out in terror, an expression used out of cultural habit and never intended as a call for divine help, had spared him who knows what kind of bodily harm.

"Ironic. One word, and that makes you believe me."

"I didn't say I believe you. We will wait to see what the transportation ministry has to say."

He walked gingerly back to the cell and found his old corner still vacant. He sat down and Ibrahim came over. "You don't look too bad." Sayid said nothing. "Do you need anything?" Sayid slowly shook his head. "Did they believe you?"

"I hope so."

"Well then, congratulations. I am glad for you."

"They nearly cut my fucking balls off."

"But you survived. Do you remember the young man in here with the bandages around his leg?"

Sayid closed his eyes and leaned back against the wall. "There were a lot with bandages."

"True. Anyway, he didn't – survive that is. They took him right after they took you and I guess his tormentors weren't as careful as yours."

"Ibrahim Fuad," a jailor called out.

"Well, time for me to go. My wife will be angry if I'm late for dinner." The jailor handed Ibrahim his personal possessions and in a courteous manner, led him out of the cell.

It took until the next morning for Sayid to be released. He was leaving the police station when the colonel came up to him. "The ministry was closed by the time we called, so we couldn't confirm your story until now. My advice to you in the future, don't go walking through neighborhoods you don't know."

"That's it? You beat me and I'm just supposed to go on as though nothing happened?"

"You're supposed to go back to your hotel, pack your bags and go back to Paris or America or wherever it is you live."

"You know I still hold Egyptian citizenship. Maybe I should file a complaint with the authorities."

"Mr. Hassan, do what you like, but the longer you stay here, the longer you run the risk of ending up in jail again. Now go."

He looked out the door and saw a cab waiting at the curb. "Is that taxi for me?"

"It's for whoever gets into it."

Sayid reached into his pockets. "I have no money."

"That is not my problem."

He walked out of the station and started heading down the street in what he thought was the general direction of his hotel. The taxi that had been waiting followed slowly alongside of him with the driver repeatedly beckoning him to enter.

"I have no money. I can't pay you." But the driver kept waiving him in. Sayid stopped and leaned into the open window. "I've lost my wallet. I have no money."

"You don't pay," the cabbie said in broken English. "Ibrahim Fuad send me." Sayid stood there and when the driver didn't leave, he opened the door and cautiously climbed into the back seat. His body was stiff and ached in places it never had before. A night spent trying to sleep on the cement floor of the prison cell hadn't helped.

"Ibrahim said I take you to doctor."

"Just take me to the Four Seasons."

"Ibrahim be mad if I don't take you to doctor."

"Tell him you took me to a doctor. Please, just go to the hotel."

He walked into his suite and his first action was to rip off his clothes, roll them into a ball and stuff them into a trash can. He noticed right away the blinking red light on his phone indicating that someone had left a message, but he was in no mood to check it. Instead he opened the mini-bar, took out a handful of small airplane-sized liquors and quickly downed two bottles of Stolichnaya followed by a bottle of Johnny Walker Black. He grabbed a couple of more drinks from the refrigerator before going into to the bathroom and filling the tub with hot water. Next to the sink basin he found a bottle of Ibuprofen and washed down five tablets with another shot of liquor, he didn't bother to look at what kind it was. In the mirror, he saw for the first time the swollen cuts on his face and the dark bruise across the side of his chest. He couldn't bring himself to look at his backside. When the tub was full, he slipped himself into the water and sat soaking for nearly an hour. After the water had cooled to the point where it was no longer pleasant to be in, he got out of the tub and gently toweled off his body. He stumbled over to the bed and lacking the energy to even crawl under the sheets, collapsed naked on top of the covers.

He had no idea how long he'd slept, except that when he awoke and looked out the window, it was night. Any thoughts of forgetting his ordeal were quickly dispelled when he got up from the bed to go to the bathroom. Each step was agony. Although he hadn't eaten in more than a day, he wasn't in the least bit hungry. He just wanted to get back into bed and hopefully sleep some more. He took another handful of Ibuprofen. The red message light on his phone was still blinking. He decided to listen. There were two messages. The first was from his contact at the transportation ministry asking him if he remembered that they had a meeting. The second was from Paul DeVeux, chairman and CEO of Argonne/DeVeux. DeVeux's message was succinct. The Egyptians had requested a new consultant and that Sayid leave the country immediately. He was instructed to get himself to the airport as soon as possible and that a ticket would be waiting for him at the Air France counter. They would discuss his situation when he got back to Paris. Sayid called Air France only to learn that the next flight he could get a seat on wasn't until morning, but there was one eleven p.m. departure that he could try and fly standby on. Frankly, he wanted out of Egypt as fast as possible, but the thought of spending the night sleeping on a chair in an airport lounge if he didn't get on that flight rather than the luxurious king-sized hotel bed made the choice an easy one.

DeVeux personally met him when he landed at Charles de Gaulle airport. "What the hell happened to you? You look like shit."

"It's a long story."

"Let's get your bags. You can tell me about it in the car."

The ride from the airport back to Sayid's apartment was the first time he'd felt some semblance of safety since the moment just before the police had seized him in that alley. He tried to explain to his boss what had happened. When he got to his interrogation, he felt the back of his throat tighten and he spoke little of it, only saying it was very rough without going into detail. He also left out any mention of Ibrahim Fuad.

"You should be seen by a doctor. I'll take you to the hospital."

"I'm really okay. I just want to go home. I'll see a doctor later."

"If you're sure."

"I am."

"Very well, but I want you to take a medical leave and use your vacation time and come back after the New Year. We don't have any immediate work for you anyway."

"Let me at least get my notes together so that whoever takes over the Egypt project won't be starting at square one."

"No one's taking over the Egypt project. They cancelled the contract."

"Shit. I am sorry Paul."

DeVeux glanced over at him as he drove.

"Don't be. I'd say you've suffered enough. If they don't want to modernize their traffic control, it's their loss, not mine. Have you spoken with your family?"

"My parents are both dead."

"No brothers or sisters?"

Sayid didn't answer at first. "I had a brother. He was killed in a car crash when he was seventeen."

"So there's just you?"

"Just me."

DeVeux arranged for Sayid to have use of a company-owned villa on the French side of St. Marten. The warm Caribbean climate and clear aquamarine seas had their desired effect, except at night when every so often, Sayid would awake perspiring and shaking. He never remembered the details of the dream that had so disturbed his sleep. The millennium arrived on schedule on January 1st, 2000, and despite the dire predictions of some, the world's computers didn't crash, nuclear reactors didn't melt down, airplanes continued to fly and trains didn't collide. A few days later, DeVeux sent an email asking Sayid if he was ready to return to work. Argonne was bidding on a contract with the Saudis and since Sayid was their only employee fluent in Arabic, he was needed. Sayid was ready, the occasional flashback to Cairo notwithstanding. It was time to get back to the real world but before leaving this tropical paradise, he decided to catch up on what had been happening by reading through some of the old copies of the New York Times that had been delivered daily to the villa, but which he had ignored.

He read a few articles on world news and some commentaries that mostly dealt with the upcoming U.S. presidential election to choose Clinton's successor. He focused more on the business section since that might actually have news that would be helpful. Three articles caught his eye. The first was an article dated November 12th about Clinton's signing of the Gramm-Leach-Bliley Act into law. He read about how the law that bore the name of the Texas senator who was chairman of the banking committee would allow banks, investment firms and insurance companies to merge. The second article was more recent and described how that same senator Gramm had managed at the eleventh hour to sneak in a small piece of legislation as an amendment to the three hundred billion dollar-plus appropriations legislation with the innocuous title of Commodities Futures Modernization Act. Gramm's bill was passed just as Congress was trying to adjourn for the Christmas recess. Apparently many members of Congress weren't even aware of what they were voting on, but if what the article said was true, then the credit default swap market was about to be shaken up. Not only would those new conglomerated banks/investment-houses/insurers find CDSs easier to structure and trade, but the law prevented these financial instruments from being regulated by states as an insurance product, even though Sayid knew that is essentially what they were.

"Adam Meecham must be turning over in his grave," he said aloud.

The final article was a small blurb announcing the resignation of Dr. Mia Jang from Micro Bio-Genetics to serve as a member of a U.S. trade commission to China. Mia was quoted as saying it was her hope that new ways of reducing the growing trade deficit with China could be worked out. Sayid looked up Mia's email address on MBG's web site and fired off a congratulatory email. Forty-eight hours later he received an auto-generated reply saying that her email address was no longer valid.

FIVE

New York

Jake Himmelfarb watched numbers flash across the four computer screens that filled nearly every square inch of his desk. As the head energy trader for Pilgrim/United Equities, he had earned his upscale private office. That office, on the eighty-fifth floor of the south tower of the World Trade Center, offered a view that stretched from midtown Manhattan on the left to the Verrazano Bridge on the right, and if one looked carefully mid-point, the Brooklyn neighborhood of his youth. Jake rarely if ever looked out the window. There were too many other sources vying for his attention, not the least of which were the computers on which he hoped to spot trends before others and pick the optimum moment to make a trade.

Jake had risen steadily up the corporate ladder since leaving MIT. Arthur Morrison was right when he told him that everything he'd need to know could only be learned on the job. He quickly grasped that much of what drove financial markets were the same forces that drove gambling, which is that despite the relative strength or weakness of the underlying asset, the cost of an investment, whether that be the price of a stock or the odds on a football wager, were often determined by the mass psychology of the purchasers, be they investors or gamblers. Many times, investors and bettors made decisions based on incomplete or inaccurate information, but Jake knew that wasn't their greatest flaw. Their greatest flaw was letting their own preferences and prejudices skew their judgment. His job was to remove his own feelings regarding companies and the products they made or the people who ran them, make valuations based on hard, impersonal numbers, and then see how those valuations compared with the selling price of those stocks, bonds or commodities in the market. At this, Jake had become very, very good. So good in fact that after First Pilgrim merged with United Investors of Mid-America to form Pilgrim/United, he was made head of energy investments, the highest position any former Pilgrim employee was given, with the notable exception of Morrison, the new company's chairman. This led more than a few disgruntled Pilgrim employees to conclude that Jake's success owed more to his prowess at the bridge table where, as Morrison's partner, they had won numerous tournaments, rather than his investing expertise. Jake had heard these rumors, but ignored them. He believed that, above all, Arthur cared most about earnings and their success at bridge wouldn't save his job if he couldn't produce results.

Jake's days were one long, frenetic stream of mental gymnastics. By the time he'd leave, never before nine at night and often later, he needed to decompress from workplace stress and the two-dozen cups of black coffee he habitually drank. This usually meant meeting his wife, the former Debbie Moshman, for an expensive dinner then hitting the club scene where they'd snort lines of cocaine through hundred dollar bills and quench their thirst with five-hundred dollar bottles of Cristal. Debbie was the first girl he'd ever slept with. When he knew her as a teenager, she was a dumpy, overweight girl with brown frizzy hair, a big nose and not the best complexion. But as a skinny kid with complexion problems of his own, he wasn't choosy. After he'd lost track of her, Debbie's father, a successful dentist, paid for her plastic surgery and weight loss treatments. It was by chance that Jake ran into Debbie at a club one night. He didn't recognize the striking blond in the tight skirt on the dance floor as his childhood girlfriend, but she recognized him. One thing led to another and, to the ecstatic joy of both their mothers, they were married at an over-the-top wedding at Leonard's of Great Neck in Queens.

The financial trends in the first quarter of the new century were all over the map, which made predicting with any certainty where the markets were

headed an impossible task. Jake watched dumbfounded as one of his computers displayed the tech-heavy NASDAQ numbers. The index was over 4,300
and climbing by the minute with no ceiling in sight. Jake's sense of these
things told him that the numbers behind those companies on that exchange
couldn't possibly justify these outrageous stock prices, but he'd said the same
thing when the NASDAQ was 1,000 points lower. He was glad to be in energy
trading which was comparatively stable.

"Jake, have you a minute?"

He looked up from his computers and saw Morrison standing at the door
to his office.

"Of course Art, come in."

Morrison took a seat on the sofa in Jake's office and Jake came out from
behind his desk and sat in a chair across from him. Morrison lit up a cigarette,
something prohibited by city ordinance, but of course Arthur assumed such
laws didn't apply to him. Jake scrambled about for an ashtray but having none,
he handed him an empty coffee cup. "Thanks. I'm here not as your boss but as
a concerned voter. Been paying any attention to the upcoming election?"

"Frankly, no. I've been a little busy. Besides it's March. The election isn't till
November, unless they've changed things. They haven't, have they?"

"No, it's still November. But if we wait until then, it will be too late to help.
I'm supporting George Bush. Can I count on your support?"

"Bush? Wasn't he already president?"

"This is his son, the governor of Texas. If we can get a Republican back in
the White House, maybe we can get some sanity into our taxes."

"Okay, Bush will get my vote."

"Your vote in this state won't mean shit. What I need is your financial
support. Can I count on it?"

"Sure. How much?"

"Two grand is the most you can give."

"No problem." Jake walked back to his desk and took out his checkbook.
"Who do I make this out to?"

"George Bush for President will work." Morrison remained seated while
Jake made out the check. "And your wife can contribute two thousand as
well." Jake didn't hesitate to write a second check and sign Debbie's name to
it. He walked back to Morrison and handed him the money. "Thanks Jake.
Remember, this has nothing to do with work."

"No, of course not."

"Are you ready for next week?" Jake wasn't sure what Morrison was referring to and didn't answer. "You know, San Diego, the spring North American championships?"

"Oh that. I'm ready."

"We'll take the corporate jet out on Monday. Try and rest. I want to win this damn thing."

Four months later Morrison was back in Jake's office asking for additional campaign contributions. Jake reminded him that he had already given and was worried that they might be violating campaign finance laws. Morrison said that the earlier contributions had gone to the primary campaign and these new contributions were for the general election. By the time the U.S. Supreme Court had made its ruling in December and George W. Bush was proclaimed president, the NASDAQ was trading in the low two-thousands. While many of the traders at Pilgrim/United were downing Maalox by the gallon, Jake felt vindicated. His energy trades had done so well that it earned him a two and a half million dollar year-end bonus. The bad showing in the stock markets did little to dampen Arthur's good mood at Bush's election. Jake had always figured that what presidents did had little to no effect on the economy, so whether it was Bush or Gore made no difference. But he knew that Morrison had a number of close relationships with members of the new administration and that would have to be advantageous.

In late February Jake was once again on a corporate jet flying with Arthur to Curacao for another bridge tournament. Arthur departed from his usual rules, which banned wives or girlfriends on these trips and allowed Debbie to accompany Jake. Jake wasn't sure whether Arthur was mellowing in his old age or had discovered Viagra because a shapely twenty-two-year-old redhead named Cherise – she apparently lacked a last name – was also on board. Jake and the two women sat in the cabin, sipping chardonnay and sampling caviar as the jet made its way out of New York airspace. When Arthur, who had been in the cockpit since takeoff, finally joined them, he announced that they would be making an unplanned stop in Washington, D.C.

In spite of knowing the statistics, Jake was always nervous when it came to flying. "Is there a problem?" There was a slight quiver in his voice.

"No problem. I've been asked to attend a meeting at the White House. Shouldn't take more than a couple of hours. You girls might as well stay at the airport. Jake, I think you should come with me."

Jake couldn't fathom why Arthur would want to take him along. Jake was a Switzerland when it came to politics, always maintaining strict neutrality. "Me? Why?"

"The meeting has to do with energy policy. I figured it wouldn't hurt to have my chief energy trader sit in."

They were picked up at Reagan National Airport in a large, black SUV with flashing red and blue lights visible through the windshield. Despite having traveled around the world, Jake had only been in D.C. once before, a seventh-grade trip to tour the monuments and museums. He stared out through the dark-tinted windows at the monuments as they crossed the Potomac, trying to remember which one was for Jefferson and which for Lincoln. "So who are we meeting?" he asked Arthur.

"The usual crowd, I suspect. There'll be people from utilities, probably coal, and of course I'm sure that Exxon and the rest of oil will be there. This was explained to me as an advisory meeting to get our input on what energy policies the new administration should pursue. Isn't it great to have a government that wants to work for you rather than the other way around?"

"And who from the government are we seeing?"

"The vice president himself."

"Really. What do you want me to do?"

"Simple, just keep your mouth shut and listen. You may learn something that could be valuable. Oh, and one other thing. If I should start to tell a joke about fags, give me a swift kick. Cheney's got a daughter who's a dyke."

Jake had always found Morrison's penchant for telling off-color jokes about gays one of his least redeeming qualities, although he certainly possessed many others. Part of it he attributed to a generational thing, part of it was that when all was said and done, Arthur was simply not a nice person. And when it came to the subject of gays, Jake's heightened sensitivity was a direct result of seeing the emotional and societal barriers that his younger brother faced daily. "I will be more than happy to give you a swift kick."

Morrison nodded. "So what do think of Cherise?"

"Seems like a bright girl."

"I don't know about being bright, but you gotta admit, she's got a great set of tits." Arthur chuckled and slapped Jake's leg.

Their SUV stopped briefly at the gate to the White House before pulling up to a side entrance where they were greeted by an aide to the vice president. After being given security passes they were taken to a conference room where a number of other businessmen were already seated around a large rectangular mahogany table. There were only two vacant seats left at the table. Arthur took the seat that was near the end and Jake realized that the other seat, smack dab in the middle, must be for the vice president. He parked himself behind Morrison in one of the chairs that ringed the walls of the room. Arthur seemed to know everyone around the table by name, which wasn't surprising. Jake recognized most of the men, especially the ones who led oil and gas companies. He reached into his briefcase and took out a pad of yellow paper and a pen.

"No notes, please." Jake looked up at the aide who had greeted them when they arrived.

"Oh, sorry." He put away the pad and waited, feeling a tad conspicuous over the reprimand.

Everyone stood as Cheney entered the room, most even applauded. The vice president went around the table and personally shook each man's hand. When he came to Jake, Arthur made the introductions. Jake couldn't deny that there was a certain thrill at being present at the epicenter of world power.

"I want to welcome all of you here to the White House and thank you for taking time from what I know are your very busy schedules to be here today. A couple of housekeeping rules before we get started – I want to assure you that your presence here will remain anonymous. I want and need everyone's candid thoughts and opinions. To that end, anything you say today will be held in the strictest confidence. To make sure it stays that way, I'd like you all to sign the confidentiality statement that Mike here is handing out."

"What am I signing Mr. Vice President?" asked one of the men.

"It simply says that you agree not to disclose any of our discussions to anyone."

"Under legal penalty?" asked another.

Cheney gave a chortle. "Well, let's just say I know people over at Langley who know where to find you, and know how to handle the situation."

Everyone laughed at Cheney's joke. Jake sort of laughed, but he didn't know that Langley is where the CIA is headquartered, and thus missed the inference.

The meeting went on for several hours with discussions, occasionally spirited, regarding energy policy and needs. After a while, Jake began to zone out and he found himself thinking about drinking pina coladas on the white sands of a Caribbean beach.

"Frank, you've been awfully quiet," Cheney finally said.

Frank Hollister was a man not many outside of that room would ever have heard of, much less recognized, but Jake knew who he was. In his younger years he became something of a legend as an Oklahoma wildcatter.

"Well Dick, I was just wondering..." It was a testament to Hollister's prestige that he used Cheney's first name when addressing him rather than the more formal "Mr. Vice President" as had everyone else.

"Wondering what?"

"Wondering when someone was going to have the balls to stop dancing around the issue and really tell it like it is."

"Go on."

"Regardless of all this bullshit about alternative energy sources, clean coal, wind, solar and the rest of that crap, this country still depends on oil, and it's going to be that way for decades and everyone here knows it. With all due respect to my brothers in coal, you can't drive your car on coal, we're not going back to powering our trains and ships on coal, and you sure as hell can't fly a plane on coal. The problem is we've got two percent of the world's proven oil reserves in this country, so we're dependent on some pretty unstable areas to get what we need. The Saudis have the most."

"We're on good terms with the Saudis," Cheney said.

"But for how long? That place is run by a single family, not exactly a recipe for long-term stability. You say we're on good terms, but what happens if those damn Israelis and damn Palestinians start shooting it up? Politically, no U.S. government's gonna back the Arabs over the Jews. Remember the embargo of seventy-three?"

"So what is your suggestion?"

"The Saudis have the most, but as you say, we're on good terms. Now Iraq is number two in proven reserves."

"In case you've forgotten, we're not exactly friendly with them."

"My point precisely. Look at the situation. You got a mad man in Saddam Hussein. He's started wars against his neighbors. He's gassed his own people. For Christ's sake, Dick, he even tried to have pappy Bush assassinated. Get rid of Saddam and everyone in that region will be better off and thank us for it. If we can take over that country, put in a government friendly to us, we'll have unlimited access to an oil supply that could satisfy our needs for the next seventy-five years."

Cheney rubbed his forehead. "One problem, Frank. How do we justify such a move?"

"I don't know, but that's what we elected you for, to figure out these things. We are, after all, talking about the security of the United States. Find a reason; make one up if you have to. Like I said, Hussein's an evil man. Wouldn't the world have been a much safer place if someone had had the guts to take out Joe Stalin back in the forties? There'd have been no cold war, and a hell of a lot of Russians wouldn't have been shot or worked to death in gulags. Get rid of Saddam, put in a good government and Americans generations from now will be singing this Bush's praises."

"He's right, you know Mr. Vice President," chimed in one of the other oil execs.

Cheney looked around the table and even though no one spoke, the consensus seemed to agree with Hollister. Cheney gave a single nod of his head. "I'll take it under advisement. Anything else anyone would like to say?" When no one responded, the vice president thanked them all and left.

"So did you learn anything?" Morrison asked Jake as they rode back to the airport.

"Nothing that will help in trading. That Hollister's something else though."

"Frank Hollister thinks he's still living in the world of John D. Rockefeller and Harry Sinclair. Forget all that crap about Iraq. This George Bush isn't about to start any wars, especially with guys like Cheney, Rumsfeld and Powell around him. They're simply too smart. I guarantee that this administration won't be invading anyone. You can make book on it."

The SUV pulled up to the curb. Morrison grabbed Jake's arm before they got out. "One last thing, don't forget Cheney's warning. Whatever was said back in that room stays back in that room. If anything gets out, they'll trace it back to the source."

"Yeah, I know. They could throw me in jail."

"Or worse."

"Worse? What could be worse?"

"They'll cut you off. More importantly, since you were there on my account, they'll cut me off. It's all about access, my boy. Access leads to success. For me to be able to pick up the phone and get right through to people like Cheney, well you can't put a price on what that's worth. So don't fuck it up."

They were soon airborne and headed to Curacao. Arthur was making jokes that only he and Debbie seemed to be laughing at, leaving Jake to wonder what she may have been doing while he and Morrison were at the White House. "I like your girl," he said to Jake as he poured himself a bourbon and lit up a cigarette. "Where have you been hiding her? Oh, and did I mention we're moving?"

"I heard you bought a condo overlooking the park. Didn't realize that you and Cherise were that serious."

"Fuck, she's not moving in with me, and I moved into the condo two months ago. No I'm moving the office. I signed a lease for office space in midtown across from Grand Central. We'll move in August when things are a little slow anyway."

"I thought you liked being in the WTC. Didn't you always say you like being high up?"

"Height is overrated, especially when the rent is double what we will be paying for the new space. More importantly, I can walk from my home to the new office."

"You walk? Somehow I don't see that happening."

"Yeah, well the doctors tell me to exercise more and get my cholesterol down."

"Ever thought of quitting smoking?"

"Every goddamn day."

"So why don't you?"

"If I quit, then what challenges are left? Oh, I know, the old joke, quitting's easy, I've done it a hundred times, blah, blah, blah. But the challenge isn't quitting, it's to keep on smoking and not die from it. Think of the satisfaction one gets from proving people with egos as big as doctors wrong." Arthur took a long drag off his cigarette and blew the smoke in Jake's direction.

SIX

At the same time Jake was flying to Curacao, Sayid was on a plane to Riyadh. Paul DeVeux wasn't sure that Sayid was ready to return to the Middle East, but Sayid was his only employee who spoke the language fluently. Sayid was confident that his experience in Egypt was a fluke and he had put it in the past; anyway, the Saudis were different. Their population was small, there was no large, organized opposition, and most importantly, they had virtually unlimited money which meant that the government could keep its citizens mollified. Still, he hadn't been on the ground for ten minutes before a Saudi policeman yelled at him for walking into a restricted zone in the airport, causing Sayid to drop his bags and freeze in place. His logical mind told him that he was probably overreacting, the result of post-traumatic stress that his therapist had warned him of. But the logical side of his brain couldn't fully overcome the emotional side.

When Sayid was not meeting with his Saudi clients, he stayed cloistered in his hotel room. As the days passed, he became aware of a certain man who always seemed to be in the hotel lobby watching his comings and goings. It reached the point where he asked the concierge whether the man was a hotel employee. Told no, his level of paranoia ratcheted up. The next time he observed the same man follow him into the lobby, he made a U-turn back outside and hid behind a corner of the building. He watched the hotel doors and as he feared, the man soon emerged, looking desperately in all directions. Sayid took a deep breath and without over-thinking, strode right up to the man. "Is there something you want from me?" he said in English. The man didn't answer, but his eyes grew wide as he seemed to cower before Sayid. Sayid repeated the question, this time in Arabic.

The man relaxed and smiled. "It's okay," he said softly and held out his hand to him. Sayid was a little taken aback, but he extended his own and they shook. Then, as quickly as he'd appeared, he walked away leaving a folded piece of paper in Sayid's palm. Sayid unfolded the note. On it was a phone number and a short message written in English. *Let's talk – I. Fuad.*

It was another two days before he screwed up the courage to call the number.

"Sayid," said the voice on the other end. "I wasn't sure you'd remember me."

"I wish I couldn't. I wish I could forget everything about Egypt."

"We should talk. There's a coffee shop down the block from your hotel. Let's meet tonight, say eight?"

He paused before replying. "I'm not sure that's a good idea."

"There is nothing to fear. It is perfectly safe."

"I'd still prefer not to."

"Okay. If you change your mind, you have my number," and Ibrahim hung up.

A day later he called Fuad back and they met that night. He found Ibrahim sitting with a few other men at a small table in the rear of the coffee shop. He walked up to the table and Ibrahim broke into a broad smile. Fuad dismissed the others and Sayid took a seat across from him.

"So, how are you doing?"

"I'm fine."

"Really?"

Sayid coughed and squirmed in his seat for a moment. "Really."

Ibrahim took a sip of Turkish coffee. "Good. I hear you are in Arabia to help the king."

"I'm doing an economic impact study on new highway construction. How is it that you know so much about me?"

"I have friends in the government. Some coincidence, huh? I was in a Cairo jail with you, then I come here only to discover that you are here as well."

"I would have thought that you'd attribute it to Allah's will or fate having pre-written our destiny."

Ibrahim smiled again. "Nothing is written, except up here," he said tapping his temple with his right hand.

"Is that from the Koran?"

"Peter O'Toole in Lawrence of Arabia. So what do you think of this country? Well country may be an overstatement. This place is more of a playground run by family of spoiled rich old men who act like teenagers."

A waiter came over and Sayid ordered a coffee.

"At least the population is taken care of, which is more than I can say for Egypt."

"Taken care of? Have you seen the way they treat foreign workers here? I'm not talking about $500 an hour consultants like you, but the people from places like Indonesia and Bangladesh who do the jobs that Saudis don't want to do but need to have done. They are little more than slaves. No, they are slaves. A repressive government, even a wealthy one that bribes its population, is still a force for degradation and should be destroyed. That, in different words, is from the Koran."

The waiter delivered Sayid his coffee. He took a sip, before whispering, "You're speaking as though you are advocating a revolution. Aren't you the least bit concerned that someone may be listening?"

"I am advocating a revolution, and I am not alone. The owner of this shop is one of us. He'd let me know if someone is listening in. What I don't understand is you."

"What don't you understand?"

"Why you are not angry, furious. You are an Arab, and you are a Muslim, even if you deny it. These are your people too who are oppressed. Mohammed calls on each of us in our own time to stand up for the oppressed."

"Of all the instruments of oppression, religion is the one most used, and the most effective."

"Spoken like a man who's spent too much time in the West. Religion has also been the instrument of greatest liberation, even in the West. Look at America. Their black civil rights leaders were all men of religion."

"An odd observation. Those guys were all Christians. I thought you considered America the instrument of Satan."

"Odd or not, it's true. America's problem is that they assassinated their good leaders because they couldn't tolerate the truth. And the first one they killed was Malcolm X, a Muslim. That was *not* a coincidence. Without America, the kingdom here would collapse, as would the government in Egypt. The only way that Muslims in general and Arabs in particular will achieve a just society is to unite against their oppressors. And the only means of uniting enough people is through faith. Let's be brutally honest – most of our brethren, through no fault of their own, are poorly educated and ignorant. It is to the advantage of the powerful to keep them that way. Islam is the only force that can bring change and restore our glory of old."

"Good luck."

"Sayid, if you aren't angry about your brothers' suffering, then at least you should be angry at the way you were treated."

"Why are you so interested in me?"

"I am interested in everyone's welfare. But Allah has bestowed much on you. You have knowledge and intelligence above many others. You are uniquely positioned to be of incredible help in the struggle."

"What knowledge?"

"You know the West. You know America. As I said, as long as America keeps a presence in this part of the world, we will never be able to get rid of the Israelis and our own corrupt rulers. You have a chance to make a difference in people's lives."

"What do you want of me?"

"Quit your job, or at least, take leave for a month. Come with me and see what we are doing. See the army we are training. If you are not persuaded to join us, then go your own way. But remember, you can be a force either for good or evil."

"An army? Where are you raising this army?"

"Afghanistan. What do you say?"

Sayid didn't answer right away. His instincts told him to bolt out of that coffee shop, but he didn't move. It had been nearly six months since Egypt. Six months of taking a sedative each night and still not sleeping well. Six months of taking notice of everyone he passed on the streets and wondering if they posed a threat. Six months since he had any sense of control over his life. He was tired of it all. He wanted his old life back, but he saw no way of getting it back. Why wasn't he angrier at being robbed of his life? His conclusion was the only way to get his life back was to stop being a victim and take a stand. Ibrahim offered a path, an honorable path paved in righteous justice. But in the end, he could not see himself as a modern-day jihadist, if for no other reason than his fear and suspicion of religious fanatics. "Quitting my job and going to Afghanistan is not for me. Sorry."

Ibrahim sighed. "So be it then." He took a sip of coffee and motioned to the waiter for a refill. "So what have you been doing here when not planning new highways for the king?"

"Not much, really. I mostly go back to my hotel and read or watch TV."

"You should get out more. There is plenty to do in Riyadh. You need to meet people. Come to my house tomorrow. I'm having some people over for dinner. Don't worry, I guarantee no politics will be discussed. What do you say?"

He was still leery of associating with Ibrahim, not because he distrusted him, but because he feared the Saudi police might take a dim view if they knew. But he was also tired of his isolated existence. "Okay, I'll come."

"Excellent. I should be going." They left the coffee shop and walked together towards Sayid's hotel, chatting about non-political subjects like soccer. "You grew up in America right?" Ibrahim asked casually.

"Outside of Boston."

"I was in Boston once. All I ever saw was the airport. I was only there for a layover. Do you know that airport?"

"Logan? Yeah I've flown out of there a hundred times."

"I'm sure things have changed since I was there. Sometime we'll have to talk about that airport."

Sayid arrived at Ibrahim's apartment the following night and was greeted by his wife and introduced to several members of his extended family. The apartment was filled with people eating and conversing. Dinner was not a formal sit-down affair, but a buffet with people eating wherever they could find a seat. Sayid filled a plate and found an empty spot on a couch in the den.

"Is anyone sitting there?"

Sayid looked up at a young woman dressed almost like a Westerner except for the scarf covering her head. With his mouth being full of food, he could only motion with his hand for her to sit. He quickly swallowed. "How did you know I spoke English?"

"Oh, you have that look about you. I'm very perceptive about people."

"Really?"

She laughed. "That, and Ibrahim told me."

"Oh. I didn't realize that he was explaining me to everyone."

"He wasn't. I asked him. In case you hadn't noticed, most of the people here are about my parents' age. You are one of the few who is under forty and not with a wife and five kids. I'm Yasmin." She held out her hand to him, which for a woman in Saudi society was a very forward thing to do.

"I'm Sayid," he said shaking her hand. "You speak with a British accent. Are you from England?"

"Originally from Palestine, but I was educated outside of London."

"What are you doing here?"

"I'm a nurse. There were no jobs in Palestine, at least none that paid anything close to what I make here. I work at a hospital with Ibrahim's brother-in-law, which is why I'm here."

"Does your family still live in Palestine?"

"My parents live outside Beirut. I go back when I can." She pulled her scarf back slightly and fanned herself with her hands. "It's awfully hot in here."

"There are a lot of people in a relatively small place."

"Wearing this on my head doesn't help."

He took notice for the first time of her facial features, which he found surprisingly soft and pleasing. "Why do you wear it?"

"You are kidding. Woman can't go out in public without it and Ibrahim's rather conservative about these things. I'm lucky to be able to wear slacks."

"Do you like living here?"

"It's better than back home. Still, for women it's like living in the first century. Even at work, I'm so limited in what I can do, especially when men are involved. You've lived in the West, right?"

"I mostly grew up in the U.S., and have lived in Europe for the past few years."

"So you know what it's like to live in a place where women are treated as adults. Tell me, did you find them threatening or less desirable?"

"No, quite the contrary."

"My point exactly. How would you feel if you weren't even allowed to drive a car? I'll tell you something – no one hates Israelis more than me. They stole my homeland and have oppressed my people, but I've got to grudgingly respect them on several accounts. They have real elections, they have a free press, and most importantly, they treat their woman like people, not possessions."

"Why don't you leave?"

"As soon as I've made enough money to pay off my education, I intend to."

Ibrahim's wife interrupted their conversation and pulled Yasmin away to introduce her to others. Sayid finished eating and walked around the apartment, occasionally downing a fig or some grapes. He eventually tired of the party and thanked Ibrahim before he left. As he waited for the elevator, Yasmin came up to him. "You didn't say goodbye."

"I'm sorry. I didn't see you. I assumed you'd already left."

"Oh." The elevator doors opened and they rode it down in silence. When they reached the ground floor she turned and handed him a slip of paper with her phone number. "I don't know how long you are staying, but if you'd like to go out to dinner sometime, call me."

Sayid was shocked by her offer. "I'm not used to girls in this part of the world being so forward. You *have* spent a lot of time in the West, haven't you?"

"See, there are advantages."

Sayid didn't wait long. The next day he called Yasmin and they went out that night, and nearly every night for next two weeks. Social mores dictated that they spend their time together in public places, which made it difficult for the relationship to progress to a more intimate level. Sayid hadn't been in a relationship for a long time and since his experience in that Egyptian jail, had not even tried. The more time they spent together, the more attracted he found himself to her. She was bright, opinionated and from what he could tell under her layers of clothing, possessed the type of slim body that he always found desirable in a woman. At Yasmin's suggestion, they took in a movie. It was a boring quasi-romantic adventure story with a plot line he found incomprehensible, but it least it allowed them to sit close to each other in a darkened room. An hour into the movie, Yasmin, perhaps by accident, let her hand fall on his thigh. It felt as though a jolt of electricity shot through his leg, and she kept her hand there. He asked her if she was hungry and when she nodded, suggested they leave the theater and grab a bite to eat.

"I wish I could kiss you," he said.

"Just kiss me?" she said coyly.

"Well, um…"

She laughed. "Look. I know it's difficult for men, especially when you're our age. We can't do much for now but I know you need to be, how do I say – relieved?"

"That's one way of putting it."

"It's getting late. I have to be at the hospital early tomorrow. Can you get us a cab?"

They took a taxi to her apartment. She got out but he remained in the back seat. "Good night," he said.

"Don't you want to come up for coffee?"

She didn't have to repeat the offer and he followed her into her building. "Is this permitted, for us to be together unaccompanied?"

"I won't tell if you don't." She laughed.

An elderly woman carrying a basketful of laundry passed them in the hallway but not before giving Yasmin a disapproving glare. "Mrs. Amahddai, this is my cousin visiting from Palestine." The woman nodded respectfully but remained standing in the hallway as Yasmin unlocked her door. "Good night Mrs. Amahddai."

She walked into the apartment, but Sayid kept looking at the old woman until he felt Yasmin tug at his sleeve. As soon as he was inside, she shut the door behind him. He started to say something, but she ripped the scarf off her head, flung her arms around his shoulders and began kissing him. "Don't talk," she whispered and led him to her bedroom.

Two weeks later, she called him in the middle of the day. He sensed immediately the distress in her voice. "I have to go to Palestine."

"When?" he asked.

"Immediately."

"What happened?"

"It's my cousin's twelve-year-old son. He was taking part in a peaceful protest when the Israelis opened fire. They claim they were using rubber bullets, but they always claim that. He's on life support. It doesn't sound good. They wanted someone they trusted with a medical background before they made any decisions, and I guess I'm the only one they could think of."

"How long will you be gone?"

"I don't know, but I'm leaving for Jordan tonight. Could you possibly take me to the airport?"

"I can do better than that," he said. "I'll go with you to Palestine."

"Really?"

"Really."

After landing in Amman, Sayid rented a car for the drive to Ramallah. Sayid's U.S. passport eased their entry at the Israeli crossing point into the West Bank. As he drove through the streets trying to find the hospital, Yasmin's phone rang. He knew when heard her say something about God's will and that it was probably for the best that the boy had died.

"When's the funeral?" he asked as soon as she'd hung up.

"Tomorrow."

"I am so sorry." The words sounded so inadequate, but there were no words anyone could say that weren't inadequate or could change the situation. "At least I'll get to meet your family."

She seemed to choke back tears. "If only."

"They're not coming?"

"Can't. The Israelis won't let them travel from Lebanon, even for a family tragedy."

"Bastards."

They watched the casket being paraded through the streets the next morning. The crowds were jostling the flag-draped coffin as it was borne on the shoulders of men whose faces were hidden behind white keffiyehs with the black chickenwire mesh pattern that symbolizes the Palestinian struggle. At times, Sayid feared the coffin would fall open, causing God knows what. The searing pain heard in the wails of the parents cut like a knife at his emotional core and seemed enough to spark a riot. Fortunately, that didn't happen. After the funeral, the crowds outside Yasmin's cousin's house were so large that they couldn't even get close. Yasmin said she was fine if they just went back to Amman without meeting the family. She'd spoken with her cousins and they all knew she'd been there.

As they drove through the West Bank, they passed by refugee camps. Yasmin explained that as a child, she'd grown up in one of them until her parents moved to Lebanon when she was eight.

"It really is a scandal that after fifty years, these places still exist," he commented.

"That is what the struggle is all about. Since the Nakba, we have been forced to a sub-human life."

"But violence isn't the answer. It will just lead to more families having funerals for their children."

"That's easy for you to say. You grew up with wealth and privilege, freedom and dignity. Your family could own their own land in America. When you have to go back to your grandparents' generation to find a time when you weren't living under the oppressive boot of an occupying force, you get tired of waiting for politicians and diplomats who offer their plans for peace, but nothing ever gets done. My ancestral home and farm and orchard is less than thirty kilometers from here, but I'll never see it again unless and until our rights of return are granted. No Israeli government will agree to that, so we are left with no option but to fight for our basic human rights."

He didn't argue her point. In fact, he felt guilty for having said anything in the first place. She was right. His life had been one of privilege. He was embarrassed and disappointed in himself for having ignored the plight of his brethren for so long.

They returned to Saudi Arabia and spent every evening in each other's company. Sayid constantly thought of Yasmin and imagined future scenarios of a life with her. She was his entire family in the world, as his immediate family was no longer living and he hadn't spoken with any extended relatives in over a decade. As it became clear that his work in Saudi Arabia was winding down and he would need to return to France, he knew he had to act. He took her dinner at one of the priciest restaurants in Riyadh, and after dessert, broached the subject. "I'll be going back to Paris next week." Yasmin went white as a sheet. "You knew this was going to happen sooner or later."

She took a sip of water. "I know. I guess I was hoping for later. I don't quite know what to say."

He took her hand under the table. "I want you to come with me. Come to Paris."

She took her hand back and pulled out a tissue from her purse. "I don't know." She dabbed at the corner of her eyes.

"What's to know? You hate it here. You've made that clear. Come to France."

"I'm just not sure. France would be beautiful, especially with you there, but I don't think I could get a job. The French are, after all, rather antagonistic toward Muslims, especially of Middle Eastern descent."

"I make more than enough money for the both of us to live on."

"It's not that simple. My family in Lebanon relies on what I make here. I send most of it back to them to live on. What would they do if I left? On the other hand, I don't think I can live without you."

"Then we'll move to America. You can certainly get a job there. They're always looking for nurses."

"America? They're run by the Jews. They'll never let me in."

He laughed. "Where did you hear that? First off, America is not run by the Jews, and even if that were true, I've known Jews for years, and they're not, despite Israel, what you think. Of course they'll let you in. As I said, they need nurses. In time, you can even become a citizen."

"Right. Like that will ever happen."

"Oh, it will happen. In case you forgot, I'm a U.S. citizen. They always grant citizenship to the spouses of citizens."

"Spouses?"

He nodded and took out the ring he'd purchased that afternoon. She looked at the ring still in the box. "What do you say?" he asked. She slowly took the ring out of the box and held it in her hand. "Try it on." She slipped it on her finger, stared at it for a second and then nodded yes. A surge of elation approaching ecstasy welled inside him and were they any place else, he would have leapt across the table and kissed her.

The following day, he took a cab to the hospital where Yasmin worked and waited for her shift to end. When he saw her leave the hospital, he jumped out of the cab and ran towards her. He was about five feet from her when a policeman stepped between them. In an instant, two other policemen grabbed Yasmin and dragged her towards a waiting police car. "Yasmin!" he screamed.

She turned and saw him. "Sayid," she screamed back, and then disappeared into the car. He started to run after the car until another policeman caught him in a bear hug and held him back. He continued screaming her name until the police car was no longer in sight.

He went to the nearest police station but was told nothing about his new fiancée. Distraught, he called the only person he knew that might be of help, Ibrahim Fuad.

"She's been arrested," Ibrahim told him.

"But why?"

"Apparently some of the money she's been sending to her family has ended up in Hezbollah's hands."

"That's crazy, and even if true, so what? Why would the Saudis care if she sends money to Hezbollah? They're not exactly a Zionist organization."

"No, but they are allied with the Iranians and are a Shiite sect. If there is one thing the Saudis fear more than the Zionists, it's the Iranians. They think they are heretics bent on overthrowing them, and they're probably right."

"But Yasmin isn't a subversive. She was only trying to help her family."

"I know, but it's not good."

"What should I do?"

"Go back to France. If you try and fight this here, they might suspect you are a radical sympathizer and throw you in jail. You remember what that's like. This will probably all pass over in a few weeks. The worst that will happen is that they'll deport her to Palestine. Don't worry."

Sayid didn't find Ibrahim's advice comforting, but he had little choice. He returned to France and called Ibrahim every day. There was no progress despite Ibrahim's assurance that things would work out. Finally, Ibrahim called him with news. "She's been sentenced to twelve years."

"What!"

"It's being appealed, but these things are rarely if ever overturned. You know what these despots are like. People have no rights."

Sayid was beyond distraught. He had no idea what to do. He contacted the French government, but they were of no help. He went to the U.S. embassy in Paris and got nowhere. Paul DeVeux recognized that Sayid was not emotionally stable enough to work and told him to take more time off. After a month, Sayid heard from Ibrahim that Yasmin's appeal had been denied, the news of which sent Sayid into a state of depression. He wandered the streets of Paris, clueless as to what he should do. As he stood on the Pont Neuf at midnight and stared back at Notre Dame Cathedral, he pulled out his cell phone and called Ibrahim in Riyadh. "I want to go to Afghanistan."

"Are you sure?" Ibrahim asked.

"Yes. I can't stay here any longer."

"Wonderful. Book a flight to the Emirates and I'll meet you there. And welcome to the fight. This time I know we'll win."

"That sounds familiar."

"It's from the end of Casablanca. Paul Henreid says it to Humphrey Bogart."

"Always with the movies."

"Get some rest. You are going to need it." Ibrahim hung up his phone.

"What time is it?" a woman's voice asked.

Ibrahim rubbed his eyes and looked at his watch. "Two a.m."

"Who calls at two in the morning?"

"That was Sayid Hassan. I'm taking him to Afghanistan."

"You have to take him?" she asked.

"He only trusts me," Ibrahim said as he crawled back into bed and cuddled up to her. "You did well, Yasmin," he whispered in her ear.

◇◇◇◇◇◇◇

In May, Jake began working on a project concerning a small oil company called Reliant Petroleum that Arthur was contemplating taking a controlling interest in. This was a departure from Pilgrim/United's past practices. Arthur's success had come from trading in equities and commodities, not in running companies. But like many powerful businessmen, he had convinced himself that success in one business would translate into success in another. Owing to his heavy workload, it took Jake until the end of June before he emailed Arthur his recommendation that Pilgrim/United not take a major position in Reliant. The company's track record was less than stellar and most of their sources of oil were in particularly unstable regions of the world, like former Soviet republics and sub-Saharan Africa. Perhaps because Jake's analysis was terse, only two paragraphs, or perhaps because of his ego, Arthur wouldn't let it go. He called Jake into his office and demanded a more detailed report with first-hand research, then handed Jake a round-trip first class airplane ticket to Lagos, Nigeria.

The flight took twenty-two hours, with most of that time spent waiting in the terminal at De Gaulle Airport between flights. Jake thought the entire expedition a tremendous waste of time. There was nothing to be learned in Africa that could substantially change his opinion, and while he was gone, his department would be in the hands of men he didn't fully trust. But Arthur was adamant and wouldn't be satisfied until Jake could produce his passport with a Nigerian visa stamped in it.

Although summer had officially arrived in New York, he wasn't prepared for the heat and humidity of Nigeria. He was met at the airport by a large man with a perpetual smile on his face and the blackest skin he'd ever seen. His name was Joshua Nduke, but everyone called him Jumbo, and he called everyone he drove around boss. Jumbo was a former cab driver in Lagos who now worked for Reliant as their official chauffeur. Jake assumed he was staying in Lagos but quickly learned that Jumbo was taking him to Port Harcourt in the delta region, a distance of around six hundred kilometers over roads that ranged from four-lane highways to little more than rutted paths. It took eight hours and after a long flight, Jake kept nodding off. Jumbo's non-stop monologue about the countryside, the people, the occasional terrorist attack, combined with the rough road surfaces managed to keep Jake mostly awake.

"Are we in any danger from terrorists?" he asked Jumbo.

Jumbo laughed. "No, boss. These men aren't too organized. Some of it is religious, some of it because of your tribe, most of it from gangs."

"Gangs?"

"Yah, gangs you know. Criminals. Young guys who take your money, watch, jewelry, cell phone. They not going to hurt you, usually."

"Usually?"

"Ha. No worry, boss. I can tell if there is danger. That is why I keep this." Jumbo stretched one hand behind the seat while steering with the other and pulled out a sub-machine gun. "There's a Glock in the glove compartment if you need it." Jake opened the glove compartment and saw the semi-automatic pistol. He had no idea how to fire the gun and found the weapons and Jumbo's confidence of little comfort.

Port Harcourt was far more developed than Jake had expected, even boasting an international airport, which left Jake wondering why he hadn't flown there directly. His hotel, while not luxurious, was at least comfortable. It didn't matter much since his plan had always been to spend one day taking a tour given by Reliant that would tell him nothing. He knew they were not likely to show him anything they didn't want him to see. After that, he'd thank them and get the next flight out of Africa.

After a decent night's sleep, Jumbo picked him up at the hotel and drove him first to Reliant's offices, then out to an oil field about twenty miles away that had been leased from the government. Jake learned from speaking with the foreman on the site that the wells had yet to produce at levels that the geological surveys said they would. The poor showings were attributed by the Reliant foreman to the poor quality of local workers and equipment suppliers. His admission was surprising since Jake had expected to hear only good news. Perhaps the foreman had no idea why Jake was there.

On the way back to Port Harcourt, Jumbo asked Jake if he wanted to see some of the countryside. Jake, figuring he'd might never be in Africa again, said he would. They drove to a small village not far from the Reliant field. Villagers, mostly women and young children, immediately surrounded their Range Rover. Jumbo stopped the SUV and encouraged Jake to get out. "Do I need a gun?" he asked. Jumbo smiled and assured Jake that he was safe, but not to eat or drink anything offered him. "Where are all the men?" Jake asked.

"Probably gone to Port Harcourt to find work or drafted by the army."

Jake got out of the SUV and immediately small hands tugged at his pants. He reached into his pockets and gave away all of the Nigerian money he had. "Are all of the villages this poor?" he asked Jumbo.

"Nah – some are much worse." They strolled by shacks constructed from scrap metal, dried mud and even cardboard. There was no running water and the only building with electricity served as a clinic. In front of the clinic sat a line of women and children waiting to be seen. Jumbo popped his head inside of the clinic and spoke with a woman dressed in white that Jake assumed was a nurse. "A doctor comes by a couple of times a month," Jumbo told him. "He should be here tomorrow or the next day."

"Why are these people are lined up now?"

"Where else have they to go? Many are too sick or too weak to travel." As he spoke, a woman carrying a small girl in her arms approached them and spoke to Jumbo in Igbo, the local tongue. "She wants to know where you are from."

"America," Jake said slowly, as if speaking slowly made it more likely she'd understand. She spoke again to Jumbo, who answered her in a dismissive tone. "What did she say?"

Jumbo waived his hand. "She wants you to take the child back with you."

"Back where? To Port Harcourt?"

"No boss, America."

The woman pushed her way past Jumbo and handed the little girl to Jake. Shocked, he instinctively put out his arms, fearing that the child would just drop to the ground if he didn't take hold of her. The exchange between Jumbo and the woman quickly devolved into a shouting match. Jake had no idea what to do. He looked down at the sickly girl who every once in a while would squirm in his arms. Her face was blank and her eyes stared vacantly back at him, not even blinking at the flies that landed on her cheeks. He smiled down at her, trying to offer some sense of comfort. Her expression gave no inclination that she was aware of his presence, but her body seemed to relax. "Jumbo, what should I do?"

Jumbo stopped arguing and walked over to Jake. He looked down at the girl's face. "Nothing," he told him as he tenderly placed his hand over the girl's forehead and closed her eyes. "She is gone."

"Gone? What do you mean? Is she's dead?"

Jumbo nodded and he took the girl from Jake's arms and handed her back to her mother. The woman let out a shriek of pain so intense that Jake felt it in his bones before she fell to her knees and was surrounded by the other women. Jake stood motionless. He couldn't remember ever having seen a dead body before and if so, it certainly wasn't that of a young child. But seeing a corpse in a coffin wasn't the same as actually seeing another human die, and that paled in comparison with actually holding that person in one's arms as their life ended. "We should be going now," Jumbo told him.

They rode in silence for half an hour before Jake finally said something. "What do you think killed that child? Is there some sort of epidemic going on?"

"She died of runs, most probably."

"Runs?"

"Runs, you know. Diarrhea."

"Diarrhea? Not something serious like malaria or AIDS or something?"

"Runs is serious. Though she might have had malaria. But most of the young ones die of diarrhea. It number one killer. You can look it up."

"I will. Does malaria cause the diarrhea?"

"Could be. I'm no doctor. Most runs come from bad water."

"Bad water? People must have been drinking this water forever. How did they survive?"

"It's much worse since the oil. The wells, and the junk they use to dig and pipe the oil, it pollutes what little good water there is. The people in these villages end up using the same water for drinking, cooking, cleaning. Their animals also use the water for their shit, as do the people. So they end up drinking bad water."

"Can't they do something about it?"

"They? You mean the government? They too busy fighting. Fighting the rebels. The Christians fighting the Islam. The army fighting each other. And it make no difference anyway. The oil companies pay the government so they can do what they want, which is to get the oil as cheap as they can."

"Don't you work for one of those companies?"

"You got me there, boss. Still, if government did its job, it could be made okay."

"What a waste."

"You can say that again, boss."

Jake returned home to Manhattan, but he'd left most of his conceit back in that African village. He had spent the flight back reading articles about diseases and economic development in the Third World. Jumbo had been right. Of all the causes of death for children in Africa, diarrhea was number one, and a lack of clean water was the major culprit. He became downright angry when he read that for literally pennies a day, medicine could be provided that would cure most of these cases.

Debbie wasn't around when he walked into their Tribeca apartment, which he was actually glad about. He needed some time alone to process the experience and get his mindset back into the familiarity of his world. He glanced at the unopened mail piled on the kitchen table and finding nothing beyond the typical junk, he tossed it aside. He poured a glass of wine, flicked on the television, stretched out on the couch and nodded off.

"You're home!" Debbie's high-pitched scratchy voice woke him. "When did you get back?"

He rubbed his eyes and sat up. "A few hours ago."

"How was your trip?"

"Long." He put on his glasses and Debbie came into focus. "You look as though you've gotten some sun. Have you been to the tanning salon again? I've warned you about those places – they cause cancer."

"No, I was at Artie's beach house."

"Artie?"

"You remember Arthur Morrison don't you? He is, after all, your boss."

"I've never heard him called *Artie* before. What were you doing at *Artie's*?"

"He called me and said he felt bad about sending you away over the Fourth of July holiday, so he invited me out to the Hamptons. Have you ever seen his place there? It's unbelievable."

"No, I've never been. How's Cheryl or Cherise or whatever her name is."

"Oh, Artie's not seeing Cherise anymore. She was way too young for him. So tell me about Africa."

Jake found his wine glass and took a sip. "Well, I wouldn't recommend it for vacationing." He took another sip. "I saw a girl die. Actually held the child in my arms when she passed."

"You're kidding."

"I wish I was."

"Oh, that is a shame."

The hair on the back of Jake's neck stood on edge. "A shame? It's a hell of a lot more than that."

"Relax honey. I only meant to say that it's sad that a child dies, but it happens. It's the way the world has always been. I only am sorry that you had to be put in that situation."

Jake shook his head before snapping back at her. "What the hell do you know about the ways of the world? You've never in your life had to worry that the water you're drinking was going to kill you. You've been lucky enough to live a life of plenty. Got news for you, Deb – most people in the world ain't so privileged. Most people don't spend their weekends sipping champagne out in the Hamptons."

"For Christ's sake, Jake, don't jump on me. You had a rough experience. I'm sorry for you. It's not that I don't care. I volunteer to help kids in Harlem stay in school."

"Serving on a committee arranging black tie fundraisers isn't exactly the hardest task."

"Fuck you, Jake. I don't have to justify myself to you."

Jake got off the couch and headed for the door. "Where are you going?" she shouted.

"For a walk. I need to clear my head."

"You sure as hell do. Don't come back until you can be more civil."

He paused at the door. "You were right, Deb. It is a shame. And the shame is on you, and more importantly, the shame is on me."

He walked for hours, wandering with no particular destination in mind. He passed by Pilgrim/United's offices on Forty-Seventh Street and eventually found himself standing in front of an apartment house on Fifth Avenue across from Central Park. He stared up at the building knowing that Morrison's condo was on the top floor. In time, the doorman came out and asked him if there was anything he needed. He didn't answer, only turned away and hailed a cab. The following morning he walked into Morrison's office and handed him a letter in a sealed envelope with a two-word sentence – "I quit."

"Is this some sort of joke?" Arthur asked after reading his resignation.

"No joke, Arthur."

"All right. Who are you going to?"

"I'm not going to anyone."

"Really? Okay then, what do you want? You need more money?"

"It's not the money. I'm just tired of this."

"Of course it's the money. Whenever someone says it's not the money, it is."

"Not this time."

"You can't just leave like this. Who's going to take your place? I've given you a lot of fucking responsibilities around here."

"Watch me," he replied and turned to leave.

"You little shit. I took you in and taught you everything and in the process, made you very rich before you turned thirty. And this is how you repay me? By walking out on me?"

"Yes, you made me rich, but I made a hell of a lot more money for you in the process."

"You see, I'm right. It is about the money."

Jake was mad at himself for stooping down to Arthur's level. "Good bye, *Artie*."

"You little fucker," he could hear Morrison shout as he left his office. "Don't fuck with me. You're screwed in this town. You think you're getting another job like this? Never, I'll see to that. I'll fuck your ass like the goddamn little fag you are."

When Jake arrived back at his apartment, Debbie was on the couch watching television. "I'm surprised to see you here at this time of day. Are you not feeling well?"

"No, I feel great. For the first time in a long time, I feel great."

"Why aren't you at work?"

"I quit."

"You what?"

"Quit."

"What are you saying? How are we going to be able to afford to live?"

"I haven't thought that far in advance."

"Shit, Jake, don't you think you should have?"

"I don't know. We can sell this place. I've always said I'd like to live in Vermont. We can move there and live in the vacation cabin all year."

"And do what exactly? All of our friends are here. My family lives here. My life is here. I don't want to live in Vermont."

"It'll be okay, fun even. An adventure. You'll see."

Nine weeks later Debbie filed for divorce. The date was September 10, 2001.

SEVEN

Pakistan, March 2002

Riding blindfolded in the trunk of a car through the streets of Lahore wasn't exactly the way Sayid envisioned going to meet Osama bin Laden, but he understood the reason why. It had little to do with Sayid's trustworthiness. If al-Qaeda had any doubts, they would never have allowed him anywhere near bin Laden. Security precautions dictated that everyone visiting a safe house had to travel in a similar fashion, probably even Osama himself. It protected the anonymity of the houses and their occupants should someone fall into the hands of enemy interrogators. Being tossed and bumped against the sides of the trunk made Sayid feel more like the victim of a kidnapping rather than a soldier in service to the cause.

The car stopped and the engine turned off. Sayid heard the men exit the car and he knew they had reached their destination. The trunk lid opened and he was helped out of the car but the blindfold was not removed until he was inside of the house.

Ibrahim was the first to greet him. "How was the trip?"

Sayid slowly rotated his head to ease the stiffness and stretched his arms. "I've got a few bruises and I'm a little stiff, but other than that, I'm fine."

"It is certainly better than the way we left Afghanistan. Follow me." Ibrahim took him to a small room that looked to be a den with a sofa and a couple of chairs. "Are you ready for this?"

Sayid nodded. "I would have preferred to have prepared a written plan."

"If you can't explain it in person, they will never approve. You know that written documents, especially ones left on computers, can leave a trail that can be traced."

"I'm always careful. I know how to encrypt everything of importance."

"That may not be good enough. Anyway, when you meet Osama, don't say anything until he addresses you."

Sayid nodded. He didn't need Ibrahim's instructions regarding protocol. Al-Qaeda's tenets of good manners, the ability to listen and obedience to superiors had been drummed into him since his first day in Afghanistan. It had been three months since he'd last seen Ibrahim under very different circumstances. Then they had just escaped into western Pakistan and the whole of al-Qaeda seemed to be unraveling. Rumors circulated that most of the leadership had either been captured or killed. Now they sat together in what, judging by the large swimming pool and manicured gardens visible through the window, was a luxurious villa.

The two were taken to another part of the house. Sayid felt his pulse quicken as he realized that he was about to meet the man who was either adored or reviled by most of the world. Either way, few men ever achieve that sort of notoriety in their own lifetime. Their escort knocked on the door and they entered a windowless room with no furniture and only cushions scattered on the floor. Sayid recognized Ayman al-Zawahiri, the Egyptian physician who was second only to bin Laden. Seated next to him was a man with a somewhat long face, black-framed glasses and a scraggly beard whom Sayid did not know. Pointedly missing was the main man himself, Osama. Ibrahim bent down and exchanged kisses on the cheek with each man. He then introduced Sayid who clasped his hands in front of himself and bowed submissively. He and Ibrahim took seats on cushions across from the others.

"Dr. al-Zawahiri," Ibrahim began, "Thank you seeing us today. I wish to present to you Sayid Hassan, a brother in jihad who has come to me with a proposal which I think deserves your consideration. A word on Sayid's background – he was educated in America and England and holds advanced degrees in engineering and economics from top universities in those countries, but we won't hold that against him." Al-Zawarhiri smiled briefly at Ibrahim's attempt at humor. The other man did not seem amused. "He joined us almost a year ago and since then has been training in Afghanistan. He was invaluable in providing logistical intelligence for our successful actions of last September. His knowledge of the airport in Boston gave the units who launched from there vital information." That last bit of information surprised Sayid. He had not realized that he had ever given any such information to Ibrahim, but in thinking about it, he did recall a number of conversations about life in America and Boston. He accepted Ibrahim's assertion that in those conversations, he may have unwittingly provided useful information. "Rather than taking up more time, I will let Sayid explain his proposal to you."

Sayid took a deep breath. "As Ibrahim said, I have studied economics. I believe we may have an opportunity to launch an economic attack against the Americans that, if successful, could damage or even cripple their economy to the point where they will not be able to afford to maintain their level of military presence in the world."

Al-Zawahiri nodded then looked at the other man who had no reaction. "Continue," he said.

"Thank you. When I was a student at MIT in Boston, I worked on a paper that laid out a business plan based on using mortgages, which are loans people take out to buy houses, that my professor at the time pointed out was likely to collapse."

"We know what mortgages are," the other man said, still looking very sardonic.

"Yes, of course. I apologize." The occasional cracks in Sayid's voice revealed how nervous he was. He momentarily lost his train of thought. Rather than appear scatterbrained, he asked for a glass of water and took a long, slow sip before proceeding. "Ah, anyway, most all of the wealth in the U.S. that is not controlled by the very rich is made up by the middle class, and the largest single investment that those people have is their homes. Changes in the banking laws have created a situation where the safeguards that previously existed to keep their financial institutions from acting in risky and predatory manners have largely been removed. With their current president, Bush, this trend is likely to continue or even accelerate. The Americans continue to reduce their manufacturing base with that slack being taken up by the Chinese, Koreans and Indians. Their technology segment has melted down and the only segment of their economy that has shown substantial growth is their service sector, which pays far less. Their interest rates are kept artificially low meaning there is a large pot of money looking for investments that could go into housing. If that pushed up housing prices, they could, in time, become over-valued to the point that they would hopefully crash."

"How much time?" al-Zawahiri asked.

"Hard to say. Two years, maybe five at the most."

"That is a long time," al-Zawahiri said.

"Yes it is," Ibrahim interjected, "but we've spent years planning missions before."

"You say that if the American economy were to collapse, they would have to withdraw their forces," the other man said. "What is to prevent those forces from being replaced by another imperialist power, say the Chinese or the Indians?"

"For one thing, neither the Chinese nor the Indians have a military that anywhere approaches the Americans in firepower and ability to deploy abroad."

"The Russians do," al-Zawahiri said.

"The Russians have memories of what our mujahedeen did to them in Afghanistan. You both know that since I assume you were there. In addition, the Russian economy has caused their military to be a shell of its Cold War self. I don't see them wanting to come back."

"What are your chances of success?" al-Zawahiri asked.

"That is impossible to say."

"Seventy-five percent? Fifty percent? Twenty-five?" al-Zawahiri continued.

"I don't think I can put a percentage on it. But I've spent years working with these people. I know how they behave and how they think. When they think that there is money to be made, they won't hesitate to act. And once it appears that an investment is profitable, they assume that its value will always continue to go up."

Al-Zawahiri appeared disinterested. The other man spoke up. "Their greed will eventually doom them. If we decide to approve this action, what would you need?"

"I won't need any personnel. Only seed financing."

"How much?" asked the man.

"Enough to put together several deals and demonstrate that there is money to be made. Once the ball gets rolling, it should take off on its own. I'd say sixty to seventy million U.S. dollars."

Al-Zawahiri threw his hands in the air. "That is a lot of money. Do you think we just have that sitting around under our mattresses?"

"I know it's a lot, but it's a small amount when compared with the size of the U.S. economy. Maybe I could do it for under fifty."

"And how exactly would you go about this mission?" asked the other man.

"I would first go back to Europe, either get my old position back in France or I have some contacts in England and Germany. Since I hold American citizenship, I could work my way into a consulting position that deals with U.S. financial institutions. Once I establish those U.S. relationships, I would structure the types of exotic investment packages that are difficult even for experienced financial managers to understand and therefore nearly impossible to assess their potential risk. As such, most people will stay away from them, which is why I need the seed money. Initially, these instruments will appear to make money, which is important because that will start the ball rolling so to speak."

"Again with the ball rolling. We are not in the business of playing football. What if they go on making money? What if they don't fail?" al-Zawahiri asked.

"The only way that could realistically happen would be for the U.S. government to step in and re-regulate the financial sector. I don't see that happening with the current administration and with Bush polling as high as he is, he's likely to be president until 2009. Things should fail long before then."

An awkward silence fell over the room. Al-Zawahiri whispered to the other man who nodded in agreement. "The problem I have," he finally said aloud, "is that there are no visible results. People will not see it in newspapers or on Al-Jazeera. Even if you succeed, our people won't have witnessed the struggle and courage of our soldiers. The Americans may not even realize that we were behind this, and if they don't realize it, how will our people realize it? Martyrdom creates symbols that people need to see. They need to know that sacrifice in the service of Allah is what will free us. Your plan has no martyrs and I'm not sure it gets us closer to establishing a new caliphate that will stretch from here across Africa to the Atlantic."

"And there is the money," the other man added.

Sayid knew he wasn't convincing them. "Look, as far as the money goes, the initial investment should easily be paid back, even make a profit."

"Really. A profit?" said the other man.

"Sure. What we will be creating is a classic scam, although if successful, on a scale the world has never seen before. Like any scam, those who get in on it in the beginning are the ones who make money. Think of it – not only could we disrupt the economies of our enemies, we could actually use their money as a source for our own funding in the process." Al-Zawahiri seemed to perk up at that last statement, but the other man remained skeptical. Sayid tried to think of any other arguments that he had forgotten to bring up. "Look, no one wants to get rid of the Saudi King or Hosni Mubarak more than me. As long as the Americans can afford to stay here, so will their puppets." He caught a glance of Ibrahim's eyes boring into him like a laser. "Of course, I mean no disrespect, and of course, I accept the wisdom of whatever your final decision is. I obediently await your answer."

He stood up and bowed to each man before leaving the room and waited outside the door for Ibrahim to join him. Nearly an hour passed before Fuad, looking rather somber, came out of the room. "I'm sorry I've wasted your time. I thought it was a good idea," Sayid said knowing what the decision must have been.

"If I didn't think the same, I would never have brought you here. But they are concerned about the length of time it will take. As you heard them say, it is important that people do not forget that we are still out here, still fighting."

Sayid accepted the situation, and although he knew that al-Qaeda had a sort of genius for their ability to take on far more powerful adversaries, he was frustrated by what he perceived as the leadership's lack of imagination for tactics not involving violence. Had he come to them with a plan to blow up the bridges leading into Manhattan, he would probably have received instant approval. But despite his paramilitary training, he realized soldiering was not his strong point, all of which raised questions in his mind regarding his usefulness to the cause. "Look at this house. I feel guilty just being here."

"You have nothing to feel guilty about. Your time in Afghanistan was not spent in luxury."

"It was still better than what Yasmin's endured rotting in some jail."

"And you thought that by going back to America and setting up your plan, you could get her out?"

"I don't know that it would have. I do know that as long as the Americans are in this part of the world, the Saudi government isn't going to change. I was trying to think of a way to bring them down and free Yasmin from twelve years in their prison. I felt it was the most effective use of my abilities."

"You may be interested in knowing that the men back there agree with you."

"They do?"

"Yes, they approved your plan." It took a second for what Ibrahim had just said to sink in. When it did, he flung his arms around Ibrahim and kissed him. "Wait, wait, there are some conditions."

"What are they?"

"First off, they approved ten million dollars in financing."

"That will be tight, but I can work with that. It just means it might take a little longer to build up interest. What else?"

"There needs to be someone watching over you. They want you to go to Berlin. There you will be contacted by a man named Klaus Voorhaus. He is one of our German associates who will get you a position with the Prussian Bourse Banque. We have a number of accounts there. You will need to make sure that any passports you use don't show your travels to countries that will raise suspicions. We can supply those. Do you need some money now to tide you over?"

"No, I've got enough. Why don't you serve as my overseer? "

"I can't get you the access you are going to need and I don't have the kind of financial experience that such a task requires. Klaus can gain you that access and he does understand these things. His father is head of the bank. Besides, I have another assignment in Indonesia. As for your superior, you will be reporting to Mustafa Abu al-Yazid."

"Who is he?"

"He was the other man in the room. Mustafa is like us, an Egyptian who spent three years in prison. I am surprised you did not recognize him. He is al-Qaeda's chief financial official, and you can thank him for getting you the go-ahead."

"How will I contact him?"

"If you need to, Klaus will get a message to him and then he will contact you."

Sayid let out a long breath. "Then I guess that's it."

"Not quite. There is something else I need to tell you." Ibrahim shuffled his feet and was obviously reticent to speak. "I waited until after you gave your presentation because I didn't want to distract you. I'm not sure how to say this."

"Go ahead."

"I spoke with my wife yesterday, and I'm afraid there's some bad news. Yasmin is dead."

Sayid felt his heart stop. His face went ashen. "What?"

"She died in prison last week. Apparently she contracted some sort of virus and they didn't bother to give her any treatment until it was too late. I know she meant a lot to you. I'm very sorry." Sayid felt his knees go weak and he slumped back against the wall. "Are you okay?" He didn't answer. "Sayid, are you okay?" Ibrahim repeated.

"When can you get me a flight to Berlin?" he whispered.

◇◇◇◇◇◇

Springfield, Massachusetts

Mia had recently finished helping her father move into his new apartment at the Faircrest assisted living facility. Since her mother's death, his health had been in steady decline with the most disheartening aspect being his diminished mental state. He was only seventy-four, but his dementia no longer allowed him to live independently. To be closer, she sold her townhouse in San Francisco and was now looking for a new place to live. Mia didn't like Springfield. A city whose most famous cultural attraction appeared to be the Basketball Hall of Fame didn't hold much appeal. Her first thought was Boston, but it was just too far from Springfield and her father wouldn't relocate. Someone suggested one of the small villages in the Berkshires, such as Lenox. She took a drive and was smitten with the charm and pace of life that seemed to stretch back to the American Revolution. There was also the bonus of cultural attractions such as the summer music festival at Tanglewood, and it seemed the perfect setting for what she saw as her next vocation in life, opening a top-flight restaurant.

Mia considered it karma when she spotted an ad in the real estate section of a local paper for a bed and breakfast. It was located in Stockbridge. She saw the place, contacted the real estate agent, made an offer and that was it. Not wanting to have overnight lodgers, she decided to convert the upstairs guest quarters into her living space while the first floor would be remodeled into the restaurant. A new, larger kitchen would be needed, but she had more than enough in the bank to cover all these expenses. The one crucial item she lacked was an executive chef. Karma once more seemed on her side when she found her chef in the most unlikely of places, a bistro in a strip mall situated between a Dollar Store and a tattoo parlor.

It was by accident that she stopped for dinner at Chez Bill's. She had made a wrong turn one day after leaving her father and ended up in front of the restaurant. Being tired and hungry she figured, what the heck, and tried it. The taste of the lobster bisque was enough to spur her to ask if she could speak with the chef. By the end of the meal, she had convinced Katherine Adams to leave Chez Bill and go with her. She offered Adams a 49% stake in the new place, but financial reward was never Mia's motivation in this undertaking. She just wanted to see if she could create something for which she had a passion.

Katherine liked to be called Kat. She was a couple of years younger and five inches taller than Mia, with hair that sported streaks of green and purple, five earrings in each ear and a small diamond piercing in her nose. Her culinary skills were for the most part self-taught. She landed her job at the bistro after bartering a deal with Bill, the tattoo artist next door who had the lease on the restaurant. Bill would give her a small tattoo if she cooked him a meal. He liked it so much that he gave her two tats and hired her to run the restaurant. But the cuisine that Kat was preparing was better suited for an upscale Manhattan neighborhood rather than this working class section of Springfield, and Bill was thinking of changing the place to a sports bar, so Kat quickly accepted Mia's offer.

Until the renovations in Stockbridge were complete, Mia was staying at a Holiday Inn in Springfield and visiting her father daily while he adjusted to his new environment. On this visit, she found him alone in his room reading a novel although she wasn't sure how much of it he comprehended. The television was on with the sound turned all the way down. "Hi daddy, how you doing?"

"I know you. You are Mia, right?"

"Yes daddy, I'm your daughter."

"That's right. Is your mother here?"

"Mother died a few years ago."

"Oh yes. I remember. What about Toni? Is Toni coming to see me?"

"No, Toni won't be coming to see you either. Toni died in China. Do you remember?"

"Yes. Toni's in China."

"No. Toni is dead. She can't come to see you."

A wave of emotional pain came over his face. "Are you sure?" he asked.

She nodded. "Anyway, have they taken you to dinner yet?"

"They took me to eat."

"Was it good?"

"No. They only gave me bread."

"I find that hard to believe."

"Then talk to them."

"I will. Are you enjoying your book?" He nodded, but said little else. She took a seat in a chair and turned up the sound on the television. After forty-five minutes or so, a staff member came into the room and informed them that it was time for visitors to leave. She kissed her father on his forehead. "Goodnight, daddy."

"You have to go now?"

"Yes, I have to go now, but I'll come back tomorrow, okay?"

"Good. And bring your sister Toni with you. She never comes to visit anymore. Will you bring her with you?"

She let out a slow sigh. "Sure, daddy."

She went back to her hotel and stretched out on the bed. She tried focusing her thoughts on the restaurant, but kept coming back to the fact that she had no close friends and a family consisting of only a father whose senility was rapidly stealing what was left of his intellect. She felt like crying but her upbringing had instilled the sense that self-pity was a shameful indulgence not to be tolerated. If for no other reason than to honor her father, she didn't give in. His parting words had revived a bitter enmity that she thought she had gotten past years earlier. If her sister were there, she wouldn't be going through this alone. Toni had been stolen from her, and although powerless to do anything about it, she found some perverse pleasure in wallowing in rage.

⬦⬦⬦⬦⬦⬦⬦

Jake stood outside the courthouse in lower Manhattan and tried to figure out exactly what had had just happened inside. It had taken less than ten minutes for a judge to grant a decree making his divorce final. Somehow, the terms were different from what his lawyer had led him to believe. Debbie, who obviously had been more judicious in her selection of an attorney, walked up to him. "Well, I guess that's it," she said.

"Yeah, I guess so. I hope you enjoy the condo, and the rest of everything else I earned."

"You make it sound as though I got everything and you did all the work."

"I don't recall you ever having a job in the four years we were married."

"Who the hell do you think took care of the household? Who decorated the apartment and made sure it was clean when you came home, made sure there was food to eat, and so on."

"Debbie, you hired a decorator, you had a maid come in five days a week, and any meals we didn't eat at restaurants, you had delivered."

"Fuck you, Jake. Everything I got, I deserve. I have no reason to feel any guilt. You – you're just a loser. Deal with it. I, on the other hand, have a life to live." She blew a sarcastic kiss at him and walked away toward a waiting limo. When the car door opened, Arthur Morrison stepped out and waved at Jake. Debbie flashed a last look back at Jake then turned to Arthur and gave him a long kiss, making sure that Jake could see her tongue lasciviously plunge into Arthur's mouth.

"Mr. Himmelfarb, here are your copies of the documents." The voice of his lawyer drew Jake's attention away from Debbie and Morrison.

"Gee thanks. What, if anything, did I end up with?"

"I thought we did pretty well. You have half of the investments at Pilgrim, although your employment contract from when you worked there makes it hard for you access those funds for quite some time, and the house and property in Vermont."

"That's it? She got everything else? The other investments?"

"Uh, well your wife's attorneys were from Putnam Barnes. They are the best. Frankly, I am pleased with how well we did."

"Oh *you're* pleased. I'm not very pleased."

"You got the house in Vermont and the farm down the road from it. That's 900 acres of income-producing land."

"Income producing?"

"Yes. The tenant farmer has dairy cows and it says here he raises hogs."

"Jesus, I own a pig farm. That will have to go. My zaydi would turn over in his grave if he knew I was producing traf."

"You can do with it whatever you like. You are, after all, the Lord of the Manor. Next time, be sure to get a pre-nup. You've got my number."

"If there is a next time and I need a pre-nup, I'll call Putnam Barnes."

EIGHT

April 2002

The two-lane road that wound its way through the Vermont country-side exposed how destructive winter is to asphalt. Potholes yet to be repaired vindictively materialized around every blind turn and Jake managed to hit nearly every one, sorely testing the tires and suspension of his BMW M3 convertible. In the two and a half years since he and Debbie had purchased the vacation home, neither had visited it. Debbie had chosen the property from an ad in the Sunday New York Times magazine based solely on the photo. They had probably overpaid but at the time Jake was making so much money he didn't care. Trying to find the place, he frequently took his eyes off the road to read the directions he'd scrawled on the back of an envelope. His lack of concentration on driving found him in the opposite lane at least three times and twice, going off the road entirely and into pasture land.

He eventually found his property perched on a hill at the end of a long driveway. He parked his car and stood outside the wooden house that reminded him of the buildings he had made out of Lincoln Logs when he was five. From the front, it was an attractive neo-rustic structure, but once he unlocked the door and stepped inside, he was really impressed. There was a large living room with glass windows on either side of a stone fireplace that ran from the floor to the two-story ceiling above, and opened to an expansive view of the valley below and the Green Mountains beyond. The furnishings were simple, yet elegantly appropriate, obviously done by the prior owners since Debbie and the decorators she used had far gaudier taste. He walked up to the second floor to see the four bedrooms. As he checked out the rooms, he heard someone shout "Anybody home?" He walked out to the hall that over-looked the living room and saw a bearded man with graying long hair tied in a ponytail and dressed in denim overalls and a red plaid shirt.

"Hey there, you must be Mr. Himmelfarb." Jake came down the stairs. "Hadley said you'd be coming by. Was kinda wondering what you looked like. Name's Francis Mazzetti. Most people call me Frank." He held out his hand.

"Please, call me Jake. Mr. Griffith didn't mention anything about you." As Jake shook Frank's hand, he had to restrain from groaning at the strength his grip.

"Well, Hadley sometimes forgets things like that. I'm the man who rents your farmland down the road. I'm also the caretaker of this place. I see to it that everything's in order for the tourists when they stay here. Zoe, she's my wife, she handles things like changing the linens and such. So what do you think of the place?"

"It's really nice. Much more than I had expected."

"It's a great property. I'm surprised you never spend any time here."

"Could never arrange it. Always too busy I guess. Can I see the farm?"

"Sure. Hop in the pickup."

As they rode the two miles to the farm, Frank gave a brief history of the area and background on the neighbors and some of the more colorful towns-folk. "We have four seasons here, summer, fall, winter and mud. As you can tell, now is mud." Jake had first-hand knowledge of the mud from his earlier accidental off-road excursions. They pulled into the farm and Frank parked in front of a modest farmhouse in sore need of a new coat of paint. "Zoe should be around someplace. I told her you might be coming by and to have some lunch ready for us."

"It's just the two of you on the farm?"

"We got a nine-year-old girl, Chelsea. She's in school now. Then there's Annie. She's twenty-two or some such and lives with us. During the growing season, I may hire a couple of men to help with the planting and harvesting. But mostly it's just tending to the animals."

"Zoe, Chelsea, Annie. Do all of the women here have names ending in 'eee'?" Frank had no reaction to Jake's attempt at humor. "So what does Annie do?"

"She helps me with the animals and making sure everything we grow is organic. She came to us last summer. Got her from one of those organic cooperatives and she's changed a lot around here. Not sure how long she'll stay."

"What kind of changes?"

"Certainly changed the fertilizers and gotten rid of the pesticides. She's also limited the amount of antibiotics we give the cows, and got rid of the hogs."

"Thank God for that."

"Yep, can't get milk from swine. Now it's goats and sheep, along with the cows."

Jake's only comment following a quick tour of the farm concerned the aroma that filled the air. A healthy, natural smell Frank said, to which Jake replied that the last time he remembered odors like that was when the sanitation workers went on strike in the city. After lunch with Frank and Zoe, Jake went into the town of Waitsfield to see the real estate agent managing his properties. He met Hadley Griffith at his office on Main Street. In his thirty-five years in the business, Hadley had seen the area slowly evolve from a quiet farming village to a vacation destination and even a bedroom community.

"Mr. Himmelfarb, welcome. Have any trouble finding your house?" Hadley spoke with a thick New England accent similar to what Jake had heard from some of the other locals. He knew it would take some getting used to before he fully understood every word.

"Not much, though the roads were a little tricky."

"Any questions regarding the property?"

"Just one. How much do you think I could get for it?"

"You want to sell the place?" Jake nodded and Hadley scratched his head. "Market is pretty soft right now. It usually picks up later in the spring on into summer when people start thinking about vacations. A lot of sales come from tourists just walking down the street and looking at photos in the window."

"But if I wanted to sell now?"

Hadley thought for a moment. "Maybe $300,000, give or take."

"That's all? There's like ten acres of land and the house is beautiful. I think we paid a lot more than that when we bought it."

"You paid…" Hadley paused as he shuffled through papers on his desk. "Give me a second – yes, here it is. You paid one point three million, but that included the farm."

"Well of course I want to include the farm. Now how much?"

"Hmm. Farmland's going for next to nothing now. I'd hope we'd get seven-fifty."

"$750,000 for the farm?"

"Seven-fifty or the farm and the house, if they could be sold. Of course, the outstanding mortgage on the properties is more than that, so you'd have to make up the difference. You know, the farm generated $19,000 in income for you last year and should be about the same this year. The rental on the house netted you another $2,200."

"This is just great. My divorce left me with assets that have negative equity."

"Aye, that's about the size of it. What would you like me to do?"

Jake sighed and shook his head. "Nothing for now I guess. Keep your ears open in case you hear of anyone looking to buy."

"I will do that. I assume you can be reached at the phone number in New York."

"No. Here's my cell. I seem to get a weak signal at the house. For the time being, it seems I'm Vermont's newest resident."

"On behalf of the community, let me be the first to welcome you."

Jake returned to his house, unpacked his clothes and began calling moving companies to have some of his possessions shipped up from the storage facility in Brooklyn. He was trying to explain to a man with a heavy Russian accent what he wanted moved when the doorbell rang. Frustrated at the Russian's lack of comprehension, he hung up and opened the door.

"Yes, can I help you?" he said.

"Hi. I'm Ann Marie. Zoe sent me over with these." She handed him two paper bags filled with groceries. "She was worried you had nothing to eat."

"Oh. Thanks." He motioned with his head for her to come in while he struggled to keep the bags from falling to the ground. "I thought Frank called you Annie."

"Yeah, everyone does, but I always introduce myself as Ann Marie O'Shea. Probably the result of the nuns from Catholic school having drilled proper manners into me."

Following behind her, he eyed her from head to toe then back again. She was not very tall, about five-two he guessed, with shoulder length red hair that hung in pigtails on either side of her face. Like a lot of people he'd seen around town, she wore blue denim overalls that made it difficult to tell what her body really looked like. She wore absolutely no make-up, but her rosy complexion seemed to glow as if a light coat of rouge had been applied. "Let me put these in the kitchen. By the way, my name is Jake."

"Frank told me."

"Can I get you something?"

"No I'm fine."

"How is it that a young girl like yourself comes to work on farm?"

"I grew up in Boston. The closest I ever got to a farm was what I could see from the highway, but I always loved animals. I ended up majoring in animal science at UVM with a minor in ecological agriculture."

"UVM?"

"University of Vermont. Anyway, I did some interning at an organic farm then spent a year in Ireland on a dairy farm. It was there I learned about cheese making."

"Cheese making?"

She reached into one of the bags and took out a hunk of yellow cheese wrapped in foil. "Try a piece."

He found a knife on the counter and cut a small slice. "That's very good. Did you make this?"

She nodded. "It's only aged three months. A cheddar like that really needs a lot longer. I'm still experimenting. I convinced Frank after we got rid of the hogs that there's a market for artisanal cheeses. We're never going to compete with the Cabots of the world, but we've developed some distinctive varieties. It could be a money maker."

"So you're planning on staying around for a while?"

"Yeah. Sure. Why?"

"Oh I don't know. I thought Frank had said something like he didn't know how long you'd be here."

"Frank's always worried about how long he's going to be able to keep farming. From what Zoe says, every year it's the same story. Spring comes, he looks at his bank account, he doesn't know if the bank will lend him money for planting, if the crops will come in and if milk prices will be high enough for him to pay back the loans. But he's no different from any farmer; they all worry about those things. In the end, he always goes to the bank and always plants."

"I have to thank you for getting rid of the pigs."

"They can be a mess, not to mention that with what pork bellies were going for, he couldn't afford to keep them. Anyway, what about you? Frank said he heard from Hadley that you're a stock broker or something."

"I used to be the 'or something.'"

"What happened?"

"I got tired of it and quit."

"Because of 9/11?"

"No, I quit some time before then."

"Were you in New York when the towers fell?" He nodded. "Wow. I cried for two days. Did you know anyone who died?"

"I used to work in the South Tower, on the eighty-fifth floor, so yeah, I knew a few people who were killed."

"God how awful. It's lucky I guess that you quit when you did."

"Actually, the firm I worked for moved out of the WTC a month before 9/11, so even if I hadn't quit, I would have been all right."

"And what do you do now?"

"I have been trying to get an organization up and running to focus on the problem of diarrhea in children in Africa. Did you know that is the largest killer of children and one of the cheapest and easiest to prevent and cure?"

"No I didn't. So how's that going?"

"Not as well as I'd hoped. I've run through a lot of my savings and then there's my divorce, which was quite costly. I had to lay off the one employee that I'd hired and I couldn't afford the rents in Manhattan any longer."

"So you're moving here?"

"It's not what I had planned but for the time being, I have no alternatives."

"There are worse places you could live."

"That's for sure. It's just hard to meet the kind of people I need to meet for funding and logistics. You know, corporate types, NGOs, etc."

"What are NGOs?"

"Non-governmental organizations."

She glanced up at the clock on the wall. "Shit, is that the right time?"

Jake looked at his watch. "Yeah, why?"

"Shit. I've got to get the cows in before dark. Gotta run."

"Okay. Thanks for the food. I'll see you around."

"You bet."

◇◇◇◇◇◇

Mia sat on the bed in her room at the New York Hilton and checked one last time the email she had printed out to make sure that she had the time right for her dinner date. It had only been a week since she and Kat had moved into her new place in Stockbridge. They had come to Manhattan to purchase furnishings for the place, with Kat concentrating on equipping the kitchen and Mia taking care of the dining room decor. But her dinner had nothing to do with the restaurant. After quitting her position on the Sino-American trade delegation, she had maintained contact with the one Chinese person that she had developed a close relationship with, Li Xuan. Li had risen to a senior post at the Ministry of Finance. He was in the city to attend a U.N. conference and when she had mentioned that she would be in Manhattan, he arranged to meet her.

"Do you know where you're going?" Kat asked emerging from the bathroom.

"The Waldorf-Astoria. Sure you don't want to come?"

"Quite. Besides, I'm meeting friends in the Village for dinner, and after that, we're all going out to some club."

"Sounds like fun."

"It will be. Don't forget, when your dinner is over, call me on my cell and I'll let you know where we are."

She arrived at the Waldorf and followed Li's instructions to go to the concierge and identify herself. Shortly thereafter, a Chinese man dressed in a dark business suit tapped her on her shoulder. She provided him with identification and he took her up to Li's suite on the 34th floor. Her escort knocked on the door and another man opened it, but did not let her inside. Instead, he stepped into the hallway and to Mia's chagrin, did a cursory frisk of her body. "That will not be necessary," she heard Li call out in Mandarin. Li appeared at the door. "My apologies for that," he said to her in English.

"It's okay. I understand the need for security."

"Please come in." He gave her a kiss on each cheek. "I'm so glad to see you again."

She walked into the lavishly decorated suite. The dining table was already set for two. Li quickly dismissed the guards and when they were alone, uncorked a bottle of champagne that had been chilling in a basket.

"How long has it been?" he asked.

"I think the last time I saw you was January 2001 in Beijing."

"Yes. I was so surprised when you told me that you were leaving your post. You had been on the delegation for so short a time."

"I know, but things happen. Bush became president. I was a pretty big contributor to the Democrats. You know how politics works."

"That is one thing I'll never understand about your government. You change parties every few years and all of your government workers lose their jobs. You never have any continuity."

"Not all of the workers lose their jobs. Most are career civil servants who are not affected by a change of administration. It's only the political appointees that go."

"Still, those are the leaders, the ones with the most power, are they not?"

"That's the price of democracy, I suppose."

Li nodded. "Well, I didn't invite you to dinner to get into an argument about the relative advantages of your government versus mine. Here." He handed her a glass of champagne. "I've taken the liberty of ordering dinner for us. I hope you like lamb."

"Love lamb."

"Good. They should be delivering it any minute."

They talked over dinner in general terms about the world, the 9/11 attacks and the ensuing war on terrorism, but they avoided any specifics when it came to China. After dinner, they sat in the living room and sipped twenty-five-year-old brandy. "Your accommodations here are beautiful. You know, I'm in the process of opening a restaurant so I'm starting to take notice of how rooms are decorated."

"Then before you go, make sure I show you the rest of the suite. I wanted to ask you, how come after you left your post on the commission, you didn't return to your old job?"

She took a sip of brandy. "My job at MBG had been filled by someone else, and as you know, MBG didn't fare so well. When their gene therapy for diabetes failed to get final FDA approval, they essentially went belly-up."

"Belly-up?"

"Bankrupt. To be honest, even if they hadn't, I didn't really want to go back to work there. It wasn't for me, which is why when I got the call about serving on the commission, I jumped at it." Li started to smile. "Did I miss something?"

"No," he said, "Maybe. Did you ever find out why it was that they called you?"

"I assumed they wanted a Chinese American who had experience with the mainland, and who was a Democrat."

"Yes, that's true..."

She knew by the way his voice trailed off there was more. "That's true – but?"

"I may have mentioned your name to Admiral Prueher."

"The U.S. ambassador?"

"Yes."

"Huh. Then I suppose a thank-you is in order."

"I'm not so sure. You only served for a couple of months and then you had no job."

"I was incredibly fortunate. When I took the position on the commission, I had to divest myself of any financial holdings that could create a conflict of interest." Li looked puzzled. "I know, another one of those inconveniences of an open government. In this case, it worked to my advantage. I sold all of my stock in MBG just before the price collapsed. I think I sold it at something like eighty-two dollars a share. Six months later it was selling for less than a dollar a share. By you getting me on that commission, I ended up financially secure. So, thank you."

"You're welcome. I have to be honest and tell you that there is something else I wanted to discuss with you."

"You mean you didn't invite me here just to see you?"

"Seeing you would be reason enough for any invitation, but I do have a proposition." He refilled her snifter with brandy. "I would like to hire you as a consultant and voice for the People's Republic here in America. You could help with representing our economic interests in Washington. Of course, you would only be dealing with economic issues, but you could explain, and perhaps influence your president and your congress. What is the term for that?"

"Lobbying?"

Li nodded. "A funny term. We would, of course, pay you quite handsomely for your services."

Mia was intrigued by Li's proposal. She had not expected anything like this. Not wanting to appear impolite, she paused for a moment as if mulling over the job, but knew pretty quickly what her answer was. "I'm very flattered that you would even consider me for such a position. But I'm afraid I have to decline the offer."

"Why?"

"I have other responsibilities. For one thing, I have this new restaurant I'm opening up and I've made some commitments to my partner, not to mention that I'm having so much fun with it."

"You can still have your restaurant."

"Stockbridge Massachusetts is not exactly commuting distance from Washington D.C. And there are other reasons."

"Like what?"

She took a deep breath. "To be perfectly honest, I have no desire to represent the interests of the Chinese government. Let's just leave it at that."

"Mia, I'm not asking you to do anything that would be at all detrimental to the United States."

She didn't feel like arguing with him. "There's another problem. My father is suffering from Alzheimer's. He's in a facility in Massachusetts, which is why I moved there. I'm his only living child. I have a responsibility to care for him."

The duty of children and parents to each other stretched back through five thousand years of Chinese history and culture, transcending the needs of any particular government. "I understand," Li said. "Please accept my sorrow at your father's condition."

She felt a palpable sense of relief that this reason had satisfied him. "Thank you. I should probably be going now."

"The evening is still young."

"I'm supposed to meet up with some friends."

"I see. Let me first give you that tour of my accommodations." He stood up and reached out his hand to her. "You've seen the living space, let me show you the bedrooms." As they walked, Li continued to hold her hand. "I'm sure the paintings are all reproductions. Whoever decorated must have been a reincarnation of Louis XIV's decorator. This, I suppose is the guest bedroom." He opened a door and she peeked in. "And this is my bedroom. You should look at the bathroom. It is bigger than many apartments back home."

She walked around the room and looked at the furniture, drapes and rugs. She was not really interested, but did not want to insult Li. She turned towards him. "It's very lovely. I..." Li silenced her by pressing his lips to her mouth and clumsily attempting to kiss her. She was flabbergasted and didn't know how to react.

"Are you sure you have to go?" he asked softly.

It wasn't as if she was repulsed by Li. Since the first time she'd met him, she'd always liked him, and had even had a passing fantasy once or twice about him. But this was too weird. She slowly nodded. "I have people waiting. Besides, you're married and I'm involved with someone." The last part of her statement had no basis in fact, but she did her best to deliver it convincingly.

Li stared into her eyes. "Okay. I'll get your coat," he finally said. He walked her to the door, opened it and the two men who had been sitting in the hallway snapped to attention. "I'll be in New York for the next month."

"Unfortunately, I'm going back to Massachusetts the day after tomorrow and I don't know when I'll be back."

"I see," he said. "Well if your plans change, you've got my email address."

"I'll be writing you. Thank you for a lovely evening." She kissed him lightly on the cheek then followed one of the security men to the elevator.

When she reached the street, she phoned Kat but the call went straight to voicemail. She hailed a cab and went back to her hotel. The bar on the ground floor of the Hilton was half-empty and Mia didn't feel like sitting alone in her room. She took a seat at the bar and ordered a glass of white wine. It didn't take long before a number of men came up offering to buy her drinks. Regardless of their age or build, they all looked the same – businessmen away from home, some probably married, all hoping to get lucky on their night in the Big Apple. She tired of having to politely fend them off and decided to go up to her room. She opened the door and was surprised to discover that she'd apparently left the TV on. She was even more surprised when she realized that Kat was under the covers of one of the beds. "God, you scared the shit out of me," Kat exclaimed.

"Sorry. I didn't expect to find you here. Are you feeling all right?"

"Yeah, I'm fine."

The door to the bathroom flung open and a shaft of light streamed in. "Hey babe, got the key to the mini-bar?"

Mia caught only a fleeting glimpse of the full frontal nudity of some man before she quickly turned away. "Oh, I had no idea you had someone with you."

"I didn't think you'd be back so soon," Kat said.

"No problem. I'll come back later." She quickly grabbed her pocketbook and leaned over Kat. "Should I get my own room?" she whispered.

Kat shook her head. "No way. He's not spending the night. I'll call your cell when he's gone."

Mia left the room and stood in the hallway trying to decide where to go and feeling a little envious of Kat. It had been a very long time since she'd been with a man. She knew this was the result of her own ridiculous standards or perhaps fears. She wasn't sure which. She could have been with Li tonight, but she knew she'd made the right decision regarding that. She could go back to the bar and get picked up, but those men did nothing for her. She opened her pocketbook, took out the paperback novel she'd started reading that morning, and headed back down to the lobby to find a comfortable chair in which to read and wait for Kat's call.

◇◇◇◇◇◇◇

Sayid was two hours into the train ride from Frankfurt to Berlin when a woman wearing a long, black raincoat and sporting dark sunglasses took a seat opposite him. She smiled briefly before burying her head in the current issue of Der Spiegel. He tried to be inconspicuous in his efforts to determine whether she was just another passenger or someone he needed to concern himself with. He had been warned that despite the long, circuitous route he had taken from Pakistan to Germany, he might come under surveillance by the authorities. He decided it was better to engage her than to sit in silence. "Have you ridden this train before?"

She looked up from her magazine. "I'm sorry, did you say something?" She spoke English with a German accent. He tried repeating the question in German, but botched it to the point that what came out was incomprehensible. "I think my English is better than your German, no?" she said.

"Undoubtedly. I've never been on this train before. I was just wondering if you knew how long it takes to get to Berlin."

"From here, I would say at least another four hours."

"Thanks." The silence returned and he still had no sense of her. He opened the laptop computer he had been supplied with and pretended to use it. Since the computer was brand new, it was devoid of any potential incriminating data. He carefully laid the computer down on the seat next to him while placing a tiny slip of paper near the touch pad before closing the screen. "Excuse me, I need to visit the lavatory."

"It's to your right at the end of the car."

Sayid headed for the restroom, glancing back twice at the woman who remained seated with her legs crossed, still engrossed in her magazine. Although he didn't need to use the facility, he went to the bathroom to kill some time before returning to his seat. When he did, the computer was where he had left it, but the woman was gone. He opened the computer and the piece of paper he had left inside was gone as well. In its place was a folded note that had been taped to the keyboard. He tore off the note and opened it.

The paper trick is not very reliable. You should really be less obvious about trying to see if a person is interested in you. I will be in the next car towards the rear of the train.

He packed up the computer and headed for the other car. He found her seated and still reading the magazine. "How was your trip to the bathroom?" she asked.

He took the seat across from her. "Should I know you?"

"Since we have yet to formally introduce ourselves to each other, the answer is no." She put down the magazine and took off her sunglasses. For the first time he could see what she really looked like; a very attractive girl who appeared to be in her late teens, but judging by her cool demeanor, must have been older. "Herr Hassan, my name is Gretchen. Klaus sent me to look out for you."

"How do I know I can trust you?"

"You don't. But since you have no idea how to contact Klaus, or even what he looks like, what choice do you have?"

"Point taken. Where is he?"

"I will take you to him when we get to Berlin. We have arranged an apartment for you. That is all I can tell you."

"All that you can tell me or all that you know?"

"What difference would that make?" She slipped back on her sunglasses and picked up her magazine.

The one-bedroom apartment was in a modern building built after the fall of the wall in what used to be East Berlin. The space was sparsely furnished, but this didn't bother Sayid. He hoped that within a few months, he'd have made enough connections to move back to America. As soon as they entered the flat, Gretchen took out her cell phone made a call. "Klaus will be here in ten minutes," she told him. "Would you like something to drink? There's some beer in the icebox. Oh, I forgot, you probably don't drink beer. There should be some juice in there too."

"Thank you. Beer is fine." He walked around the apartment, checking out the bedroom, kitchen and bath. After more than a year of living in the primitive conditions of Afghanistan and Pakistan, the accommodations felt downright regal.

There was a knock on the door and Sayid returned to the living room in time to see Gretchen let a man in and give him a kiss. She relaxed her embrace and turned to Sayid. "This is Klaus." Klaus broke away from her and reached out to shake Sayid's hand.

"How was your trip?" he asked.

"Long. When can I start work?"

"In a couple of days I will present you. You will have to convince my father of your value to the bank. I frankly do not know enough of what you are planning to do to be of much help beyond making the introduction. Ibrahim told me very little."

"In broad terms, I want to be dealing with the Americans, so I will do anything that will help me with that."

"PBB has almost no presence in the U.S., so this may not be the best fit."

"Other than the money you handle for our mutual associates, do you have any accounts for the Saudis or the other Gulf States?"

"I handle all of our Mideast depositors."

"And I assume the amounts are significant."

"Billions."

"Then tell your father that those depositors are hinting that they want to move their funds to U.S. banks." Klaus looked lost. "Make up something like with the large American military presence in their countries, they feel an obligation to invest more in American securities. If PBB had a New York branch office, they could handle all of their needs, not to mention the fees and commissions that the bank would earn. Plant the idea in your father's head in advance, then bring me in."

Klaus nodded and brushed a piece of lint off of Sayid's shoulder. "You are going to need a bit of a makeover. Gretchen brought most of your clothes from your apartment in Paris. They are hanging in the closet in the bedroom."

"I saw that, though I must be twenty pounds lighter than the last time I wore them."

"Then you are going to need new ones. Gretchen will take you shopping tomorrow." She dismissively shrugged her shoulders. Klaus grabbed a handful of Sayid's hair. "And get this cut," he told her.

"Whatever," she said.

"Anything else?" Sayid asked.

"Lose the beard by morning. You can keep a moustache if you like, but I recommend no facial hair."

"Is that all?"

"One final thing. I took the liberty of getting your background from the Argonne web site." He reached into his pocket and handed Sayid a sheet of paper. "If you intend on returning to America, you're going to have to have a different identity. Being an Arab is not going to open any doors. You might pass as a Greek or a Spaniard."

"My Spanish isn't very good, and my Greek is non-existent. What about Italian? I'm not bad at that."

"Italian it is. Here, read this. It's your resume, once we fill it in with your new name. Memorize it."

He took the paper from Klaus. "And what have I been doing?"

"For the past year, you have been living in Bangladesh working with a company that provides micro-financing loans to startup entrepreneurs. It's a legitimate company that will corroborate that story."

"How did you arrange that?"

"We gave them $25,000."

"That was enough?"

"Things are very cheap in Bangladesh, including bribery. That is enough money for them to make five hundred or more loans. That's about it for now. Gretchen will come get you in the morning."

Sayid nodded. He scanned over the resume as Klaus and Gretchen started to leave. "Wait, so what's my new name going to be?"

Klaus stopped at the door. "Choose one yourself. Even here in Germany things have changed since 9/11. We have a large Turkish community and Muslim sounding names are not an asset. Remember that Atta, the leader of the attacks on America, planned most of the operation from Hamburg. The BND is still on high alert for anything suspicious. Just pick a name that you can remember. Believe it or not, usually it's best to pick something that sort of sounds similar to your real name so your response is natural."

"Understood. Gretchen, I'll see you tomorrow?"

"Around ten," she replied and then hesitated for a moment after Klaus had walked out the door. "How about Stephen for a name?"

"Doesn't sound very Italian," said Sayid.

"Then make it Stefano. Stefano Assan – Stefano Assanti."

"Sounds as good as any."

Sayid met Klaus on the street in front of the main entrance of the bank. "You clean up very well," Klaus told him. "Gretchen did a fine job picking you out a suit. It's conservative without being old-fashioned. What do you think of her?"

Sayid didn't know what to answer. "I get the feeling she doesn't care much for me."

"What makes you think that?"

Sayid threw his hands up. "I don't know. She doesn't say much, as if talking to me she found distasteful."

Klaus laughed. "She doesn't talk much to anyone, but she thinks Muslim men oppress their women."

"She's not entirely wrong about that. Why does she help us?"

"She helps me, not your partners. She's a dedicated anti-imperialist and anti-globalist, and will go along with anyone who helps those causes." They started up the marble steps of the bank entrance. "And, it doesn't hurt that she's real good between the sheets," Klaus added.

They made their way to the office of Klaus's father, Gunther Voorhaus, where they found him seated behind a large desk. "Father, this is Stefano Assanti. I mentioned him to you the other day in regard to my idea about opening a New York branch. Steve, my father, Gunther Voorhaus, the president of the Prussian Bourse Banque."

"Herr Assanti, welcome." The senior Voorhaus reached across his desk to shake Sayid's hand. "Please, sit down. Klaus has told me something of you but I'd like to hear it from the source, if you will."

"A pleasure to meet you, sir. Please call me Steve."

"You have an impressive resume. What can we do for you?"

Sayid cleared his throat. "As you can see from that resume, I've spent the last year working in Bangladesh, trying to help that very impoverished nation. It was a wonderful experience, and I regret none of it, but it was draining. In the U.S., they call it burnout. I'm ready to get back to living in the West. An executive recruitment firm that I was using connected me with Klaus."

Gunther nodded his head. "Well, you certainly deserve it. I see you lived in America for some time. Why not go back there or to Italy?"

"Since you've seen my resume, you see I have citizenship in both places but the Italian economy is, well you know, a mess as always. I think it will give me an edge to represent a German firm in the U.S. And I also think from what Klaus has told me, I can fulfill PBB's needs."

"Perhaps, but the clients that my son is responsible for are very particular, and very wealthy."

"I am aware of Klaus's book of business. If you'll look at my resume, you'll see I have firsthand experience with the Arab culture. I worked in Saudi Arabia for several months and am fluent in Arabic."

"Which father, is exactly why I brought Stefano to you."

Gunther leaned back in his chair nodded. "I have taken a serious look at what Klaus said regarding opening a branch in America. Heaven knows those bastards at Deutsche Bank are big there."

"And we don't want our Middle Eastern friends thinking that Deutsche Bank would be a better place to park their money, would we?" said Klaus.

"We most certainly do not. I am convinced of the need to establish a New York office. Klaus, since you are PBB's main contact point with the Arabs, I think you should go to New York and manage the setting up of things there. Today is Thursday. Have a budget on my desk by next Tuesday for staff, rent, equipment, supplies – you know the drill. I'll present it to the board at the weekly Wednesday meeting, although that is just a pro-forma step."

"What about Steve?"

"Oh, I thought that was obvious. Once things are up and running, I assume you will be coming back to Germany. Herr Assanti will be our Director of U.S. operations, assuming that he still wants to work for us."

Sayid flashed a broad smile as he stood and reached out his hand to Gunther.

"Absolutely."

Gunther took his hand. "Then welcome aboard, Stefano. Do not disappoint us."

"I will not, sir."

NINE

September 2002

Manhattanites who had spent much of August vacationing in the Hamptons, Maine or on Martha's Vineyard had returned to their lives and jobs in the city. The relative quiet of late summer New York had evaporated along with the heat and humidity, but the city and its residents still hadn't returned to their pre 9/11 state of mind. And lest they ever forget, the gaping hole where the towers once stood was there to remind them. Sayid, or Steve as everyone now knew him, had spent the summer laying out the groundwork for his business plan based on his vague recollections of the student project he, Mia and Jake had developed a decade earlier. On more than one occasion, he had contemplated tracking down one of his old classmates to get their input, but obvious security concerns always nixed that idea.

Klaus had spent the summer flying back and forth between New York and Berlin. Sayid always preferred it when the younger Voorhaus was out of the country and not meddling in his work. They had managed in less than four months to establish a U.S. office of PBB in lower Manhattan off Wall Street, replete with furnishings and a staff of seven employees. All was progressing nicely yet there were still several problems. For one thing, Sayid recognized early on that if his plan for using mortgage-backed derivatives were to succeed, he would need a legal framework upon which the securities could be based. A simple document would not suffice; he needed the paperwork to be of such complexity that not only would the buyers and sellers be unsure of all the provisions, even the lawyers drafting the documents might not comprehend all of its implications. And if such complicated transactions were to gain the acceptance of large investors, the documents would need to have been drawn up by a law firm with a reputation above reproach. Klaus, through his connections, provided a list of large, old-line firms to choose from. He settled on one that had previously done work for PBB. It wasn't that their hourly rates were any lower than the others, he simply figured that using a firm with which the bank had an established relationship with would make things go more smoothly.

There were other issues facing Sayid but the hardest was keeping his attention focused on what was for the most part, tedious and boring minutia. A year of living in primitive conditions, not knowing whether your next meal might be your last, had diminished his white-collar skills. Like an athlete out of training, he needed time and practice to get back into "game shape." Now that summer had ended, he felt his confidence returning and was ready to strike his first deal. He approached Klaus to secure the necessary funds.

"How much do you need?"

"After thinking about it, I want to go with the full ten million."

"That's very bold, or very reckless. Are you sure you want to risk it all in one shot?"

"No, I'm not sure. But I need at least that much to put together a CDO that will have any of the characteristics I need. The worst thing to do would be to slowly dribble away the funds without any impact on the market."

Klaus went to his computer and accessed the al-Qaeda account. "Very well then. There is nine point three million, give or take, in the account."

"What happened to the other seven hundred thousand?"

Klaus hemmed for minute. "You know, the exchange rates fluctuate daily, affecting the balance and of course, there are fees."

"What fees?"

"Look, Steve, maintaining these accounts for your people incurs a great deal of risk, to PBB and to me personally. There are people at the bank I have to keep happy so that they look the other way, if you know what I mean. Seven percent is not that much. If you think you can find someone to do it for less, be my guest."

"Those funds have been on deposit since the spring. Shouldn't they have earned interest?"

"Have you looked at the rates lately? Yes, the funds earned some interest, but the places I can park that money without raising suspicions are limited. Maybe the fees amounted to more like eight or nine percent, so I'm giving you a break. As I said, you can go to another bank if you think you can find one."

Sayid knew he had no choice. "No, I'm not changing banks, but you had better be careful that you can justify yourself because Mustafa al-Yazid is not someone you'd like to disappoint."

"Let me worry about al-Yazid. Do you have a deal lined up?"

"I have all the paperwork. I just need to find the right investment house to go through."

Klaus let out a derisive laugh. "Don't you think you are, as they say in English, putting the cart before the horse?"

"The legal framework is the foundation on which this plan relies. I've got that. Now I just have to make some connections."

Klaus pulled out his Blackberry and began scrolling through his contacts and calendar. "Have you got a tuxedo?"

"Why do you ask?"

"Next Thursday night, there's a charity dinner in town for some organization called KISS. Not sure what that stands for. Anyway, I can get us two tickets. They're fifteen grand a piece."

"Fifteen grand? They had better have some very good food for that price."

"Don't worry. PBB will pick up the tab. The important thing is that the room will be filled with investment bankers and hedge fund managers. It's time that you and PBB let this city know that we're in town. You might want to do some online checking to see who attended last year."

"How would I do that?"

"You can find anything these days on the Internet. Check the newspapers for archives of their society page, or the organization must have a web site."

"I'll look into it."

The private car arrived to pick Sayid up in front of his apartment. He climbed into the back and found Klaus with a glass of Scotch in hand. It quickly became clear that the drink wasn't his first of the evening. "Care for one?" he asked Sayid.

"I'm okay."

"Oh yeah. I forgot you guys don't believe in this stuff. Afraid you're not getting into paradise or something?" Sayid declined to respond although it occurred to him that Klaus was providing a good example of the Koran's wisdom on the subject. "So, did you research who's going to be there?"

"I went over last year's list. Some of them certainly won't be back this year."

"And why's that?"

"Because a year ago, they were in their offices in the World Trade Center."

Klaus tried to stifle a burp. "Too bad for them."

The ballroom at the downtown Marriott was already filled with guests by the time they arrived. Immediately Klaus, with Sayid in tow, headed for the bar and ordered another cocktail. Sayid stuck with club soda and lime. "Come with me," Klaus said. They dodged servers carrying trays of hors d'oeuvres and snaked their way through the crowd. "Hello, Alan. Haven't seen you in quite some time."

The man Klaus was addressing took a few seconds to recognize him. "Klaus," he finally said, "surprised to see you here."

"The bank has decided to open a New York office."

"Really. How's your father doing?"

"He's good. Let me introduce you to Steve Assanti. Steve is heading up our New York office. Steve, this is Alan Schwartz, head of Bear Stearns."

Schwartz held out his hand to Sayid. "Mr. Schwartz, a pleasure to meet you. I hope we can do some business together in the near future."

"I hope so too. Have you got your card on you?"

"Of course." Sayid reached into his inside coat pocket and handed over a card.

Schwartz glanced at the card before putting it in his pocket. "Thanks. Have your secretary call mine and set up a lunch. Oh, excuse me, I see Hank Paulson over there."

Schwartz walked away and Klaus leaned over and whispered in Sayid's ear, "See, this is easy. Unfortunately, Alan is probably the only person I know in this room, but he's been involved in investment banking most of his career. He understands the derivatives market as well as anyone. Just go around and mingle. Give me some of your cards to hand out." Klaus downed the rest of his drink and headed off to the bar.

Sayid stood off in a corner trying to decide what to do. He was still uncomfortable in social situations with large numbers of strangers, but he knew it was something he needed to get better at.

"You look a little lost." An attractive woman seemingly materialized from out of nowhere.

"Excuse me?" he said.

"I didn't mean to offend. I don't recognize you from last year. My name is Debbie." She held out her hand to him. "I'm on the KISS board."

"Oh, I'm Sayee – Steve."

"Having trouble remembering your name?"

"Um, perhaps I should have eaten something before getting this drink. No, this is the first time I've been to this. I'm only here because my partner thought it a good business move. I don't even know what KISS stands for."

She gave one those knowing laughs. "Don't apologize, most everyone else is here for the same reason, although etiquette prevents them from admitting it. By the way, KISS stands for Keep Kids In Safe Schools. I know, it should be KKISS, but the double Ks at the beginning made it sound as though you had a stuttering problem when you said it. I've always thought that whoever comes up with these names first comes up with a catchy acronym and then finds the words to match it."

"You're probably right."

"If you don't mind me saying so, for someone who wants to make business connections, you seem to be avoiding the action."

"Right again. I've been out of America for the last decade, working in Europe. Everyone here seems to know one other and I don't want to intrude."

"Honey, shyness is not an admired trait with this group. Come with me." She took his hand and led him across the room. "Steve, this is my fiancé Arthur Morrison, head of Pilgrim/United. Artie, this is Steve, uh, you know Steve, I'm sorry I don't recall your last name."

Sayid had hoped to meet Morrison. He couldn't believe his luck at having Morrison's fiancée make the introduction. He handed Morrison his card. "Assanti. I'm heading up the New York office for the Prussian Bourse Banque."

Morrison looked at the card. "I didn't know PBB had opened an office here. Nice to meet you."

"It's been only opened for a few months. And incidentally, we have met before."

"We have?"

"It was a long time ago. Like you, I studied at MIT."

"Is that where we met?"

"I had the pleasure of playing against you once in a duplicate bridge game."

Morrison's eyebrows perked up. "Oh, you play bridge?"

"Not in a while. I couldn't find anyone in Europe to play with on a regular basis."

"Oh, God. Now you're going to starting talking about cards," said Debbie. "My work here is done. I'll leave you two alone." She gave Arthur a kiss on the cheek and walked off.

"I'm impressed that you would remember a game from years ago."

"I was just a student then, and you were already well known." It suddenly dawned on Sayid that perhaps he'd just committed a breach of security. If Morrison were so inclined, he might decide to research his MIT background revealing his true identity.

"Really. Tell me, did I win that night?"

"To be honest, I don't recall. I was only at MIT for one semester as an exchange student. Do you still play bridge?"

"Haven't much. I'm looking for a new partner. Finding a wife is easier."

"What happened to your old partner?"

"Funny you should ask. He too was a student at MIT. Maybe you knew him, Jacob Himmelfarb?" Sayid coolly shook his head. "It's a big school, and Jake was a dick. I don't know where he is now. He quit on me. I think he flipped out or something. Last I heard, he was living on a farm in Vermont or Maine or someplace like that. So tell me Steve, have any interest in playing sometime?"

"I'd love to play again, though like I said, I'm a little rusty."

"It'll come back quickly. How about tomorrow?"

"Tomorrow?"

"Why not. There is always a penny-game of Chicago going on at my club. Play with me. As I said, I've been looking for a new partner. If you're half the player Himmelfarb was, this could be the start of a new partnership."

"Sounds like a plan."

◇◇◇◇◇◇

"Things will get crazy once the colors change in a couple of weeks. Are you sure you don't want to rent out the house? I can get you two grand for a week."

Jake thought over Hadley Griffith's offer. The real estate agent had been hounding him all summer to rent out his house. No doubt the commissions were Hadley's motivation, but truth was that Jake could use the money. His savings, or those that he had access to, were dwindling. Living in Vermont, much to his surprise, was growing on him. The slow pace of life and the friendliness of the locals was a tonic after the frenetic world of New York. He liked Frank and Zoe, and had grown particular fond of their daughter Chelsea. It almost made him regret that he and Debbie had put off having children, although when he really considered that possibility, he always ended up thankful they had none.

And then there was Annie. He couldn't quite figure out what he thought of her. She was bright, funny and with that head of flowing red hair, quite attractive. She clearly had talent when it came to cheese making, a skill, really an art, which Jake had grown to appreciate. But Annie's sexual orientation meant that a romantic relationship was clearly not in the cards. Some men, even gay men, are intimidated by and biased against lesbians. Jake reasoned that these men either fear that gay women have secret a desire to castrate all men, or their male egos are too fragile to deal with a woman who would out-of-hand reject any sexual overture. Jake harbored no such prejudices, and in fact, found the abstract image of Sapphic love rather erotic. Yet he had a much better reason than a sexual fantasy for appreciating Annie being a lesbian. He'd come up with a plan to turn the farm and its cheese production into a real business and, borrowing from what Paul Newman had done with his food products, have it provide an income for his fledgling clean-water foundation. To accomplish that, he needed Annie's expertise and a relationship between them other than one based on achieving the same business goals could only be detrimental.

Jake's visit with Hadley was really just an excuse to come into town. He knew Annie's routine and that she'd be in town at the same time buying groceries and supplies. It spoke volumes about Jake's insecurity when it came to making any kind of proposal that he felt it necessary to "accidentally" run into her on the street. He could then offer to buy her lunch, during which he'd, as if off the top of his head, pose the idea. He'd rehearsed the conversation in his mind a dozen times, each time trying to imagine a different reaction and coming up with what he thought were convincing reasons. It was a lot of wasted energy on his part, for Annie immediately signed on to his offer, and AV Fine Cheeses, the AV standing for Aqua-Vitae, water of life, was consummated over two hamburgers and glasses of lager at the Village Pub.

TEN

February 2003

It had been a good ski season in New England, despite the below-normal amount of precipitation. With temperatures colder than average, the resorts were able to make plenty of snow. This resulted in excellent conditions, both for the skiers and the businesses that depended on them. The slopes were well groomed and with the cold, dry weather, there were few of the icy patches that often plague skiers on the east coast. The only drawback to the lack of natural snowfall was that the ambience of winter, the snow-covered grounds, trees and buildings, was absent. On the positive side, with the roads being clear, even the less avid skiers were inclined to travel.

For dedicated skiers, the Berkshires aren't nearly as popular as Vermont, New Hampshire or upstate New York. The mountains aren't as high, the trails not as long, and the facilities a notch below those in neighboring states. But they have one advantage – they are easier to get to for a large number of people living in the crowded northeast. Napa-East, Mia's restaurant in Stockbridge had only been open since October, and despite a shaky start that led to a less than favorable review in the Boston Globe, it was gaining a reputation for its nouveau-American menu and its extensive wine cellar.

Running a restaurant took up far more time and energy than Mia had imagined. Possessing a type-A temperament, she was used to working hard and the fourteen-hour workdays didn't faze her. But she had no conception of the controlled chaos of a restaurant kitchen. She liked her world to be organized, prepared and smoothly functioning. Organization and preparedness are necessary for any restaurant to succeed, but there are unexpected glitches nearly every night. In the early days, Mia would run into the kitchen and, as Kat put it, freak out when a meal was taking too long to get to a table, a piece of meat was over or under cooked, or the wrong side dish was put on a plate. Kat was experienced enough to know these were minor problems that would be corrected once the line chefs and servers grew comfortable with her vision of the workflow. Seeing that Mia's anxiety was actually making matters worse, Kat banned her from the kitchen. Despite the bruise to her ego, Mia recognized the improvement and was actually happier running the front of the restaurant.

Even the breaks that came with the restaurant being closed on Mondays and Tuesdays didn't offer Mia much of a respite. While Kat took advantage of the off-time to go snowboarding, Mia felt obliged to take the forty-five minute drive to Springfield to visit her father. She had gotten to know the staff pretty well at Faircrest and was generally impressed with the care he was receiving. Perhaps it was the result of being able to put the letters M.D. after her name, but if her medical degree was getting her father better treatment, so be it. That she no longer practiced medicine did not cause the slightest bit of guilt in using the title doctor when introducing herself to Faircrest caregivers. She had read many horror stories of care at nursing homes that could only be classified as abusive. She was determined that her father would not experience anything like that.

Upon entering the facility that day, she spotted her father's neurologist and quickly engaged him in conversation. Again, being a physician allowed her to learn far more detail than family members are often told. The doctor had started her father on a new medication. There were no guarantees of course, and the medicine was by no means a cure, but it might delay the progression of his dementia. Walking through the halls, she passed signs pointing to what was kindly called "the memory care unit." She had seen that ward when she first toured the facility before her father moved in. She knew that the people living behind the locked doors spent their days sitting in chairs or confined to beds, often in silence, their minds having failed before their hearts or lungs or kidneys. It was not the kind of fate she wanted for her father but she knew it was what likely awaited him. She entered his room and found him sitting in a chair watching television. A young female staffer was just finishing making his bed. "How are you doing today, daddy?"

"He's doing well today, aren't you Mr. Jang?" the girl said.

"Yes. This is my daughter Mia. This is Jenna."

Mia was impressed by her father's cognizance. Just the week before it had taken almost fifteen minutes before he seemed to really know who she was. She could only hope that the new medication was the reason. "Shall we go out to lunch today?"

"I get my lunch here."

"I know you do, but I thought maybe you'd like a change."

"Oh. Okay."

"Good." She took off her coat and sat on the small sofa next to him. "What are we watching?"

"The news. I don't know what this Iraq stuff is about. They keep saying that we are going to go to war with them. Why?"

She wasn't sure how much he would comprehend, but the fact that her father was interested in world events was heartening. "Saddam is an evil man and he is developing what they call weapons of mass destruction, like chemical and biological weapons."

"He is? Well that is bad."

"Do you remember what happened on 9/11 with the planes flying into the twin towers and the Pentagon?"

"Of course I do. What do you think, I can't remember that?"

"I'm just making sure. Sometimes you…" she stopped, not wanting to be disrespectful.

"Anyway, they say that the Iraqis helped the people who attacked us. They also say that Saddam is trying to build nuclear bombs. Can you imagine a terrorist attack with an atom bomb?"

"We are sure of this?"

"The government has intelligence. The British concur, so it must be true."

"Then we have no choice," he said.

"I'm afraid we don't. So what do you feel like eating? I hear there's a good Chinese restaurant not far away."

"It won't be as good as your mother's."

She agreed, but said she wanted to try the restaurant anyway. What she couldn't tell was whether he remembered that his wife was dead, and she wasn't about to pursue it with him to find out.

◇◇◇◇◇◇

"This is all such crap."

Annie looked up from the bench where she'd been testing the PH level of the milk that would, in time, turn into her version of English Stilton. "What are you talking about?" she asked.

Jake stood a few feet away leaning against a wall and reading the Week in Review section of the Sunday New York Times. "All this Iraq hysteria, it's crap."

"How so?"

"This stuff about building WMDs. I don't believe it."

Annie, satisfied that things on the cheese front were going well, wiped her hands on a towel and walked over to Jake. She peeked over his shoulder to see what he was reading. "All these people can't be wrong. Hussein's a mad man. Another Hitler. Didn't they say he was involved in 9/11?"

"So you have been following this stuff."

"What, you think you're the only person in this town who reads a newspaper?"

He turned the paper to the next page. "I have my suspicions," he said under his breath. "Look at that guy," he said, pointing to a picture of the vice president. "I wouldn't trust him as far as I could throw him."

"You think he's making it up?" Jake nodded. "How could he do that? And why would all the others, like Rice and Powell, not to mention the president, lie?"

"You can't be serious. Bush is so dumb that he might not even know he's lying. As for Rice, I don't trust her. As for Powell, I get the feeling that Cheney's screwing him. Powell is first and foremost a soldier and he knows how to follow the chain of command."

"But what makes you so sure that they're lying? You don't have access to the information that they have so I don't see how you come to your conclusions."

"I met him once."

"Met who?"

"Cheney."

"Really."

"I was at a meeting at the White House led by him two years ago. I heard him speak, and heard the advice he was being given, and I just have the feeling that something isn't right about this whole Iraq thing."

"So what are you going to do about it?"

He was dumbfounded by the question. "Do about it? There's nothing I can do about any of this. I'm just some schmuck up here in Vermont trying to make cheese. It's not for me to *do* anything." She dismissively closed her eyes and walked away. "What?"

"We all have a responsibility to act when we know things aren't right. Look at you and your clean-water initiative."

"Jesus, Annie, what would you have me do?"

"I don't know. Something. Go to the TV stations. Go to CNN or go to the newspapers. Get your story out."

"I'm not sure there is a story. It's only my suspicions."

"But if you're right, then hundreds, thousands, maybe tens of thousands of people's lives are at stake. Can you live with that?"

He folded the paper in half and laid it on the table. "I wouldn't know who to go to, and if I did, would anyone listen?"

"You won't know unless you try."

He rubbed his eyes. "I suppose I could ask my cousin Rosalie. She works at the Times, or at least she did last I heard."

"There you go," Annie said stirring a large stainless steel pot filled with milk.

Jake drove to Manhattan to meet with his cousin Rosalie Berk. Rosie was a couple of years his junior and the daughter of his uncle Lenny. "How's your dad?" he asked when they met in a coffee shop a block from the Times headquarters.

"You heard he's got cancer."

"Shit. You're kidding. What kind?"

"Lung. Diagnosed last November."

"What's the prognosis?"

"You know these doctors, they never really give you an answer. I was sure your mother would have told you about this."

"I don't speak with my parents very often. I don't think they approve of my life choices, which isn't so bad because they used to rant about my brother David to me all the time. Now, he's the one in a stable relationship, albeit with another man, and I'm the divorced one who walked away from a seven-figure income to go make cheese in Vermont."

She reached across the table and pulled on his dread-locked hair. "Well what do you expect from your parents? Look at you. The beard, the long hair, what gives?"

"Since I've been living in Vermont, I've kinda gone natural, I guess."

"You look like a fuckin' hippy or something. People do what you're doing either when they're twenty and too dumb to know better, or when they're fifty and having a mid-life crisis. I haven't heard from you in like three years. Then you call me and here we are. What's up?"

"If someone had information about this Iraq shit that's not getting out to the public, who at the Times should they speak with?"

Rosalie sat back in the booth and took a sip of her coffee. "Someone in security, national or international, I suppose. Why?"

"Do you know anyone?"

"A couple of people."

"Could you set up a meeting?"

"A meeting for whom?"

"For me."

"You? What the hell would you know about Iraq?"

"Could you set up a meeting?"

"I suppose I could, but I won't unless you tell me more."

"Let's just say I know things. I met with Cheney once, and something's not kosher about this."

"Not kosher?"

"Yes. Please Rosalie, would you, as a favor to me, set it up?"

She shook her head. "If it wasn't for the fact that my father adores you…"

"Then you'll do it?"

She let out a small sigh, and wrote a name and phone number on a paper napkin and slid it across the table. "Alice Shepherd. She works on international stories. Give me a day or two to speak with her first. I'll call you after."

"Thanks, Rosie."

Rosalie didn't wait to act. The next afternoon Alice Shepherd showed up at Jake's hotel room, tape recorder in hand. She handed him her business card and placed the recorder on a small table between them as they sat across from each other. "This is Alice Shepherd. I am a reporter for the New York Times. It is…" she glanced at her watch on the inside of her left wrist, "four-forty p.m. on February 20th, 2003. I am sitting with Jacob Himmelfarb. Mr. Himmelfarb, could you please identify yourself for the record and consent to my recording this interview."

"Yes. I'm Jacob Himmelfarb, and I agree to this recording."

"Thank you. Now, Mr. Himmelfarb, would you please state your background."

Jake took a sip of water and nodded. "I am currently the owner of the AV Cheese Company of Vermont. Up until July 2001, I was the chief energy trader for Pilgrim/United Investors here in New York. On February 26th 2001, I attended a meeting held at the White House in Washington D.C. regarding energy policy."

Alice held up her hand as she made notes on a yellow legal pad. "Are you sure of the date?"

"Yes because I was, at the time, on my way to a bridge tournament in Curacao. I checked online to confirm the dates of that tournament and I remember arriving in Curacao the day before it started."

"Good. As you may or may not know, my newspaper, along with other news sources, has been trying to identify who attended those meetings and what was discussed. Can you identify any of the participants?"

"Lets see. The meeting was chaired by Vice President Cheney. There were some members of his staff there along with CEOs and execs of companies, primarily oil, gas, coal and utilities."

"And investment companies?"

"I believe that at the meeting I attended, Pilgrim was the only investment house there."

"Can you identify any of the others by name?"

Jake scratched the side of his head. "Well, my boss Arthur Morrison was there, and to be truthful, I can't say for sure who the others were."

"You didn't write any of this down?"

"No. We were asked, told really, not to take any notes. Oh I do remember one other guy, Frank Hollister, a Texas oilman." He looked up at Alice and noticed her frowning. "Is there a problem?"

"No. Can you recall what was discussed at that meeting?"

In spite of her assurance of keeping an open mind, he sensed her skepticism. He had to assume that this was normal for reporters and tried not take it personally. "Yes. Most of the meeting was about further de-regulation of the industry and the need to open up Alaska and the Continental Shelf to more drilling."

"That's not surprising. I think we all assumed that a Republican administration led by men who made their money in oil would take that position. Anything else?"

"Towards the end of the meeting, Hollister offered a proposal that seemed to draw unanimous agreement, including Cheney. He reminded the vice president that opening up new areas for exploration, while a good idea, had two problems. First off, it would take years before any oil and gas that might be discovered would reach the market. Second, and more importantly, there was no guarantee that oil would be found."

"He's right on both accounts," she said.

"Yes he was. Then Hollister pointed out that the Saudis have by far the largest known proven reserves, but that the nature of our relationship with them, while beneficial, left pricing and availability beyond our control. He also pointed out that the unstable nature of Middle East politics could jeopardize that relationship in the future."

"What else?"

"Hollister said that the country with the second largest supply of proven reserves was Iraq. He suggested to Cheney that a change in government there from Saddam to a more friendly government could secure that supply for the U.S. market. When Cheney asked Hollister what he was implying, Hollister told him that the U.S. should invade Iraq, depose Saddam and replace him with a friendly government."

"What did Cheney say?"

"He responded that attacking Iraq was not something that the administration could do without some sort of justification or provocation. Not liking Saddam Hussein was not a sufficient enough reason, to which Hollister responded by telling Cheney to find a better reason. Make up a reason if necessary. Iraqi oil could supply America's needs for most of the rest of the century. It was a matter of national security."

Alice leaned in towards Jake. "He really said make up a reason?"

"Yes he did, which the vice president didn't dismiss out of hand. He really seemed to accept it as a plausible course of action."

Alice reached down and turned off the tape recorder. "You do realize what you're implying? Two weeks ago, just blocks from where we sit, the secretary of state addressed the UN Security Council with the head of the CIA sitting behind him, presenting evidence that Iraq is pursuing WMDs in violation of UN resolutions. Are you saying they just made it all up?"

"I don't know. What Powell said could be true, I mean, Saddam is certainly acting as though he has WMDs. But what if it's not true? Cheney didn't have a problem at that meeting when advised to make up a reason to invade. What if that's what's happening now? Don't you think Americans have a right to know about this and decide for themselves?"

"As a reporter, I always fall on the side of the public's right to know. But you have some problems. Do you recall signing any sort of non-disclosure agreement when you attended that meeting?"

"I might have."

"Then you are setting yourself up for a possible prosecution. Are you prepared for that?"

"Not really." Jake slumped back in his chair. "But if it might prevent an unnecessary war, it's a risk I'll take."

"I'm impressed by the nobility of your altruism. But what if what Bush is saying is true? What if the Times prints your story, people get all riled up and the U.S. backs down. Then Saddam gets an atomic or biological weapon, arms terrorists with it, and sets it off in downtown Manhattan? Could you live with that?"

Jake's stomach started to churn. "Jesus, I don't know." He picked up a glass of water and drank all of it. "So, are you going to publish this?"

Alice turned back on the tape recorder. "Let me ask you this, Mr. Himmelfarb. Can anyone corroborate your story? Can you provide any independent evidence that this meeting you attended took place at the White House, and that you were there?"

"Arthur Morrison could verify my story, but he won't. We didn't part ways on the most amicable of terms, and Arthur's a big Bush-Cheney supporter.

You said that the White House refuses to release any details of these meetings, so you may just have to take my word on it."

"Even if I do that, I need some independent confirmation of what was discussed. My editor would never approve an article with these allegations without it."

"Maybe you could try contacting Frank Hollister. He'd probably hang up on you, but he's an old coot who, if you're clever enough, you might get to admit to what he said."

"Frank Hollister won't hang up on me."

"So you know him?"

"I know of him, but never met him."

"Then how do you know he'd talk to you?"

"I didn't say he'd talk to me, I said he wouldn't hang up on me. That's because Frank Hollister died last August."

"Oh, I guess I missed that. So this story goes nowhere."

She turned off the recorder and put it in her pocketbook. "With what you've told me, I'm afraid not." She stood up and held out her hand to him. Jake remained slouched back in his chair, not sure why he'd bothered making the trip to New York, and not even sure that it would have been a good thing if he'd succeeded. "You okay?" she asked.

He took her hand and gently shook it. "Yeah, I'm fine. I'm sorry if I've wasted your time."

"Not a waste of time. If it makes you feel any better, I believe your story."

"Thanks."

She started to leave, but paused by the door. "Look, I'm not promising anything, but I'll do some checking around and see if I can find out anything. I'll speak with Judith Miller at the paper. She's an expert on this stuff and she'll know if the White House is ginning up their evidence. Don't worry, I'll leave your name out of it. If I find out anything, I'll call you."

He watched the door close behind her, and knew he wouldn't be hearing from her.

◇◇◇◇◇◇

Sitting in his office a mile from where Jake's interview had just ended, Sayid was briefing Klaus Voorhaus on the progress of his scheme. In less than a year, he had managed to establish a base in New York from which to operate, create credibility for his concept, and make connections with enough money managers to have brought off four collateralized debt obligation deals. Klaus was impressed, as was his father back in Berlin, but the total dollar value of the deals came to less than thirty-five million, not enough to catch the attention of the major banks, investment houses and fund managers that would be needed if his plan had any chance of succeeding. He had managed to resell the initial CDO investment that the al-Qaeda seed money had financed for a two million dollar profit and was putting the finishing touches on a new deal. He had expected to have access to close to twelve million in funds, but Klaus argued that he was only authorized to release ten million. "If you have a problem," Klaus said, "take it up with Mustafa al-Yazid."

"The only way I can get in touch with al-Yazid is through you. You have to tell him I need access to the full twelve million. I could really use triple that amount."

"I'll try, but he's very difficult to get in touch with. I have no idea where in the world he is, and it can take a month before I get a reply. Even after that, he'll probably have questions before authorizing more funds. It could take until summer before you have an answer."

Sayid threw up his hands. "I can't work this way. I need resources. I need to be able to do my job without someone scrutinizing my every move." He took out a cell phone and a small, black address book, which he started to thumb through.

"What are you doing?" asked Klaus.

"I'm calling Ibrahim Fuad. He'll get to the bottom of this."

"You shouldn't keep names and numbers in a place where the authorities may find them."

"You don't need to lecture me on security. Any vital information written down here is in my own code. It means nothing to anyone else, which is why I don't store numbers in my cell phone. Besides, these are pre-paid disposable cells. I have a dozen of these and toss them into the Hudson after any compromising conversations." He took out a piece of paper and began deciphering Ibrahim's number.

"You can't call him."

"What's the matter, Klaus? Afraid that my superiors may take a dim view of the fees your bank has been assessing on their accounts?"

"I have nothing to fear from them. This is what I'm talking about." He walked over to the computer on Sayid's desk and did a quick Internet search. He found what he was looking for at a number of locations and clicked on a link to the Washington Post's site. "This is from December."

Sayid sat down in front of the screen and began to read an article entitled "Indonesian Police Raid al-Qaeda Safe House." He only got as far as the second paragraph before he stopped. "How long have you known this?"

"Since it happened. I'm shocked you didn't know. It was big news back in Germany, but maybe that was because two German nationals were killed."

Sayid re-read the sentences in disbelief. *Authorities confirmed that two Indonesian security officers were killed in the shoot-out, along with at least five suspected terrorists. Identified among the dead were Mohammed Sukahn and Ibrahim Fuad, both alleged to have been high officials in al-Qaeda.* He put the cell phone back in his pocket and shut down the PC.

Klaus lit up a cigarette and blew the smoke in Sayid's general direction. "So my friend, you're just going to have to make do with the resources you've got." Sayid got up from behind his desk and started to leave. "Where are you going?"

"I've an engagement to play bridge."

"Shouldn't you be more concerned about work?"

"This is about work. Make sure the door to my office is locked when you leave."

Sayid met Arthur at Morrison's bridge club. The two hadn't yet established a partnership that Arthur felt ready for tournament play, but the games at his club provided a venue to hone their skills as a team. Around ten p.m., their game broke up, more a result of their opponents owing each of them several thousand dollars than for the stated reason of the lateness of the hour. Arthur, in a good mood following their success, invited Sayid to stay and have a drink at the bar. Sayid had never been to the club's bar, but it was just as he'd pictured, a dark room with heavy oak paneling and high-backed leather chairs. He'd half expected to see the mustachioed old rich man with a top hat and a monocle from the Monopoly game he'd played as a kid sitting in one of those chairs, reading the results of his stocks off a ticker-tape. "What are you having, Steve?"

"I'll take a glass of red wine."

"Good healthy choice. That's why the French can eat all that fat and not drop dead from heart attacks. Barkeep, a red wine for my friend and I'll take a Johnny Walker Blue." Morrison offered Sayid a cigarette, which he declined. "The goddamn government's making it so there's no place you can smoke anymore. Thank God for private clubs. Soon, you won't even be able to smoke here, and then they'll ban you from smoking in your own house. Wait and see."

"Governments want to control people's lives."

"You're damn right they do. I don't think I could sleep at night if Gore was in the White House. So tell me, how's business?"

"Not bad. I'm just finishing another CDO, which leads me to ask, when is Pilgrim going to get into that market?"

Arthur tossed a handful of cashews into his mouth. "We've done some work with derivatives," he said over the crunching of the nuts. "Problem is, I don't really understand them, and I don't think anyone on our staff does either. That, quite frankly, scares me."

The bartender delivered them their drinks. "I don't think that the lawyers who drew up the documents even understand them," Sayid said. "But if you look at the long-term marketplace, housing offers a vast, stable source of assets from which the middle class can draw on to invest with. What these financial instruments allow is method by which those investments can be quantified. How many hedge funds do you control?"

"Seven."

"And of those, the minimum investment is what, half a million?"

"It starts there. Some have larger requirements."

"So you're limited as to your source of investors."

Arthur put out his cigarette. "But on the flip side, we don't have the SEC breathing down our neck and passing judgment on our every move. That's the way I like it."

"And that's the way these derivatives work. It fits with your philosophy."

"Perhaps we should take a look at them."

"That would be great. I could sure use an influx of capital."

"I didn't say we'd do it, just that we'd look at it." He lit up another cigarette. "If you really want capital, you should hit the sovereign wealth funds."

Sayid knew in general what Arthur was talking about, but had no idea how to approach it. "Do you know that market?"

"Me personally, no. I have enough problems dealing with my own government. The last thing I want to do is spend time dealing with foreign governments. But that's where there's capital. Take the Arabs, they've got money."

"I don't want to deal with the Arabs. I still haven't forgiven them for 9/11."

"I fully understand and share your sentiments. What about the Indians or the Chinese? What with our trade deficits and their high savings rates, they've got money."

It was a market that Sayid had never considered. He had been exclusively focused on developing a domestic U.S. market that would eventually collapse under its own weight. He immediately recognized he'd made a basic mistake in his assumptions. Financial markets had become so intertwined throughout the world that a plan as audacious as his would, of course, have to take a global perspective if it was to succeed. "I can't believe I've been so stupid," he said under his breath.

"What did you say?" asked Arthur.

"I was just wondering if you know anyone dealing with the Chinese or the Indians."

"Henry Paulson at Goldman Sachs has a long history with the Chinese."

"At the risk of sounding forward, could you get me an introduction?"

Morrison erupted with a bellowing laugh loud enough to draw the attention of the four other people in the room. "For all the good that would do you. Paulson, to put it politely, hates my guts. He'd rather have this whisky glass shoved up his ass than give me the time of day." Talk of having objects "shoved up someone's ass" struck a nerve in Sayid. More than three years had passed, and he was still haunted by his Cairo experience. "No Steve, the last thing you want Paulson to know is that you're a friend of mine. Why don't you try calling him yourself? I doubt you'll get through, but you never know."

"I doubt I'll get through too, but what have I got to lose?"

"Exactly. Shit, I told my wife I'd meet her for dinner at ten. It's almost eleven. I gotta get out of here. Order another drink on me if you like." Morrison threw the rest of his Scotch down his throat, grabbed his coat and was gone.

Sayid remained in the chair sipping wine, trying to think of what he might say that would get him a meeting with Henry Paulson. "Problems?" the bartender asked as he brought him a fresh drink.

"Just trying to figure out how to meet a particular person."

"A girl?"

Sayid looked up at the bartender and realized he'd spoken without thinking first. "Yes, a particular girl."

"I'll give you the advice I give all my clients in your situation. Forget about her. If she's not interested, move on."

Sayid handed his empty glass back to the bartender. "It's a little more complicated than that."

"That's what they all say." The bartender bent down close to Sayid's ear and whispered, "There aint nothing that one girl's got that you can't get from another. When the lights are out, pussy's pussy, if you know what I mean." He did one of those little semi-macho hand slaps that men of a certain generation do when discussing sex with other men. "If you can't get what you need from this girl, go get it from someone else. Huh?" He looked at the bartender's nodding head, and slowly began to nod synchronously. "There you go."

"Thanks." Sayid started to reach for his wallet.

"Nah, no tips allowed here. Club rules."

Sayid took a couple of sips from the second glass of wine, then put the goblet down atop a folded fifty dollar bill before leaving. As soon as he reached his apartment, he turned on his computer and Googled a name. More than twenty thousand hits almost instantaneously came back. After a searching through a number of sites, he found what he was looking for and quickly made a phone call. "Yes, is this the Napa-East restaurant in Stockbridge? I'd like a reservation for Saturday night, say around eight. Number in my party? Just one."

◇◇◇◇◇◇◇

It was another paradoxical quandary of the modern world, one that the people who first traveled this stretch of Massachusetts in horse drawn wagons two hundred and fifty years earlier never dealt with. As Mia was driving back from seeing her father, the late afternoon light was quickly fading, turning the February sky from slate gray to charcoal and eventually to black. The forecasted snowstorm seemed to materialize before her eyes. Flakes that at first were small and fine became thick and dense as they danced in the headlights of her Lexus SUV. *Why does it choose this moment, the first time all winter, for the forecast be right?* The windshield kept fogging up, hence the source of her dilemma. Every time she turned on the defroster, unless she set the temperature to cold, essentially turning on the air conditioning, the glass didn't clear. It might not have been so bad if the electric seat warmers were working, but the one on the driver's side had quit two months earlier and she'd never gotten around to taking it to the dealer to be fixed. Thus her dilemma – comfort or safety. She opted for the latter.

She was sick of listening to the same CDs and made a mental note to put new ones in the changer, the same mental note she often made but always managed to forget. Radio was worse. The only FM stations that came in clearly played country and western music or hip-hop. Music seemed to have disappeared entirely from the AM spectrum, replaced by talk-radio shows dealing with either politics or sports. The subject matter made little difference since the people who either hosted or called into those shows all sounded like the same angry, middle-aged white man in need of getting a life. So Mia drove on entertaining herself by singing songs, often repeating the lyric in the old James Taylor song about the first of December being covered in snow, along with the turnpike from Stockbridge to Boston. It wasn't December, but the Mass Pike was quickly turning white.

She pulled into the garage behind her restaurant, converted from the original carriage house, and ran to the rear door that led to the kitchen. Kat, standing before tall pots of simmering water looked at her as she whizzed by. "A little late," she said.

"I know, I know," Mia replied as she threw her parka into a corner.

"The roads bad?"

"Not *that* bad, but a few flakes and people freak out and go like ten miles an hour. Is it crowded out there?" she asked nodding towards the dining room.

"No, it's quiet. We got a lot of cancellations."

Mia was at least thankful for that affect of the storm. Saturday nights were the busiest. All the time she was driving, she worried that her assistant wouldn't be able to manage in her absence. The loss of income from one slow night could be absorbed much more easily than a damaged reputation from disgruntled customers. She made a quick stop in the bathroom to look in the mirror. Her cheeks were still rosy-red from the cold although her face felt as though it were perspiring. She rebuttoned the top of her blouse, ran a brush through her hair, applied fresh lipstick and headed to the dining room. "Hi Ken, where's Liz?" she said as she passed by the bartender too quickly to catch his answer.

"Mia, you're here," said the young hostess as she was scratching out another reservation from the book.

"Yep, Lizzy. Finally," Mia replied in a breathy voice. "Everything going okay?"

"Everything's fine. As you can see, not many diners tonight."

"Let's just make sure we treat the brave souls we have extra well. Give everyone a glass of champagne on the house."

"I'll tell the waiters. Oh, the gentleman seated at table six was asking for you. Do you know him?"

She looked over at table six. "Can't tell from here. Did he give his name?"

"His reservation is under the name Stefano Assanti."

"Don't recall knowing any Stefanos. I guess I should go over." On the way, she stopped by the bar and had Ken fill a champagne flute as a gift for the diner. "Hi there. Everything okay?" She placed the glass on the table without looking at the man's face. "We just wanted to offer you a little champagne in appreciation of your braving the…" and then she looked up at Sayid. She recognized him immediately. "Oh...My...God! Is it you?"

He pushed back from the table and stood. "It's me."

She grabbed him around his shoulders and hugged him. "I can't believe it. It must be ten years. How the hell are you?"

"I'm good. Living in Manhattan. And you?"

"As you can see, I own this place along with Kat, the chef. What are you doing here? Come for the skiing?"

"No, I had a meeting in Albany and was heading back to the city."

"Stockbridge isn't exactly on the way. And to think, you picked my restaurant to stop for dinner. What are the chances?"

"In the interest of full disclosure, I didn't choose to eat here by accident. Sometimes when I have time to kill, I go on the Internet to try and find out what's up with old friends. I've been following your career, and was surprised to discover you living here. Last I'd read you were serving on some sort of government panel."

"Seems like a lifetime ago. This is much more fun, though to be honest, much more work. And what of you? I thought you were living in England."

"I went to graduate school in London, but have lived most of the time in Paris."

"Oh Paris. I love Paris. Why did you leave?"

"I got an opportunity with a German bank who wanted to expand their operations in this country. Frankly, I was glad for the change. Paris is very expensive and the French reputation of being surly with non-natives is not undeserved."

"I've always found the French to be fun."

"They treat women differently, especially beautiful ones. I guess that's why their art is so good. I, on the other hand, was an amalgam of their two greatest prejudices, Arabs and Americans. But along with their art, they do well with food and wine. Which reminds me, the bouillabaisse was outstanding, better than I've had in Marseilles. My compliments."

"Kat does do fish and soups well."

"And thank you for the champagne."

He lifted the flute towards his mouth, but she grabbed his hand before the glass touched his lips. "We can do better than this." She called over a waiter and handed her the glass. "Take this back to Ken and bring us a bottle of Veuve Clicqout Rose."

"Very expensive, no?"

"What else is it for? So, you found me on the web. Gosh, I still can't believe it's you. I should try looking on the web sometime. I wonder whatever happened to Jake Himmelfarb."

"I can tell you that."

"You Googled him too?"

"Didn't need to. I happen to know his old boss very well. He quit his Wall Street job two years ago and moved to a farm in Vermont or New Hampshire."

"Jake living on a farm? I'll believe that when I see it. That's not the Jake I remember." The waitress showed up with the champagne, popped the cork and poured two glasses for them. "You planning on driving back to the city tonight?"

"I had been."

"The roads are getting bad. It's going to take you forever. Why not stay here with me. I have a guest room upstairs that's never been used."

"I hate to impose."

"It's no imposition. Besides, if you drive you're not going to be able to help me finish this bottle, and it would be a crime not to drink it all." She picked up her glass and held it out.

He flashed a smile. "You convinced me." He lifted his glass. "To old friends."

She smiled back, repeating the toast.

Kat put another log on the fire and announced she was tired and going to bed. She gave Mia a sly glance as she walked by on the way to her bedroom, the kind of glance that said *he's awfully cute, make sure he wears a condom.*

"She's really nice," Sayid said.

Mia put on a Miles Davis CD and crouched down in front of an antique wooden chest that served as a liquor cabinet. "What can I get you to drink? I've got some port, cognac, a bunch of single malts."

"I'll try the Scotch." She pushed aside bottles and called out several brands. "You pick," he said.

She grabbed a bottle of Glenfarclas 105 and a couple of glasses. "I have to ask you something. Liz, our hostess said your name was Stefano. Did she mis-hear your name?"

"I use Steve or Stefano as a business name. Since 9/11, Muslim-sounding names can close doors in your face faster than saying you're from the IRS. I use a little white lie so people think I'm Italian."

She handed him the glass of Scotch. "That's so unfair."

"Unfair or not, it's the way the world works."

"Sadly true," she said. Sayid took a big sip of the liquor and his eyes almost popped out of his head. "Sorry, I forgot to warn you. This Scotch is like a hundred and twenty proof, so sip slowly."

"How come you left the government?"

"It was a political thing. New administration, they wanted their own appointees, yada-yada. Frankly, I was glad to leave."

"Do you keep in touch with anyone from your days there?"

"No. Why would I?"

"I don't know. Actually, not true, I do know – not why you'd keep in touch, but why I asked. I have been working on a new investment vehicle that is really starting to take off. My problem is that I'm running into reluctance with investors."

Mia sat down next to Sayid on the couch. "I've got some money, although a lot of it is tied up in this place. But I might be interested."

"The kind of investments I'm talking about may be just a bit beyond your means. We're talking hundreds of millions, billions, even more."

Mia raised her eyebrows at hearing the number. "Even more?" He nodded. "Well, that is a *just* a bit beyond my means. But the people I knew were all government types, not investment bankers."

"You specialized in China, right?"

"Only China."

"The Chinese have mountains of money and it's controlled by the government, so government types are what I'm looking for. I think this would be a good investment."

Mia took another sip of Scotch. "To be honest, the Chinese government is the last thing I want to help."

"I guess their wealth has come at the expense of our industrial base."

"My loathing is personal, not patriotic. I hate them. Before 1948, my family was very prominent. My grandfather was a professor in Beijing. My father barely escaped with his life when Mao took over. All of that I could forgive, but I'll never forgive them for taking my sister's life."

"Then why did you serve on a trade commission with them?"

"I don't know. I was bored with my job. I liked visiting China, and as much as I hate the government, I did like some of the people." She knew there was a deeper reason, and she knew by the way Sayid sat silently staring at her, that he knew as well. "I suppose in my own naïve way, I was hoping that by connecting with enough party members with influence, I could find out what really happened to Toni."

"Your sister."

"Yes, but I never did find out anything. They all held to the Party line, that Toni was killed in an auto accident hundreds of miles from Beijing. They never produced her body, never told us where she was buried, never gave us any closure." The room was dim, lit only by the glow from the fireplace, but Sayid had an odd look to him such that she couldn't tell if he was disturbed or relaxed, or both. "Good Scotch, huh?" she said, to which he slowly nodded. "What kinds of investments are you selling anyway that need billions?"

"Mortgage-backed derivatives." He let that sink in before continuing to describe the investments in more detail.

"Granted, it's late, I'm tired and a little drunk, but sounds like something from MIT," she said.

"It should. It's basically the plan that you, me and Himmelfarb used for our thesis in that econ class."

A silly smile appeared on her face. "You're crazy. Perhaps you don't recall what Meecham thought of our idea. He said, and I paraphrase, that the concept was almost guaranteed to result in a disastrous collapse."

"Oh I remember. Meecham even destroyed a house of cards before our eyes to prove his point."

"He always did have a flair for the dramatic. But his point was, it was a very shaky, unstable model to use for investing. Have you found a flaw in Meecham's thinking?" He shook his head. "Then why pursue this?"

Sayid paused, making it seem as though he were rehearsing his answer in his head before verbalizing it. "The greatest threat to this country comes not from Arab terrorists. They're too disorganized to do much more than they've already done. The real threat comes from countries like China who artificially keep their currency low to bolster their exports. If we keep going in this direction, we'll wake up one day and find that we have no steel mills, make no electronic or computer products, and our automobile and airplane factories will be empty buildings. The only jobs available will be flipping burgers at McDonalds."

"But Sayid, don't you fear the risk to our own economy? I mean, wouldn't this certainly affect American investors as well?"

"It's a risk, but look who would be hurt. Not the average guy, but the Wall Street types who, if we're being honest, are making obscene amounts of money that have no relation to their contribution to society. I deal with them every day and they make me sick."

"But you take the money like they do."

"True, but I didn't go into business thinking I was going to get rich on the backs of the working class."

She shook her head. "Don't you think you're being just a little bit full of yourself here?"

"How so?"

"Do you really believe that one person has the power to affect the entire international financial structure? You think this is really going to hurt the Chinese? Come on Sayid, these things are way too complicated for you to pull off by yourself."

"Perhaps, but at least by trying, I sleep better at night." He paused for a long time staring at the whisky slowly swirling in the glass in his hand. "I have another, more personal motive." He didn't say another word.

"And?" she finally asked.

"I too lost someone I loved." He finished the whisky in one gulp and put the glass down. Mia, sensing pain in his voice, refilled the tumbler. "I was engaged to a woman, a nurse. Her name was – her name was Jasmine Kim. She was a nurse and an American of Korean descent. She went back to South Korea to do volunteer work. She was in a village near the demilitarized zone. I am sure she was on the southern side, but somehow, she ended up in the hands of the North Koreans. When they found out she was an American, they accused her of being a spy and threw her in jail."

"My God, Sayid. What did our government do?"

"Not much, but then again, there wasn't much they could do. We don't have diplomatic relations with the North, and that country is ruled by a mad man."

"How long will she be imprisoned?"

"Forever."

"What! They gave her a life sentence?"

"Essentially. You see, after six months rotting in a North Korean jail, Jasmine contracted some infection and died in prison."

"Oh how awful." She put her arm around his shoulders. "I am so sorry."

"Thanks."

She picked up his glass, took a sip of the Scotch and handed it to him. "But there is one thing I don't quite get. I can see why you hate the North Koreans, but what does that have to do with wrecking the Chinese economy?"

"I'm an economist. There is no way I could wreck the North Korean economy because frankly there is nothing to wreck. The place is beyond a basket case, with a per capita income that ranks behind places like Uzbekistan and Sudan, and a population that faces perpetual famine. The only way that their government stays in power is because of the support they get from Communist China."

"So you're thinking is that if the Chinese faced an economic crisis…"

"Then they'd have to cut their expenditures, and one of the most likely places to cut would be foreign aid, most of which goes to Korea, and that might cause the government there to fall. Anyway, I thought it worth asking of you since I knew you had connections, and as an added bonus, I could pay you a commission, which judging from the success you've had, you probably don't need."

"I hope you're not being sarcastic. Tonight's crowd was way down because of the snowstorm. It's usually packed on a Saturday."

"No, I wasn't being sarcastic. I know how well you must be doing because when I tried to get a reservation, I was told the earliest available was ten p.m.

I came in earlier figuring I'd just wait at the bar, hopefully with you. I'm really sorry if I offended you."

"Don't apologize. You didn't offend me. I'm impressed that you think on such a grand scale. I don't know anyone who thinks that way. Besides, don't you have to have some kind of license to pay a commission on investments?"

"Usually you do, but there are always legal ways around that. You just call the payments something else, like a finder's fee or consulting expenses. Wow, all of a sudden, I'm really feeling this drink. I think I should go to bed." He leaned over and kissed her on the cheek before heading off to his bedroom.

"I've put some towels on your bed. Sleep well. Kat makes a great breakfast." She heard the door close to the guest bedroom. She marveled at his audacity. The idea that the Chinese communists could be severely hurt was alluring, but from what she knew of the workings of business and government, there was no chance he'd succeed. She sat in front of the fire looking out the windows at the snow as it fell past the streetlights below. It hadn't let up all night and if it continued till morning, the roads would be impassable. On the positive side, a good season for skiers had just gotten better.

ELEVEN

June 2003

The drive from Waitsfield to Bennington took three hours, but Annie appeared determined to make it in two. Jake usually did the driving on these excursions to local farmers markets, but this morning he was still reeling from the effects of one too many margaritas the previous night. Annie was doing her best imitation of a NASCAR driver as she negotiated the roller-coaster back roads through the Green Mountains. It took every ounce of control for Jake to keep whatever was left in his stomach in his stomach.

"I don't know why you complain about this car. For a wagon, I think it handles great." Jake didn't reply. He kept his eyes closed hoping that by not seeing the twists and turns, he'd feel less queasy. "Jake? Are you awake?"

"I heard you. A Subaru Outback is no BMW M3."

"I wouldn't know. You never let me drive your old car when you had it."

He didn't have the energy to argue. He'd switched to the station wagon for two reasons – he needed more room to transport cheese samples and he needed a four-wheel drive vehicle to navigate Vermont winters. The Subaru was perfect at both, but it didn't have the same thrill or boost to the ego that the M3 provided. "Let's stop in the next town," he said.

"We're supposed to get to Bennington before nine."

"I just need some coffee, besides, we're gonna need gas."

"Whatever."

She seemed very testy. Jake thought better of making a comment that it must be that time of month.

The morning at the farmers market passed excruciating slowly, with sellers outnumbering buyers two to one. Most of the time, Jake sat alone at their booth reading a newspaper behind wheels of Stilton, cheddar and a variety of goat cheeses. He doubted the value in attending these things but Annie insisted it was a cheap method to get their product known in the marketplace. Having no better alternatives, he agreed, but still complained when on days like this, no one seemed to be interested in even sampling, much less purchasing. The one consolation was that Annie's mood had brightened considerably since earlier that morning. He watched as she walked around the market talking and laughing with the other vendors and sampling their products, and felt just a bit jealous at the ease with which she engaged strangers. He knew that his inclination towards being an introvert had always held him back but he could never overcome it.

Annie returned to their booth. "Any action?"

"The fat guy in the Hawaiian shirt with the fanny pack said the cheddar was too sharp."

"What did you say?"

"I told him that I was thankful he didn't like it because if he did, there wouldn't be any left for others."

"You didn't?"

"No, but I wanted to."

"Well if it stays like this, I say we split at two and go home. It'll be good to get back before dinner. I'm going to grab something to eat. Can I bring you back anything?" she asked.

"I'll take a sandwich, corned beef on rye with mustard if they've got it. If not, get me a turkey or roast beef with mayo." She nodded and left. He returned to reading his newspaper. A minute later, he sensed a woman standing across the table from him. "Forget something?" he asked without looking up.

"I was just interested in trying some of your cheese."

Realizing that the voice was not Annie's, he dropped the paper on the ground and stood up, not bothering to look at her while he searched for a knife. "What would you like to try first? We sell the most cheddar but I'm partial to the goat cheeses and the Stilton is very popular."

"I'll start with a goat cheese."

"Great. Let's start with this one, it's on the creamy side, and then we'll go on to the harder ones." He spread some on a cracker, handed her the sample and looked at her face for a reaction. The sight of her made him feel faint and he dropped the knife and sat down.

"That's really good," she said. "I'll try some others." Like an automaton, he robotically spread the same cheese on another cracker and held it out to her. "I think that's the same one I just tried."

He stared at her and she, appearing somewhat fearful, stepped back. "You don't remember me, do you?" he finally said.

She slowly shook her head. "No. I don't think we've met. Are you sure you're not confusing me with someone else?"

"Quite sure, Mia."

She took another step back and for a moment, he feared she was about to walk away. "I'm sorry, but I can't recall…"

"It's Jake. MIT. A dozen years ago or so."

She lowered her sunglasses and peered over them. "Jake, uh Jake Himmel…"

"Himmelfarb. Yep, it's me."

Her jaw dropped. "Oh my God, it is you. I would never have guessed. I mean, look at you. You look so different. The long hair, the beard, the…I don't know…the everything."

"I'd recognize you anywhere, though your hair's quite different. I remember it being jet black and down to your ass."

"Yeah, I know. Now I wear it cropped at the neck. It's a little more adult."

"Not like mine, I suppose. Also, the color's a little different."

"The red highlights were Kat's idea."

"Kat?"

Mia looked around the market until she spotted her. "She's the tall girl over by the asparagus. She's my partner."

Another shock to Jake's system. "Oh, gee. I had no idea. I mean, I never would have guessed that."

"Guessed what?"

"Guessed that you had that sort of orientation, uh, sexually you know."

Mia burst out laughing. "Now that's the Jake I remember. She's my business partner, not my lover. We own a restaurant down in Stockbridge, Massachusetts. We come to farmers markets in the area to get fresh produce all the time. Don't recall ever seeing you here before."

"So you're not a lesbian."

"As I recall Jake, you should know the answer to that from personal experience."

"You recall correctly. It's just that I sometimes get the feeling that the result of being with me causes women to swear off being with men." She couldn't stop laughing. "So what's this about a restaurant? I thought you were a doctor."

"It's a long story. And what are you doing selling cheese?"

"Also a long story. You had lunch yet? We should grab a bite and catch up."

"Don't you have to attend to your stand?"

"Eh, fuck it. You're like the third person who has stopped by all day. Besides, my associate just went to get us some sandwiches and should be back any minute. I'll just leave her a message."

"What about the sandwiches."

"I can eat crappy sandwiches anytime." He scrawled out a note and taped it to the table. "Let's go."

They found a small café and took seats across from each other in a booth. Mia ordered a glass of chardonnay while Jake, still not fully recovered from his hangover, ordered coffee. "Odd that I'm the one with the wine," she said. "When we dated, I couldn't drink anything alcoholic while you always ordered beer."

"Yeah, but you smoked a lot of pot as I recall."

"I sometimes still do."

"Really. Gosh, I haven't smoked in years."

"I wouldn't were it not for Kat. She's a bit of a party girl, and who can blame her. She works most nights until well past midnight and needs to unwind."

"I think I'd like her."

"You would. So come on, tell me what you're doing selling cheese. Last I heard, you were working on Wall Street."

The waitress came by with the drinks and asked if they were ready to order. They simultaneous answered "not yet." "I did," he said. "Quit that two years ago."

"Why?"

"I had a four-year-old girl die in my arms in Africa, and somehow making gobs of money for really rich people didn't seem like the best use of my time."

"And selling cheese is?"

"I own the company that makes the cheese. AV Cheeses. The company's profits go toward a foundation I started to provide clean drinking water for Third World countries."

"I'm impressed."

"Don't be. To date, the foundation has yet to provide a single drop of clean water for anyone, and AV hasn't made enough money to pay the salaries of its employees."

Mia took a sip of wine and flashed him a coy little smile. "Don't worry. You'll make it. I've a good feeling about you."

"From your lips to God's ears. So tell me, what happened to becoming a doctor?"

"I am a doctor, or at least, I've the degree and I still have a license in California. Frankly, that was more for my father. I never really wanted it. Let's see, after cutting short my residency, I went to work for a biotech firm in Silicon Valley, made a shitload of money, left there when I was appointed to a trade commission to China under Clinton, and left that after Bush was elected. After that, I had no idea what to do. My father developed Alzheimer's, so I moved back east. With no real direction, I decided to open a restaurant. My two passions in life are cooking and art. I'd like to open a gallery in Stockbridge next to the restaurant."

"No Mister Jang?"

"I was married once, briefly, to an Indian doctor."

"Indian woo-woo-woo," Jake said smacking his lips with his hand in the stereotypical war chants of Native Americans, "or Indian-Indian?"

"Indian-Indian. Turned out he was already married to a woman back in Bombay or Calcutta or wherever the hell he was from. A detail he conveniently failed to mention. Fortunately we were married for such a short time that there were no kids. So that ended. And you? No Misses Himmelfarb?"

"Like you, there was, but that also ended in divorce. Again, no kids."

"Do you regret it?"

He chuckled. "Not in the least. She ended up marrying my old boss, a man that, to put it mildly, I have very little affection for. It's funny because after I quit, I tried to think of ways to get at him, and couldn't. Then Debbie marries him and that's better revenge than anything I could have come up with."

"Funny how that happens. Ever hear from the Egyptian kid?" she asked.

"Last I heard he was studying in England, but that must have been ten years ago. You?"

"I know he was working in France."

"Good for him. Me, I have no desire to get back into that scene. Do you?"

"Sometimes. Perhaps it's still guilt from my father. I think he envisioned his daughter as doing more than running a restaurant. I have to admit, when I was working in high-powered positions, I got a certain ego boost out of it."

"I fantasize sometimes about going back to Manhattan as a triumphant business man with a cheese empire, and the great philanthropic institution which it supports. Most of the time, I'd be happy if just one fewer child died as a result of my efforts." He couldn't stop staring at her face and into her eyes. For all the time that had passed since he'd last seen her, he'd never forgotten her, even to the point that he'd sometimes imagine her when he was with other women, and that included Debbie. "I wrote you several times after you went to med school. You never answered."

"I remember. I'm sorry. I guess I was busy or something. No, that's not true. I wrote you several letters."

"Really? I never got them."

"Because I never sent them. I couldn't see the point. God, Jake, we were so young then, and my parents – and your parents – would never have accepted us being together. It was just best to end it, don't you think?"

He picked up his coffee and took a sip. He'd always assumed she'd simply moved on after him without giving it much thought. "You broke my heart." She said nothing. "I've been dumped by other girls, obviously, but you're the only one I can honestly say that about."

Her eyes glistened over. "Oh Jake, why do you bother saying things like that?"

"Because it's true."

"I'm sure you've broken many girls' hearts."

He thought about it for a moment. "You know, I think I can honestly say I haven't."

"I don't know what to say."

"There's nothing to say. I'm not mad at you or anything. If I should be mad at anyone, I should be mad at myself. I could have done more. Gone to see you in Baltimore or something."

"It wouldn't have done any good. I was too trapped by my family history."

"And now?"

She took a sip of wine. "We're very different people from who we were in college. I mean, what do we have in common?"

"We're both living in rural New England, both doing things that neither of us ever imagined, and certainly had no training for. And they're both food-related."

Her lips twisted into that odd smile that only she could produce, half-sarcastic and half-naïve. "We don't really know each other anymore."

"Are you seeing anyone? I'm mean in a serious way."

"No, not even in a casual way. You?"

He shook his head. The waitress stopped by again and they both sensed the need to place an order. The conversation drifted from various topics such as art and politics. Mia mentioned in passing that she was looking to buy an apartment in Manhattan to have a base there, but Jake didn't really retain much of what she said. A third of his life had passed since he'd last spoken with her, and she was different than the memories of her he'd kept. He doubted whether anything could reignite their relationship. It had happened such a long time ago and in retrospect, lasted a very short time. By the end of lunch he had reconciled himself to the reality that they had gone their separate ways. They left the restaurant, splitting the check and strolled back to the AV booth.

"Jake, where have you been? I thought we were packing up early. It's like three-thirty already."

"Annie, this is an old friend of mine from college, Mia Jang."

"Oh." Annie stood back to look at her. "Hi. Nice to meet you."

"And you," Mia said. "Listen, I should find Kat. We really need to get back to Stockbridge. It was nice to meet you Annie." She hugged Jake, much tighter than he'd expected, and whispered in his ear. "It was so great seeing you. Call me some time." She relaxed, stepped back from him, and handed over a business card. "Please, stop by and have dinner." He glanced at the card, than looked at her. "Really. Please do."

He was a bit surprised at her sincerity. "I will, really."

She kissed him once on the cheek and walked away.

"She seems to like you."

"You think?"

"Yeah, Jake, I think. Are you going to call her?"

He looked again at her card. "I don't know."

"Why not?"

He let out a long sigh. "I don't think it'd work out. We knew each other a long time ago back in college. And…"

"And?"

"And, well, she's the one who got away. After all these years, I'm afraid that my memories have built her up into something that she could never be, or for that matter, anyone could, which is odd because we only dated for a couple of months."

"Was she your first?"

He softly smiled. "Not physically the first, but my first real infatuation."

"I see. Bret Stricker."

"Bret who?"

"My first real crush, of course that was in seventh grade, but every once in a while, I think of Bret." Jake stood there looking at Mia's business card. "I'm guessing that this girl is in your thoughts a little more often than Bret is in mine." She took the card from his hand. "Huh. Napa-East. I was just talking with the chef of this place, a really neat woman. She liked the hard goat cheeses, and the Stilton, though she was confused at the name you chose for it."

"What's wrong with Chamberlain Stilton?" he asked.

"She thought it strange to name an English cheese after a British prime minister known for a piece of something, or maybe she meant peace. History was never my strong point. I said that you, as the boss, reserved for yourself the right to name varieties."

Jake shook his head. "I think she may have said appeasement, but it wasn't Neville Chamberlain who I was thinking of, it was Wilt."

"Wilt?"

"Yeah Wilt, as in Wilt Chamberlain. He was one of the greatest basketball players ever, and probably the greatest center. He once scored one hundred points in an NBA game."

"I think you're being too clever by half. No one's going to make that association with the cheese. Besides, why does scoring a hundred points warrant getting your name on a food product?"

Jake took a cracker and spread some of the white Stilton liberally laced with blue-green streaks on a cracker. "Stilton reminds me of his nickname Wilt the Stilt. Since I was a kid, I've always loved sports, and have made some money betting on them," he mumbled through a mouthful of cracker. "But it wasn't Wilt's athletic prowess that I most remember him for. In his memoirs, he wrote that he had sex with 20,000 women, though not all at the same time I imagine."

Annie burst out laughing. "That's the most ridiculous claim I've ever heard. Twenty thousand? That would mean having sex with three different women every day, without taking a break for holidays, for like twenty years. I may not be good at history, but I can do math."

"Like the hundred points in a game, it's a record that will never be equaled."

"Yeah, right." Annie said as she started to pack up the cheeses and other goods for the trip back. "I'm surprised his dick didn't fall off from over-use."

Jake handed her the slicing knives and started to wipe off the trays. "You know what they say, use it or lose it. So I'm sure his schlong was fine, and being who he was, I'm sure his schlong wasn't schlort."

"Because he was black?"

"Because he was seven feet tall."

"Oh hey, don't think of me as racist." He waved his hand aside in a way that conveyed that he didn't. "Anyway," she continued, "I'll never think of the Stilton in quite the same way. And about that use it or lose it rule, don't you think it applies to you?"

"What do you mean?"

"When was the last time you got laid, or for that matter, had a date with a girl?"

He stopped packing and scowled at her but knew she had a point. He couldn't recall exactly how long it had been since he'd experienced either. "The options regarding amorous liaisons in our little hamlet of Waitsfield are rather limited."

"That's a fucking copout if I ever heard one. There are tons of snow bunnies that come for the slopes and the après-ski. And there are almost as many up here for the summer. Use it or lose it, Jake." She picked up the last box of cheese, loaded into the back of the Subaru and slammed the tailgate shut. "Call the Chinese girl."

He got behind the wheel and she took the passenger seat. He started the ignition, but turned to her before putting the car in gear. "Bret? Your first crush was on a boy?"

"I was twelve years old. Now I know better."

Mia walked past the other stalls in the farmers market, purposely trying not to find Kat too quickly. She took out her cell phone and punched a number from the speed-dial listings.

"Hey," she said when the other party answered. "I just met with Jake Himmelfarb. We don't need to worry about him. He's totally not interested in Wall Street stuff, so he won't be a problem." There was a moment of silence on the other end. "Sayid, did you hear what I said?"

"Yeah, sorry. I was just reading my email. That's good about Jake. I met with Li for the third time and have received a verbal commitment, but he'd like to see you first. Also, I've set up meetings with a bunch of mortgage companies to educate their brokers on various marketing and re-fi techniques. It's starting to come together. This may just work after all."

"Okay. Tell Li I'll be in the city next week and I'll get in touch with him then."

"Good. Why are you coming down?"

"I want to look at an apartment."

"Are you moving to Manhattan?"

"No, I just want to buy a place so that I have somewhere to stay when I'm in the city. I really don't like hotels."

"Listen, if you need a mortgage, I have some ideas about that."

"I bet you do. Ciao." She flipped her cell phone closed and went to find Kat.

TWELVE

"Take the next exit." It was the first time Annie had spoken in over an hour. Jake wasn't sure if something was bothering her or if, as she professed, was merely tired.

"How far after we get off?"

"On the map, it looks to be another fifteen or twenty minutes to Stockbridge."

Jake couldn't decide whether or not coming on this trip was a good idea. When Annie first told him of the order from Napa-East, he urged her to personally deliver the product to the restaurant. Only later did he discover that she and Kat had been communicating regularly for the past month. He sensed Annie's ill ease at his insistence on coming along, which perhaps explained her aloofness. An uninvited houseguest is at best awkward, but he hadn't worked up the nerve to do what he should have done weeks ago and call Mia. Taking a passive-aggressive approach of just showing up was right in his wheelhouse.

They found a parking space directly in front of the restaurant which, being nine-thirty in the morning, was closed. After repeated knocks on the front door and no response, Annie called Kat from her cell phone. Moments later the door opened and Kat, smiling broadly, gave Annie a hug. "Kat, this is my boss and the owner of AV, Jake."

Kat stood in the doorway for a moment giving him the once-over. "So this is Jake Himmelfarb."

He was a little taken aback that she seemed to know about him. "That would be me." He held out his hand but she quickly eschewed it in favor of a hug.

"Well, you're not exactly what I pictured. Come on in."

"What exactly did you picture?"

"I don't know. Mia showed me a photo of you from college. You were – how do I put this without offending – kind of nerdy looking. Of course nerdy describes Mia, so I can see why the two of you were friends."

"Mia mentioned me to you?"

"Quite a bit since last month. She's been wondering why you haven't phoned. I told her she should call you, and even gave her the AV number, but you know how stubborn she can be."

"Yeah, I've been real busy too, which is why I decided to come along. Is she around?"

"Now that's a problem. She's in New York for a few days to settle on an apartment."

"An apartment?"

"She's bought a place down in the Village off Washington Square. I've only seen pictures. I won't say how much she spent on it, but I can't believe what real estate goes for in the city these days. She says before 9/11, things were going for thirty percent more. In the last few months, prices have started climbing again and she wanted to get a place while they were still affordable. Personally, I'll never have enough to buy what she considers affordable, but that's Mia."

"Is she planning on moving to Manhattan?" he asked.

"No. She says she still instends to live here. She claims to hate hotels and just wanted a place to stay in the city. She calls it her pied-à-terre, wouldn't you know. Typical. I don't know if she told you, but she's bought the building next door and plans turning it into an art gallery. I think she's crazy, but if she goes through with this gallery thing, she says she'll be spending a lot of time in Manhattan. Anyway, I assume you're staying over tonight. Follow me." Jake picked up on a certain vibe between the women, which probably explained Annie's hesitancy about him being there.

After they had unloaded the cheese from the back of the Subaru and brought in their bags, Kat took them on a walking tour of Stockbridge. She explained that many of the tourists came for the music festival at Tanglewood and that the economy depended on the summer months to turn a profit. The previous summer had not been good, which many of the merchants attributed to the residual effects of 9/11. So far this summer, things were looking much better. Jake only vaguely followed what she was saying. His thoughts were occupied with Mia.

It was just after midnight before the last of the diners left Napa-East and the staff had gone home. Annie and Jake had spent most of the evening drinking wine on the small balcony off the second floor residence that overlooked the street. Kat joined them, still dressed in her white chef's uniform, and uncorked a bottle of Malbec. "Thank God tomorrow's Monday and the place is closed. I wonder how Mia's doing." No sooner had she spoken than her cell phone rang and she glanced at it. "Speak of the devil…hey, what's up?"

Jake stared intently at Kat trying to determine what was being said on the other end. Kat's side of the conversation consisted of terse responses like "uh huh" and "right" and "wow." As she talked, Kat pulled from her pocket a small plastic bag filled with marijuana and with one hand began rolling a joint. Without missing a beat, she lit it from a candle on the table, took a puff then handed it to Annie. Jake had never seen Annie use any drugs and was curious as to her reaction. Casually, she took a long drag off the joint and handed it to him. He declined with a wave of his hand and she gave it back to Kat.

"Listen, you will not believe who I'm sitting here on the porch with," Kat said. "No – wait – I'll let you hear for yourself," and she shoved the phone next to Jake's ear.

"Hello," he heard her say on the other end.

"Hi. It's – uh – Jake – uh – Himmelfarb." His words stuck in his throat.

"Jacob. What the heck are you doing there?"

"I'm here with my head of production. We came by to personally deliver your order."

"Fuck, why didn't you call? I'm so pissed I missed you."

"It was all sort of last minute, my coming along that is." He could hear the sounds of traffic in the background coming from her phone. "So you bought a place in the city."

"I did. Moved in last week. I'm standing here on my balcony looking out on Fifth Avenue. I can see Washington Square which even at this hour, is still full of people."

"I haven't been to the city in a year."

"I've got plenty of room if you ever need a place to stay."

"Is that an invite?"

"Absolutely. Just call me first."

Kat grabbed the phone back from him before he could say another word. "Why doesn't he come tomorrow?" she asked.

Jake began to squirm in his chair. "I can't do that," he whispered to Kat as he tried to take back the phone. Laughingly she pushed him away.

"Good. I'll tell him."

"Let me have that!" He lurched for the phone but couldn't wrest it away from her.

"Ciao," she said and quickly slapped the phone shut. "There. It's settled. She's expecting you for lunch tomorrow around eleven. I'll give you her address."

"I've got to take Annie back to Vermont tomorrow."

"I'll take her back." The joint had gone out so Kat re-lit it and took another puff. "Look," she said blowing out the smoke, "I'm not stupid. The only reason you came was to see Mia. Now you will."

He let out a long sigh. "Give me a hit of that."

Mia stared out at the Manhattan skyline. She had been standing on a balcony but it wasn't the one in her apartment. She glanced at her Blackberry and reviewed the upcoming schedule for the week, trying to figure how a visit from Jake would impact it.

"Are you coming in?"

She turned around to see Sayid standing at the open sliding glass door. "Yeah, I'll be right there." She put the Blackberry back in her pocketbook. Sayid's apartment was on the Upper West Side. She felt good that the small dinner party that she'd planned and he'd just hosted had achieved its purpose. Back in the living room, Li Xuan and Klaus Voorhaus were lighting up cigars as Sayid filled four snifters with brandy.

"So Mr. Li, we have a deal, yes?" Sayid asked as he handed him a glass.

Li looked at Mia. "I think so, and you can thank Madame Jang."

"Five hundred million, was it?" Klaus said.

"Two hundred," Li corrected.

Sayid took a sip of the brandy. "You buy many more times that amount in U.S. bonds, don't you? And the return on those is a fraction of what we are offering."

"That may be so, but your securities are not guaranteed by the American government. They are not guaranteed at all."

"That is what risk-reward is all about," Sayid said.

"I understand that, Steve. Two-hundred million dollars is still a major investment by my government."

"Two hundred million *is* a lot of money," Mia interjected. "And if, in time, everything works as we expect it to, I'm sure that the Chinese will be eager to invest more. It's getting really late. I'm exhausted so if you don't mind, I think I'll be going."

Li put his cigar down and stood up. "I must go too. Mia, let me have my driver drop you off."

"That'd be great."

"Mia, you left your jacket in my bedroom." Sayid tilted his head in the direction of the bedroom as a signal for her to follow. "I thought we'd do better with Li," he said quietly when they were alone.

"I know. What are you gonna do?"

"I know that I'm missing something," he said. "It's hard to compete with the feds for a safe investment."

"If you recall, that's the point of this whole thing. These investments, in the end, aren't safe. That is why Meecham nearly flunked us." She took her jacket from him. "I'll try and convince Li to go more, but he's pretty conservative and I don't want to over sell."

"I wish I knew what more I could do."

"Maybe you can get Klaus to have the bank guarantee Li's money," she said, half laughing.

"That's it!"

"I was kidding."

"No, that's what I'm missing. To seal the deal we need to have the money guaranteed. Don't you remember? Meecham talked about this, talked about using credit default swaps to insure the investments."

She looked a bit bewildered. "My memory's not the best, but from what I recall, Meecham was even more skeptical about those than he was about derivatives."

"So much the better. The more tangled this gets, the harder it will be to prevent a collapse."

"But who are you going to get to write a swap?"

"Well, we're talking about insurance, so I guess I'll try insurance companies."

"That might not be so easy. They're not stupid. Those guys understand risk."

"They're just like the rest. If they see something they think they can make money on, they'll move. Anyway, if not them, there are other sources. Banks, hedge funds, you know, the usual suspects. As Meecham used to say, greed is never an orphan. I have my work cut out for me."

"And I guess, so do I."

"Driver, after you drop me off at the Waldorf, please take Ms. Jang wherever she wants." Li's instructions were given in Mandarin, but Mia understood. They got into the back seat of the limo and Li raised the glass partition that separated them from the chauffer.

"My place is down in Greenwich Village. It may be quicker to drop me off first."

"Perhaps, but it's late and I need to pack and be up early in the morning, so I hope you don't mind if I'm taken home first."

"Of course not. I appreciate the lift."

Li opened a small cabinet that had several bottles of liquor and two glasses. "Care for a night cap?"

"No, I'm fine. Packing you say? Are you going somewhere?"

Li took one of the glasses and poured himself a Scotch. "Yes, I'm flying back to Beijing tomorrow."

"Oh, for how long?"

Li took a sip of the whisky. "I'm not really sure. At least until September when the UN goes back in session. Of course, when it comes to predicting what any government has planned for you, you never know. Maybe they'll send me to a re-education facility."

She clutched Li's arm. "Is there a problem?"

He gave a short laugh. "No, no problem. I was only trying to make a joke. Obviously, it's not something I do well."

Mia realized that her opportunities to influence Li were rapidly dwindling. She needed to act now, but she had no plan. The limo turned onto 59th Street and headed east. She gazed at the horse-drawn hansoms in Central Park going by with couples sitting arm-in-arm, savoring their romantic rides. By the time they turned onto Park Avenue, she knew what she had to do, but if she was going to succeed, she needed to give the impression of being impetuous. The limo pulled up to the Waldorf, and Li reached out his hand to her. "This is my stop," he said. "I wish you a good rest of the summer, and we will speak soon."

Mia didn't let go of Li's hand. "I can't believe I won't be seeing you for such a long time."

He looked confused. "It is only a couple of months."

"I know, but we've been seeing a lot of each other lately. I've kind of gotten used to..." She paused mid-sentence. "Why don't you invite me up for that night cap? We can have a bon-voyage toast."

Li looked even more confused. "Okay," he said haltingly. "I'll have the driver wait here."

He started to roll down the glass partition, but she stopped him. "I wouldn't want him to have to sit here. Send him home. I can take a cab."

"Are you sure?" Mia nodded and they got out of the car. As they rode the private elevator up to Li's suite, Mia slipped her arm around Li's and leaned her head on his shoulder. It had been a long time since she'd tried to seduce a man, and never had she the need to use sex, or the prospect of sex, as a method for achieving an alternative goal. The fact that she knew he desired her was a plus, yet it was going to take some degree of skill for her to seem sincere, a skill she didn't know whether she possessed. But she couldn't think of any alternative. Li unlocked the door to his suite and dismissed the guard stationed in the hallway. "What can I get you?" he asked.

"Have you any champagne?"

"I'll check." He disappeared into the kitchen and she tossed her pocketbook on a table, slipped off her heels and stretched out on the couch. He returned holding two glasses in one hand and a bottle of 2000 Perrier Jouet in the other. He popped the cork and handed her a glass.

"To a safe trip and a quick return," she said holding out her glass.

"To friendship," he replied.

She took a long sip. "Mmm, excellent."

"I suppose. Frankly, I can't tell the difference."

Mia took another sip and felt a surge of nervous adrenaline turning her stomach into knots. She needed a moment alone to steady herself. "Excuse me, I have to visit the powder room."

"It's down the hallway on the right."

She picked up her purse and headed off. "I'll be right back."

"I'll be waiting."

She closed the door behind her and turned on the exhaust fan to mask any sounds. She took out her cell phone and called Sayid. "Hey, it's me. I'm still with Li. He's going back to China tomorrow. Have you got anything?" She knew it was a stupid question because she had only left him forty-five minutes earlier, not to mention it was the middle of the night.

"Actually, yes," Sayid answered. "I've spoken with a guy I know in Singapore. It's afternoon there. He reminded me of a mutual friend that we have that works out of London for AIG and he said they've already done a bunch of swaps. Mostly they were doing municipal bonds, but he said they've actually done some mortgages. I know this guy pretty well. We were classmates at the London School."

She was stunned that Sayid had acted so fast. "Can I tell Li that AIG will insure his risk?"

"It's only six in the morning in London, so obviously I won't have a better sense until I speak with him."

"I can't wait that long," she said.

"Well do whatever you have to."

Mia let out a deep breath. "Okay. Listen, give me a call back in a half-hour."

"Why?"

"Just do it." She shut off her phone, flushed the unused toilet and headed back to Li. She found him asleep on the couch, snoring loudly with champagne spilled across his lap. She finished off the rest of her drink, went to the kitchen to get a towel, returned and began sopping up the spilt wine. Her cleaning woke him.

"Oh, what happened?" he asked.

"You nodded off. You're obviously very tired. Maybe I should be going."

"No no, I'm fine. Stay…please." She nodded, put the towel aside and sat next to him on the couch. "Can I ask you a question?" he said.

"Of course."

"What is your interest in these investments that you brought Steve and Klaus to me?"

She'd anticipated this question and was somewhat surprised he hadn't asked it sooner. Her planned response went something along the lines of saying how she had a shared sense of loyalty to the U.S. as a citizen and to China based on her heritage, and wanted to do something that would benefit both nations and strengthen ties. But at that moment, that sounded as insincere as it in fact was. He'd see right through it. "Honestly?" she asked.

"Of course."

"I've known Steve for years. He's quite brilliant, which I think you've already determined on your own. He knows his stuff."

"That's not an answer."

"No, it's not. The truth is if you make an investment, I'll earn a finder's fee off it."

"Oh. I see. I thought you are quite well off financially. Why do you need money?"

"To begin with, starting a restaurant is very expensive and I have yet to recoup what I've put into it. Then I had an opportunity to buy the adjoining property, which I did. I'm turning it into an art gallery. Art is an obsession of mine, even more than cooking. I've dreamt of becoming an art dealer, discovering the next Picasso, that sort of thing. The demographics of the Berkshires leads me to believe that there's enough disposable income to support a high-end gallery. What I hadn't realized was the amount of capital that starting up such a place requires."

Li nodded. "And how much is Steve paying you?"

"I'm not sure that's any of your business."

"On the contrary. It is my business since my country is investing a lot of money based on my recommendation."

"If you put it that way." She refilled the glasses with champagne. "I'm getting a flat fee of $10,000."

"Ten thousand? That's a pittance," he said with a wave of his hand. "It will hardly be enough to make any impact on what you're trying to do."

"I know. There is the possibility of a bonus."

"What sort of bonus?"

"If you invested a half-billion, I'd get $50,000." She took a sip of champagne. "Of course, what I was really hoping was that you'd consider a really big stake. Then I'd really get a nice remuneration."

"How nice?"

"If you invest a billion, I'd get 75 basis points. At two billion, they'd double it to 150."

"A hundred-fifty points of two billion, that's what, thirty million? I hate to be the bearer of bad news but my government isn't going to put two billion at risk."

"I certainly understand that. I'm hoping that in time, your initial two hundred million will grow as will the amount of new money your government will want to invest. I know it's not up to you."

Li said nothing for several minutes. "There are no guarantees that even if this initial investment works out, I will want to invest more."

"*You* invest more? I thought you only offered your opinions and that it was some government committee or such that made these decisions."

"Technically that's true."

She was ready to make her move. "Can I change the subject?" She slid up precipitously close to him and softly began to stroke his arm. "Right now, I'm more concerned about you…and me…and the fact that I'm not going to be seeing you for some time than I am about collateralized debt obligations or finder's fees or…" she moved her lips close to his ear and whispered, "art galleries." Then she lightly began to nibble his earlobe followed by kisses on the side of his neck until she slowly worked her way down to his mouth. It could have been straight out of a badly written dime-store romance novel, with the exception that Li's body would never be confused with the idealized Adonis's that grace the covers of those books. But if she was feeling somewhat embarrassed by the triteness of her seduction, he seemed to enjoy it. They kissed for what felt like hours to Mia, but in fact, was only a few minutes. "You're clothes are still damp from the champagne," she finally said. "Don't you want to get out of them?"

"Let me go to my bedroom and change." He stood up. "I'll be right back."

She stood up with him. "Why don't I just follow you?"

"Yes, why don't you."

As soon as they entered the bedroom, Li went to the bathroom to change. Mia, not wanting to prolong this any longer than needed, slipped off her dress, keeping on her bra and panties, and climbed under the covers. "Have you any condoms?" she called out.

Li returned from the bathroom wearing a robe. "That's not necessary. As a good party man, I long ago had a vasectomy. We have to be an example, you know."

"You can still contract diseases, vasectomy or not."

"I'm not worried about getting any diseases from you." He shed the robe and stood naked, though not very aroused, at the side of the bed.

"No you won't get any diseases from me. I was referring to my health."

He smiled. "You are safe," and he started to climb into the bed.

She held out her arm to stop him. "Even so, I am a doctor. I too have to be an example." Li stood motionless at the edge of the mattress. She wondered, even hoped, that her insistence on a condom might be a barrier to any further intimacy. Li took out a condom from a drawer in the nightstand. Mia took that as evidence that either she wasn't the first woman to share this bed or that he was being less than honest about that vasectomy, or both. He fumbled as he tried to tear open the wrapper. "Let me do that," she said taking it from him. Mia thought she was experienced enough with Chinese men to know what they liked and more importantly, what they didn't. Were Li a Caucasian, she'd have no qualms about orally stimulating him, even using her mouth to slip the rubber on. But Chinese men, especially of Li's generation, were reticent about oral sex, and any such stimulation may have had the reverse effect. Even if he was receptive, he certainly wasn't going to reciprocate on her, so the fact that the condom was lubricated was inordinately helpful.

Li pulled back the covers revealing Mia. "You are so beautiful." She smiled, sat up in the bed, slipped off her remaining clothes and stretched out so that he could admire her. She then took his hand and motioned for him to lie down on his back. They kissed, Li put on the condom and was about to climb on top of Mia when her phone rang. "What's that?" he asked.

"Shit. It's my cell."

"Let it go."

She nodded and continued kissing him but then stopped as the phone kept ringing. "No, I'd better get it. If someone's calling me at this hour, it might be an emergency. My father's not been well." She got up from the bed, went to her pocketbook and flipped the phone open. "Hello?"

"It's me," said Sayid.

"Oh. What's up?"

"You told me to call you."

"Oh that's really good news," she said.

"What? What are you talking about?"

"No, no. I'll tell Li next time I see him."

"Mia, what the hell is going on? Are you okay?"

"Yeah, everything's great. I'll talk to you later. Gotta go." She shut off her phone and climbed back into bed. "Now, where were we?" she said in her sultriest voice.

"Was it about your father?"

"Uh, no. Actually that was Stefano."

"Assanti? What was he calling at this hour about?"

"Oh, he's found a way to insure your investment, if you want to."

"Insure it?"

"Yes. He's got an insurance company to underwrite whatever you invest via a credit default swap."

"Whatever I invest? Up to what limit?"

"As much as you want to put in. Naturally you'll have to pay a premium, but it shouldn't be much considering the returns the investment will yield."

"Really. Which insurance company?"

"Um, I think he said AIG. Ever heard of them?"

"Of course. I believe they are your country's largest insurer."

She knew that Li was intrigued, but she knew there was other work to be done first. "Anyway, enough about your financial needs. It's time to address some of your other needs." She switched off the lamp on the nightstand knowing this would be much easier for her in the dark. She had never before made love to a man that she really had absolutely no desire for, and she didn't know how she'd react. Maybe if she thought of someone else, it would work better. He rolled on top of her and they resumed kissing, but being that close to him, feeling his breath, taking in his smell, made it much too personal. She rolled him over again on his back and climbed on top. This allowed her to sit up straight with the feel of him inside of her their only contact. Now he was only a disembodied penis. It could have been anybody's. She fantasized about other men, from movies, from TV, even from posters plastered on the sides of bus stops. She began to think about her new apartment. A new dresser was going to be delivered later that day but she needed to furnish the rest of the place. Maybe she'd go furniture shopping in SoHo, or perhaps up to Bloomingdales. Damn, was that sale at Bloomie's still on or had it ended yesterday? There was an appointment to see her lawyer on Wednesday, after which she might drive back to Stockbridge or maybe stay in the city and do more shopping.

Then she remembered Jake. Shit, Jake was coming today. What the fuck was that going to be like? Jake. Since that night Sayid had shown up at Napa-East, she kept thinking about that last semester at MIT. Of all the men she'd known, none was like Jake. None had a mind quite like his, and she'd been with a number of really smart men. None of them seemed so utterly uncon-cerned by what others might have thought of him. None cared as sincerely as he did for those worse off. And none ever seemed to take the unbridled joy in her that he did when they made love. Perhaps that was just youthful exuberance back then. She knew that her memory was being selective, that Jake was no saint. Like any human, he certainly had his faults, not the least of which was his tendency to be condescendingly impatient towards those less intelligent. But compared to this old party apparatchik whose carnal desires she had taken upon herself to satisfy, Jake was a fantasy. Perhaps he had no interest in her any more. He had probably changed. She certainly had, but for a moment she pictured them in bed together back in her old student house in Cambridge. She quickened her pace over Li. She nearly called out Jake's name but luckily remembered where she was. She wanted to be done with this already, but having gone this far, she might as well make a good show of it. She began to moan, then to curse, then to scream out "I'm coming," first in English, and when that didn't have much of an effect, she switched to Mandarin. At last she could feel Li begin to tense up and then let out a low, primal grunt before he pulled her down to his chest. She stopped her humping, but he continued with several thrusts before she felt his body go limp. At last it was over. She quickly rolled off him and made her way to the bathroom where she sat on the toilet, wiping herself off with tissue. Although the condom or the vasectomy had done its job, she still wanted to be clean of him.

She went back to the bedroom and found Li sitting up in bed smoking a cigarette. "Care for one?" he asked.

"No thank you. That was more incredible than I'd imagined."

"You enjoyed?"

"God yes," she said. "Didn't you?"

"Very, very much. I'm just sad that I have to leave in a few hours."

"Me too." She slipped on her under garments. "It's going to be a long, lonely summer."

"Well, I'm sure you'll be busy. You have much to do with your new apart-ment and your new gallery."

"The apartment isn't that big a deal, and as for the gallery, that's still a pipe dream."

"I would think your finder's fee from Assanti should get you well on your way. After all, thirty million should help, shouldn't it?"

"Really?"

"Really. Actually, if AIG is going to guarantee it, who knows, maybe more."

She bent down and kissed him one last time. "Who knows?"

Mia managed to flag a taxi on Park Avenue, which considering the hour was fortunate. She gave the address to the cabbie and stretched out on the back seat, absolutely sure she'd fall asleep before they'd gone two blocks, but she didn't. She re-played the last few hours over and over in her head, as though she were watching a TV show that she'd recorded on her DVR, skipping over the dull parts as she'd skip over commercials, and rewinding snippets of conversation, trying to discern any inferences or meanings that she'd missed on first viewing. She kept coming back to one thing – she'd used sex as a tool. It was something she'd never done before, could never recall even considering before. She didn't know whether to feel a sense shame or accomplishment. Other people did it all the time, men as well as women, but that was no comfort. In the end, she decided that the best way to come to terms with it was to say it was necessary and try not to dwell on it lest her whole attitude toward sex be jaded by the experience. Li would be gone for months so certainly she'd not be in that situation with him any time soon. *Hopefully never*, she whispered under her breath.

She took out her cell and called Sayid who didn't answer. She didn't leave a voicemail, but simply closed her eyes and slumped back in seat. Seconds later, she flipped open the cell and hit re-dial. A groggy-sounding Sayid picked up this time.

"Hey, it's Mia."

"What time is it?"

She glanced down at her wristwatch. "Ten after four."

"In the morning?"

"Unless there's a solar eclipse blocking out the sun, it isn't afternoon."

"Shit, why are you calling me?"

Suddenly, Mia had an urge for a cigarette. She didn't know why since she never smoked, but her last image of Li was him smoking in bed, seemingly savoring the nicotine. Somehow, a cigarette seemed right after a night of inter-national intrigue. "I've got good news. Li's in for two."

"That's not news. The Chinese had already committed to two hundred million."

"Well my dear, you can add a zero to that number."

She heard an audible gasp on Sayid's end. "Two billion, with a 'B'?"

"That's right, dearie."

"Jesus. How'd you pull that off?"

"Never mind. Couple of caveats though – you are going to pay me three hundred basis points on this."

"Wa-wa-wait a minute, we never discussed any points to you."

"Okay, I guess I'll just have to inform Li that the deal's off."

"Um, no, but sixty million? I can't swing that."

"Steven," she was careful not to use Sayid's real name as the driver, despite his marginal fluency in English, could nonetheless hear her end of the conver-sation. "Certainly a number of parties to this transaction are taking their fair share. Frankly, I don't care who the fuck's portion it comes out of, but I need three hundred points. I've literally worked my ass off to do my part, and if you want the Chinese money, Li needs to be paid. Understand?"

There was silence for a minute until Sayid spoke. "Okay, I'll work it out. I suppose you'll want it wired to some off-shore bank account."

"No, not at all. You can put it in my Citibank account, and I'll expect a 1099 for tax purposes. I want this all legal and above board. I've got nothing to hide."

"What about Li?"

"Let me worry about Li."

"You know, I'm not sure exactly how legal this is for you."

Now Mia really wanted a cigarette. "What are you referring to?" she snapped back.

"I'm not sure, but with that much money and it being a percentage of the investment, I think you probably need to register as an agent of a foreign gov-ernment, or something."

She took a deep breath, like she had taken a drag on a cigarette. "Don't worry about it. Three hundred points. Understand?"

She heard a sigh. "I understand. Anything else?"

"Li wants the insurance on his CDO. He's expecting AIG to write a CDS on this."

"Why the hell is he expecting to get AIG?"

"Because I told him AIG would write it."

"Fuck, Mia, I told you that in confidence. It's by no means a done deal. I haven't even spoken with them yet."

"Then I suggest that as soon as we hang up, you give them a call. It's the middle of the night here, but it's morning in London."

"I'm not sure I can pull this off."

"Just....Fucking...Do It!" she said with a quiet, but deliberate cadence. "Get it done. As I said, I've done my part, now goddammit, do yours. Call London. Get AIG. Convince them there's money to be made. Unless, of course, you don't want the Chinese, but other future investors will also want protection." There was only silence coming from Sayid's end. "You still there?" she asked.

"Yeah I'm here. What if I can't get AIG?"

"That, sweetie, is not an option."

"I'll see what I…" Mia slapped her phone closed, cutting Sayid off. *Shit,* she thought, *I had to fuck that man. All Sayid has to do is make a few calls.* Only then did she think about the money she'd demanded from him, and only then did she have a sense of being a prostitute.

As soon as she got to her apartment, she went straight to her bedroom and immediately stepped out of her dress, leaving it on the floor. She went to the bathroom and began filling the tub with very hot water. The apartment had recently been renovated and one of the improvements was the installation of a Jacuzzi. She lit a couple of scented candles and then slipped into the water until all but her head was covered. She closed her eyes and tried to allow the stress to flow out of her. The smell of Li, which was primarily one of cigarettes, seemed to have leeched on to her body. She sniffed a hank of her hair and realized that was the main source of the odor. Shampoo would take care of that. The mental picture of Li inside her would not be as easily washed away. She sat up and turned on the spa jets to full force, then positioned herself in such a manner so that the gushing water would cleanse her of him. This had the unexpected effect of being mildly arousing, which was the last thing she wanted. "That's certainly more stimulating than Li," she said out loud and then laughed. She stretched out again in the water and allowed the pulsating jets to provide a full-body massage. After ten minutes, the timer automatically shut off the jets, signaling it was time to empty the tub, shower and shampoo.

After drying off, she went straight to bed, not even bothering to put on clothes. She was sure that sleep would come the second her head hit the pillow. When it didn't, her first thought was to take a couple Benadryl tablets, but it being five in the morning, she didn't want the effects to ruin the rest of the day. She decided on doing something that she hadn't done since she was a teenager, meditate. When Mia had declared herself a Buddhist in high school, her father insisted she attend meditation classes at a local Zen meeting house. She didn't get very far, certainly not even close to attaining enlightenment. She doubted that such a state even existed. Satori, nirvana, these were just catchphrases of the Buddhist marketing plan to attract adherents, probably no more real or effective than Wonder Bread's claim of "building strong bodies 12 ways." Still, the lure of enlightenment was far more attractive than the advertising hooks of her parents' church – heaven and hell. Mia never forgot some of the meditation techniques. She sat up in bed, assumed a half-lotus position, and began taking very long, slow breaths, visualizing the air molecules as they entered her lungs and exited into the room. She sensed her pulse rate fall as her conscious mind gradually went blank, and she had no recollection of her body when it fell back onto the sheets and sleep came.

The doorman was taking a particularly suspicious attitude towards Jake. "She's not answering, just like she didn't ten minutes ago, or the time before that, or before that. Why don't you come back later this afternoon?"

Jake looked at his watch. "No, I'll just wait in lobby if you don't mind. She said to meet her here around eleven. I guess she's running late."

"It's your life," replied the doorman.

Stupid thing is I should have gotten her phone number, Jake thought to himself. "No, the stupid thing is that I didn't call Annie, who's still with Kat, who does have her number," he whispered as he took out his cell and made the call. Mia's number attained, he wasted no time calling her. Her line rang but she didn't pick up and when he heard the voicemail prompt, he hung up. Feeling stupid at not having left a message, he redialed the number. He rehearsed what he'd say, wanting to sound entertainingly clever but not off-putting. Just as he was prepared to speak, Mia picked up.

"Hi, it's me, Jake." He winced as the words came out of his mouth.

"Oh, Jake. Where are you?"

"Down in the lobby."

"Shit, what time is it?"

He glanced at his watch. "Twelve thirty."

"My God, that late? Hold on, I'll let you up."

He paced nervously across the elevator's small floor as he rode up to her apartment. He took a deep breath before knocking on her door and heard her call out that she was coming. The door opened and she stood there in bare feet wearing a ragged T-shirt and boxer shorts. Her hair was unkempt and she looked as though she'd just hopped out of bed, but he couldn't help but notice that even in that state, he found her damned attractive. She smiled broadly and planted a kiss on his cheek. "Where are your bags?"

"I left them in the car."

"Why didn't you bring them up?"

"I dunno. I guess I wasn't sure what my plans were."

"You're not going back to Vermont today. I was hoping you'd stay for at least one night."

"I didn't want to impose."

"Oh Jake, don't be ridiculous." She playfully punched him in the stomach. "You're staying the night. We'll get your clothes later. Come on in, I'll give you the Manhattan tour of the place, which lasts all of thirty seconds."

"I know. I used to live about ten blocks from here."

"That's right," she said, leading him into the living room. "I'd forgotten that."

The room was bare of any furniture, save for a couple of folding chairs and a floor lamp. A cardboard carton served as a coffee table and a large-screen television sat against one wall. "I love what you you've done with the place," he joked.

"I know, I know. I can't decide on how to decorate. The good thing is there's plenty of room. I've got an inflatable air mattress, which is pretty comfortable. I slept on it for the first few nights until my bed arrived."

Jake took that to mean he'd be sleeping on the mattress. This wasn't so much a surprise as a mild disappointment. She had said she wasn't seeing anyone but it was unrealistic to think that they'd sleep together. His goal for now was just to keep things between them light. "You got the essentials, especially the TV. It's really big."

"Tell me. I ordered it over the phone last week from J and R and I didn't realize the size of it. What's worse is that they screwed up the order and delivered two. The other one's in the bedroom, which is really stupid. I have to confess though, I kinda like it. I can actually see the damn thing when I'm in bed without my contacts in. Come, I'll show you." He followed her into the bedroom in which there was only a king-sized bed, the sheets on which had not been made, and a television identical to the one in the living room. On the floor was a smattering of dirty clothes, the most prominent of which was a black, very expensive-looking cocktail dress.

"Excuse the mess," she said. "Until the dresser comes, things are just all over the place." She picked up the dress and hung it in the closet in a manner that seemed purposely inconspicuous, making it all that more obvious to Jake. "So, what do you feel like doing?" she asked closing the closet door.

"I have no preferences."

"We could schlep around the Village. There are some furniture places I've wanted to check out. Or if you prefer, we could go to a museum, MOMA, the Met or some other place."

"The Village would be fine."

"Great. Let me change and we'll be off."

"I'll wait in the living room."

"Help yourself to a drink," she shouted from the bathroom. "There's soda in the fridge, and I think there's some wine or beer if you'd like."

He took out a Diet Coke and popped it open. "Did you just get up or something?" he shouted. There was no response. He didn't know if she hadn't heard him or chose not to answer, but he didn't bother to repeat the question.

They spent the afternoon traipsing through boutiques and galleries in the Village and SoHo. They couldn't decide on where to go for dinner and in the end, went back to Mia's and ordered in Indian food. They sat on the living room floor and dined on samosas, kabobs and other dishes out of cardboard boxes. "So tell me about your marriage," Mia asked.

"Not much to tell," he replied as he finished off a leg of tandoori chicken. "Debbie was a girl I knew since we were both kids, although when I met her again after moving back to New York, she looked nothing like I'd remembered. Not that looks are what's important but they don't hurt. Anyway, unbeknownst to me, my boss seemed to take a fancy to her and he was a lot wealthier than yours truly."

"Arthur Morrison?" she asked.

"One and the same. Artie sent me to Africa on the pretext of checking out some oil company."

"And while you were away…"

"The cats did play. He invited her out to his place in the Hamptons for the weekend and as they say, the rest is history."

"What a fucking douche bag."

"Him or her?"

"The both of them," Mia said, taking a swig of beer.

"In the end, it turned out for the best."

"How so?"

"I found out what the world's really like. I think I told you that I held a child as she died in my arms. The glitzy clubs, fancy cars, big houses, all that I had thought was important since leaving school – it was all so trivial, if you know what I mean."

She nodded her head. "So you decided to become a philanthropist."

He laughed. "No, to be a philanthropist implies you have money to give away."

"You weren't making a lot of money?"

"Yes, but once I decided it would be better served by using it on people with far less, my darling ex decided I'd left my sanity in Nigeria, so she left me."

"For Morrison?"

"For Morrison and his credit cards."

"Any regrets?" she asked.

"Only that it took me so long to realize the truth about her, and myself."

They sat there eating in silence for several minutes. "You know," Mia finally said, "I think I met them both a couple of months ago."

"Really?"

"I met Morrison for sure at some fundraiser. And I think I recall someone saying that his wife was one of the organizers, assuming that he's still with your ex."

"That he is, and that was certainly Debbie. Why were you there?"

Mia quickly picked up a lamb chop and started nibbling on the bone. "Huh?" she finally said.

"Why were you at the fundraiser?"

She swallowed and wiped her mouth on a napkin. "Um, I think someone advised me that it would be good for making contacts. For the gallery, you know. Those are the people who buy. But getting back to you, you said you aren't seeing anyone. What about that cute little Annie?"

He rolled his eyes. "She's not exactly my type. Besides, sleeping with your employee is generally not a good idea."

"That's for sure. I was only kidding about Annie anyway. I know she's interested in my chef."

For the second time in three minutes, Jake found himself spitting beer out of his mouth. "What?"

"Oh come on Jake. You didn't know that Annie and Kat are an item?"

"How would I know that? I didn't even know she knew you or Kat until two days ago."

"Oh yeah. Annie's been to our house three or four times in the past month."

"Jesus. I didn't realize that Kat is gay," he said shaking his head.

"She's actually bi, but it's not that big a deal."

"No, I didn't mean to imply, oh fuck, I don't know what I meant. Well, if they're happy, who am I or anyone else to say? After all, my brother is gay. My cousin's a lesbian, so why shouldn't my head of production also be lesbian. It's just that I'm so oblivious when it comes to these things. No wonder I don't get laid. Everyone I know is gay." She started laughing uncontrollably. "You think this is funny?" She nodded her head. "Funny for you, not so much for me." Then he started to laugh.

"Oh Jake, we need to find you a nice Jewish girl."

"There's an oxymoron if ever I've heard one."

"Come on now. Besides, think how happy you'll make your mother."

"The hell with my mother. What about making me happy?"

"Now, now, Jacob. That's going to be my goal in the coming months. To find you a nice Jewish girl."

"You'd have more of a chance making peace between the Arabs and the Israelis."

"You'll see." She began to yawn. "All of a sudden, I'm really tired. Tomorrow, we're going to Bloomie's."

"Why?"

"Because," she said tossing the remnants of their dinner into the trash, "their semi-annual sale is ending, and what better place to find a Jewish girl than at Bloomingdales."

"No JAPs though."

She wiped her hands on a towel and headed to her bedroom. "No JAPs. Good night." She closed the door.

He lay on the air mattress flipping through the TV stations. He eventually settled on a Yankees game. They were playing Seattle on the west coast and although it was eleven-thirty, the game was only in the second inning. He found that despite the bed being as comfortable as Mia had said, he couldn't sleep, and he knew the reason. Sleeping twenty feet away was the one girl he had ever desperately wanted to make love to, and that desire still tormented him. By the seventh inning with Yankees losing by eight runs, he decided to change the channels. When he happened upon *Casablanca*, he put the remote down. He'd seen the movie a dozen times before, but watching Bogie and Bergman never grew old. When the movie ended, it was nearly three in the morning. He decided it was time to turn off the set and try and sleep. He had lain in the darkness for only a few minutes when he heard the door to Mia's bedroom open. In the shadows, he watched her silhouetted body walk softly towards him and crawl under the sheets next to him.

"Did I wake you?" she whispered.

"No," he whispered back. "I couldn't sleep."

"Me neither." She rolled on top of him. Their lovemaking was slow, but with a familiarity of a couple who had been together for many years. In many ways, in Jake's mind they had been since every woman he'd ever slept with was always compared to her. When they finished, Mia slowly crawled off the mattress and started to go back to the bedroom.

"Where are you going?" he asked.

"Back to bed. I'm tired."

"But I was kind of hoping..."

"Hoping what?"

"Hoping that you'd be next to me the rest of night."

She audibly sighed. "My bed's more comfortable. I need sleep." She walked toward the bedroom stopping at the door. "Aren't you coming?" He rolled off the mattress and stumbled to her side. "But," she cautioned, "I need sleep, so don't keep me awake. And don't snore. I remember you used to snore sometimes." He snuggled next to her in the bed, kissed her and then she said, "Goodnight."

"Can I ask a question?" he said.

"Jake, I'm really tired."

"Just one. What about that nice Jewish girl?"

She rolled on her side away from him as he wrapped his body around her back and clutched her hand in his. "You said no JAPs. I know you white boys think all Asians look alike, but I'm Chinese, not Japanese."

THIRTEEN

February 2005

he invitation had been sitting unopened on Sayid's desk for three weeks. It had come the day he left for Paris and when he returned, it was lost among the pile of mail that his secretary had left for him. The purported reason for the European trip was to put his old Paris apartment up for sale. In the nearly three years that had elapsed since his return to the States, Sayid had spent less than two weeks back in Paris. With favorable market conditions, selling the flat made economic sense, yet during his Paris stay, he'd spent little time dealing with its sale. The real reason for his visit was for a series of clandestine meetings with Klaus and various al-Qaeda operatives to brief them on the status of his operations. The final meeting had been a one-on-one session with Mustafa al-Yazid, who had now assumed a far greater role in running the overall operation of the organization, to the point that many Western intelligence sources regarded him as a target more valuable than anyone else, including al-Zawahiri or even bin Laden.

The meeting with al-Yazid had gone well. The collateralize debt obligation derivative investment vehicles that Sayid had promulgated were catching fire.

With the types of returns they were yielding, mainstream brokerage houses, funds and investment banks couldn't get into this market fast enough. The unexpected bonus, to Sayid's way of thinking, was the credit default swaps often linked with the CDOs. None of this was lost on al-Yazid, who had a strong financial background, but he was growing skeptical that any of this would lead to the financial ruin that Sayid had promised. The original seed money that the terrorist organization had given Sayid had quadrupled in value. Sayid was shocked that during their meeting, al-Yazid had expressed an interest in investing more in derivatives, not in the hopes that this would speed up a market collapse, but because al-Yazid wanted to make money.

It took twenty minutes of persuading before Sayid had convinced him not to do so. Eventually these investments had to fail, as no one could really determine what they were worth. In such an environment, they would surely end up being way over-valued. While some people would make money, many more would suffer losses, and since you could never be sure when the market would implode, you would always be at risk. "But what difference does that make if your investment is guaranteed by a swap?" al-Yazid asked. Sayid explained that the total value of all these insurance swaps was estimated to be as high as fifteen trillion dollars, which was more than half the value of all companies traded on all of the U.S. stock exchanges. The "insurers" of these swaps couldn't possibly pay off if they needed to, hence they would collapse as well. What Sayid didn't tell him was that, in fact, no one knew the total amount insured by these swaps since CDSs were not regulated by any government body and their total value or risk was, for the most part, not reported to anyone.

He flew back to New York not entirely sure that al-Yazid wasn't going to be another derivative investor, which would be the ultimate irony. Despite having a successful meeting with the al-Qaeda commander, he continued to ruminate over al-Yazid's parting words that were clearly meant as a warning. He told him that he while he understood the need for Sayid to take on the trappings of Western liberal capitalism, he was concerned that Sayid was being seduced by that culture and might lose his connection to, and faith in, the one true religion. That would be a crime worse than having never believed at all, a crime that the Koran identified as a capital offense.

Sayid chucked the bundle of junk mail in a wastebasket, but as luck would have it, the invitation ended up on the top of the pile with its fancy linen stationery clearly distinguishing it from the other mass solicitations. He retrieved it from the basket and noticed that the outside address, Mr. Stefano Assanti and Guest, was hand written in fine calligraphy. He flipped the envelope over, but the return address had no name, only the Fifth Avenue address of the sender. He opened the invitation. *Arthur and Deborah Morrison request the pleasure of your company for cocktails at their home in celebration of their second anniversary on February 10, 2005 at 8:30 pm. RSVP regrets only.*

"Shit," he said, realizing that the party was scheduled for that night. He summoned his secretary and told her to get Morrison on the phone while he looked through the rest of the mail, wondering what else he had missed. Minutes later his secretary informed him that Morrison was on the line.

"Art? Steve Assanti here. How the hell are you?"

"Pretty fine. Looking forward to seeing you tonight."

"Yeah, about that. I just got back from Paris this morning and saw the invite. I know it's late, but I've been up for like thirty hours straight, and I'm afraid if I came, I'd fall asleep on your sofa. So I'm going to have to take a rain check."

"Ah, that's too bad. I haven't seen you in months. We really need to just get together some night and bullshit about what's going on. I hope you're still intending on partnering for the ACBL spring championships."

"Definitely, on both."

"Good. How's next Wednesday?" Morrison asked.

"Um, hold on, let me check my calendar. Yeah, I can do Wednesday. Shall we say lunch around one?"

"I was thinking more of dinner, at my place. Debbie's great at entertaining. Say eight?"

"Eight it is."

"Perfect. And bring a date so Deb has someone to talk to, otherwise I'll never hear the end of it."

Morrison hung up and Sayid began to stew over who to ask. In all the time he been in Manhattan, he had formed no relationships with any women beyond those tied to work. As he flipped through his Outlook contacts, none seemed a likely candidate. He knew there was only one name that held any possibility. He took out his cell and called her.

"Hey, it's me" he said when Mia picked up. "Where are you these days?"

"In Stockbridge," she answered. "Why?"

"I need a favor. Can you be in the city next Wednesday?"

"What for?"

"I need a dinner date."

"I don't know. What's the occasion?"

"I've been invited to Art Morrison's for dinner."

"Hold on." He could hear other voices in the background and Mia saying something about needing to go somewhere quiet because she had an important art buyer on the phone. That was followed by the sound of a door closing and what sounded like a toilet flushing. "Sorry about that, but I wanted to go where no one would hear us."

"And you chose the bathroom?"

"It's private. Arthur Morrison, huh? Look Sayid, I'm not driving all the way down there just to attend some lavish, but undoubtedly boring party that Arthur Morrison is throwing. Get someone else to go with you."

"It's not some party. Just dinner, the four of us."

"Four?"

"Yeah, you, me, Art and his wife."

"Oh." Mia's tone suddenly changed. "Arthur's wife is going to be there?"

"Yes. That's why I need you, so that his wife won't feel left out if the conversation turns to business or bridge, which it probably will. I wouldn't ask except that Morrison has a lot of money under his control, and I couldn't think of anyone else."

She hesitated, but knew that the Morrisons fancied themselves as art collectors. "Okay, but you'll owe me."

"Thanks Mia. Meet me at my apartment at seven-thirty."

Mia sat on the toilet seat for five minutes as she thought about what dinner with Arthur and Debbie Morrison would be like. Arthur could either be charming or boorish, sometimes both within the span of minutes. As a bonus, Debbie was Jake's ex, and that alone might have gotten her to go. She shut off her cell and left the bathroom. "I've got to go the city next Wednesday."

"What for?"

"Big collector in from England."

"Okay, I'll go with you."

"Don't be ridiculous, Jake. It's just for the evening and I'll be tied up with this guy and his wife. I'm lucky to see them before they fly back to London. I'll be back on Thursday."

Arthur Morrison had purchased his Fifth Avenue apartment for the tidy sum of twenty-six million, and it looked it. Mia found it ironic that they both had residences on the same street, albeit Arthur's location overlooking Central Park might as well have been in another state from hers in the Village. She was dressed in a tight-fitting red strapless cocktail dress, accented by a small diamond choker and diamond stud earrings. Sayid was impressed and knew that Morrison would be as well. Debbie greeted them at the door and showed them into the living room where Arthur, martini in one hand and phone in the other, was having a heated conversation liberally punctuated with expletives. "His bark is worse than his bite," Debbie said apologetically. "What can I get you to drink?"

"I'll have a glass of red wine," Sayid said.

"Wine's fine with me," Mia concurred.

Arthur shouted a parting curse into his phone and then turned to his guests. "Sorry about that. You know how business is. Steve, great to see you," he said placing a fatherly hand on Sayid's shoulder. "And who is this lovely creature?"

"I'm Mia," she said, extending her hand.

He took her hand and in one motion, brought it up to his lips and placed a light kiss on it. "Enchanté," he said.

"Oh Artie, you're so full of shit when it comes to this stuff," Debbie said, returning with two glasses of wine.

"Am not." He leaned close to Mia's ear. "She's just jealous," he whispered.

After dinner, Debbie offered to take Mia on a tour of the apartment while the boys retired to the study. Unlike most Manhattan apartments, the Morrison residence was over 10,000 square feet on two levels, so the tour actually took some time to complete. Each room had an array of fine artwork, paintings, drawings and sculpture, all of which caught Mia's attention. And try as she might, she couldn't help liking Debbie, although she couldn't forget what she'd done to Jake. In her defense, she'd only heard Jake's side and knew in situations like theirs, there were always two sides to the story.

Arthur bade Sayid to have a seat as he filled two Waterford crystal tumblers with whisky. "This is twenty-five year old single malt. Costs like two hundred for a fifth, but it's worth it."

"I think I've already had enough to drink tonight," Sayid said.

"You've never had Scotch like this, and anyway, you only had a drop of wine."

"More like half a bottle."

"As I said, a drop." He handed Sayid a glass. "Salut."

"Salut," Sayid took a sip and even though he almost never drank hard liquor, he was surprised by how smooth the Scotch was. "My, that is very good."

"I told you." Morrison walked over to the bookshelf, opened a humidor, took out two cigars and snipped the ends off. "This is the only room Debbie allows smoking in. I had to have special air filtration installed. These, by the way, are Cubans. I have them flown in from Montreal. I know they're fucking communists, but Fidel can't live forever, and I haven't found a Dominican that really matches." He handed a cigar to Sayid and extended a lighter to him before lighting up his own.

Sayid took a small puff and nodded approvingly.

"Steve, let me get right to the point. I've been meaning to speak with you for some time now. The other houses – Bear, Lehman even Goldman – they're all getting big into CDO derivatives. I think it's time to get into that market."

This was precisely what Sayid was hoping for. He took another sip of whisky. "Well Art, if you want, I can get you in touch with some of my people and put together something."

"Not interested in having your people put something together."

"Then why bring this up?"

Arthur took a long drag on his cigar. "My net worth is something north of half a billion."

Sayid tried to look impressed, but he was already well aware of Morrison's net worth. "That's a lot of money."

"Yes it is, but that's not what I want. I want to be north of a billion."

"How far north?"

"The fucking Artic Ocean north. No, the fucking North Pole north. I'm talking Bill Gates north, and I think these instruments can get me there sooner."

"They probably can. So let my people..."

"I don't want your goddamn people. I want you. You were way ahead of the curve on these things, and quite frankly, I don't understand them, and quite frankly, I get the impression that nobody else in my shop understands them either."

"You offering me a job?"

"Yes. Quit PBB and come work for me. I'll make it worth your while."

"I already make a good salary."

"Whatever they are paying you, I'll double it, hell, triple it. Plus you'll get options." Morrison freshened Sayid's drink.

"I don't know, Art. I have a lot of freedom where I am and to be honest, I'm not sure I would do well working under you."

"I'll give you all the autonomy you need. Ask anyone who works for me. I don't give a fuck about how you go about your job – I only care about results."

Sayid began to weigh the offer. With Morrison's backing, his scheme would have resources that PBB couldn't match. But PBB had the approval of al-Yazid, which Morrison would never get. "Tell you what Art. Let's do a couple of deals together first and see how it goes. If I think we can work together, then maybe I can look at changing the address on my business card. How's that sound?"

Arthur's jaw clenched tight. "It's not what I was planning but it's a start. Give me a call when you've got something and I tell you, my friend, you will come to work for me someday." He held his glass toward Sayid.

Sayid responded in kind. "Someday, perhaps." Sayid finished off his drink and suddenly felt the alcohol begin to cloud his brain.

Morrison refilled both glasses. "Okay, enough business. Now tell me, where did you find that gorgeous creature?"

"She is very attractive, isn't she?"

"Attractive?" Morrison puckered his lips and tweeted a short whistle. "She's a knockout. I've never had an Asian woman. Is it true what they say?"

"What do they say?"

"That they're pussies are like their eyes, slanted."

The comment made Sayid cough. "I'd never heard that."

"An old joke. Hey, I'm just yanking your chain, though I wouldn't mind being yanked by her. She's got a great ass, nice and round and firm, not flat like Deb's, not that my wife's ass matters since she's made it abundantly clear that I'll never get up that hole. But Mia's ass, I'll bet you've been up there." Sayid, not knowing how to respond said nothing. "Ah shit, I didn't mean to embarrass you. Deb makes up for it. I may not get her ass but she's got one great tongue. Best goddamn blowjobs I've ever had, which is probably why I married her. Mia give good head?"

Sayid's mind was spinning. He didn't want to lower himself to Morrison's level of crudity, but he didn't want to alienate him either, so he simply nodded. He glanced down at his watch.

"Shit Art, look at the time. I'm flying to LA in the morning, so I should be going." He put out his cigar and stood to leave.

Morrison escorted him back to the living room where they found Mia and Debbie drinking coffee. Sayid explained that he and Mia needed to be leaving. Arthur began to help her with her coat. "I'm so glad to have met you Mia. Hope to be seeing a lot more of you in the future."

"Thank you both for a great meal and a lovely evening," she replied.

"Our pleasure," Debbie said.

Morrison showed them to the door. "Call me when you've got something," he told Sayid, "and don't take too long. I'm not known for my patience."

Riding the elevator down, Mia noticed that Sayid seemed to be having trouble keeping his balance. "Are you okay?"

"Sure." He straightened for a moment before falling back against the wall. "Perhaps I had a bit too much to drink." He was beginning to slur his words.

They caught a cab on Fifth Avenue and Mia instructed the driver to take Sayid home first. She soon found him slumped against her, clumsily pawing at her dress. "What's with you tonight?" she asked.

"I have a confession," he said, but didn't elaborate.

"What?" she finally said after several blocks.

"Huh?"

"You said you have a confession."

"Oh, yeah. I've never had oral sex."

Mia shook her head, unsure she'd heard correctly. "Excuse me?"

"I've never had oral sex."

She knew he was drunk, and knew it probably best to just let it go, but for some reason, she was curious. "Do you mean you've never received or performed?"

"Either. Both."

She tried to remember back. "It seems to me I recall one night at MIT when we smoked pot and had sex."

"I've never forgotten." His words were surprising because until that moment, she'd totally forgotten the incident. "But we just did it normally."

That last word struck her. She'd never viewed oral sex as not normal. Anyway, she had so little memory of the event that she couldn't dispute his recounting of it. "You're really drunk. We need to get you home and get you to bed before you vomit all over the place."

The cab pulled up in front of Sayid's apartment and Mia gave the driver instructions to wait. She helped Sayid out of the taxi and into his building. "Give me your keys," she told him when they reached the door to his apartment. Once inside, she helped him to his bedroom. He collapsed on his bed as she went into his bathroom and started the shower. "I think you'll feel much better if you get under the water and wash yourself off before you go to sleep."

"Are you getting in there with me?"

"No I'm not. I'm going home."

"You're not going to suck me off?"

"What?" she asked incredulously.

"You're not going to give me, you know, a blow job?"

"You'd have a better chance of finding bin Laden at a bar mitzvah."

Sayid sat up on the mattress. "Please?" he asked again.

"You are so fucking drunk." She opened her purse and took out a hundred dollar bill. "Here," she said tossing the money at his face. "Go out and find a hooker to give you your blow job. My treat." She turned her back while he tottered on the edge of the bed. "And don't call me for a while." She slammed the door and left.

Riding the elevator down, she couldn't help but think how strange Sayid's behavior had been. She never thought about the fact that they had slept together that one time, it simply hadn't meant that much to her. She tried remembering how it had happened, and all that came to mind was that they'd been out jogging, she'd been angry at Jake for some reason, they'd gone back to her apartment, she smoked a lot of dope but Sayid declined, and then she, as the phrase of the times went, jumped his bones. It never happened again, but obviously, it had left an impression on him.

She walked out of Sayid's building only to find that the cab she assumed was still waiting for her was nowhere in sight. A weird night had just gotten weirder. It was unheard of for a taxi to leave without collecting the fare. She walked down 72nd Street towards Broadway where the chances of catching a cab at that hour were certainly better. She didn't notice the headlights illuminate and the engine turn over on the black limousine twenty feet behind her. Seconds later, two men emerged from the limo and came up to either side. "Come with us please," one said.

She froze. Thoughts flooded her brain. *Am I about to be robbed? Am I about to be raped? God, let it be robbery. Shit, What if I'm being robbed and raped?* She hadn't anticipated the paralysis that overcame her. She didn't fight, didn't struggle, didn't even scream as each man grabbed one of her arms and turned her one hundred and eighty degrees around. They walked fifteen feet to the limo and the rear right door flung open. She peered inside and, to her relief, Li Xuan was sitting in the rear seat extending his arm, beckoning her to enter.

"Sha-sha," she exclaimed using the pet name she had for him. "You scared the hell out of me." She slid next to him and lightly placed a kiss on each cheek. "When did you get back in town?"

"A few weeks ago." He reached over and closed the door, then rolled up the glass partition that separated them from the driver.

"God, your men scared the shit out of me."

Li lit up a cigarette. "I apologize for that. You haven't responded to my phone calls."

She feigned surprise at his statement. "What phone calls?"

"I've left half a dozen voicemails. No answer."

Mia had heard the messages but didn't want to talk to him. Lately Sayid for some reason seemed less interested in the Chinese money. Perhaps he'd given up on his idea of wrecking the Chinese economy. Perhaps he had established enough credibility with Li that he no longer needed her, or perhaps Sayid had come to the conclusion that Meecham's original analysis of the plan was wrong and that in fact, these investments were sound. Whatever the reason, Sayid was refusing to pay Mia anything more than a token finder's fee and that just wasn't worth it to her. She saw no point in maintaining contact with Li.

"I lost my cell two weeks ago and didn't get a replacement until yesterday. By the time I did, my voicemail had hundreds of messages, and I just haven't had time to go through them yet." It was a plausible enough sounding explanation that, had it not actually happened to her six months earlier, she would never have come up with so quickly.

It seemed to satisfy Li. "I have been looking forward to seeing you again. I want to show you something." He reached inside his coat, took out an envelope and laid it on the seat between them. "Open it up."

She picked up the envelope and took out two first-class airplane tickets to Switzerland, one with her name on it and one with Li's. "Oh," she said, trying to imagine what Li had in mind. "That is so nice of you. I'd really love to go to Zurich on vacation, but right now, I'm so backed up with work, what with the gallery and the restaurant, that I just can't get away."

"I wasn't planning a vacation."

"No? Then what are the tickets for?"

"If you notice, they are one-way tickets. I bought a villa near Lucerne. You will love the Alps." He leaned over and kissed her but she remained icily detached. "Is there a problem?"

"What are thinking? You can't seriously expect me to just up and quit my life here and move to Europe with you."

"Why shouldn't I? I have managed to put away some money. I bought the villa for us."

"What about your wife?"

"I will see that she is well taken care of. We can be very happy there and Swiss extradition laws will keep us safe."

"Safe from what?"

"From your government and my government, should any financial irregularities ever arise in the future."

"For God's sake Sha-sha, I don't know what to say. We haven't been seeing each other for over a year..."

"That was not for my lack of trying," he interrupted. "Every time I call you, you always have some excuse."

"We both lead busy lives. I assumed that like me, you'd come to realize that our relationship wasn't going anywhere and was essentially over."

"I never assumed that."

"I don't know what to say," she repeated and felt herself beginning to sweat. Li had obviously put a lot of thought into this and she didn't know how to go about convincing him that she wasn't going to be a part of his plans. "I'm involved in a relationship." She closed her eyes and fell back against the seat. She was the one who'd made sex a part of their relationship and had used it solely to lure him into investing with Sayid. It was clear that he saw the two of them as a couple and now he seemed sincerely hurt by her rejection. She felt bad about that but her decision was never going to change.

Li also sat back and took another drag on his cigarette. "With the Jew?" he said quietly. She opened her eyes and turned towards him. "Yes, I know all about your dalliances with Mr. Himmelfarb. I didn't know whether it was serious." He let out an audible sigh. "Judging by the amount of time you spend with him, I should have realized it was."

She felt the hair on the back of her neck stand up. "Have you been spying on me?"

"Don't be naïve. My government has invested a lot of money on your recommendations. It would have been irresponsible of me not to have done background checking."

He spoke in a calm, but eerily threatening tone. "I'm going," she said as she reached for the handle, but the door was locked.

"We are not yet finished," he said.

"I am. Let me out." He grabbed her wrist and bent it back. "Goddammit, you're hurting me."

"Don't be in such a hurry. I'll take you home. As I was saying, we have items yet to discuss." He released her arm.

She began to massage her wrist. "What items?"

"I have," he paused, "certain needs that you can still fulfill for me." He crushed out his cigarette in the ashtray in the door's armrest, unzipped his pants and exposed himself.

She gave a sarcastic laugh. "That you can take care of with you own hand. It's far too small an item for me to waste my time with." Immediately she regretted the insult.

"You can make it a bigger item."

"Forget it, Sha-sha."

"Why? Does the Jew mean that much to you?" His voice grew slightly louder and more animated. "I wonder how he'd feel if he knew how much time you are spending with Steve Assanti? Or should I say Sayid?" She turned sharply in his direction and stared at his face. The corners of his lips moved just slightly up. "It would be a shame if some rather compromising photos showed up in Himmelfarb's mail box."

"I don't have the slightest idea what you're talking about."

He rolled down the window and motioned to one of his agents to hand him a camera. "We took these tonight. That dress you are wearing is very fetching."

She watched the images of her and Sayid taken earlier that night as the flashed by on the camera's LCD display. "So what of it? There's nothing in these pictures that is compromising."

"Taken by themselves, that is true." He reached down to the floor, picked up a large envelope, took out several photos and them handed to her. "But placed in context with these, they do not paint a very pretty picture." She looked at some grainy black and white photos of her walking around naked in her apartment, and then Sayid, also nude appearing with her. "I know you're wondering how I got these, and to be honest, they are fakes. Isn't it marvelous what can be done with digital images and a computer these days."

She shoved the pictures back in his lap. "He won't believe this."

"Are you sure? Anyway, is Himmelfarb and the American Government aware of Mr. Hassan's associates? And I'm not referring just to Hassan's German banker friends, but to his contacts with men of Middle Eastern descent with some rather nefarious connections. Also, there is the little matter of all the money you made on my investments."

"That's all been declared. I've paid my taxes. I've nothing to hide."

"Nothing? Did you ever register as an agent acting on behalf of the Chinese government? I believe that failure to declare is a federal offense, punishable by large fines and jail time. And when they follow your connection to Hassan, they will find his connections with terrorists, and that, they take a very dim view of indeed."

She felt his eyes boring straight into her. Much of what he said, like the references to terrorists, she took as bullshit, no more real than those faked photos of her cavorting around naked with Sayid. But could she risk it – risk having Jake see the fake photos, risk prosecution, risk that there might be some truth to the terrorist connection? It was probably easier for the time being to just mollify this pathetic old man and deal with it later. After all, they hadn't had any contact in well over a year. Maybe he just woke up that morning feeling particularly horny. She reached down to his penis and began to caress it, hoping that he'd be satisfied with a simple hand job. "I'm sorry I was so cross. It's been a long day. I guess I'm tired," she said as she felt his erection grow in her hand.

"There now, that's much better," he said. "Okay, you can climb on top now." It was not what she was hoping to hear, so she just continued to stroke. "Stop. Get on me now."

She dutifully withdrew her hand, took off her coat, pulled her panties down and her dress up and then straddled him. Between the threatening circumstances and her own dryness, the act was far more uncomfortable than she'd ever experienced. For this she was grateful. She didn't want to feel anything less than total disgust but she also knew she couldn't show that to Li.

"That's a very a pretty necklace," he said. What a stupid dick this guy is, she thought. Here I'm being basically raped by this asshole and he bothers to give compliments. "My wife would like such a necklace."

She stopped moving, reached behind her neck and unclasped the diamond choker. "Here, give it to her as a present from me." She handed it to him, hoping that in return, he might let her leave.

"And the earrings?" he said. She slowly took out the studs and gave them over as well, then started to move off him. "Where are you going?" Despite feeling like she wanted to vomit, she resumed the sex.

When he finally indicated that he was finished, she again tried to move off of him, but he kept her on top of him by holding down her shoulders. "That takes care of one of my needs, now I have just a couple of others." He moved his hands around her neck and slowly pressed his thumbs against it. "From now on, when I call you, if I leave a message, I'll expect a call back in less than an hour. If you're in New York and I want to see you, I'll expect you to be at my residence in less than an hour."

"Can you take me home now?" was her whispered response.

"In time. I have one more issue. On doing an audit on my transactions, I found about a hundred and fifty million dollars unaccounted for."

"That you'll have to take up with Assanti. I know nothing about that."

"I prefer to have you take care of it. You made what, thirty, forty million off my accounts? That will be a start. Where you get the rest is your problem, not mine."

"I don't have that kind of money sitting around in a bank. Most of it is tied up in artwork. And there is no way I can come up with anything like a hundred fifty million dollars."

It came flying at her so fast that she had no time to prepare for the back of Li's hand as it smacked against the side of her face. "You damn whore," he shouted and slapped her again. "Do not tell me you can't. You can and you will. Do we have an understanding?"

She knew if she tried to speak, she'd start to cry and whatever else happened, she wasn't going to let that happen in front of him. She slowly nodded. "Good. You have about a million and a half in your Citibank account. I'll expect to have that transferred to me by Friday."

She was beginning to wonder what Li didn't know about her. "I assume to the same account at the Bank of China that we'd used before." She spoke just above a whisper.

Li cleared his throat. "No. Use this account." He handed her a business card of a Zurich bank with a numbered account written on the back. "Are we clear about everything?" She again nodded. "All right then, you can get off now."

She rolled off him and on to the seat, pulled up her panties and slipped on her coat. "Can you take me home now?"

Li looked at his watch. "It's late and I'm tired, as is my driver." He unlocked the car doors. "Find your own way home." She opened the door, but he grabbed her arm before she could leave. She couldn't look at him. "We could have been happy in Lucerne. Then again I suppose, once a whore, always a whore." He released his grip.

She felt like a zombie walking down 72nd to Broadway. As if on autopilot, she went into a Duane-Reade drugstore and bought an instant ice pack to put on her mouth where Li had struck her. She caught a cab back to her apartment and went straight to her kitchen, took a bottle of Grey Goose vodka from the freezer, poured a tall glass and headed to the bedroom. She'd always assumed that she could never hate anyone enough to murder them, but at that moment, were it within her means, she'd have murdered Li. And no simple execution for him – she wanted him to suffer as she'd suffered. As a physician, she knew she'd be suffering psychological repercussions from Li's assault for some time to come. Her cell rang. Fearing it was Li not wanting to waste a moment to test her, she didn't look at the phone. Only after the ringing stopped did she dare to see that it was Jake who'd called.

She drank half of the vodka while she tried to compose a story to say to him. She looked at the clock on her nightstand. One-thirty. Proabably best to wait until morning, she thought. She finished the vodka and was about to get ready for bed when Jake called again. "Hey, hope I didn't wake you." he said.

"No," her voice cracked as she answered.

"What's wrong?" he immediately asked.

Let me get this right she thought. "Oh Jake, I was attacked tonight."

"My God! Are you okay?"

"I think so."

"What happened?"

She took a breath. "I had dinner with my potential client on the upper west side. Afterwards, I was walking down 73rd, or maybe 72nd towards Broadway to catch a cab. It was dark and a man came up behind me and grabbed my purse. I screamed but no one was around. I should have just let him take the damn purse and ran, but when I struggled, he pushed me down. Then he dragged me in an alleyway and…"

"And what?"

She heard the anxiety in Jake's voice. "And he started to rape me."

"Oh Jesus."

"I pleaded with him to stop. I gave him my jewelry, you know, the diamond choker you bought me for my birthday. He took it, but that didn't stop him. I guess I was lucky because a group of college kids were walking on the other side of the street and I managed to scream and he ran off."

"My God! Did you call the police?"

"No."

"Why not?"

"Jake, I worked in an ER once upon a time and saw a number of sexual assaults, and saw how the cops handled it. I wasn't going through that."

"Did you at least go to an emergency room?"

"I just told you, I worked in one. If I'd gone, I'd still be sitting around waiting to see a doctor, who'd call the police, who'd get a rape kit, etc., etc. My only injury is where my face hit the pavement when he pushed me down. I've got medical training. I know nothing's broken. He didn't ejaculate. I'll go tomorrow or the next day to my OB/GYN to get a test for an STD and to make sure everything is okay down there, but I'm sure it is."

"I'm coming down tonight."

"Jake, honey, it's the middle of night. I'm really going to be okay. I just want to go to bed. I'll call you tomorrow. Good night."

"I love you."

Only after she'd hung up did it strike her what he'd said. He'd never said it before, but then again, neither had she. She tore off her clothes not caring that she ripped her dress. She was never going to wear it again anyway. She took a quick, hot shower then fell on her bed, but couldn't sleep. She tried meditating, but it didn't help. She lay in the dark, eyes wide open, until at around quarter to four, she heard what sounded like the door to her apartment unlocking. She pulled up the covers to her face so that only her eyes peered out. A light went on in the hallway and she heard footsteps approaching her bedroom. The door slowly swung open and silhouetted against the light stood Jake.

She sat up from beneath the blankets. "I didn't mean wake you," he said, "but I was damned sure you weren't going to be alone."

FOURTEEN

It was a sudden shudder from Mia, not the ringing of his cell phone that awoke Jake. "What time is it?" he asked her.

She reached over his chest and picked up his watch from the bed stand. "Quarter after five. I wonder who is calling." She put the watch back and curled up around her pillow in a fetal position. In the three weeks since the rape incident, Jake had been with her constantly. She had, on a number of occasions, tried to convince him that she was fine and he could go back to his place in Vermont and run his company and foundation. Stockbridge was not Manhattan. She was safe. His response was always the same – he wasn't needed for making cheese and the foundation, such as it was, could be run from anyplace. She didn't argue, especially at night. "I hate it when the phone rings in the middle of the night," she said.

Five-fifteen wasn't exactly the middle of the night, but was very early. He went over to the dresser and picked up his phone. "It was my brother," he announced and called him back. "Hey David, what's up? Goddammit, when? Fuck, how's Rosalie? Uh-huh… When's the funeral? Yeah…okay, See you then. Bye."

He got back into the bed. "Who died?" she asked.

"My uncle Lenny."

"Oh, I'm so sorry."

He wrapped himself around her. "He had lung cancer. Actually, it's a blessing I suppose. I know he'd been really sick and in a lot of pain."

"You never told me."

"You've had enough to deal with. Anyway, when he was diagnosed, it was stage three or four and they gave him six months. That was more than three years ago, so for his last act, Lenny beat the odds, which for an old gambler, isn't a bad way to go out. The funeral is day after tomorrow."

"So soon?"

"Jews like to get you in the ground fast. It's supposed to be within 24 hours, but these days we make accommodation for out-of-towners. I have to go."

"Of course."

"Um, would you come with me?" He was sure she was going to say no and began to think of reasons to convince her, so he was surprised when she readily agreed.

The funeral home was a large neo-classical building in Queens designed to hold up to four funerals concurrently. Jake and Mia were greeted by a heavyset middle-aged man in a black suit sporting a black skullcap on a shiny bald head. "Is that the rabbi?" Mia asked.

"Doubt it. Probably just one of the undertakers."

"How does he keep that hat from falling off?" she whispered.

"Superglue."

They were directed to the hall on the second floor where the service for Lenny would take place. A line of mourners stretched out from a small waiting room where his mother and father, aunt Gertrude and cousin Rosalie sat accepting condolences. A man looking like a taller, younger and clean-shaven version of Jake walked up behind them and tapped Jake on the back. "What's with the beard? You becoming a Lebovitcher?"

Jake turned around. "Just saving money on razors," he replied as he gave the man a bear hug. "This spindly schmuck is my little brother, David. David, meet Mia Jang."

"So this is the famous Mia you've been talking about forever. I'd assumed you were a figment of my brother's imagination."

"Forever?" she said.

"Forever. Or at least since he went to college." David stood back and looked her over. "My apologies, Yakov. She is as stunning as you said. I thought your description of her was just an amalgamation of all those Asian porn stars you like to watch."

"Gee, thanks David."

"Mia, how do you tolerate my brother's sense of humor, or rather lack of such? Anyway, come with me and let me introduce you to my partner, Ben." He took her hand and led her off. One thing Jake always admired about David was how easy he was with strangers. The genes for being gregarious had obviously skipped him and gone to his younger brother.

"Jacob? Is that you?" Howard Podansky was an old friend. Jake couldn't help but notice that he looked like a younger, slightly thinner version of the funeral worker who'd greeted them at the door.

"Howie, my God! Haven't seen you in what, twenty years? I didn't recognize you."

"Nor I you. I heard you were making big bucks on Wall Street, but you don't look like my stock broker."

"I quit that years ago. I live in Vermont mostly now and own an artisanal cheese company and run a charitable foundation."

"That doesn't sound like the Jake Himmelfarb I remember. As I recall, you were the kid who used to win all the other kids' quarters when we'd skip Hebrew school to play poker in the dairy kitchen at shul."

"You remember poorly. It was the meat kitchen. The dairy kitchen was always crowded with old ladies. So what are you up to these days?"

"I'm a CPA living in Brooklyn Heights. Married, two daughters aged five and three. Very exciting life."

"How come you came?"

"David called me. We're actually fairly close. His daughter attends the same daycare as my youngest and they're best friends. So who's doing the service?"

"I don't have the faintest. Lenny wasn't very religious." He started to laugh. "I remember one Yom Kippur, I think it was the year after my Bar Mitzvah so I guess I was fourteen. Anyway, during a morning break, Lenny comes up to me and asks me if I want to go to Belmont. He assures me we'll be back before the closing service. I naturally agree. Of course we don't get back until way after dark. We go to my folks' place where everyone's eating their break-the-fast meal. Gussie is beside herself. My mother is hysterical and my father is screaming that he's ordered sturgeon and the deli's delivered whitefish. We walk in and Gussie runs up to Lenny, throws her arms around him and thanks

God for having sealed him in the book of life. My mother isn't as generous. She goes up to her brother and demands to know where he and I have been. Funny, she didn't seem that concerned that I had been missing. Anyway, when Lenny says we were at the racetrack, my mother and father go ballistic. How could he spend the holiest day of the year gambling on horses? And what kind of uncle corrupts a young boy? Lenny's response was simply, 'What's the big deal? We didn't eat.'"

Howie howled at the story just as Mia returned. "That sounds like Lenny. I just hope you don't get Shmuluvitz to do the service. My grandfather's funeral was here and he did that one. I think that Rebbi Shmuluvitz is a little too fond of the Slivovitz. His whole eulogy was some incomprehensible rambling about being a king and wearing three crowns. "

"Howie, let me introduce you to my friend Mia."

Howie turned to her. "Just a friend?" he asked.

"Jake is rather shy about using the adjective of my sex before the noun friend. I'm not so reticent. I refer to him as my boyfriend."

"Jake always was the luckiest kid I knew. Oh, there's Rosalie. I'll catch you two later."

"Remind me who Rosalie is?" she asked when Howie left.

"She's Lenny and Gussie's, that's short for Gertrude, daughter. She's a writer at the Times. I think that woman standing next to her is her partner."

"Your family's got a lot of gay members. I think it's great how accepting they are."

"Don't give them too much credit." The line started moving. "I guess we'll see them after the service. And by the way, when did you ever call me your boyfriend?"

When the service was over, the man from the funeral home who had first greeted Jake and Mia when they arrived announced directions for those travelling to the gravesite, as well as the schedule for minyan services for the coming week to be held at Jake's parents' home. Jake explained the Jewish customs of mourning – the immediate family spends the next week at home while visitors supply their meals and allow them to hold twice-daily prayer services. Yet it didn't end there. The first thirty days were the period of intense mourning with the following ten months considered a less intense period. Only then was the headstone placed on the grave, signaling the end of mourning.

"I had no idea," she said.

"Yeah, Jews do death well."

"Going to the cemetery?" David asked Jake.

"I suppose. Where is it?"

"It's out in Elmont."

"So perfect, right near Belmont race track. Are you okay with going?" he asked Mia.

"Of course."

"Why don't you both ride with me and Ben. Howie's going with us too." Jake agreed and the five of them piled into David's car, with Mia seated in the back between Howie and Jake while David drove with Ben in the front seat.

"Smuluvitz came through as always, again with the three crowns." Howie said. "I'm sure he was tipsy. He kept getting Lenny's name wrong. Lou, Leon, Larry. I was waiting to hear Lavern."

"Didn't you just love when Dot shouted 'It's Leonard!' at him?" said David.

"Dot?" Mia whispered to Jake.

"Dot, or Dottie or Dorothy. My mom. Cyrus is my father. Dot and Cy," he explained.

"Hey, anyone want to smoke?" asked Howie.

"After that," said David, "I need to."

Howie reached into his coat, took out a joint and lit it up. "This is really good stuff." He handed it to Mia, who promptly took a deep drag on it, coughed as she exhaled then handed it on to Jake. "So what do you do for a living?" she asked Howie.

"I'm a CPA. Very exciting work."

Jake took a hit of the pot then handed it Ben who took the joint, but didn't smoke any. "Do you want some honey?" he asked David.

"You know I probably shouldn't, but I just had a drug test last week and won't get another for at least six months. Why the hell not." David took the joint from Ben, took a hit and handed it back to Howie.

"They give you drug tests where you work?" Mia asked.

"David works in a rather high security place," Jake explained.

"Really," she said. "What do you do?"

"I'm in computer security. Mostly I spend my time verifying that the data systems that banks use are secure."

"The Himmelfarb math genes," she said.

"I suppose, but unlike my brother, I actually make a living from that aptitude. And it's how I met Ben. He works for Citibank in IT."

"I've made money off my math abilities," Jake protested. "Uncle Lenny could tell you, if he wasn't so dead."

After the burial, they returned to Jake's parents' apartment, which was already filled with people. "You ready to meet my parents?" Jake asked. Mia nodded. "No one's ever ready. Maybe you should ask Howie for some more pot. Just don't take them seriously. I don't. As for aunt Gussie, she'll probably add 'ala' to the end of your name. I don't know where that comes from, but she'll call me Jake-ala, my brother's David-ala. I think she even calls her daughter Rosala. She doesn't add that to names of adults, her definition of an adult being anyone her age or older. If she can't remember your name, you'll just be Tattala, which I suppose is the generic form."

They washed their hands using a pitcher of water that had been left outside of Cy and Dottie's apartment. Jake explained it was another Jewish custom when returning from a cemetery. They walked into the apartment that was packed with family and friends talking loudly and eating bagels and sandwiches off food platters. "Why are there sheets over the mirrors?" Mia asked.

"Another custom in a shiva house," he explained.

"And I thought the Chinese had an abundance of traditions. I had no idea that Judaism was so steeped in rituals. The Jews that I've known were totally secular like you."

"Both cultures are really old. When you've been around for all those millennia, you end up with a lot of mishegas."

"Misha-what?"

"Craziness."

She laughed. "I think it's kinda neat."

"Come on. My father's over by the booze." They pushed their way through the crowd and found Cy acting as bartender."

"Boychik," he said grabbing Jake by the collar and kissing his forehead. "I'd thought by now you'd have lost the beard. I can't tell if you're a hippie or a black-hat."

"Hey pop, how's it going?"

"How's it going? We just buried your uncle. How should it be going? Here." He handed Jake a glass filled with Canadian Club whisky. "And who is this?" he asked looking at Mia.

"This is my friend, Mia Jang."

She held out her hand, but Cy hesitated. "Friend?" he asked slowly with his voice rising up in a glissando of half an octave.

"Girlfriend," Jake reluctantly elaborated.

"You've got an oriental girlfriend?"

"Asian, dad. She's a woman, not a rug."

"What, what – what'd I say?"

"He's just being ornery, Mr. Himmelfarb," she said.

"Well," Cy said, "I'm just a little surprised. Not that you're ori... Asian, but that such a pretty girl like you would put up with my bedraggled son." He pushed her hand aside and held out his arms. "I don't want a handshake, I want a hug." After they released from their embrace, Cy poured two more glasses of whisky, handing one to her and keeping the other for himself. The three held out their glasses to each other.

"L'Chaim," Mia quickly said, eliciting looks of wonder from both Jake and his father. "L'Chaim," they both echoed.

"Have you introduced Mia to your mother yet?" asked Cy.

"Not yet," he answered.

"Oy gevult. Better let me. Come, darling." Cy took Mia's hand and led her off.

Jake trailed behind them. A number of people had lined up to pay their respects to his mother, so they stood and waited for the crowd to disperse before making the introductions. Then Jake heard the familiar sound of his aunt's voice call *Jake-ala*. "Aunt Gussie," he said, walking over to where she sat on a small, hard chair.

"Rosalie, come see your cousin."

While Jake chatted with his aunt and cousin, he was aching to hear what was transpiring between Mia and his mother, and paying no attention to anything Gertrude or Rosalie said.

"Dot, I want you to meet Mia," he heard his father say.

"Hello, dear. I noticed you at the funeral." Dorothy said holding her hand out. "Did you know my brother well?"

"Actually, no," Mia confessed.

"Mia is a friend of Jacob's."

" Jacob's friend?" Dorothy asked.

"Yes. Mia is his very good friend. His girlfriend."

"Oh. I didn't know Jacob was seeing anybody. He never tells me anything. How long have you known about this?" Even from where he stood, Jake knew his mother was speaking as though Mia weren't there. He inched closer to them.

"Five minutes," Cy replied.

"Is it serious?"

"I don't know," he answered. "Is it?" he asked Mia.

"You'd better ask Jake that, but as far as I'm concerned, I'd say yes."

"Oh," said Dorothy. "She's not Jewish." Jake cringed at hearing that and knew he had to get over there immediately, but Gussie was deep in conversation about Rosalie and Rosalie's job and her partner Alice, and he didn't want to be rude.

Cy smirked. "Noooo. Gee, Dot, I'd never have guessed. You're so perceptive. What gave it away?"

"Gai kakhen afenyam," she told her husband. "Let me warn you about the Himmelfarb men dear, if you haven't already learned from my son. They think they're so smart and so clever. But they're no different from any other man. They're all obnoxious idiots. Come, sit here by me," she said patting the chair next to her. "We have much to discuss. Cy, go bring her a plate of food. She's all skin and bones. And bring me a cheese Danish."

When Jake saw Mia sit down next to his mother, he took this as a signal that his mother wasn't going to have a coronary and it was best to leave the two of them alone. Other visitors came up to see his aunt and cousin, so he excused himself and went to get some food. He started to assemble a sandwich from one of the deli platters when a woman walked beside him and grabbed a pickle off of the tray. "You're Rosie's partner Alice, right?" he asked her.

"Yes. And you're her cousin Jake."

"I didn't think you'd remember me."

"Remember you? Are you kidding? I wish I could forget you. Every night when I watch the news and they announce the names of those boys killed in Iraq, I remember what you told me before we got into that mess. You were right, and I feel so damned guilty."

"Guilty? Why?"

"Because I did nothing with what you told me."

"At the time, you were right. You acted as any responsible journalist would have. What I told you could not be verified. What else could you do?"

"I don't know. Something."

"You've got nothing to feel guilty about."

"Tell that to Karen Rogers."

"Who's she?"

"She lives in my apartment building, with her three kids. Two months ago her husband came home from Iraq in a flag-draped coffin."

"I'm sorry," he said.

"Me too. Good to see you again. If you ever come upon information again, call me."

"That's not going to happen. I live a quiet life in Vermont now," he said.

"Lucky you." She chomped on the pickle and walked away.

That was cheery he thought. "Mr. Jakie!" He instantly recognized the voice as that of Mirabella Cuerto, the maid who had been cleaning his parents' apartment for years.

"Mirabella," he kissed her on the cheek. "It's been like forever."

"It has," she said with her heavy Guatemalan accent. "I know your mama needed someone to set up and clean, so I come in on my off day."

"That's so good of you."

"Of course I do it. Your family is my family. Only problem is I have to leave by three and I'm afraid people will still be here."

"Don't worry about it. If you have to go, then go. Others will clean."

"No, I know your mama. She's very fussy about cleaning. It is just that I have to go to a closing on a house."

Jake smiled. "You're buying a house. That's wonderful. After all these years and all that hard work. Definitely go to the closing. I'm so happy for you."

"It is not that big a deal."

"What do you mean? It's a very big deal. To finally have a home of your own, it's the American dream."

"I've been through six of these closings so far. All you do is sit around a big table and some lawyer keeps shoving papers for you to sign."

"Six closings? What, have you been refinancing?"

"I no refinance. This is the sixth house I buy."

"Sixth house? How is that possible?"

"The mortgage man, he arranges it. I buy the houses, they give me the mortgage then I rent the houses for a little while until the price goes up and then I sell it."

"So you own like two houses at a time, one to live in and one to rent."

"Not really. I only sold two houses so far. With this new one, I will own five, four of which I will rent until the price goes up enough."

"And the banks are loaning you all the money," he said incredulously.

"Si. Eat now. I go make fresh coffee."

Howie walked up to him just as he was biting down on his sandwich. "So what do you think?" he asked.

"About what?"

"I don't know what the fuck what."

Jake wasn't sure what to make of Howie's semi-coherent rambling. "Are you all right?"

"I need to eat something," Howie replied as he grabbed a paper plate and plopped a dollop of potato salad on it. "This is a like a trip back to the eighties, only everybody's older, yet oddly, much unchanged."

Jake glanced over to where Mia appeared to be in intense conversation with his mother. "That's what I'm afraid of. Maybe it's because we smoked dope like we did back then. But I gotta say, I don't think my mother could possibly have talked to a shiksa, had I dated one back then, as much as she's talking with Mia."

"That's because back then, the closest we came to a shiksa was a Penthouse centerfold whose pubes had conveniently been airbrushed out of the photo to entice our oversexed, adolescent minds. You wanna step outside and have another smoke?"

Jake's forehead crinkled at the suggestion. "It's like fucking two-thirty in the afternoon. We already got high much earlier than I've ever do."

"For old time's sake?" Howie asked.

"Eh, what the fuck," and out they walked. After they had smoked another joint, they walked around the neighborhood, noting the places where many of the old mom-and-pop stores that used to line the streets had since morphed into national chain stores such as Starbucks and Kinkos. Before they returned, Howie offered Jake a joint to take back and smoke with Mia, adding that the best sex he had with his wife was always after they'd smoked marijuana. Jake didn't object. Jake returned to his parents' apartment and couldn't believe that Mia and his mother were still deep in conversation. "I think we should probably be going," he told them.

"Show her your old room," Dot ordered.

"Nah ma, Mia doesn't want to see any of that."

"Yes I do. I'd love to see where little Jakie grew up."

"Show her!" his mother again commanded. Jake, his shoulders slumped, led Mia away. "And stand up straight."

They walked to the room that Jake and his brother had shared as children. "This is the shrine," Jake said opening the door. The walls were still covered with posters of sporting events and rock bands, and the beds were neatly covered with Yankee-themed sheets. "I think my mother has saved every damn thing I ever brought home."

"You exaggerate," said Mia.

"No, what my brother says is true." David was standing at the door. He walked over to the desk upon which sat a PC. "This," he said pointing to the computer, "is about the only thing that wasn't here when we grew up. The rest is authentic. My mother saved every report card, class picture, award, test or paper that we ever brought home."

Mia was skeptical. "Every one?"

"From kindergarten through college. It was becoming a fire hazard so I told her the paper had to go."

"Oh, that's such a shame. I would love to have seen what Jake wrote in second grade."

David turned on the computer. "You can. Dot wouldn't part with anything until I agreed to scan it all so she'd have it." He took a blank CD that was sitting on the desk and put it into the computer drive. "As soon as this thing finishes booting up, I'll burn you a copy."

"Oh God, David, you wouldn't."

"Yes," Mia insisted.

"I'll wait for you two in the living room."

"Did she like your room?" his mother asked him.

"It was the cultural highlight of her year." David and Mia returned as she triumphantly held up the CD in her right hand. "Well, we really do have to get back to the city."

"You coming to any minyans?" Dorothy asked.

"I'll be here tomorrow morning," he answered.

"And what about the evening?"

"Don't push it, ma."

Mia embraced Dorothy. The sight was so unthinkable that Jake wasn't sure if what he was witnessing was actually occurring or the manifestations of a THC induced hallucination like in those 1930s anti-pot movies. Before they got into Jake's car, he had enough sense to hand the keys to Mia. "So?" he asked as they headed towards the tunnel to Manhattan.

"So what?"

"So what did you think of that?"

She smiled and shook her head. "You know, for a funeral, I'm afraid to confess that I had a good time. I actually enjoyed myself. I loved meeting your friends and family. I absolutely adored your father, and your brother. Howie is hysterical, especially for an accountant."

"And my mother?"

"I like your mother, and I think she likes me. She told me that if I could get you to do just one thing, I'd have her blessing to, let me get this right, 'shtup' you. Is shtup what I think it is?"

He nodded. "What do you have to do?"

"Get you to shave off that beard. She wants to see your old, uh, is the word 'punim?'"

"That's the word."

"Well, will you?"

"Do you want me to?"

"God, yes. I've been wanting you to shave it off for a long time now."

"Why didn't you say so?"

"I don't know. Will you?"

He sighed. "Yeah, sure. Why not? Anyway, I heard the oddest thing today. My parents' maid had to leave to close on the purchase of a house."

"What's weird about that?"

"Well, she's just an immigrant domestic worker from Guatemala. And working for my parents, she's making on the low end of that pay scale."

Mia frowned at Jake. "I think it's wonderful that people can still pull themselves up economically. I'm surprised that you, of all people, would be so condescending about it."

"I was happy for Mirabella. Believe me, that wasn't what surprised me. It was when she told me that it was the sixth or seventh property she was buying. She buys houses, rents them for a short time and sells them. I can't understand how she'd qualify for mortgages to buy all those properties. The houses don't have a guaranteed income, and she couldn't possible demonstrate enough income to support the loans. Then she told me the interest rates, which were quite low. They were all balloon loans that would reset in several years at much higher rates. I warned her to make sure she sold the houses before the rates jumped. I hope she understands the implications if she doesn't."

Mia honked on the horn. "Idiot jerk, changing lanes without even signaling," she snarled. "Look, I'm sure the banks wouldn't do anything beyond reason. If they are okay with it, I'm sure your maid will be fine."

Jake hoped she was right. She probably was. There was something about Mirabella's story that sounded oddly familiar. He just couldn't place where he'd heard it before.

FIFTEEN

Mia got out of a taxi at Columbus Circle and headed for Jean-Georges. She spotted David as soon as she walked into the main dining room. He was sipping a Côte-du-Rhone at a table towards the back. "Sorry I'm late," she told him as she kissed him on each cheek.

"No problem. You told me to block out the whole afternoon. I thought Jake was coming with you."

The maître d' pulled out a chair for her and asked if she cared for a drink. She picked up the wine bottle on the table and examined the label. "This is fine for me," and he filled her goblet. "Jake had to go up to Vermont. Some problem on the farm – something about a worker sick with the flu and he needed to pitch in."

David rolled his eyes. "I love my brother, but I've got to tell you, I'm dubious about this farm and cheese-making thing. It's going on three years now, and the operation has yet to turn a profit."

"He does it for the foundation, not for income."

"The foundation raised a grand total of fifty-six thousand dollars last year, and none of it was from the sale of cheddar. It came from donations. I alone gave ten grand. He took only one dollar in income from his farm, and none from the foundation."

"He must have money saved from his Wall Street days," she said chomping on a breadstick.

"Most of his assets were gobbled up in his divorce, not that that bitch Debbie needs it. I heard she married Art Morrison, so she's loaded. My only hope is that when she dumps Morrison, or he her, that she takes him to the cleaners."

"Not likely. Unlike your trusting brother, you can bet that Morrison had her sign an ironclad pre-nup."

"You seem surprised at Jake's financial situation. You've being seeing each other for some time. I'd have thought that by now, you'd know each other's lives inside out."

She took a sip of wine. "Everything's a process. We're not married so when it comes to our professions, we each respect the other's privacy. If and when he wants to share, I'm happy to listen."

"You still have the restaurant in Lenox?"

"Stockbridge, and yes, I still own half of it, but I'm not involved in the day-to-day operations. I leave all that to my partner. If you think farms are money pits, try owning a restaurant. That dollar Jake made last year was one dollar more than I made from Napa-East."

"And the gallery?"

"That's done a little better, especially since the economy has picked up. Which brings me to Frederick Evanson. I recall you telling me at your uncle's funeral that he's one of your favorite painters."

"God yes. Why?"

"Because I've just signed up to represent him. There's going to be a show of his oils at the Strathmore gallery in April followed by a showing at my place in the Berkshires in June. I'm expecting that between the two, everything will sell out. That is why I asked you to clear your schedule. After lunch, I thought we'd go to his studio to select pieces, that is, if you're interested in coming."

"Interested? Are you shitting me? I'd love to. God, I can't believe my idiot brother picked an art dealer for his squeeze. Jake's idea of great art is dogs playing poker."

"I know, what are you going to do? He does like nudes," she said.

"He likes porn." They both laughed as the waiter delivered appetizers to the table. "I don't recall ordering."

"I took the liberty before I came," she explained. "I know the chef."

"Really. What are we having?"

"To be honest, I don't have the faintest. I simply told him to make us whatever he thought we'd like. I can't tell you how nice it is to share a meal with someone who's willing to be adventurous. Jake's palate abhors the unfamiliar, although I keep trying."

They ate their way through five courses and downed one and a half bottles of the red wine. Before the waiter brought dessert, David excused himself to go to the restroom. Mia accepted the bus boy's offer of coffee, and as she sat sipping, a familiar voice came from behind. "How have you been?" The voice sent a chill down her spine. "We need to talk before your friend returns." Li took the chair just vacated by David. "By the way, who is he?"

"That's none of your concern." She slowly put her cup down on the table, trying her best to conceal her shaking hand.

"Everything in your life is my concern. Especially when it comes to the money I've yet to receive."

"I sent you over a million dollars."

"That leaves only a hundred and forty-nine million still owed the Chinese people."

She let out a derisive snivel. "The Chinese people, that's a joke. You think I'm so stupid not to realize that you had me wire the money to a numbered Swiss account and not the Bank of China? You're keeping the people's money."

"I'm a person, and I'm Chinese, so I'm one of the Chinese people."

"Don't try sounding witty or clever, Sha-sha. You don't have it in you. I'm working on getting you some more money. It's just that I have no liquid assets right now. You should know that. You seem to know everything else about my life."

He reached across the table and took one of the chocolate pastries off her plate. "I do know everything about your life. How you come up with the money is not my concern. Sell off some of your less liquid assets if you have to. I'll expect a deposit in that account by the end of next week. Shall we say five million? No, let's make it ten. It's coming on two months since your last payment. I need to know I can trust you." He popped the pastry into his mouth. "I can trust you, dear, can't I?" he mumbled.

"Yes," she replied softly.

He swallowed the chocolate. "Good, because I'd hate to have to disseminate certain information to other parties in interest." He got up from behind the table, walked behind her, placed both of his hands on her shoulders and bent down next to her ear. "And while we're on the subject of trust, I haven't seen you socially in a very long time. Come to my place tonight, say around eleven."

"I have to tell you, I just started having my period this morning, and I don't think you'd find it appealing." It was a good excuse, especially since it was true.

"Oh, in that case, I'll look forward to seeing you next week. By then, you'll have sent my funds, correct?" She closed her eyes and nodded once. "Good. I'll call you." He kissed the back of her neck and stood up. "By the way, the dessert was excellent," and he walked away.

She picked her napkin off her lap, dipped the corner into her water glass and wiped off her neck where he'd just planted the kiss. When David returned, he immediately noticed the distressed look on her face. "What's wrong?"

She tried to inconspicuously wipe a tear from the corner of her eye. She shook her head. "Nothing. Just my contacts are bothering me. Enjoy the chocolates."

"Bullshit. You are not the girl I left here five minutes ago. You look like your dog was just run over by a car."

Mia looked around the restaurant. She took a sip of water, and while holding the glass at her lips, spoke. "Do you see those men standing near the front getting ready to leave?"

He peered over her shoulder. "The Chinese guys?"

She nodded. "Check out the shortest one."

He spotted Li. "What of him?" She felt her eyes well up, but was determined to do her best not to cry. "What is it?" he asked again.

"Forget it. I don't want to burden you with this."

"Burden away. You're practically family. Even my mother likes you."

"She doesn't approve of me."

"She doesn't approve of anybody her sons see. You could be fucking Moses's sister Miriam and she'd find fault. But you're the first gentile lover for either of her boys that she invites to Friday night dinner. I think Debbie was married to Jake for ten months before she received such an invitation." That brought a smile to Mia. "Now that we've cleared that up, tell me what's the deal with the old guy." She turned around to look for Li. "Don't worry," David added, "he's left."

She finished off her coffee. "Okay, but not in here. Let's go for a walk."

They crossed the street and headed into Central Park. It was warmer than usual for the end of March and Mia took off her jacket and draped it over her shoulders. She didn't know where to begin or how much to reveal to David. She'd only known him for a little more than a month, but in that short time, she'd developed a sense of trust, perhaps because of the nature of his job. David, as an expert in IT security, was entrusted with a great deal of sensitive knowledge and information. He'd done work for the military, the CIA and the NSA. If they could trust him with their secrets, who was she to doubt his ability to keep things in confidence. The difference, of course, was that her secrets involved his family, not the security of the United States, or so she thought at the time.

They'd walked for nearly a quarter of a mile, and all Mia had spoken of was how beautiful the weather was and how the crocuses and daffodils were sprouting from the ground. "We didn't come here for a nature walk," he finally told her. "Get to the point of what is troubling you."

She nodded. "Last month," she paused to take a breath," I was assaulted." She waited for a reaction from David, but got none. "You don't seem surprised or shocked."

"To be honest, Jake told me some of it. He didn't go into any details, just that you'd been raped. He only told me because he was concerned for your welfare, especially with having to meet my family at Lenny's funeral. I said it was probably the best time to meet my parents since they'd be distracted by all the other people around and not be their usual overbearing selves."

David had never indicated that he knew of the attack, which she took as a good sign that his sense of propriety could be trusted. Even so, she felt it necessary to qualify what she was about to reveal. "David, what I'm going to tell you now has to remain just between us. I don't want to say anything that might get back to Jake, and that he might find hurtful. If you feel you cannot keep things from your brother, I understand and respect that, and we'll just forget we ever had this conversation. So, can I trust you that this conversation stays between us and only us?" He didn't answer right away. While his hesitation might have been construed as a sign that she shouldn't trust him, she took the opposite view, that he was actually processing what she'd said and considering his answer rather than just blurting something out. He assured her that he'd hold whatever she told him in the strictest confidence, like a priest or a psychiatrist. The only problem she had with that response was that priests and shrinks are required by law to reveal any knowledge of a crime. It had never been her intention to commit any such infraction, but based on what Li had said to her, she wasn't sure she hadn't.

"I wasn't completely honest with Jake about the rape. I wasn't assaulted by some stranger on the street. It was in the back of car, and I knew the man who did it."

"The guy you pointed out at Jean-Georges?"

"His name is Li Xuan. I've known him for years."

"Why didn't you go to the cops?"

"I couldn't. You see, I did have a relationship with him at one time. And although that ended shortly after Jake and I started seeing each other, there was a period when they overlapped."

"But that was like over a year ago, right?" She nodded. "And once the two of you were serious, you ended it with this Li guy, right? So I don't see what the problem is. Jake would certainly understand that. You should still go to the police."

"That would be useless. To begin with, it was two months ago. There is no physical evidence available, and also, he didn't exactly rape me in the traditional sense. One could draw the conclusion that it was consensual."

"Was it?"

"No."

"Then why would one draw that conclusion?"

"Because," she gulped, "Li had some incriminating evidence on me. Some of it was faked, some not, but even so, he threatened to reveal it to Jake. I didn't want to risk it."

"So you were coerced by this asshole. That, my girl, is still rape in my book. Jake isn't stupid. If you could tell what he had on you was fake, so could Jake, and I'm sure, so could the police. I'd still go to them."

"Li's a Chinese government official, and very high up. He has diplomatic immunity. The worst that would happen is that he'd be asked to leave the country, but since he's at the UN, I doubt even that. He uses his government connections to have me spied upon. After he assaulted me, he forced me to wire him money to his personal Swiss bank account."

"Talk about chutzpah. He rapes you and then blackmails you into paying him. How much did you pay?"

"About a million and a quarter."

Mia walked for several paces before she noticed that David had come to a complete stop behind her. "A million and a quarter? Dollars?" he shouted.

She walked back to him. "Not so loud please. Yes. I know I'm an idiot, but I didn't know what else to do. I was hoping that once he got that money, he'd be satisfied and leave me alone."

"A million and a quarter?" he repeated incredulously. "I had no idea you had that kind of money lying around."

"I did well back in the tech boom of the late nineties. It's what allows me to pursue my follies like a restaurant and an art gallery. It was worth it to me if it would get Li out of my life, and out of Jake's."

"God, you must really love that dufus brother of mine. I love Ben, but I'd never spend one point two-five mil on him."

"I shouldn't have either because it isn't working. Li came up to me while you were away from the table. He wants more money."

"Tell him to go fuck himself."

"He wants that also. He's expecting me to see him again at his apartment in the Waldorf next week. And before that, he wants ten million dollars more transferred to his account. I don't have that kind of money, but if I did, I might pay it. But the one thing I won't do, that I positively refuse to do, is to sleep with that creep again."

"Why would you even consider paying him?"

"Because." She shut her eyes and sighed. "Because he can link me to some financial dealings that might not have been completely above board. I've had some government experience. I served in the Clinton administration. Federal prosecutors take a dim view of governmental misconduct, especially considering my past and this Bush-Cheney administration. You've no doubt been reading about how they've politicized the Justice department. Think what political capital they'd gain by having a former member of a Democratic administration brought up on charges concerning Communist China. I don't know what to do, and I don't expect you to tell me what to do. I just needed to unburden myself to someone. I'm not sure I'd even care about facing a trial if I was sure that Jake would understand."

"Okay, now you're starting to sound like a soap opera. Don't underestimate my brother. When I was seventeen, I wanted to come out, but was terrified of my parents' reaction. I confided in Jake. True to his fashion, he had no idea that I was gay, which considering how much money I spent on clothes back then, should have been obvious. But also true to his nature, Jake insisted that he be there when I told Cy and Dottie. My parents' reaction wasn't as bad as I'd anticipated. My father thought I'd grow out of it and my mother wanted me to see a shrink. I was ready to accept that but Jake wouldn't. He made them confront the reality, that I was gay, that it wasn't a choice, and that they could either accept it or risk doing irreparable damage to themselves and me. He asked if they'd prefer I was dead. When put that way, their attitude changed. Acceptance came. Not right away, but in time, and much sooner than had he not been there. So as I said, don't underestimate Jake. And as for what you should do, can I think on it?"

She nodded and then wrapped her arms around him in a tight hug. She glanced at her watch while they were still embracing. "Shit, look at the time. We'll just barely have time to get down to Frederick's studio, if you're still interested."

"Shit, yes I'm interested. Let's go."

They spent nearly three hours going over Evanson's bold landscapes of forests so deconstructed as to appear to most observers as pure abstracts. Mia sensed a detachment, almost disinterest in David. Was it the result of her confession or simply being overwhelmed in the presence of the artistic genius she believed Evanson possessed? She wasn't sure but with the task of selecting oils at hand, she didn't have the time to worry about it. Frederick and Mia finally settled on twenty-three oils to display for the first show, with an additional ten as backups for the second showing in Stockbridge. As she was saying goodbye to Frederick, she glanced at David who looked as though he were standing on another planet. "David, are you ready to go?"

"Yeah, yeah. I must apologize Mr. Evanson. I've been consumed by this problem at work, which is such a waste since I just adore your work."

"Really? And call me Freddie, everyone else does. I thought you were bored by this whole production."

"Jesus, God, no. I'm a big fan of your work. I saw your show in Barcelona four years ago, and was blown away."

"It's kind of you to say that. Which of these oils do you like?"

"I like all of them."

"I noticed you spent a lot of time looking at that one of the nude in the meadow." Evanson tipped his head in the direction of a small, unframed canvas hanging on a wall.

"Freddie, there's a nude in that painting?" Mia asked. "Do you want to include it in the show?"

"No," he replied. "I'm not ready to sell it yet."

"Suit yourself. We really should be going, David. It's nearly eight and you still have to go back to Brooklyn." They left the Evanson's loft and headed for the subway, stopping just before the steps leading down to the station. "Thanks for today," she said. "I really appreciate having someone to vent to."

"No, thank you. To spend the day in Frederick Evanson's studio with the artist himself, I still can't believe it happened. Ben's going to be so jealous."

"Next time we'll bring him along."

"Listen, I've been thinking about your problem."

"Any ideas?" she said knowing that there was no solution.

"Not yet, but do you happen to have the account that you wired that money into for that creep?"

"Not on me, but I can get it. Why?"

"Email it to me when you get a chance."

Two days later Mia got a phone call from David. "Have you checked the balance in your account lately?" he asked. She opened her computer and clicked on the link to her Citibank account expecting a balance of less than a thousand dollars. Instead it was over a hundred thousand.

"That can't be right," she said.

"It was just a test. I needed to see if it could be done."

"You did this? How?"

"My dear, I spend all day designing and testing data security software for financial institutions."

"I thought you did spy work for the government."

"I did several years ago, but our present government thinks that a person's sexual orientation is a big a security risk. Too vulnerable to coercions, although I suspect it has more to do with the right wing fanatics this administration coddles to. Fortunately, banks care more about protecting their money than they do about who someone is fucking. They also pay a hell of a lot more than does the government. I was poking around the inscrutable Mr. Li's Swiss account. For all the secrecy that the Swiss promote about those numbered accounts, their IT security was state-of-the-art for 1995. It took me less than fifteen minutes to get into Li's account. From there I traced back the funds you transferred and reversed a hundred grand."

"That's amazing, but won't Li notice it?"

"Which is why I only did the hundred. If I'd done the whole amount, he'd have come after you, but I coded the reversal as a bank error in the original transfer. Besides, he's got over three mil in that account. He may not even catch it until I pull out the rest that you gave him." Mia said nothing. "You still there?" he asked.

"Yes. I don't know what good that would do, other than to make Li angrier with me. He'll just come after me harder."

"I suppose. It really frosts me that that son-of-a-bitch is getting rich off you. Maybe I should have the Chinese government reimburse you. After all, he represents them. You wouldn't object to that, would you?"

"Not in the least, but could you really do that?"

"In theory. The Bank of China's security is far more sophisticated than the Swiss. It's too bad you don't have an account number for them."

"Uh, actually, I do."

It was nearly midnight when David called again. "The fucking Chinese were a hell of lot better than I thought."

She felt her heart sink. "Well, thanks for trying."

"Have a little more faith in me. I said they were good, I didn't say they were impregnable. Nothing is impregnable."

"So you're going to keep trying?"

"No, because ten minutes ago, I gained access to the account you gave me. There's like six hundred million dollars in it, which explains why they guard it so well. How much do you want?" Again there was silence. "Mia? How much? I was going to do the one and a quarter million you gave Li, but I think you should get little more to cover the lost interest earnings and pain and suffering. Your thoughts?"

"One hundred fifty million."

She heard David laugh on the other end. "Why not just take the whole six hundred mil? Look girl, if I transfer one and a quarter, or even as much as two million, it may not be noticed, especially the way I will cover my tracks. They might not even bother to try and trace it because the amount of time they'd spend wouldn't be worth it. But for a hundred fifty million, they'd spend the time."

"I'm counting on them to," she said.

"Huh?"

"I don't want it transferred to my account, but to Li's Swiss account. And when you do, don't cover your tracks so well that they can't figure it out. I'm not saying to make it obvious, just make it hard enough that it looks like whoever took their money didn't want to be discovered, yet with enough evidence that they will be."

"You are a devious little girl. I'd better watch myself around you. It's brilliant, but when Li sees that much money showing up in his account, mightn't he get suspicious? If he figures out where the funds came from, he might give it back to cover his ass."

"If you can make it look like the funds came from me, he won't question it. How long will this take?"

"I'll work on it this weekend. By Monday morning, it should be complete."

"My God, David, are you sure you really want to do this? I mean, if anyone found out, it would wreck your career, maybe even send you to prison. You've got a young daughter. I can't ask you to take that risk."

"You didn't ask. I offered. It's not like I'm profiting from this. It's not even like you're profiting from this. The only one who's being impacted is Li, who's a criminal. There is a phrase in the Torah, *Justice, justice you shall pursue*. As I see it, that's all I'm doing."

"Okay, but bad things can happen even to people doing good. Just be very, *very* careful please."

"I always am."

The following Monday, she was eating breakfast at a coffee shop in the Village and speaking with Jake who was still in Vermont when a two-word text from David showed up on her cell. 'It's done.' She got off the phone with Jake and called Li. "Sha-sha, I can't see you this week. My father has taken a turn for the worse and I have to go be with him."

"You wouldn't be trying to deceive me?" he replied.

"No I wouldn't, but if you don't believe me, I'm sure you can confirm this from your other sources."

"Yes I can. Have you handled that other financial transaction that we discussed?"

"Even better, I've taken care of the entire debt."

"Well, that is good news. I knew you wouldn't disappoint me."

"And as such, I don't see any need for further communications between us. This is the last time we shall be speaking, ever."

"Well, I'm not so sure about that. I'd miss your comforting presence."

"With the money at your disposal, there are a million women who'd be happy to comfort you."

"I'd have thought a hundred and fifty million women," he said.

"That is the number. Goodbye, Sha-sha. Don't call me again." She slammed shut her cell phone not waiting for his response.

She left the city that afternoon to return to Stockbridge. As she had told Li, her father had gone into hospice care. She spent the next week at his bedside. Jake, still tied up with production issues at AV, only managed to be with her once during that time. When her father finally succumbed, she was alone with him at his bedside. For all the strife there had been between them, their relationship had mellowed in his final years. With his mind and memories slowly drained by dementia, their roles had flipped to where she was the parent and he the child. In many ways, this was the most disturbing part of his illness, and she couldn't help but wonder whether his fate awaited her. If it did, there would be no child to care for her as she had for him. She was determined to keep it that way.

In June, on the day of the summer solstice, she did what she'd been doing every day since she'd last spoken with Li. She ran a Google search on Li Xuan to see if there was any news. Nearly every day the same hits showed up on the list in the same order, but that day, a new link appeared to a posting from the Shanghai Daily. She clicked on it and read that Li had been dismissed from his official position with the government and had been arrested for malfeasance, but it gave no details.

That weekend, David, Ben and their daughter Abigail came to Stockbridge to see the Frederick Evanson show. She took David into her office and showed him the article. "I'm just sorry that I couldn't get you all your money back," he told her.

"You did way more than enough. I'll never be able to thank you."

"Just keep my brother out of trouble. You got him to shave that beard, maybe get him to get a haircut."

"That may be harder than hacking into the Bank of China." They laughed and went into the gallery to view the show. She walked two paces behind

David and Ben, holding Abigail in her arms so that they could concentrate on the oils.

"Oh, this one's my favorite, Nude in the Meadow," David said as they came to one of the last paintings. He turned around to Mia. "Didn't Freddie say he didn't want to include it?"

"Freddie?" Ben exclaimed.

"You convinced him," she said. David bent close to the picture, and noticed the red circle sticker covering the price indicating it had been sold.

"I knew it wouldn't last," he said, "not that we could have afforded it."

"Yeah, it went fast. Freddie didn't want to sell it, but when I told him how much the owner deserved it, he relented." She put down Abigail and lifted the painting off the wall. "You might want to get it reframed," she said as she turned and handed it to David.

SIXTEEN

August 2006

I t was just a glimpse, a split-second sighting on the fringe of his peripheral vision, obscured by waiters delivering meals and the cigarette smoke that hung over the bar like fog on the Thames. Just a glimpse, but enough to cause Sayid's pulse to quicken.

"Monsieur Hassan, it's been a long time since we've seen you."

"Oui Henri, a very long time. I'm living in America now. Just in Paris to finalize the sale of my flat, but I had to have one more dinner here."

"I hope the duck is to your liking."

"It's excellent. Just as I remembered. Let me ask you, I saw this woman at the bar a minute ago. She was seated at the end, but I don't see her now. I was wondering if you know who she is?"

"I don't know exactly who you saw, but if you wish, I can ask the bartender."

"Would you, please?"

He knew it couldn't be who he thought it was. Yasmin was long dead, and it was not the first time he'd seen a woman whose likeness was reminiscent of her. This girl wore the clothing of a Parisian and her hair was cropped short with streaks of various colors. Still he wanted to meet her if for no other reason than to fulfill the fantasy of being with Yasmin.

"Georges does not know her name," Henri reported back. "She's been in a few times. He thinks she works in one the boutiques in Louvre-Tuileries. He doesn't know which. Is that any help?"

Sayid shook his head. "It's not that important."

After leaving the restaurant, Sayid took a cab to Rue St-Honoré and walked up and down the avenues surrounding the Louvre, stopping outside shops to peek through their storefronts at the people inside. After an hour, he decided it was fruitless to continue looking for her, but he did remember that he still needed to buy a few gifts to bring back to New York, including a bottle of fine cognac for Arthur Morrison and a designer pocketbook for Debbie. Pilgrim/United's book of business in derivatives was over ten billion and on pace to double that volume by year's end. In addition, their brokerage in default swaps was responsible for half a trillion dollars of risk assumption. Spending a few hundred bucks on a bottle of booze and a grossly overpriced piece of leather was a bargain.

He walked into a handbag and luggage store. A matronly looking woman asked if he was looking for something in particular and he answered a designer pocketbook. She showed him several bags but he couldn't discern any appreciable differences between them. "It's for a younger woman," he explained.

"You wish to spend a thousand Euros on a little girl?"

"Oh no, not a child, she's in her early thirties I'm guessing."

"Well this is very popular," she said holding a Chanel bag. Sayid shrugged his shoulders. "Non? Perhaps a Vuitton?" He was still non-committal. "Let me get you another opinion. Jeannine!" she called. "She's closer to your age. Jeannine!"

"Quoi!" a voice answered back.

"Venez-là"

From behind a curtain she appeared as though she were making an entrance on stage. "Quoi, quoi," the girl said without looking up at Sayid, but he was stunned. There she was, the girl he'd seen at the restaurant.

"Monsieur, this is Jeannine. She speaks English, better than moi. She will help you."

"What you looking for?" she asked in that dismissive tone for which the French are famous. He said nothing. He just stood there staring at her eyes. "Do you want to buy something or just take up my time?"

"Pardon me, it's just that you look so much like a girl I used to know."

"Wonderful. Now you buy something or not?"

When he still didn't respond, she started to walk away from the counter. "Yasmin." She stopped for the briefest moment before continuing to leave. "Yasmin," he repeated.

This time she stopped and turned to him. "Did you say something?"

"Her name was Yasmin."

"Oh, your old friend. I thought you might have said Jeannine, which is my name." She came back to the counter. "So what kind of bag you looking for?"

"One for a woman in her thirties. An American. Hopefully, something that she couldn't buy in New York."

"Your girlfriend?" she asked.

He shook his head. "Wife of a business associate."

"You live in New York?"

"Yes. Do you mind if I ask you a question?"

"Depends on the question."

"I'm guessing from your accent that you're not a native. Can I ask where you come from?"

"You're not being honest with me monsieur. You never said your name."

"Stefano Assanti. And why do you say I'm not being honest?"

"Because it wasn't my accent as much as the way I look that makes you ask. Right?"

"A little of both. You dress like a Parisian woman, but you look Middle Eastern. Don't be offended. I myself was born in Egypt."

"My parents were Algerian. I have lived in France a long time."

"One last question. When do you get off work?"

She looked at her wristwatch. "The store closes in ten minutes, so I'll be leaving in a half hour or so, that is assuming you don't make us stay open any longer than necessary."

"Do you want to grab a drink or something to eat after you get off?"

"Thanks, but I have a husband to get home to."

Sayid nodded his head. "I see. Well, then I'd better not keep you any longer. Pick me out a pocketbook. Anything you'd like up to fifteen hundred Euros."

"Ah Monsieur Assanti, her husband must be important." She opened the glass case behind her and took out a blue leather bag. "I like this one. It's a Michele, and is eleven hundred. What do you think?"

"Fine, I'll take it." He handed her his Amex card. She processed the sale and then wrapped the pocketbook in a box. All the while, Sayid kept looking at her, imagining that had Yasmin lived, how much she might look like this girl. He took the package from her, thanked her for her help, and left the shop. He'd walked less than half a block before he heard her calling after him. He turned back and saw her running towards him.

"Monsieur Assanti," she said as she tried to catch her breath. "You forgot your credit card."

He took the card from her. "Shit, that wouldn't have been good. Thank you, Jeannine."

"You welcome…Stefano, or should I say…Sayid?"

He stumbled three paces backward. "There is only one way you could know my name." She didn't answer. The possibility was beyond comprehension. "My God," he whispered.

"Come," she said. "There's a small cafe down the street. We can talk." She took his hand. He followed her, feeling as lightheaded as though he'd swallowed a bottle of Ambien. They sat at an outside table away from the other diners. "I don't know where to start," she said.

"Is it really you?" She nodded. "They told me you were dead."

"I know. They tell you what they want to. As you can see, I'm quite alive."

"Why didn't you get in touch with me?"

The waiter delivered the coffees they'd ordered. She lit up a cigarette, slowly blew the smoke out the side of her mouth and took a sip of coffee. "How could I do that? You were in Afghanistan and not exactly available. Plus those people we knew in Riyadh were not very pleased with me. They told you I was dead because that is what they wanted."

"Why would they want that? They are fighting to free our people, and not just the Saudis and Egyptians, but the Palestinians as well."

"And you think having them in charge will make any difference?"

He didn't answer. "Yasmin, I loved you. I would have done anything for you."

She crushed out her cigarette in the ashtray and immediately lit up another. "I am sorry. You were a nice guy, and I did like you. But you were set up from the beginning."

"What are you talking about?"

"We did not meet by chance. You remember Ibrahim? It was his doing. He wanted us to be together, then apart. He staged my arrest. He told you I was dead, which as I said, was what they wanted. He was a shit."

"Ibrahim was martyr. He gave his life for jihad. I read how he died fighting in Indonesia."

She laughed derisively. "Some martyr. He died in Indonesia all right, but it wasn't fighting. The fat slob had a heart attack fucking two whores in a Jakarta brothel."

"But the reports of a gun battle with the police?"

"All made up. It was to everyone's benefit to have his demise promoted that way. For al-Qaeda, much better to have a fighter dying a martyr's death, and for the Indonesians, much better to have killed a terrorist than have a fat tourist drop dead in a prostitute's bed."

"How do you know all this?"

"Let's just say I heard from someone who knows and leave it at that."

"And what about your family back in Palestine and Lebanon. Have you just abandoned them?"

"I have only been to Palestine once in my life, and that was with you. My family lives in Algeria."

"And the funeral we saw for the Palestinian boy?"

"Was just some Palestinian boy. Ibrahim had heard about it and thought seeing it would sway your sentiments into joining him. He was right, I guess."

Sayid shook his head. "Why was he so interested in having me join up? There are so many others he could have much more easily recruited, and to be honest, would have made much better fighters."

"But none with your knowledge of the Boston airport in the months before 9/11, and few with as much first-hand experience of how young men behave in American society so as not to stand out. That you had all of that experience with international finance was just an unexpected bonus. When he told me that you had come up with some plan and you were going back to Europe or America, I asked if I could join you. I was sick of living like someone's child or possession, which is all that women are in that society. He refused to let me go.

I'm not sure whether it was because he didn't trust me or because he wanted to keep screwing me. Whatever, when he got wind of my plan to get out of Arabia and find you in Germany, he ordered me eliminated."

"I can't believe it. How did you get out?"

"I did a favor for the boy they sent to execute me. In exchange, he let me escape. I got out with nothing but literally the clothes on my back. I still held a French passport, so I came here, changed my name and the color of my hair, and got on with the rest of my life. The one thing I couldn't risk was contacting anyone with any connection to the organization, including you." She glanced again at her watch and put out her cigarette. "I really have to be going."

"Where? To your supposed husband?"

"That part is true. I am married, with a two-year-old son." She leaned across the table and kissed his cheek. "Au revoir. I'm glad that you've left that crowd behind and are doing so well in America. I really did like you. Take care of yourself." She left the cafe. He knew he'd never see her again. He could only guess what kind of "favor" she must have done to facilitate her escape. The experience of seeing her again left him numb and terribly confused.

SEVENTEEN

November 2006

The first measurable snowfall of the season was a reminder that soon skiers from New York and Boston would be descending on Vermont. Jake hated when that happened. The roads were clogged, the stores crowded, and getting a table at any restaurant, regardless of its reputation, was not worth the trouble. The truth was that even though AV Cheeses was on pace to have its best year, he was tired of owning it, tired of owning the farm, and with his own savings all but gone, tired of feeling poor. Mia had offered to invest in the operation, but he knew that was purely a gift to him. His refusal of her offer wasn't so much a result of hurt pride as the realization that profits from artisanal cheeses would never produce the kind of money that would make an impact on his foundation.

After weeks of considering his options, he decided it was time to tell his board of directors that he was calling it quits. The board, which consisted of himself, Frank, Zoe and Annie sat around his dining room table, unaware of why Jake had asked them over. "We haven't had a meeting in a long time, and I checked our bylaws, and we're supposed to do this at least once a year."

"Since when did you ever care about bylaws?" asked Annie.

"Whatever. As you all know, AV is doing pretty well, thanks to the efforts of all of you, and I am truly grateful for that." He poured a glass of water and took a long drink.

"But?" said Zoe.

"But, I don't think I can continue."

"What are you saying? That you're quitting?" asked Frank.

"Um, yeah, that's what I'm saying." He looked at each of the others around the table. He'd expected more of a reaction, but they all remained rather stoic. "Well?" he finally said. "Don't any of you have questions?"

Zoe spoke first. "Frankly we're surprised that you stayed with the company for this long. We'd been expecting this for some time. We understand you can't go without an income forever. And to be honest, you spend so much time in New York or at your girlfriend's in Massachusetts that you don't really do that much for the company. My only question is what do you plan to do with it, the company that is?"

This was the topic that Jake was dreading, for he knew it wasn't going to sit well with them. "I've made some inquiries, and I believe I've got a buyer for AV."

"Who's that?" asked Annie.

"It's called Heldstrum. It's a Danish company that distributes foods worldwide."

Annie groaned. "I know who they are. They're big agro. How much are they offering?"

"One and a half million."

"What about the farm?" asked Frank.

"That, I'm guessing, will be part of the sale since the farm is now owned by the company, not me."

"Would you consider selling to anyone else?" asked Zoe.

"Did you have anyone in mind?"

"How about Frank and me? We've lived on that land for a decade now. Raised our daughter in that house." Jake rolled his eyes. "What?" she said. "Don't you think we can afford it?"

"I don't know how to say this without sounding condescending, but frankly, no."

"Actually," Annie said, "the farm is appraised at nine hundred thousand. If Frank and Zoe could get a loan, would you consider financing the balance?"

Jake shook his head in disbelief. "First off, Heldstrum is also going to buy my house, this house. And second..."

"What if I bought this house?" Annie interrupted.

"And second," he continued staring directly into Annie's eyes. "I can't believe that a bank is going to give any of you a loan. It's not that you're not trustworthy but folks, let's be honest here, none of you can demonstrate the kinds of assets or income that banks want to see before they lend out their money."

"Would you at least give us a chance to see what we can do?" asked Zoe.

Jake didn't want to be harsh with these people whom he sincerely cared about, but he couldn't risk the sale to Heldstrum not going through. "Nothing's going to happen until after Thanksgiving, but that's in just three weeks. I can give you until then, but it's not much time. I'm really sorry. As I said before, I know how hard everyone's worked, which is why I've insisted that Heldstrum keep all of our employees, and that they give you all significant raises."

"We appreciate that Jake," said Zoe as she stood up. "Three weeks is better than nothing. Well, Frank, Annie, we've got work to do."

Jake remained seated at the table after the others left, dumbfounded that they could be so delusional as to seriously believe that they'd be able raise the money. Certain of their failure, he called his lawyer to see how negotiations with Heldstrum were proceeding and was told that for tax purposes, it was in everyone's interest to complete the sale before the New Year. He then called Mia in Stockbridge with the news and said that he'd be moving back to Manhattan, and did she want to help him look for an apartment that weekend? She questioned why he needed an apartment when hers was quite large by New York standards. "Are you inviting me to live with you?" he asked.

"For someone as smart as you think you are, you're really clueless. Yes I'm inviting. Are you accepting or not?"

"Gosh, it's a big step you know. Are you ready for this?"

"Jesus, Jake, what's so big about it? It's going on two years that we've been seeing each other. We're not kids anymore. As it is, we virtually live together. Buying or renting your own place in the city is a superfluous waste of money, don't you think?"

"I suppose so. Okay then, let's do it."

After the call ended, he turned on his laptop and Googled movers. He called several, all of whom asked if he knew how much furniture and other possessions he'd be taking. He told them he'd get back to them, grabbed a pad of legal paper and began cataloging what to take. He quickly realized that with the exception of his clothes, there was no reason to take anything. Mia's apartment was fully furnished. Then he made one more call to his friend Howard Podnansky. "Howie," he asked, "don't you have an uncle who's a jeweler?"

"He's a dealer, primarily diamonds."

"Can he get me a good deal on a stone?"

It had been years since Jake had spent Thanksgiving with his parents. He always managed to find some excuse to avoid the ordeal of a day of having to listen to his mother's harping on his lack of a wife and children or the arguments that she invariably got into with her brother Lenny. All of this was made worse by having to eat her overcooked turkey moistened by her concept of gravy, which was little more than the fat from the bottom of the roasting pan. But this was the first Thanksgiving since Lenny's death, and Mia urged him that they both go. Only later did he learn that his brother had triangulated with her to convince him to attend.

The Himmelfarb house, even without Lenny, was a noisy place. The concept of an indoor voice was alien to these people. They all spoke as though the person they were talking to was on the other side of the Grand Canyon rather than across the table. Adding to the cacophony were the two televisions, one showing football games that nobody watched while the other had cartoons that David's daughter was glued to. Were his phone not set to vibrate, Jake would have missed the call. Normally he would not answer a call from an unrecognized name, but he jumped at the excuse to step outside for the quiet of the street.

"Is this Mr. Himmelfarb? My name is Craig Chandler. I'm a mortgage broker in Burlington."

"I don't have any need for a mortgage," he explained. "As a matter of fact, I'm in the process of selling my house, and I'm not buying a new one at this time."

"Yes well, I represent the Mazzettis as well as Ann O'Shea. I'm arranging their financing."

Jake held onto his cell by securing it between his ear and shoulder while he blew on his hands. He'd gone out without a coat and the late November air was colder than expected.

"Financing? For what?" He assumed that Zoe, Frank and Annie had listed him as a reference on some application and this guy was doing his due diligence. The thing that struck him as odd was that he'd called on a holiday.

"Why for your house of course."

Jake's head snapped up at hearing the answer and his phone almost fell to the ground. "My house? Who did you say you were?"

"Craig Chandler. I'm a mortgage bro.."

"Yeah, mortgage broker. But who said they were buying my house?"

"No, just Ms. O'Shea's buying your house. The Mazzettis are buying the farm."

"Is this some sort of a joke? Who put you up to this?"

"I can assure you Mr. Himmelfarb, this is not a joke."

Jake could tell even over the poor cell phone connection that Chandler wasn't endowed with much sense of humor. He was dead serious. "This is the first I've heard of this."

"That's strange. They are under the impression that if they bought the properties, that would also give them ownership of the cheese corporation. They said you gave them until Thanksgiving to make an offer. Is that true?"

Jake rubbed his eyes. "Geez, uh, yeah I may have told them some such thing. But I never gave them a price. I don't even know what the price is."

"Which is why I'm calling. I need to get one, at least an asking price for now, so that I can give it to my underwriters to see how much we'll qualify them for. What do you want me to put down? I've gotten appraisals. The farm is eight-fifty and the house is four-sixty-nine. Do you want me to just go with the appraised value?"

Jake didn't know what to say. The deal with Heldstrum was nearly complete. The sale of AV, including the farm and the house, would, after paying off all the expenses and the mortgages, net him a little over a half a million dollars before taxes. He didn't want to hurt Zoe, Frank or Annie, but he didn't want to lose the money. "I need one and a half million," he finally blurted out.

"One – point – five," Chandler repeated in a calm and deliberate voice on the other end. "And how much for the house?"

"Huh?"

"I assume that one-five is for the farm and its dwellings. Is it not?"

Jake shook his head in disbelief. "Uh, I guess."

"So how much for the house?"

Jake laughed to himself. It was like being in a Samuel Beckett play, the conversation was that absurd. "I don't know. How about seven-fifty."

"Seven hundred fifty it is. Thank you."

"That's it?" Jake asked.

"Well, it's above my initial appraisals, but I can have them re-appraised to get them more in line with what you're asking. I know you told them Thanksgiving was their deadline, but would it be okay if we extended it until tomorrow? With the holiday, it's sometimes hard to get people to do what needs to be done."

Jake knew it was ridiculous. Even at the original appraised values of the properties, Zoe, Frank and Annie would still need to come up with down payments of twenty percent, and they most certainly didn't have that kind of money sitting around. "Sure. Take the whole weekend if you want."

"That's very kind of you. The Mazzettis and Ms. O'Shea spoke highly of you. I'll call you Monday morning then. Have a good a holiday."

The line went dead. Jake slowly closed his phone and slipped it in his pocket. He'd forgotten how cold he'd felt earlier. Surreal experiences sometimes have that effect.

Jake and Mia spent the following Saturday shopping on the Upper West Side for Christmas/Hanukkah gifts. He had all but forgotten the call from Chandler. As they stood in the checkout line at Barneys, his phone rang. The caller ID flashed the name 'Burlington Mort.' "I should take this," he told Mia. "Do me a favor, just buy my mother a gift card and I'll pay you back." He flipped open his phone and walked several feet away.

"Hello, Mr. Himmelfarb. I've got an approved amount for your house and farm."

"So soon? I thought you wouldn't have anything before Monday."

"We work fast here. I haven't contacted the buyers yet because the numbers are somewhat less than the ones we discussed the other day. I wanted to run them by you first to see if there was still interest on your end."

Here we go, Jake thought. He felt guilty over the disappointment these people who he considered friends would feel when told they couldn't afford the purchase. "What's the number?"

"I can do one million, one hundred fifty thousand."

The amount was three hundred and fifty thousand less than if he sold to Heldstrum, yet it might be worth it. "Uh, maybe, but they'd still need to come up with over two hundred grand for the down payment. I guess I could owner-finance that amount."

"Oh no, that won't be necessary. We do a package deal of second mortgages which will cover that."

"One hundred percent financing?"

"Absolutely. We even do a hundred twenty-five percent. Last month one of my partners did a one-fifty. Now I know you said you wanted two and a quarter million for both, but this is only a little less."

"Your definition of little is different from mine. It's less than half the price I gave you."

"I'm sorry. I wasn't being clear. The one point one five was just for the farm. I was able to get eight hundred seventy-five for the house, which is actually a little more than you were asking. So taken together, that's just under two million. And since there's no real estate agent to pay, you'll come out pretty well. So can I tell the buyers that you'll accept these numbers?"

"Jesus. Yeah. Okay. By all means, tell them. But let me ask you this. At those numbers, how can they afford the payments?"

"If they meet their projected sales from the cheese company, they'll cover the loans. Their rates will average just under three and a quarter APR."

"My God, I haven't been keeping up with these things. Have interest rates really fallen that low?"

"That rate is for the first two years. After that, it can reset but hopefully before then, the profits from the company will have increased enough that we can refinance them to a fixed rate. We do this all the time."

"What bank are you using?"

"Initially, the loans will be issued by Green Mountain Federal Savings Bank. But that will in all likelihood be sold before the first payment comes due. The market is huge for buying up mortgages. Almost every loan we do these days gets sold."

"And who's buying these loans?"

"You know, I don't really know for sure. Other banks, I suppose, but there are institutional investors that have gotten into buying and selling. Even some hedge funds. But before I let you go, how is the week of December eleventh sound for closing? Any day in particular?"

"Do it the eleventh."

"That's what we'll shoot for. If it's okay with you, we usually use Yankee Title. Their offices are here in Burlington."

"That's fine with me."

"My secretary will call you next week with directions and an exact time. Thank you for your help."

"No, thank you." He walked back to Mia who was just finishing paying for the gifts. "You're not going to believe this, but Heldstrum is not buying AV."

"Shit. What happened? I thought it was a done deal. Did they get cold feet?"

"Not at all. I just got a better offer. In two weeks, the deal closes."

"Really? So, I guess that means in two weeks, we will officially be living together."

"As they used to say, living in sin."

EIGHTEEN

December 2006

Sayid had become a creature of habit. Every morning he'd wake up at five-fifteen, check his email over a bowl of oatmeal and then head to his health club to exercise before going to work. Regimentation, even without the paramilitary training, was part of his DNA and it served him well. Sticking to a predefined daily routine limited one's chances of finding oneself in an unexpected situation that could lead to a misstep. This morning he was watching CNN on television while jogging on a treadmill. The story that the congressional Iraq Study Group was releasing their final report was mildly interesting, even though the recommendation that the U.S. greatly scale back their presence in Iraq had been widely reported. He sensed from meeting with al-Yazid that al-Qaeda's preference was that America remain heavily engaged in Iraq, leaving them free to consolidate their presence in Afghanistan and Pakistan. He reached for his Blackberry to enter the ISG web site address to download the report, but before he could, a call from Arthur Morrison popped up on the screen.

"Hey Arthur, what's up?"

"What the hell is all that noise? I can barely understand you."

"Sorry. I'm on a treadmill at the gym."

"At six in the morning?"

"It's the least crowded time."

"Which is why I refrain from exercise. You got lunch plans for today?"

"I don't think so. Where do you want to meet?"

"Come up to my office. I'll have something brought in. Say around one."

"I'll be there." The Blackberry slipped as he tried to put it down on the treadmill's console. "Fuck," he said as he hit the stop bottom and stepped off the machine. The screen was scratched but other than that, it seemed to be working. He forgot about the Iraq report and started wondering what Morrison wanted. Most likely it was to do another mortgage-backed derivative. Arthur liked to do deals over meals, but they usually took place at particular restaurants that he fancied. He commented more than once that everyone seemed more comfortable at neutral sites causing things to fall into place quicker. So why meet this time at his office? He got back on the treadmill and checked how far he'd run - just over two miles. He usually did five, and never less than three, but he wanted to get to his office and prepare for Morrison. A little over two miles would have to do.

He arrived at Morrison's office fifteen minutes ahead of schedule even though Arthur was notorious for showing up late. Morrison's secretary escorted him to the conference room and informed him that Morrison was tied up on an overseas phone call. She brought him a cup of coffee and a New York Times and left him alone. It was only minutes before Arthur came in and took a seat at the table. "I took the liberty of having lunch ordered. Sandwiches should be here soon." Arthur glanced at the article Sayid was reading. "A panel of politicians for politicians is supposed to tell us what to do with Iraq. They," he pointed to a picture of Congressional leaders on the front page, "must have to pass some sort of stupidity test to get their jobs."

"And what does that say about the people who vote them in?"

"That they're dumber than dirt. But this Iraq group wants us to pull out with our tails between our legs."

"And you believe that would be wrong?"

"You're damn right that'd be wrong. Think of the chaos we'd be leaving behind. In no time another Saddam would come to power, more repressive and more anti-American. Shit, we would have wasted our boys' lives for nothing."

"And what is the alternative?"

"Just the opposite. Put more troops in and get rid of the radicals once and for all. We'd end up with a government we could rely on, and that would help both them and us."

Sayid put the newspaper off to the side. "Well it doesn't look as though that will happen."

"Don't believe what you read in papers, especially the Times or the rest of the liberal media. This president isn't going to shrink from his responsibilities. You can bet on that." There was a quiet confidence in Arthur's voice that left Sayid with the impression that he knew more than he was letting on. It was ironic that Mustafa al-Yazid and Arthur Morrison should want the same American foreign policy. "You know, you of all people should be thankful for what Bush and Cheney have done."

Sayid didn't know what Arthur was referring to, but wasn't going to pursue it. "Enough politics. Why am I here?"

"Two items. The spring ACBL championships are in St. Louis in March. Can I count on you?"

"Let me check." Sayid took out his Blackberry but the unit didn't respond. "Damn this thing."

"Maybe the battery is dead."

"No, I charged it last night. I dropped it earlier, but thought it was working. You said March. I'm supposed to be in Berlin at some point in March for semiannual meetings with PBB, but I don't recall exactly when."

"That brings me to my second item. PBB. I want you." Arthur threw his hands in the air as if exasperated. "Now I know we've discussed this in the past but before you say no again, let me make my point. You've made how much money for PBB?"

"Off the top of my head, I don't know."

"Whatever it was, I'm sure they haven't paid you what you're worth."

"They take a conservative approach. They possess a very old-world view, having been around since the middle of the nineteenth century."

"My point exactly. To them you are just some nice young Italian who's managed to carve out a little niche for himself. You've made them money, but you'll never be more than an afterthought to them. They don't understand how business gets done on this side of the Atlantic. They have no idea how much more is out there, but I'm guessing you do. So my question to you is this. Do you want to be an afterthought or do you want to build real wealth?"

Arthur hadn't brought up the subject of Sayid coming to work for him in months. Sayid's initial reaction was the same as it always had been, but this time he thought it over. He had no need for recognition from PBB. They were simply a means to an end, but their lack of backing was having a negative impact. He had expected that, by now, there would be more grumblings in the financial community regarding collateralized debt obligations and credit default swaps, but dissenting voices, whether from analysts or regulators, were few and far between. Everyone was making too much money to complain. Until someone big ran into trouble nothing would happen. Leaving PBB for Pilgrim/United had risks. His al-Qaeda comrades might take a dim view of such a move. PBB and Klaus Voorhaus were entities that they had confidence in from years of working together. But were he to go to Pilgrim, he'd have a green light to do most anything. "How much autonomy would I have?" he finally asked.

Arthur's eyes lit up. "How much do you want?"

"Complete. These deals happen in a kind of counter-intuitive manner. On the one hand, their structure is incredibly complicated, requiring a lot of legal prep work, which can be time consuming."

"Which means lawyers, which means fucking expensive."

"Yes. On the other hand, often you're in a situation where an opportunity comes up and you have to act fast and just hope that your instincts are good enough so that the legalese won't end up, as they say, biting you in the ass. So I need to know that if I say yes to a deal, your legal team won't leave me hamstrung."

"I can assure you that won't happen."

"And that you won't be looking over my shoulder questioning my decisions?"

Arthur got out of his chair and walked over to a credenza on which sat a pitcher of water and several crystal glasses. "As long as you're making money, I don't give a crap what you do." He opened a door in credenza and took out a bottle of whisky. "I should have been born forty years earlier when the men who sat in these offices thought nothing of drinking during the day." He filled two glasses and handed one to Sayid. "So are you coming on board?"

"We haven't discussed salary." Sayid didn't really care about the salary. He just wanted a few minutes more to consider the repercussions of the move.

"PBB paid you three hundred fifty grand last year. Don't bother to deny it. I've got my sources. I'll triple that to an even million."

"If you triple it, the amount is one million, fifty thousand."

Morrison laughed. "I'm glad you're good with numbers. Steve, your base salary is meaningless. You know what my base salary was last year? Seventy-five thousand dollars. You know how much money I earned? Sixty-seven million give or take. It's all in the stock options and bonuses. If the extra fifty G's will make you happy, then take it, but don't forget where the real money is."

Morrison had just given Sayid the chance to take his company, a rather good-sized fund manager and investment bank, and if he did things right, drive it into bankruptcy. The hell with al-Yazid and the rest of the leadership. They were either too stupid or too caught up in violent jihad to recognize the brilliance of what he was doing. And he hadn't forgotten what Yasmin had said. He still believed in the need to overthrow the autocrats in the Middle East, and that as long as the West in general, and America in particular, remained entrenched there, that wouldn't happen. What al-Qaeda seemed to have forgotten, or never knew in the first place, was that it was America's economic strength that enabled her military strength. With or without al-Qaeda's blessing, he was going ahead. He took the glass from Arthur's hand. "You've got yourself a new employee." They both downed their drinks and shook hands. "And I'll take the extra fifty grand."

Morrison laughed. "Excellent. Talk with my secretary Caroline as soon as you're ready to start, which I assume will be no later than the first of the year."

"That should be doable."

"And one last thing, make sure she knows to block off the second week in March on your calendar."

"What's happening in March?"

"St. Louis." Sayid looked quizzically at Arthur, not making the connection. "Remember, the bridge tournament?"

"Right." He started to pick up his Blackberry. "I'll put it in my calendar right now, if this damn thing will work."

"Have Caroline get you a new Blackberry and she'll put it in your calendar. Now that you're working for me, you'll have no excuses not to go, right partner?"

"Right, partner," Sayid replied.

◇◇◇◇◇◇◇

The glow from Jake's laptop computer cast a pale light on the bedroom walls. Even though they'd been seeing each other exclusively for nearly two years, living together felt different, not as formal as being married to Debbie, yet not as casual as before. After the sale of his properties and AV, he had enough money to buy his own apartment in Manhattan, but he was ready to make a commitment. In two weeks his brother David was going to marry Ben in Massachusetts, and that may have influenced his thinking. Mia had offered to host the reception at Napa-East, including the food and drink, as a wedding gift. The generosity of the present shocked Jake and when he questioned her about it, she simply answered that she and David had become close, and it was a slow time at the restaurant anyway. While he knew that the two of them talked often, mostly regarding their mutual love for art, he also knew that with ski season underway, the stuff about it being a slow time for the restaurant was bullshit. He guessed that between the cost of food, booze and personnel, combined with the loss of revenue on a Saturday night, Mia's gift must be costing her at least fifty grand. Either the art gallery was a cash machine, or she had far greater financial resources than he imagined.

He sat at a small desk surfing the Internet and doing his best not to disturb Mia who lay sleeping a few feet away. "Shit," he blurted out.

Mia shuffled under the covers. "What time is it?" she asked.

"Sorry, didn't mean to wake you." He looked at the bottom corner of the computer screen. "Around two-thirty."

She rubbed her eyes. "What'cha doing?"

"Nothing really. A little insomnia. Go back to sleep." She pulled the covers up and buried her face in the pillow. "Damn," he whispered.

"I heard that," she said keeping her eyes closed. "What are looking at? Porn?"

"That wouldn't be as disturbing," he replied. She pushed back the covers and got out of the bed. "Where are you going?" he asked.

"The bathroom."

He went back to reading. She returned and stood behind him, peering over his shoulder at the computer screen. "So what is so disturbing?"

"Ever since I sold the farm and house to Annie and the Mazzetti's, something's been eating at me."

"The check bounce?"

"No, nothing like that. I got all the money."

"Then what's the problem?"

"I can't understand how they got approved for the mortgages. I signed their paychecks. I know how much income they could demonstrate."

"That's the bank's problem, not yours. Obviously the bank thinks they can afford it. I'm going back to bed." She kissed him on the cheek and got back under the covers.

"It will be their problem if they can't make payments."

"Jake, you can't worry about what other people do with their lives. I'm sure they've planned out their finances. They'll be fine." Mia pulled the blanket all the way over her head.

"I hope so. They're not alone though."

"Huh?" she said from below the covers.

"I mean to say, they've taken out balloon mortgages that will reset in a couple of years. Banks give these out at low teaser rates, which is I guess how they qualify people who otherwise wouldn't. Remember at Lenny's funeral when my folks' maid told me she was in the process of buying her seventh house? I've been reading about what's going on in the mortgage world. It's unbelievable. Mortgage companies then sell these loans to other banks or brokers who bundle them together and sell them again. Doesn't any of this seem oddly familiar to you?"

She pushed the blanket off her face. "No. Should it?"

Jake pushed his chair away from the desk. "Think back to when we first met. What do you remember from that time?"

"Back at MIT?" she asked. Jake nodded. "I remember we used to smoke a lot of pot and spend all day in bed making love."

"Yeah, well I was referring to the economics class we were in together."

"Your memory is better than mine. Why don't you come back to bed?"

He slipped in beside her. "Really? You don't remember Adam Meecham and the project we did together?"

"Um, vaguely. Why?"

"He was going to flunk us on our project."

"I never flunked anything in school."

"No we got As. But the point was that our project described a business that was pretty much like what is going on with mortgages today."

"So we were prescient. Ahead of our time. No wonder we got an A. I'm going back to sleep." She rolled over with her back facing Jake.

"It's kind of eerie. I've been reading about this online. It's almost as if they've copied our business model, right down to those credit default swaps. I read a quote from a professor at the University of Maryland who estimates that the face amount of credit default swaps may be as high as seventy trillion dollars. That's trillion with a 'T'. The market cap of all publicly traded stocks in this country is like a third of that."

"So we could have been rich beyond all get-out," she murmered.

"But it doesn't make any sense. Meecham threatened to flunk us because the underlying premise of our plan was fatally flawed. With all the mortgages bundled together, then sliced and diced and repacked and resold, eventually their true worth would be undeterminable."

"Maybe Meecham was wrong."

"Maybe, but with the way banks are handing out loans like candy at Halloween, something's going to go poof. Housing prices can't continue rising forever." He sat up in the bed and stared across the room at the computer which he had left on. "What was the name of that other guy?"

"What other guy?"

"The other guy at MIT who did the project with us. You remember, the Arab kid. Abdullah or Mohammed or something."

"I don't remember any Abdullah." He got out of bed and went over to the computer. "What are you doing now?" she asked. "You going to Google Abdullah or Mohammed? You'll get a bazillion hits."

"No, I just came over to shut the thing down."

"Oh. Anyway, why do you care about Abdullah or Mohammed?"

"I don't know. I haven't thought of him in years. You sure you don't remember him?" She didn't answer. "Mia, you asleep?"

"I'm trying to."

"Sorry, again." He climbed back into bed and wrapped his arm around her.

"He was Egyptian, I think," she said softly. "My memories of those days are a little hazy. I smoked an awful lot of pot back then."

"Didn't we all."

"I know he went to grad school in London, then I think he stayed in Europe, but that was more than a decade ago. I guess you could try looking him up in England if you really want to."

"No point in that." He closed his eyes and drifted off. Mia lay next to him, her eyes wide open.

David's wedding reception went off without a hitch. Gay unions, especially in Massachusetts, had become so commonplace that few found them to be anything other than ordinary. Around ten p.m., Jake, who'd drunk a lot of champagne, decided he needed to clear his head in the crisp air of a January night in the Berkshires. He spotted Alice Shepherd standing with Howie Podnansky, and detected the telltale aroma of marijuana. "What, not enough booze in there for you two?"

"Oh Jakie, you've gotta try this shit," Howie said holding out a joint.

"I think I already drank too much."

Alice took the joint from Howie. "But this stuff is really good. Kat, you know the chef, gave it to me." She coughed and handed Jake the joint.

"The chef gave you this?"

"Oh yeah. We've been hitting it off all night. She's very funny and very attractive," she said.

"Attractive?"

"Honestly, Jake, you have to know she's a dyke, or at least bi."

"Should my cousin be worried?"

Alice reacted by laughing uncontrollably. Jake didn't know what was so funny, then looked at the joint in his hand and had an answer. "Rosie's got nothing to worry about. Besides, Kat told me she's been in a long on-again, off-again relationship with someone you know."

That bit of information surprised Jake, and he decided that maybe a hit off the joint might be helpful before he asked the obvious follow up question. "Someone I know?" he said.

"Her name is Annie. I thought Kat said she used to work for you."

"Oh, Annie. I'd forgotten that the two of them were seeing each other." In his impaired state, the thought that Mia might be romantically involved with her chef had crossed his mind, even though he had no reason for such an assumption.

"Anyway," Alice said as she took the joint back from him, "no inside news on what Bush and Cheney are up to these days?"

"I'm sorry to say that my inside days with our government are long over. Actually, I'm not sorry to say."

"What the fuck are you two talking about?" Howie finally asked.

"I report on national security. Jake here gave me an inside scoop several years ago which I, being a young and inexperienced journalist at the time, ignored."

"What was the scoop?"

"Ignore her, Howie. She's high and her memory is a little skewed. But let me ask you this. You're an accountant. Have you taken notice of what's going on with housing and mortgages?"

"We've already had this conversation. It's crazy, I know, but it's the new math. Rates keep falling and home prices keep rising. I've got clients that have refinanced their homes four times in the last two years and cashed out the equity. It's like free money."

Jake took another hit off the joint, which by now was nearly gone. "Shit," he exclaimed as he singed his fingertips and dropped what was left of the joint into some slush on the sidewalk. "Fuck, sorry about that."

Alice started laughing again. "Forget it. Kat gave me more." She reached into her pocket and handed him another joint. "Keep it and smoke it with Mia later. Weddings always make people horny, and smoking a little dope always makes sex better." Jake and Howie stared at her. "Well, at least it does for me."

"I've been telling that to Jake for years," Howie added.

"I suppose," said Jake. "But getting back to mortgages..."

"Fuck mortgages!" Howie shouted. "This is a wedding. We here to celebrate, not stress over economics. If it bothers you so much, why don't you just short bank stocks?"

"Huh?" mumbled Alice.

"He's advising me to invest money by betting against financial institutions."

"Huh?" she repeated.

"It's complicated. I'll explain it to you some day," Jake said.

"Nah, don't bother. I don't understand finance. Now, if you want to tell me about a terrorist plot, that I can write about."

NINETEEN

March 2007

Sayid pushed the button for the ninth floor and fell back against the rear wall of the elevator cab. As the doors were closing, he spotted an older couple he knew lived in the building coming towards him, their arms full of grocery bags. His first instinct was to reach out and stop the doors from closing, but he was exhausted and just wanted to get into his apartment. Anything causing delay, even something as trivial as having to stop on another floor, just wasn't going to happen. The woman shouted just as the doors sealed shut. Her bad luck. It was after ten p.m. and the flight back from St. Louis had been oversold, delayed and so turbulent that the pilot never turned off the seatbelt light. He needed sleep more than that couple needed to wait a minute for the next elevator.

The elevator emitted an irritating beep as it passed each floor. Sayid felt his Blackberry vibrate with an incoming call and he glanced at the number. It was the same one he'd received at least dozen times since leaving for St. Louis, from some guy named Rashid that he didn't know and whose voice messages never gave a reason for the call. Possibly it was some salesman or broker, but judging by the name and his accent on his messages, it was more likely to be someone connected to his Arab associates. Either way, he'd chosen to wait until he returned to New York to deal with the man. He shut off the phone. He started to unlock the deadbolt on the door to his apartment, but was surprised to discover it wasn't engaged. He usually locked both the deadbolt and the lock in the handle whenever he traveled, but this time he must have forgotten. Once inside, he left his suitcase and computer in the entranceway, figuring he'd wait until morning to unpack, and tossed his coat on top of them. He went to the living room to make a cocktail. He filled a glass with bourbon and took a sip.

"You know that is forbidden."

The voice in the dark sent a jolt through him. He choked on the whisky in his mouth. "Who the fuck is there!" A lamp came on. Two men he didn't recognize were sitting on the couch. "Who are you? What do you want? Look, I've got no jewelry or valuables, but you can take my watch and whatever money I've got in my wallet." He started to unclasp his watch.

"Relax, Sayid. We don't want your money. We've been trying to talk to you for weeks now. I left a number of messages, but you didn't call me back."

Sayid took a deep breath and a good look at his visitors. They were definitely of Middle-Eastern extraction. The one doing the talking looked to be in his early forties, nicely dressed but with a scraggly beard of black and gray that managed to look as though it hadn't been shaved in three days. The other, who kept silent, was a thin young man appearing to be still in his teens, wearing a sweatshirt and expensive looking blue jeans. "How the hell did you two get in here?"

"We have our methods."

"And what is it you want from me?"

"Mustafa has concerns. As I said, you haven't returned my calls."

Sayid took another sip of whisky. "I've been out of town. I didn't talk to anyone while I was gone."

"Yes, away playing card games. Don't you listen to your messages?"

"I assume you are the Rashid who called, but since I've never heard of you, and since there was little I could do for you or anyone else while away from my office, I decided I'd wait until I got back."

"Your office. That is one of Mustafa's concerns. You left your job at the PBB to go work for some American company that we know nothing of. You should have gotten permission before making such a change."

"It was an offer that came up suddenly and I had to make a decision. PBB wasn't giving me the support or access to the capital markets necessary to achieve my goals." He glanced at the younger man whose blank expression reflected a total lack of comprehension.

"Don't you mean our goals?"

"Yes, of course. Our goals. It's late and I'm exhausted." He finished his liquor and refilled the glass. "Either of you care for one?" he asked holding up the tumbler.

"That's another of Mustafa's concerns."

Well Mustafa can go fuck himself he thought as he sipped the booze. "It's part of my training. When you're on a mission in a Western country, you have to blend in with the society. Allah understands and forgives. Now if you two don't mind, I'm really tired and I still have to unpack. Leave me a phone number and I'll call you tomorrow."

"It's not me you need to speak with, but Mustafa."

"Fine. Leave me his number."

The older man stood up. "He does not use phones. Someone else may be listening or worse, tracing his location and launching a rocket from a drone." He tossed what looked like a plane ticket on the coffee table. "Don't bother unpacking. There's a room reserved under Stefano Assanti at the Baglioni Hotel for tomorrow night."

"Where's the Baglioni Hotel?"

"In Kensington." Sayid stared blankly at the ticket. "London. England. Your flight leaves from Newark at six a.m."

"I can't go now. I've been away from work for almost two weeks. It will look suspicious, especially to my boss."

"Since you've been spending the past two weeks playing cards with Mr. Morrison, I'm sure he'll understand. I believe the two of you won some sort of tournament, so he should be in a forgiving mood. Just call in sick." Rashid nodded to his young companion who stood up and demonstratively pulled a pistol from his sweatshirt pocket and shoved it into his pants behind his back. "Don't disappoint Mustafa or..."

"Or what?" snapped Sayid.

"Let's just say that he'll lose whatever little confidence he still has in you. You'd be a security risk. Need I say more?" Sayid slowly shook his head. "We'll show ourselves out. Have a good trip, and get some sleep. You will need it."

◇◇◇◇◇◇

Jake didn't know what to make of the phone call. A man going by the name Dougan and identifying himself as a federal agent had asked him to come down to his office, for what, the agent wouldn't say over the phone. Jake's first reaction was that it was a prank, but he couldn't fathom who'd want to pull off such a thing. When the address turned out to be that of a federal office building, he called back the agent and asked if he needed a lawyer. Assured that he didn't, he went to the meeting alone, although he couldn't stop hearing in his head the voice of his late uncle Lenny admonishing him to never meet with any cops, especially the feds, without an attorney.

Just getting through the lobby was worse than going through airport security, with metal detectors, photo-IDs and pat-downs. Trying to lighten the situation by joking with the uniformed officers had only made things tenser. He was told to wait for someone to escort him up to Dougan's office. From that point onward, he kept his mouth shut until a youngish looking woman approached and introduced herself as Hannah Longworth, Dougan's associate, and led him to the elevator.

As they rode up, Jake noticed the photo-ID tag and the letters FBI on it. "So Dougan is an FBI agent?" he blurted out.

"Didn't he explain?"

"No he didn't. I wasn't sure. He only said federal agent, so I thought FBI or IRS or even SEC. I mean, what do I know? I guess I'm babbling, but I'm a little nervous. Should I be nervous? I mean, am I under investigation for something?"

"Relax, Mr. Himmelfarb. You're not the subject of an investigation. Ron will explain it. Here we are." The elevator doors opened and before them stood a tall well-tanned man in a gray pin-striped suit holding a mug in one hand and stack of manila folders in the other.

"Mr. Himmelfarb, thanks for coming in. I'm Ronald Dougan."

Dougan handed the folders to Longworth then held out his ID for Jake to inspect. Immediately his eyes locked on the words Central Intelligence

Agency. He had pictured Dougan as being an old Irish cop with a pronounced beer belly, so his being rather buff came as somewhat of a surprise, but nothing like the shock of those words. "CIA?" he said exhaling a long breath.

"Yes, Jake. Do you mind me calling you Jake?" Jake shook his head. "Good. Call me Ron. Yes, CIA. I thought I told you that over the phone."

"No you didn't. I'm pretty sure I'd remember that. I thought you were the FBI like Miss Long …a… Long…"

"Longworth, and while we're on the subject, call me Hannah."

"Great, we're all now on a first name basis, nice and chummy." Jake tugged at his collar, trying to feel less clammy. "So why does the FBI and CIA want me?"

"Let's talk." Dougan and Longworth led him past rows of modular office units where men and woman sat working in front of computers. They entered a small room with a round conference table upon which Dougan set down the folders and his mug "Can I get you anything to drink?"

"Coffee'd be nice" Jake replied and Dougan poked his head back into the hallway and called for someone to get them all coffee. He closed the door behind him and motioned for Jake to sit down.

Dougan sat across from him and smiled. If it was meant to put Jake at ease, it had the opposite effect. "I was speaking a while back with a mutual acquaintance and your name came up." Dougan paused as he emptied two packets of sugar into his mug. *Mutual acquaintance? Who could they possibly know in common?* Jake wondered. "Alice Shepherd," Dougan finally said.

"Alice Shepherd? How do you know Alice?"

There was a knock at the door. Longworth got up and took a tray with a carafe of coffee, packets of sugar, powdered creamer and Styrofoam cups from someone whom Jake took no notice of. "Alice and I go way back," Dougan said as he started to fill the cups with coffee. "How do you take it?"

"Black's fine," Jake said.

"Anyway, Alice was telling me that you had some kind of theory regarding what's happening in the financial markets."

Jake was totally lost. *Financial markets? Why would the FBI and especially the CIA be interested in what was going on with mortgage-backed securities?* "I vaguely recall telling her about derivatives, but isn't that something for the SEC or FDIC or Federal Reserve to be looking at?"

Dougan nodded. "Perhaps, but our concern has more to do with international connections." Dougan opened a file and pulled out a sheet of paper.

"Before we go any further, I need you to understand that anything we may discuss here is to remain in the strictest confidence, not to be shared with anyone. Do you understand?"

"I suppose."

"If you do, then please sign this." Dougan handed Jake the sheet of paper and a pen. "It says that you understand what I just said about not revealing anything we talk about, and that if in the future should you reveal any information, you will be subject to criminal prosecution for felony violations of numerous federal intelligence and security laws, punishable by fine or imprisonment or both."

Jake's eyes opened wide. "Is that a threat?"

"It's a fact," said Longworth.

"Maybe I should have my lawyer review this before I sign."

"That's your right, but you'll have to pay legal fees and come back down here again."

Jake paused a moment before picking up the pen. "What the hell." He scrawled out his signature.

"Good. You may be happy to know that you've just been given security clearance, limited as it may be. And now that that's out of the way, I believe you know some of these people." Dougan took an eight by ten photograph from the folder and slid it across the table.

Jake picked up the photo of a four men dressed in tuxedos, along with a couple of women wearing evening gowns, all holding glasses of champagne and smiling. "Well, this guy is Art Morrison, head of Pilgrim/United where I used to work. And the blond woman on his arm is his wife Debbie."

"Deborah Morrison, whom you used to be married to, right?" Longworth asked.

"Right, but if you already know this, why am I here?"

"Do you recognize this man?" Dougan pointed to the man standing next to Morrison.

Jake shook his head. "Don't think so. Who is he?"

"His name is Klaus Voorhaus. He is a vice president with PBB." Dougan must have been able to tell from his blank expression that Jake didn't recognize the initials. "The Prussian Bourse Banque."

"A German bank, I take it. So what's the connection?"

"Klaus's father is PBB's CEO."

"Last time I heard, nepotism doesn't violate any laws. If it did, our current president would be up for impeachment."

"It's not nepotism were concerned with. We've been following the money flow for some time of people who are connected with people who don't like us."

"Ron, I get it that spies like to be cryptic and all, but I'm not following you. People who know people who don't like us? What the hell does that mean?"

Dougan took a sip of coffee. "Eight blocks from here there's a big hole in the ground with the ashes of three thousand Americans mixed into the mud. Do you understand now?" Jake slowly nodded. "We have it on pretty reliable intel that the younger Voorhaus has been laundering money for years for terrorist groups, including al-Qaeda."

"So why don't you arrest him?"

"It's not him we want so much as the people whose money he's been moving." Longworth said. "If we take him down, they'll just find someone else to take his place. We want him to get to them."

"I wish you luck. Really I do, but why do you need me?"

Dougan began to flip through his files. "It seems that Voorhaus has been trying to establish a presence for PBB in America. Why, we're not really clear about, but PBB has been doing business with a number of Wall Street investment houses, including some of those derivatives that you mentioned earlier."

"Look, since you gave me security clearance, you've obviously done a background check on me and you know I left Pilgrim back in 2001 and haven't seen or spoken to Arthur Morrison in years, or for that matter, my ex either. And I don't know this Voorhaus character from a hole in the wall, so I don't see that I could be much help."

"But you were an employee of his and you still hold assets in a pension plan at Pilgrim. You are entitled under ERISA to review plan documents, including financial records in which the plan's assets may be invested. Hannah, in addition to being a field agent, also happens to be a lawyer. She can go with you as your attorney in case Morrison gives you any resistance, and once you're in, she'll know what to look for."

"Why don't you just subpoena the records?"

"As I said, we don't want raise any suspicions with Voorhaus and especially the terrorists he's in cahoots with."

Jake again picked up the photo and stared first at Morrison, then at Debbie, wondering what Arthur had gotten into. "Who is the guy standing next to Voorhaus?" he asked.

Longworth bent over to see who Jake was referring to. "His name is Stefano Assanti. He's an Italian national who used to work at PBB, but now works for Morrison. The Italian police say his record is clean."

"For whatever that's worth, coming from the Italians," Dougan added derisively.

"Ronald, be nice now. Why do you ask?"

Jake shook his head. "He looks kind of familiar."

"You know Assanti?" Dougan asked.

"I don't recall meeting anyone by that name. I guess not."

Longworth took the photo from Jake and handed it back to Dougan. "Well then, we should be going," she said.

"Going?" asked Jake.

"Yes, you and I have an appointment at eleven-thirty at Pilgrim."

"Geez, you guys move fast. Suppose I had refused to sign that confidentiality letter?"

"We were betting you wouldn't," said Dougan. "Welcome aboard."

"Do I get a badge or something? Do I have to take some sort of oath?"

Longworth chuckled. "No badge, and no oath. You've already signed your life away to us." Jake froze. "Just kidding. If it makes you feel any better, we can get you a photo-ID. Can you do that, Ron?"

"I'll look into it."

Jake and Hannah waited in the reception area of Pilgrim's midtown office for someone from human resources to take them back. Jake passed the time leafing through a four-month-old New Yorker magazine while she was busy reading and replying to emails on her phone. Neither noticed when Arthur Morrison walked through the door. "Jacob Himmelfarb, what the hell are you doing here? I thought you abandoned civilization to herd goats in New Hampshire."

Arthur's voice was only slightly preferable to that of fingernails on a blackboard. "Vermont, Art, and no, I'm back in the city," he said without looking up from the magazine.

"Come looking for a job?"

"From you? On my list of things I'd like to do, that ranks somewhere below walking barefoot through a field of fire ants."

"I'd be more than happy to arrange for the ants."

Hannah quickly stood up to get between the two. "Mr. Morrison, I'm Hannah Longworth, Mr. Himmelfarb's attorney." She handed him a business card that made no reference to her being with the FBI. Arthur handed it to the receptionist without looking at it.

"So what kind of trouble has Jake gotten himself into that he needs a lawyer? Killed anybody?"

"Not yet, Artie," Jake said with a devilish grin.

"What we are here for," Hannah intervened, "is to inspect the documents relating to the tax returns, investments and other agreements that involve funds in which Mr. Himmelfarb still retains assets." Morrison scowled at Jake whose smirking smile grew in proportion to the rise of Arthur's irritation. "Of course, if you're telling us that you are not going to give us the access we're entitled to, my recourse will be to the Department of Labor, Pension Benefit Guarantee Corporation and the SEC whose lawyers will be a lot more intrusive than will we."

"Don't threaten me, honey. I've got nothing to hide."

"Then you shouldn't have any objections to sharing the information," she replied.

As he glared at Hannah, another woman came up behind Arthur. "Excuse me Mr. Morrison," she said sheepishly.

Arthur pivoted around to her. "Who are you?" he snapped.

"Jen Carter, from HR. I'm here to show these people back. We've set them up in an office."

Arthur seemed to snarl at the girl. "Give them whatever they want," he shouted as he pushed his way past her.

"Just pissing Arthur off like that was worth all the trouble," Jake whispered to Hannah as they followed behind Carter. They were given a small interior office to work in. It had a four-foot-square table upon which files were stacked two feet high. On the floor were more than a dozen cardboard boxes bulging from the folders jammed inside of them. "Where the hell do we start?" asked Jake.

Hannah laid her briefcase on the table. "Can we get Internet access?" she asked Carter.

"I'll have someone from data processing come by and set you up. Anything else I can get you?"

"Not for now."

"There is one thing," Jake said as Carter was leaving. "Is Mr. Assanti around?"

"I haven't seen him today. Do you want me to check on it?"

"If you wouldn't mind."

"No problem."

Carter left them alone and they sat down. "Why did you ask about Assanti?"

"I'm not really sure. You said he worked at PBB, which is where Voorhaus works."

Hannah raised a finger to her lips to signal Jake to stop talking. "You never know who may be listening," she whispered.

"You think they bugged us?" he whispered back.

"Probably not, but it's best to be safe. Just pick up a file and start looking for anything suspicious."

"How will I know what's suspicious?"

"You'll have to rely on your instincts. Just keep track of the files you've examined so that you don't waste time looking over the same info." They spent the rest of the day scanning through documents and got through less than a tenth of the ones in the room. Around five, Jen Carter returned to ask them how things were going.

"There's a lot to go through, but we're getting there," Hannah replied.

"Good. I've had the rest of the documents brought up for you. There out in the hallway."

They stepped out of the office and saw stacked against the wall at least double the number of boxes as were in the conference room. "Shit," exclaimed Jake.

"Have fun," Jen said and started to leave. "Oh, you were asking earlier about Mr. Assanti. It seems that Steve was called quickly out of the country. Some sort of family emergency back in Italy, I think."

"Any idea when he's coming back?" Hannah asked.

"He didn't say."

◇◇◇◇◇◇

Sayid stood waiting for his suitcase to pop onto the luggage carousel in the baggage claim area of Gatwick airport. He was pissed at having to acquiesce to Mustafa's demands. The implicit threat to his wellbeing didn't bother him nearly as much as the notion that Mustafa would pull the plug on his operation. He no longer needed al-Qaeda's funding; in fact, he hadn't seen any transactions that he identified as belonging to them in months. What he feared was that they might somehow decide to sabotage his scheme, why and how he had no idea. There was no logical reason for them to do this, but he knew that logic wasn't always the basis of their actions.

Between the jostling from other passengers reaching to grab suitcases off of the conveyor belt, he thought he heard his name, but ignored it. At last his bag came up. He pulled it off the belt and bent down to look at the nametag to confirm it was his. There was a tap on his shoulder. "Mr. Assanti?" He stood up and faced the woman who spoke.

"Yes."

"I'm here to pick you up."

"Really. I didn't know anyone was doing that."

"Yes, it was arranged by our friend." She was an attractive blonde who spoke with what sounded like a slight German accent. "If you've got everything, follow me. I have a car."

As they drove out of the airport parking lot, he kept staring at the woman seated behind the wheel to his right. "Mind if I smoke?" she asked.

"No, go right ahead."

She reached for the pack cigarettes resting on the console between them and with one hand, managed to get one to protrude from the pack, which she clamped between her lips. She held out the pack to him. "Care for one?" she mumbled, careful not to let the cigarette fall from her mouth. Sayid shook his head. She tossed the pack back down on the console and pushed in the lighter on the dashboard. Once the cigarette was lit, she took a deep drag and brushed back her shoulder-length snow-white hair. All the while, Sayid kept glancing at her. "How was your flight?"

"Okay." They continued driving toward downtown London while he tried his best not to conspicuously stare at her.

"You don't say much," she said.

"Just tired, I suppose." He couldn't stop looking at her.

"Something wrong?" she finally asked.

"No. It's just that you look familiar. Have we met before?" He suddenly felt stupid, as though he'd just given one of the lamest pick-up lines out there. He might as well have said *Come here often?*

"Actually," she took another drag on her cigarette, "we have."

It was not what he'd expected. "Really?"

"Years ago. I took you to meet Klaus."

It all came back to him. "Greta was it?"

"Close. Gretchen."

"Whaddaya you know. I thought you and Klaus broke up."

"I wouldn't say we broke up, since that implies some sort of serious relationship existed. I never considered my time with Klaus serious. And what about you? I never heard from you again. What have you been doing all this time?"

Sayid was puzzled by the question, as well as by the fact that Gretchen was driving him to meet Mustafa. "You don't know?"

"They don't tell me much. You can understand that." She parked the car in front of a row house in East London. The neighborhood was populated by immigrants, mostly Bangladeshis, and in need of urban renewal.

"Is this it?" he asked.

"Knock on the door. It's the green one. They're expecting you." She reached for another cigarette.

"Should I take my bag?"

"You can leave it for now."

He nodded, left the car and walked up to the house with the green door. He knocked and a short woman opened it. She was dressed head to toe in the traditional black abaya clothing worn by conservative women in the Persian Gulf. Once inside, two men led him up a flight of stairs to an interior room with no furniture other than chairs where he was told to wait. Twenty minutes passed before the door opened and in walked Klaus. "Sayid, it's been some time. How are you?"

"I'm all right, though I didn't expect to see you here."

"Nor I you." Voorhaus reached into his pocket and took out a small plastic baggie filled with a light brown powder. He took a pinch of the powder, held it up to his nose and inhaled. "One of the great perks of working with these Afghan guys is they have the best supply of H. Care for a snort?" Sayid knew about Klaus's penchant for substance abuse but with heroin he seemed to have graduated to a new level. Sayid shook his head. "Suit yourself. Do you have any idea what this is all about?"

Again Sayid shook his head. "I thought it was because I left PBB to go to Pilgrim. I was surprised to see…" Before he could complete his thought, the door opened again. In walked Mustafa accompanied by the two men who'd earlier escorted Sayid and strangely, a woman dressed similarly to the woman who had opened the door. She was thinner and several inches taller than that woman, and although her face was hidden by a black veil, she just seemed younger.

"Gentleman. Thank you for coming," Mustafa said.

"I didn't think I had a choice," replied Sayid.

"You didn't. Would you care for something to drink? Tea or coffee perhaps?"

The reason for the woman's presence as a waitress now seemed clear. "I'm okay," said Sayid. Klaus also indicated that he didn't want anything.

"Very well. Please…" Mustafa motioned with his hands for them to take seats which they did next to each other while he sat in a chair facing them. The other two men stood in the back by the door, and to Sayid's puzzlement, so did the woman. "I have some concerns regarding our funds," Mustafa continued. "I've had our accounts audited and there are discrepancies which I'm hoping you can explain."

"What sort of discrepancies?" asked Sayid.

"There seem to be funds unaccounted for." He reached into his pocket and unfolded a sheet of paper. "By our calculations, we should have well over thirty million Euros more in our accounts at PBB than is reflected on our statements. The investments we made in those American bonds that you, Sayid, have been marketing seem to be the major source of the discrepancy."

Sayid now wished he'd asked for some water. "I'm not sure what you're referring to. You'd have to show me the statements. As far as I know, everything was accounted for. The last time I looked at your block of business, and it's been a couple of months, the original ten million dollars had increased more than ten-fold."

Mustafa stared into Sayid's eyes. "I'm talking about thirty-six million, six-hundred and ten thousand or so Euros. That is the amount unaccounted for. We transferred fifty million to you last November to be invested, but the statement we received two weeks ago reflects less than half that amount."

"I never saw a transfer for that amount," Sayid said. "I'll have to look into it."

"We already have," Mustafa shot back. "Funds are missing, and they go back to PBB and their New York branch."

"I...I really don't know what to say. There has to be an explanation."

"There is. Someone has been skimming off our funds. Skimming really isn't the word. Stealing is the word, and it's not just the stealing of money that's at issue. By taking our funds, you have hindered our operational abilities."

"But I didn't take any of that money."

"The funds are given to PBB, and shortly thereafter, you leave PBB, without our approval, and go work for some American. I find that rather suspect."

"I don't know what to say."

Mustafa raised his eyebrows. "Stealing our money was an attack on us. We are soldiers, and we respond as any soldier does when attacked." He nodded to the woman. She walked over and stood directly between Mustafa and Sayid. Sayid felt his heart pounding as she calmly withdrew her right arm from beneath her robe. In her hand was a pistol with a silencer on the muzzle. She slowly raised the gun and aimed directly at his head. Sayid closed his eyes. *So this is how it ends,* and he waited for the inevitable. After what seemed like an eternity and nothing happened, he opened his eyes and looked up at her. Even in the dull light of the room, her iridescent blue eyes flashed from behind the traditional Muslim veil. It struck him that he'd never seen eyes like that on any woman dressed as she was, and then he noticed a wisp of blonde hair peeking out just below her head covering.

"Es tut mir leid, meine lieben," she said, then quickly pivoted and fired a single shot into the center of Klaus's forehead an inch or so above his eyes. Klaus's body immediately went limp as his neck snapped back from the bullet's force. His body slid off the chair and onto the floor. There was surprisingly little blood, but Sayid knew the execution was real. Klaus was dead. The two men who'd been standing by the door came over and dragged his corpse by the armpits from the room as Gretchen followed behind.

"We've known for some time that Voorhaus had been stealing, but until we had another way of investing our assets, we tolerated it." Mustafa reached into his pocket and took out a pack of Camel cigarettes. "Care for one?" he asked. Sayid didn't smoke, but this time he held out a trembling hand and took one. Ironic, he thought, that Mustafa would smoke an American brand. "Now, we have other matters to discuss. An opportunity has arisen for us to launch the kind of attack on our enemies that could very well hasten our final victory.

However, it will require a substantial financial investment that is beyond our current resources. I have been watching your activities and I am most impressed with your success."

"My..." Sayid's throat was so dry he could barely speak. "My success? I haven't succeeded yet."

Mustafa laughed. "Of course you have. Oh, I know you planned on bringing financial ruin upon the Americans, but as I told you before, I never thought your plan had much chance of working. But you can make money. I'm going to put at your disposal 170 million U.S. dollars."

Sayid was still so distracted he wasn't listening to what Mustafa was saying. All he kept thinking about was the look in Gretchen's eyes followed by the look of astonishment on Klaus's face when she turned to shoot him. "I'm sorry. What were you saying?"

"You will invest our funds for us."

"Um, sure, whatever. What do you want to invest in?"

"As I said, we need to make a substantial amount of money."

"How much were you looking at?"

"One billion."

"Billion? That is substantial. And how much again are you investing?"

"One hundred-seventy."

Sayid's lips puckered before he let out a long sigh. "It is possible, no guarantees, but in eighteen months, with a little luck, we might get close."

"Eighteen months is too long. By then, the window of opportunity may well be gone."

"I don't think it can be done any quicker."

"With the help of Allah, it can. It has to."

"Can I ask what the money is for?"

"You don't need to know, but you're a bright man, perhaps you can guess. Now, the German girl will go with you to the airport. You will be flying to Rome." He handed Sayid the plane ticket and stood up.

"Shouldn't I be returning to New York?"

"Flight records are easily traced. It will look suspicious if you flew here for a few hours then returned. You are supposed to be Italian, so take some time. The girl will appear to the outside world to be your girlfriend. We have a safe house on the Amalfi coast where you can relax and plan how you intend to fulfill your assignment. God be with you."

"The girl is going with me?"

"Yes. A prop if you will. When you go back to New York, she'll stay with you."

"I don't see why."

"It's important that you seem as typical as any other American, and not raise any suspicions. You never know who may be watching."

Sayid didn't like the idea of Gretchen being around. He was used to living on his own, but there was no point in arguing. As for being watched, he sensed that the only one watching him would be Gretchen, Mustafa's eyes and ears so to speak. And now he knew why Mustafa had taken the unusual step of using her, rather than one of the men or even himself, as Klaus's executioner. When it came to sending a warning, Mustafa was never one for subtlety.

◇◇◇◇◇◇

For nearly two weeks, Jake and Hannah spent ten hours a day in the small office at Pilgrim poring over files filled with correspondences, contracts, statements and receipts. It was clear from the outset that Arthur's strategy was to overwhelm them with so much information that if there were anything out of line, they'd probably not take note of it. Their lack of progress was getting tiresome, and Hannah indicated that unless they came up with anything soon, she was ready to shut it down. "I was on the NYU Law Review, but I can't make sense of this contract," she exclaimed as she flung a thick binder across the table. "It's purportedly a mortgage-backed CDO, but it's really eight hundred pages of legal gobbly-gook, so arcane and twisted in construction, it may as well have been written in hieroglyphics. Who understands this stuff? Yet there appears to be three quarters of a billion dollars riding on it."

Jake picked up the binder and started leafing through it. "And this isn't disturbing? I mean, I've been thinking for months now that what's happening in the mortgage world is heading for a meltdown."

"That may be, but it doesn't appear to violate any securities laws."

Jake closed the binder. "What do you want me to do with this?"

"I got it from the file box on the floor, the one labeled 'BE-BH'. You can put it back in there."

Jake opened the box and put the notebook in the front. He noticed that one of the other files was labeled 'B/H-W.B.' which he found odd compared with the way other files had been labeled. He opened the file and the first item in it explained the mystery. "Would you look at that," he said.

"What is it?"

"A letter from Warren Buffett to Morrison declining to take a stake in what Arthur was peddling." He showed her the letter written on Berkshire-Hathaway stationery.

"I guess Buffett couldn't understand this stuff either. That should tell you something about these things." She handed the letter back to Jake and he put it back in the file.

There were a dozen or so letters on Berkshire letterhead written over the past six months, all declining Morrison's offers, but it was the last item in the file that Jake read over twice to make sure it was what he thought it was. It was simply a receipt for artwork, probably misfiled by some clerk, and anyone other than Jake wouldn't have given it a second thought. "My God," he said barely audibly.

"What?" Hannah asked. When Jake said nothing, she came over and grabbed the receipt. "Granted, three and a half million is a lot to pay for a painting from an artist I've never heard of, but unless you can find a pattern of egregious spending, which I haven't, I'm not sure you've got anything there." She handed the receipt back to him, but he didn't put it back in the file.

"I wonder who S.H. is?"

"Huh?"

He again showed her the receipt. "At the bottom, the approval is initialed by S.H."

She squinted at the writing. "That could be S.A. Maybe it's Stefano Assanti, which reminds me, I had the airlines checked out, and our Mr. Assanti did fly to Rome last week. I assume he is still there because there is no record of any reservations on flights back. Anyway, just put that back. We're done here. Let's go." She packed up her files and laptop computer. Jake started to put his coat on but when she wasn't looking, he took out his cell phone and slipped it underneath some papers sitting on the table. "Ready?" she asked.

"Sure." They walked out of the small conference room that had been their office for the past ten days and found Jen Carter to thank her and let her know they were finished and that she could have the files returned to storage. "Shit," Jake said as he ran his hands through all of his pockets. "I must have left my cell back in there. I'll be right back." He jogged back to the conference room and before he retrieved the phone, he opened the carton with the Berkshire-Hathaway files and took out the receipt and stared at the name of the gallery printed at the top. "Berkshire Fine Arts" and the name printed in smaller letters just below, "Mia Jang – Owner." He folded up the invoice and stuffed it in his wallet, unsure of what to make of it, and not sure he really wanted to know.

TWENTY

With more than a month having passed since the discovery of the receipt in the files of Pilgrim/United Investors, Jake still hadn't broached the subject with Mia. A number of issues held him back, not the least of which was that it would likely be a violation of the limited security clearance from the feds, and that had the potential of landing him in jail. But he knew it wasn't the threat of prison that kept him from confronting her. Rather it was the reality that she'd received a large sum of money from a company that he had history with, a history that she was well aware of, and she had not seen fit to mention it to him. Mia was in California meeting with a wealthy collector in Palm Springs. He'd declined her invitation to join her, citing his niece's fifth birthday party. It was a lame excuse, but she didn't argue.

Jake sat in their Manhattan apartment passing the time surfing the Internet while old Three Stooges movies played on the TV in the background. He checked his email, which, except for one from David reminding him of Abby's birthday, all turned out to be spam. By accident, he clicked on one that promised to enlarge his penis by two inches in two weeks. Before he knew it, he'd downloaded a virus to his computer that his anti-virus software, for whatever reason, didn't detect. In short order, his laptop was rendered unusable. David told him to bring it over when he came to the party. With only Moe, Larry and Curly as company, Jake decided that the best way to enjoy them was to get high, even though it was early afternoon. He rarely smoked pot – that was more Mia's cup of tea – but he knew where she kept her stash. He went into her closet and behind boxes filled with shoes she never wore, he found the Tupperware container inside of which were a couple of small, brightly colored glass pipes and a plastic baggie filled with a half an ounce of marijuana. He picked up the container and below it spotted the CD that David had made on which could be found the Dorothy Himmelfarb collection of souvenirs of his life, many of which he'd undoubtedly find embarrassing.

He went into the bathroom to smoke so the exhaust fan would expel the distinct acrid odor. He returned the Tupperware to Mia's closet and looked again at the CD. *Asshole brother of mine,* he mumbled as he picked it up. He thought of looking at the scans of what his mother had saved if for no other reason than to delete them. There were problems with that. His computer was fried by what he called the penis virus and files stored on a CD, unless the CD is rewritable, which this one was not, are not erasable. He went back to the bedroom and sprawled out on the bed to watch the Stooges. To his disappointment, the episode airing was with Joe instead of Curly. Joe was no Curly. He might have tolerated Shemp in Curly's stead, but Joe was unwatchable. He left the TV on anyway. With his own laptop not functioning, he decided to use Mia's, which, for some reason, she'd left behind. He opened it and to his surprise, discovered that she'd not shut the system down, but merely put it into its hibernating mode. Once the screen was illuminated, he noticed at the bottom an icon for her email, meaning that she'd left access to it open. Jake closed his eyes and took a deep breath. Were he not under the influence, his inhibitions might have prevented him from violating her privacy, but folded up in his wallet was that receipt, which seemed to compel his hand to move the mouse over the icon and click on it.

She's worse at deleting old messages than me, he thought when seeing that her in-box had hundreds of unread messages. As soon as he read the first one, an ad for a sale at Macy's, he realized that by merely viewing the messages, they were being checked as read, which meant Mia would know he had been in her account. He was careful from that point forward only to look at the subject line of any unread messages. He went through the list, which was in chronologic order, with the newest ones first. When he got to the end of the current emails, he clicked on the folder titled "BFA" which he correctly assumed were where the older emails pertaining to the art gallery had been archived.

Past the RSVPs to show openings, past the messages from artists inquiring about representation or insisting on higher prices for their work, after the insurance premium notices, he found what he was looking for, messages from sassanti@pilgrimunitedinv.com. The most recent had been sent three months earlier confirming the transfer of 2.4 million into the gallery's account. It was followed by prior emails negotiating her fees for consulting, although exactly what the consulting entailed seemed intentionally vague. Some referred to artwork for M's office, some for M's home and some for her Asian client. M was obviously Morrison. Earlier emails talked about residuals on investments owed to Mia and should they be handled through the gallery or sent as they'd done earlier. Jake would be the first to admit that he understood next to nothing about the art world, but the terms residual and investments seemed out of place.

He reached the end of the messages in the BFA folder and began looking through the other folders. Whenever he found emails involving him, he read them, trying to recall his state of mind at the time they were written. He came across one sent by his brother as a reply to one that Mia had sent first, and was embarrassed at how clueless he'd been at that time regarding her feelings about him. At the end of the email was a sentence again thanking David for all he'd done in taking care of her problem. Jake didn't know what to make of that.

In the background he heard an ad for pizza come over the TV, which brought on a marijuana-induced urge to eat. Having come across nothing that could shed new light on Mia's dealings with Assanti and Morrison, and feeling guilty at having invaded her privacy, he decided it was time to close her computer and get some food. Then he noticed a greyed-out icon of a file folder on the desktop enigmatically labeled "h-li-doc." He clicked on the icon and the computer responded by saying the folder was encrypted and asking for a password. Jake entered "April27," Mia's birthday, which he knew was her password for turning on the computer, but that was rejected. Feeling egotistic, he tried his own birthday, but that too was rejected. He tried 0427 which was her ATM PIN, and when that failed tried 1008 which was his PIN number. Nothing worked. He sat for a moment before remembering that Mia's old password for her computer was "Toni," her deceased sister's name. Still no access. *Just as well* he thought, but before leaving, he tried one last code that he had seen her use before, 06041989, the date of the massacre at Tiananmen

Square where she was convinced Toni had been killed. The computer icon disappeared for a moment before a listing of files showed up.

He sorted the listing by date with again the most recent ones listed first. The newest one was an email from Assanti saying that the payment for the 2.4 million would be the last one. An email sent a month prior from Assanti was a reply to an email from her that had asked for a five million dollar payment, citing the "purchase" price of one hundred and sixty million from the final 2005 transaction. He tried to recall what was happening in 2005, but he was sure that she'd never mentioned any art sale of that size, and the fact that the word purchase was surrounded by quotes, again seemed out of place. Further adding to the mystery was that, unlike other emails from Assanti that were signed SA, this one was signed SH. It was probably just a typo, but he looked down at the computer's keyboard and noticed that the "H" was five keys away from the "A," and that for most typists, it would be entered by the index finger of their right hand whereas the A would be entered by the left hand's pinkie. He pulled out the receipt he'd taken from Pilgrim and looked at the initials authorizing payment. They could have been SA, but the A looked more like an H.

He scrolled down the list of files back to the earliest ones. The first thing that jumped out was the reply email address, "sassanti@pbbank.de." This meant that Mia's contact with Assanti pre-dated Assanti's employment with Pilgrim, which also meant that her connection to Pilgrim did not necessarily come from Arthur. He wasn't sure if this info was more reassuring or more troubling, but judging by the transaction amounts, Assanti must have some incredible art collection, even if he was using his employers' money to funnel the purchases. Then he saw an email dated from late 2004 from Mia to Assanti that was stunning. The body of the message was uncharacteristically filled with four letter words chastising Assanti for his failure to secure AIG. At the end, she expressed her anger and disappointment, closing with the sentence, "I've done everything in my power, including taking personal risks, to make this venture a success. It's now up to you. Mia."

"What the fuck?" he said out loud. AIG? What does an insurance company have to do with anything? A sickening feeling hit him, overpowering any hunger that the pot had earlier brought on. He read the rest of the documents and it appeared as though she had been dealing with Assanti for years. He Googled Stefano Assanti and found a surprising large number of hits, but nothing prior to 2002. He clicked on a link to a Forbes article on Assanti's hiring at Pilgrim which included a photo of him and Arthur. He enlarged the image and was surprised again by how familiar he looked. He sat with his eyes closed desperately trying to remember where he knew him from, but nothing came to mind. He clicked on the browser tools button and cleared out all of the search history so that she wouldn't see what he'd been doing. He turned off the computer and grabbed a jacket before leaving the apartment for the Apple store in SoHo. David had always said that Macs were far less vulnerable to viruses than Windows PCs. He was going to find out.

◇◇◇◇◇◇

Sayid's heart was pounding in his chest. With each stride he felt blood pumping through his arteries, to his arms, lungs and especially the muscles in his legs. He left Central Park on the west side near the Museum of Natural History. He ran past the glass cube with the giant globe that houses the planetarium. It reminded him of a child's toy for the Brobdingnagians in Gulliver's Travels. The aching in his thighs let him know that he'd gone much farther than usual, but that was by design. It was going on six weeks of living under Gretchen's constant oversight. She'd moved into his apartment ostensibly to enhance the charade of being his girlfriend. He missed his independence. He was angry with Mustafa for insisting on her presence and what had started as merely a dislike of Gretchen had grown into resentment bordering on hatred. He found her constant questions regarding the investments, investments that she could have no possible understanding of, demeaning. Running gave him time alone to clear his head and time away from Gretchen who did God knows what when he wasn't with her.

He couldn't figure her out. What was a German girl doing with radical fundamentalist Muslims? She didn't act like a Muslim woman. She obviously dyed her hair, painted her eyelids, drank beer, smoked cigarettes, and dressed provocatively in very tight jeans and skimpy halter-tops. The one concession she made to the faith was in her choice of cuisine. She did all of the cooking for the two of them, and was surprisingly skillful at it. It was her one saving grace and she always observed Islamic dietary rules, which ironically meant shopping at kosher markets.

He paused outside his apartment building until his breathing returned to normal. He would have waited longer to enter had he not been covered in sweat and in need of a shower. He unlocked the door to his unit and noticed that Gretchen wasn't sleeping on the couch as she had been when he'd left. With luck, she'd gone out shopping. He kicked off his running shoes, ripped his sopping wet T-shirt over his head, pulled his running shorts off and headed for the bathroom wearing only boxer briefs. To his disappointment, he heard water running in the sink, which meant she was in there. He knocked on the bathroom door. "Are you going to be long in there? I need to shower."

"Just a couple of minutes," she answered. "Come in and start the water if you like."

He opened the door and was greeted by the sight of her standing in front of the mirror putting on makeup, stark naked save for the towel wrapped over her head like a turban and a thin silver necklace with a couple of gold rings around her neck. "Shit. Sorry," he blurted out. "Why did you tell to come in?"

"What's the big deal? We live together now." She didn't skip a beat in applying her eye shadow. He didn't know what to say, but knew he should leave immediately. Yet he didn't, perhaps because her thin, but very athletic-looking torso seen from the back was disturbingly enjoyable. She put down her eyeliner and turned to face him. "If it bothers you so much, you can leave." He said nothing. She took two steps towards him and placed her hand over his crotch. "Or are you afraid that this bulge is betraying you," she said mockingly. He grabbed her wrist and bent it back. "You're hurting me," but he wasn't hearing her. He'd lost all sense of reason or fear. With his hand clenched tightly around her arm, he dragged her out of the bathroom and threw her down on the bedroom carpet. He ripped off his undershorts and forced himself into her.

It was over fast and only then did he realize that she hadn't shouted or screamed, fought back at him by scratching, biting and clawing, cried or done any of the things he'd expect a rape victim to have done. In fact she'd said nothing until he rolled off of her. "Feel better now?" Her words, as always, were delivered in an emotionless monotone voice and there was no way to tell whether she was being dismissive, angry, accusatory or actually wanted to know how he felt, leaving him to wonder whether he'd just sexually assaulted her or she'd just seduced him. She got up and went into the bathroom. He lay confused on the floor for a moment before following her.

"What the hell does that mean?"

She resumed putting on her makeup. "It's a simple question. I've been around you for a month and a half, and in that time, I've observed you haven't had sex once, and judging by how tense you've become, probably a lot longer than that. Maybe now you can concentrate on your job and obtain the money we need."

"I could have fucking killed you just now."

She shrugged her shoulders. "Not likely." She twisted out her lipstick and began applying it on her lips. "After all, which one of us has the experience in killing?" She puckered to smooth out the gloss. "There." She held up the lipstick inches from his eyes. "Looks like a little cock, don't you think?" Then she rolled it back into its case. "Don't worry, yours is a little bigger."

"What kind of a slut are you?"

She pulled the towel, which had amazingly stayed in place through the assault, off her head and wiped herself off. "The kind that does her job." She shoved the towel into his stomach. "Now shower and go do yours." She started to leave, but he again grabbed her wrist.

"Just a second. That's bullshit about you being concerned that my sex life, or lack of, was hindering my work."

She stared down at his hand that was still clenched on her arm and didn't reply until he let go. "Maybe," she finally said. "I mean, I think you are really wound tight and I don't know whether sexual frustration is part of it, but I know you resent my being here. It wasn't my idea and I'd much rather be somewhere else, but the leadership is placing a lot of trust in you. The imperialist Western governments have been successful at limiting our ability to move money. Funds are getting tight. We're risking a lot on you, more than we can afford, but the opportunity we've been presented is too good to pass."

"How much do you know about the organization?"

"Enough to know that the success of the global revolution may rest with you. Anything that hinders you hinders the cause. I thought that your anger at me was distracting you. If raping me released your hatred, well, it had to be done."

He felt guilty. "You think so little of your body that you'll let anyone fuck you if it helps the cause? I suppose you fuck Mustafa too." She said nothing and again started to leave. "Wait. I'm sorry for saying that. And I'm sorry for assaulting you. I can't believe I did that. I could have really hurt you."

She turned back and placed her hands on his shoulders with her thumbs resting lightly below his Adam's apple. A slight smile formed at the corners of those freshly painted lips and it seemed like she was about to kiss him. In one motion, she took her hands off him, lifted the necklace over her head and before he realized what had happened, it was around his neck. "This necklace is only silver plated. Its core is of high tensile steel." She pulled down on the ring pendant, which snapped the necklace tightly around his throat to the point that Sayid felt his windpipe constrict. "I could have, at any time, choked you." She released the pressure, lifted the necklace off his neck and replaced it around hers.

He reflexively gasped. "But you didn't. For the life of me, I can't figure you out. You flaunt Islamic traditions and rituals. Are you even a believer?" She slowly shook her head. "Then why? Why the hell are you involved with al-Qaeda?"

"I could ask you the same. I've been around you long enough now to know you're not too anxious to live in their vision of a perfect world." She pulled a towel off the rack and wrapped it around her body. "Okay, so neither of us is too keen on their vision, but I spent a lot of my youth in the Middle East, which is where I learned to speak Arabic. My father worked for a company that stationed him there. I didn't live in Germany until I was almost twenty. But I saw how oppressed people were, and governments were the oppressors, which led me to being what I suppose you'd call an anarchist. Al-Qaeda is a useful ally in breaking up the hegemony of the industrialists who are enslaving the world. The G-8, the IMF, they're all in it together. If that means I have to defer to men like Mustafa in their presence, dress like a nun or whatever, that's a small price to pay. In this case, they are on the side of good."

"Your Manichean world view is rather simplistic. I guess that's why you get along so well with Mustafa." If she took umbrage at the criticism, once again she didn't show it, leading Sayid to conclude she didn't understand what he said. "Manichaen means..."

"I know what the word means," she interrupted. "Were you aware that it's derived from the third century Persian Gnostic religion?"

"Of course," he replied, although in fact he wasn't aware. "So I guess that explains how you could murder your ex-lover."

For the first time, Gretchen let a tiny bit of emotion show as her eyes closed and the veins in her neck bulged slightly. "When I first met Klaus, he was as committed as I was to striking out at the industrialists. He hated what his father stood for. You know the elder Voorhaus was in the Hitler Youth and his grandfather was an official in the Nazi party, so he came from a long line of fascists, which he wanted to be cleansed of. But Klaus had weaknesses. He liked fast cars and faster women. I was okay with that, but, as you may have observed yourself, Klaus also developed a taste for cocaine and heroin. Towards the end, his habits made him succumb to the bourgeois lifestyle of his father, and he ended up embezzling from al-Qaeda. He betrayed my cause and Mustafa's cause. He was a dead man. Whether I pulled the trigger or someone else did doesn't really matter, does it?"

"But you were his lover, right?"

"Not for some time. He kept pressing me to have a group swing with him and other women, and I just wasn't into doing that. I mean, I'm as liberal minded as anyone when it comes to sex, but just because I believe consenting people can do whatever they like with each other doesn't mean I have to participate. Truth be told, Klaus was a lousy lover, so offing him wasn't that hard. As I said, he was a traitor."

"So because he wasn't good in the sack, you felt nothing about blowing his brains out. What does that portend for me?"

"If by some cosmic chance we should ever screw again, you'd better be a lot more attentive to my needs than you were ten minutes ago." She leaned next to his ear and whispered. "But the odds of that ever happening are practically nil." She planted a kiss on his cheek then stood back. "So go take your shower and then get to work. A billion dollars is a lot of money, and Mustafa is not one with a great deal of patience."

She walked away leaving the door to the bathroom wide open. He stood under the stream of hot water trying to come to terms with what Gretchen had said. He'd always been under the impression that for women, sex was inextricably tied to emotional commitment. Apparently that wasn't true. He thought of Yasmin. Was she any different from Gretchen? Were all women like this? Then he remembered the billion dollars and the question of why Mustafa would be willing to risk what was probably the lion's share of al-Qaeda's liquid assets was even more disturbing than the fact that he'd just raped Gretchen. But his opinions of her had changed. For one thing, he realized that beneath that icy, at times stoic to the point of seeming idiotic façade was a first-rate intellect. He also realized his anger towards her was gone, much as she'd predicted it would be. And although he could envision perhaps liking her, he knew he'd never stop fearing her.

◇◇◇◇◇◇◇

For two days Jake surfed the Internet in an attempt to learn more about Stefano Assanti. Although he was able to construct a plausible history of a man born and educated in Rome, this information was gleaned mostly from documents or articles about Assanti that had as their source, Assanti himself. No actual references to Assanti in newspapers or other official public documents could be found that pre-dated 2003. With Mia scheduled to return from California that night, he was desperate to know what her relationship with Assanti was. He needed help, and the logical choice would have been to ask his brother who could gain access to information not available to the public. The problem with using David was that he was close to Mia and if Jake's suspicions turned out to be totally unfounded, it could do irreparable damage to everyone's relationships. That only left two other possibilities, Ron Dougan or Hannah Longworth.

He tried Hannah first, but the message on her voicemail simply said she'd be out of the office for the next two weeks. She did give the name of another agent who could be reached in case it was an emergency, but he saw no point in that. Dougan, judging from his outgoing message, was available but away from his desk. He left a message asking for a return call. As soon as he'd hung up, his cell started ringing with Mia's name displayed. He didn't answer it. A few minutes later, it rang again from Mia but he still couldn't face talking with her. "This is ridiculous," he muttered when it rang a third time. He'd have to face her in a few hours and if he couldn't speak to her over the phone, how could he speak with her face to face. He flipped open his phone without looking. "Hey sweetie, how's it going?"

"Uh, this Ronald Dougan. I may have called the wrong number. I was trying to reach Jacob Himmelfarb."

"Oh no, agent Dougan. This is Jake. I thought you were someone else."

"I see. What can I do for you?"

"I know we struck out at Pilgrim, but I was wondering, how sure are you of Stefano Assanti?"

"Why do you ask?"

"Well, Assanti worked for Voorhaus and it seems logical that if you suspected Voorhaus having ties with terrorists, then Assanti would as well."

"We thought that, but we've thoroughly checked on Assanti, and we're quite sure that he's legit. The Italian's have supplied us with certified copies of everything from his baptismal certificate through his college diploma from the University of Rome."

"Have you questioned Assanti yourself?"

"We didn't want to as we felt it would tip off Voorhaus, not that it matters anymore."

"Why do you say that?"

"Voorhaus is dead."

"Dead?"

"Scotland Yard found his body three weeks ago in some grimy back alley. He'd been robbed so there was no identification on him and no one had reported him as missing which is why it took so long to identify the body. They'd assumed he was just another derelict drug addict that was the victim of a deal gone wrong."

"Why did they assume that?"

"The toxicology reports showed a large amount of heroin in him, along with traces of other drugs. We've known for some time that Voorhaus was a user. I guess it finally caught up with him. If it weren't for his dental records, we probably still wouldn't know. Of course, all of the forensic evidence at the crime scene was pretty much lost."

"So you don't know what killed him."

"I suspect the bullet they found in his brain in the autopsy had something to do with it."

"Yikes."

"Yeah, yikes."

Jake drove Mia's car out to the Newark airport to pick her up. He'd urged her to take a cab, but she liked having someone to greet her when she landed. Besides, it would be easier to see her in a public place. He waited by the security station where departing passengers stood in long lines, taking off their shoes and filling plastic trays with laptop computers and anything made of metal. Another post 9/11 fact of life that everyone seemed to have grown inured to. He spotted her walking towards him from far away and the sight of her still elicited the same desire as the first time he'd seen her in Meecham's economics class at MIT. He wished he could go back to those simpler times. He'd never experienced emotional paralysis like this. She smiled broadly and threw her arms around his neck. "Hey stranger. Miss me?"

"What do you think?" he replied as he kissed her.

TWENTY-ONE

January, 2008

"We need to talk." The four most dreaded words any man ever hears from a woman. They signal an impending conversation that is either the result of dissatisfaction borne from a lack of attention, sensitivity to emotional needs, perhaps financial strains, or any number of perceived faults that men are usually not aware of as problems. Whatever the reason, the talking is rarely pleasant and more often than not, the topic of taking a break from one another, whether temporary or permanent, eventually comes up. This is especially so if the reason for the conversation involves an attraction to a third person.

Jake didn't know what to say in response to those four words, especially since they came over the phone. In the end, he just mumbled "Okay" and left it to her to respond.

"Okay," she replied back. "But this is something I'd rather not discuss over the phone. I'll be back in the city tomorrow night. Will you be around?"

He thought it a strange question. "Of course. Where else would I be?"

"I don't know. I guess I'm just a little haggard. It's been a crazy week up here at the gallery. I'll see you tomorrow."

"Drive carefully. I love you." The phone clicked off without her customary reply. He didn't know what she wanted to talk about, although he had his suspicions. It had been more than six months since he'd discovered her communications with Assanti, and in all that time, he rarely felt completely at ease around her. It was not so much a sense of alienation as it was the need to always be on guard about what he said. Several times he had tried to give her openings to explain her connections to Assanti and Morrison without directly posing the question. He'd mention seeing Morrison around town or an article that appeared in the financial or social sections of the Times or some other paper, but she never responded. He knew by what he'd seen on her computer that she'd been involved in some way with Assanti for a long time, but his name never came up in conversation. He had reached the point where he began to doubt what he'd actually seen on her computer. It was only that once and he had been under the influence at the time. *We need to talk.* "Great," he said under his breath.

He returned to reading an article in the Wall Street Journal about some concerns that the Federal Reserve had regarding an unexpected rise in the rate of home mortgages that were at least ninety days delinquent. An executive at Bear Stearns was quoted as saying it was just a temporary anomaly brought on by loans with adjustable interest rates all resetting at once, and by springtime it would correct itself. He reread the words: *There is nothing to worry about.* "Oh really," Jake said out loud. "So it begins."

◇◇◇◇◇◇

Sayid was not surprised to find that Gretchen had prepared a sumptuous dinner of grilled lamb, couscous and chopped salad. In addition to her other talents, he'd grown to appreciate her culinary skills. It was as though she had dual-majored at school in home economics and paramilitary training, or maybe she was the offspring of an old affair between Che Guevara and Julia Child. The result of his gastronomic indulgence was that his pants were feeling a bit snug in the waist.

"Mustafa wants an update," she told him as she cleared the plates from the table.

"What kind of update?"

"He wants to know how much money you've made."

Sayid rubbed his eyes with the palms of his hand. "I'll call him tomorrow."

"No. You are not to contact anyone in the organization. Mustafa made that clear to me."

"No one made it clear to me."

She brought her laptop computer over to the table and showed him an email from Mustafa advising her that they had discovered a security breach and instructing Gretchen on how all communications between al-Qaeda command and her, as well as Sayid, were to be handled.

"How come I never received this?" he asked.

"I don't know. They don't tell me more than I need to know. But with a security leak, we have to limit communications to the absolute minimum until they can identify the source and extent of the leak. So how much money is available?"

"I'm guessing if we liquidated all of the investments, it could yield four hundred, give or take."

"Four hundred million?"

"Maybe four fifty, possibly as high as five. Prices are still rising, but that won't last forever. If they want my advice, they should sell now."

She shook her head demonstratively. "Can't do that. You know how much they need."

"I know finances may not be your strength, but even you have to appreciate that in a little over six months, I've managed to triple the value of the investment. That's no easy feat."

"You have another six months to reach the goal. If you continue at the same rate of return, you should make it with time to spare."

"Let me try and make this as simple for you as I can. The whole purpose of what I've been doing for the past five years was to wreck the American and European economies, which would force them to withdraw their armies, and cause a drying up of oil dollars. This would greatly increase the chances that the governments in the Gulf and Egypt would fall."

"But that hasn't happened. The American stock market is at record highs. It may never happen, or at least not until after you've made us the money. That's what Mustafa and the rest of the leadership have concluded. The money is needed to fund a more traditional method of attacking our adversaries."

He got up from the table and grabbed a beer from the refrigerator. "The leadership is as stupid as the investors I deal with every day. It's going to fail. Of that I'm sure." He chugged down the entire bottle and went searching for a second one. "How is it that you, an infidel in their eyes, not to mention being a woman, have gained their trust?"

She walked over to the refrigerator, pushed her way past him and took the last beer for herself. "I've proven my abilities. You've seen some of my work in person. But in this case, I am the source of why they need the money. I probably shouldn't reveal this, but if you want to know what the money is for, I'll tell you."

"I suppose you're gonna say they're buying a nuke."

"Two actually." He was shocked by how casually the words came from her. She took a sip and handed him the bottle. "I know an ex-Soviet general in Chechnya. He can get us two one hundred and twenty kiloton weapons. That's ten times the power of the bomb dropped on Hiroshima."

"Shit," he said quietly.

She looked straight into his eyes. "Do you have a problem with this?"

"Shouldn't I? I never signed on to kill thousands, maybe millions of innocent civilians."

"Civilians aren't innocent. They elected into power the men making war. Their taxes pay for the bombs dropped on truly innocent people and for the salaries of the soldiers who drop them."

Sayid's head was spinning. "You have to know that if we set off a nuke in Manhattan or Washington, the retaliation would be on an unimaginable scale."

"You've made assumptions that aren't necessarily true. You assume that America is the only target. There are many others, such as Tel Aviv, Riyadh or even Moscow. And whoever the target is, including America, would have to know exactly who the attacker was to retaliate."

"Nuclear weapons leave fingerprints. Their source can be determined. And if the leadership decides that Tel Aviv is the target, the Israelis will stop at nothing to track us down and kill us all. Remember what happened to the Munich attackers. If it's Russia, they may start World War Three and end life for all humanity."

"If that's the result, then that's the result. But I've been assured by the leadership that they will not use the nukes without first providing a warning, which is why we need to buy both. But you have only made enough money to barely buy one, which if we did, would mean detonating it without warning. So, are you on board with this or not?"

Sayid knew if his response to that question were negative, Gretchen would in all likelihood kill him on the spot. If, on the other hand, she was telling the truth, then perhaps there were worse things than al-Qaeda having nuclear weapons, but he couldn't think of any. "Yeah, I'm on board," he finally said. "But I have to tell you, the markets may collapse before we have a billion. I just can't be sure. As I said, I thought they would have collapsed long before now. Do you think we should risk letting the investments ride?"

Gretchen nodded, which caused Sayid to do something he'd never done before – secretly pray – pray that the mortgage bubble would burst before Mustafa asked for the money.

◇◇◇◇◇◇

Jake found a spurious excuse to visit his brother so as not to be home when Mia returned. As the evening droned on past eleven-thirty and no excuse for staying could be fabricated, he realized that he couldn't put off the inevitable. He returned to the apartment and was relieved to find that Mia had already gone to bed. As quietly as possible, he climbed in and rolled on his side away from her. "You're home. I didn't hear you come in. Where were you?"

Mia's voice was not entirely unexpected. He reached over to his nightstand and turned on the lamp. "I was at David's."

"I thought you'd be here."

"I wanted to. It took much longer than I'd expected."

Mia sat up in the bed. "Can we talk now?" He wanted to say no, but that wasn't really an option. "I'm not quite sure how to bring this up, but there's a big fundraiser next month with lots of well-healed types that I need to attend. Will you come with me?"

"Is this what you wanted to talk about?"

"Uh, yeah. Why?"

"Oh, nothing." All the anxiety over her wanting to talk suddenly seemed so foolish. "Sure, I'd be happy to go with you."

"Great. I really appreciate it. It makes it so much easier to approach these fat cats if I can introduce my boyfriend to them. It's a great opportunity for you too. You should try and hit up as many as possible for Water of Life. But I have to warn you that Arthur and Debbie Morrison are going to be there. As a matter of fact, Debbie is the chair of the charity. Are you okay with that?"

He shrugged his shoulders. "Why shouldn't I be?"

"Well, I have a confession to make."

This piqued his interest, and he sat up and faced her. "What's that?"

"I have had some dealings with Arthur and Debbie in the past. I never mentioned it because I know that your history with them is somewhat painful, but they have been really lucrative clients."

"Really? I had no idea."

"Yeah. Arthur always wanted things run through his company, why, I don't know. Maybe it had something to do with taxes or maybe he was doing something not quite kosher, but that wasn't my concern. Anyway, I'm sure we will have to meet with them and I just wanted to make sure that you're prepared."

For the first time in six months, he felt a sense of complete ease in her presence. In fact, for the first time in six months, he suddenly had a great desire to make love to her. Her using the word "kosher" made him realize how acculturated she'd become with him. "Not a problem. I'll be on my best behavior." He rolled on top of her. "However, I could use a little something for my trouble."

She laughed. "I think I can accommodate that."

The ballroom at Ritz-Carlton in Battery Park was nearly full by the time Jake and Mia arrived. Jake spotted the mayor, Michael Bloomberg, holding court with a small entourage that included Arthur and Debbie. He tried his best to appear outwardly calm but Morrison always put a knot in his stomach. Debbie being there only added to the tension. He felt ridiculous wearing a tuxedo, but Mia dressed in a flowing turquoise strapless Vera Wang evening dress was so stunning that he was actually relishing the moment when she'd introduce him as her boyfriend. Mia was off somewhere mingling with potential clients when a waiter carrying a tray of champagne glasses walked by. Jake grabbed two of the flutes, one intended for her, but downed both in seconds and went looking for more.

"You're looking well."

Jake wasn't ready for the unmistakable Long Island timbre of Debbie's voice coming from behind and he gagged on the champagne in his mouth forcing some of the bubbly up his sinuses. He grabbed a napkin and turned to face her. "Not as good as you, I'm afraid," he replied, wiping his face.

"After all these years, don't I even get a kiss?"

He thought it a weird request, but if for no other reason than to demonstrate some sense of civility, he leaned over and gave a perfunctory peck on her cheek. She responded by wrapping her arms tightly around his neck and kissing him on his cheek, but in a manner diametrically opposite of his. "I mean it," she whispered in his ear. "You really look good, and happy. Life must be treating you well." She released her grip then took the napkin from Jake's hand to wipe her lipstick off his face. "I suppose we have Mia to thank for that."

"You know about me and Mia?"

She licked the napkin and finished removing the last of the lipstick from his cheek. "Of course. She told me about the two of you from the start. I guess she was worried I might have problems using her as my art consultant and dealer, which of course was nonsense. I mean, she has one of the best eyes in the business. Everyone knows that. Why should the fact that her lover happens to be my ex have any impact on her doing her job? But I appreciated the candor and assured her that you and me are ancient history." A server carrying another tray of champagne came by and she took two fresh glasses and handed one to him. She tapped her glass against his and took a sip. "We are ancient history... aren't we?"

The seductive tone in her voice was unsettling. He wasn't sure what her agenda, if she had an agenda, was. When he thought logically about her question, the answer was obvious, but when it comes to sex, no one ever uses logical reasoning. That's one of its greatest attractions – the chance to ignore the brain's response to social norms or logic and act on those primordial impulses encoded in our DNA millennia ago. "What exactly are you saying, Deb?"

She laughed. "Oh come now, Jake, I'm just having some fun with you. I know you and Mia are serious, and I've got Artie." She again leaned close to his ear and whispered. "But, if you ever feel the need for a little change of pace, give me a call. You still have the best tongue I've ever known." She then stuck her tongue into his ear causing the champagne flute to drop from his hand and shatter on the floor.

"Oh, there's Mia," he gasped. "Hey Mia," he called out and waved his arm over his head in an effort to grab her attention. To his relief, she saw him and came over. Debbie backed away slightly from Jake but kept her arm wrapped around his. "Mia, I believe you know this woman."

"Hi Deb," Mia said as the two women exchanged kisses on each cheek. "I saw you earlier, but you were engaged with the Mayor." Jake wondered whether Bloomberg's ear had also experienced Debbie's oral advances. "I see that you and Jakie are catching up on old times."

"Absolutely," Debbie said. "And you call him Jakie. That's so cute."

"I heard his mother call him that and it kind of stuck."

"How are Cy and Dot? I haven't seen them since we were married."

"They're fine. Buying a condo in Florida, even though my father swore he'd never leave New York. Something must happen to old Jews when they reach a certain age that pulls them down there, like salmon swimming upstream to die."

"But the salmon go there first to spawn before they croak," Debbie said. "Maybe seniors go to Florida to fuck."

Jake extricated his arm from Debbie's. "Thanks for the wonderful mental picture."

"Why shouldn't old folks enjoy sex?" Mia asked.

"I'm all for old folks enjoying whatever they can, but excuse me if I'd prefer not to picture my parents screwing. I can just hear my father complaining about his aching back and my mother just complaining."

Both women giggled. "Well give them my best when you see them." Debbie gave him one last quick kiss on his lips. "And save a dance for me later. Call me next week, Mia. I have some ideas about redecorating the place in the Hamptons I want to run by you. We'll do lunch."

Debbie walked away and Mia turned to Jake. "Was that weird for you?"

"You have no idea." He looked around for a server with appetizers, as he hadn't eaten since breakfast. "Can we leave soon?"

"In a bit. You know, you really should try and mingle with some of these people. There's a shit load of money in this room that Water of Life could use. I'm happy to introduce you to those I know."

Jake nodded in Arthur's direction. "What about him?"

"Morrison?" she said. "He's the last person I'd think you'd approach, and you certainly don't need any introductions from me."

"I wasn't referring to him, but the guy Arthur's talking to. He looks familiar. Do you know who he is?"

Mia didn't respond at first, but squinted. "I took out my contacts earlier because they were bothering me. I can't quite make him out."

"Well let's go up and see." He started to walk towards Morrison when she grabbed his arm.

"Oh I recognize him now. His name is Assanti. Uh, Steve I think. He works at Pilgrim under Arthur. I've met him only once or twice. If I recall, I think he's Italian, but I don't think he'll be of much use."

"Probably right, but I've got to meet Morrison at some point and if this Assanti's important enough to show up at this event perhaps he has some authority when it comes to corporate donations." Jake headed off but Mia hesitated, looking for another server with a tray of champagne.

"Mr. Morrison," said Jake boldly as he held out his hand to Arthur.

Arthur's eyebrows rose and his forehead curled back into his expensive, but not undetectable toupee. "Jake Himmelfarb. I'm a little surprised to see you here."

"Why's that?"

Arthur shook his head. "Maybe because Debbie runs this little shindig."

"Oh that. Listen, Art, I'm over that. I'm happy for you…and for Debbie."

"Oh really?"

Jake paused a moment. "Yeah. Really. I'm glad she's happy, and why not? I've got my own relationship. Mia Jang. I think you know her."

"Of course. I believe Deb mentioned that to me."

"I'm glad you didn't hold me against her. And as for Debbie, she's now your headache, and that's a comforting thought."

Arthur laughed. "Ah Himmelfarb, you always were the biggest pain-in-the-ass motherfucker who ever worked for me."

"Then why'd you keep me around for as long as you did?"

"Because up till now, you were also the goddamn smartest."

"Up till now?"

"Till now. Now, I've got someone who'd I've have to put a step above you. Have you taken a look at the value of your Pilgrim portfolio since you fucked around with that lawyer last year?" Jake nodded. "Then you know how much money you've made."

"I'd cash out today if I could. Something's so out-of-kilter that the markets are bound to correct."

"Hah. You're just jealous of the fact that my current superstar outshines you. Here, let me introduce you to him." Arthur walked a few paces to his right, grabbed Sayid's arm and pulled him over to Jake. "Jacob Himmelfarb, meet the man who's going to let you retire in comfort, though God knows you don't deserve it. This is Stefano Assanti, head of derivatives and swaps at Pilgrim."

Jake held out his hand and after a brief awkward pause, Sayid responded in kind. "A pleasure."

Jake didn't let go of his hand. "Excuse me, but you look very familiar. Have we met before?"

Sayid shook his head once. "Not that I recall. Have you spent much time in Tuscany?"

"Never been."

"Such a shame. It's the most beautiful part of Italy. If you ever plan on going, let me know and I'll tell you the best places to stay."

Gretchen tugged at Sayid's sleeve. "Aren't you going to introduce me?" she asked.

"But of course. This is Jacob Himmel…, I'm sorry, I don't recall your last name."

"Himmelfarb. And this lovely lady is?"

"This is Gretchen. She is my…" Sayid paused, not quite knowing what to say.

"I'm his girlfriend," she finished.

"Nice to meet you. Judging by your accent, I'd say you're not originally from around here."

"Germany. That is where Stefano and I met."

"He's a lucky man." Jake smiled politely at her and surveyed every inch of Sayid's face before turning back to Morrison. "Arthur, since you're doing so well, and Pilgrim's doing so well, don't you think it would behoove you to donate a little of your success to allow an infant in Africa to drink a glass of water without risking cholera or dysentery?"

"Your little foundation?"

"Over ninety-eight percent of our funds go directly to provide benefits and givingwell dot org gives us a gold rating, which only one other charity achieved, so what do you say?"

Jake could tell that Arthur feigned being impressed. "What do you think, Steve? Can we earmark some funds for Jacob?"

Sayid's eyes darted around the room. "I suppose. I'm not sure. I'd have to check to see whether Pilgrim's annual giving hasn't already been allocated. Now if you'll excuse me, there's someone I need to talk to. Mr. Himmelfarb, a pleasure to meet you," and he disappeared into the crowd.

"I tell you what Jake," Arthur said. "If Assanti can't find anything in the budget, let me know and Deb and I will personally make a donation."

"Nothing's stopping you from giving regardless of what Pilgrim can or can't give."

"You've a point, but if Pilgrim makes a donation, I feel as though I've made one since in the end, the money comes from my own pocket."

Jake was in no mood to argue the point. Mia finally appeared, which gave Arthur the opportunity to ask her to join him for a dance. She was reluctant to accept the offer, relenting only after Jake urged her on. He watched as the two of them took to the floor, and although no one would ever mistake them for Fred and Ginger, he had to admit feeling a bit jealous at their grace. When he could no longer bear watching, he made his way over to one of the bars to get a drink. In line in front of him stood Assanti ordering a Dewar's on the rocks. Jake couldn't resist the temptation to find out more about him. "Mr. Assanti," he said, but the band was so loud, he realized he'd have to shout. "Hey Assan –", before he could finish the name, a somewhat obese matronly woman pushed in front of him on her way to the buffet line.

"Yeah what?" Sayid replied without turning to see who had addressed him. The bartender handed Sayid his drink, and for a brief moment, he stood motionless, before turning around to face Jake. "Oh, it's you," he said haltingly. "Did you call me? It's hard to hear over the music."

"Yeah, before Mrs. Jabba-the-Hut in the gold dress over by the roast beef barged in front. I just wanted to give you my card. I don't want you to forget about my foundation." Jake reached into his wallet and handed over the card.

"I won't forget. Arthur won't let me." Sayid took the card but avoided making eye contact. He downed half of his Scotch and excused himself.

"Good. I'll look forward to hearing from you," Jake shouted. Only then did he notice Gretchen standing nearby sipping champagne and staring at him as though he'd just yelled some obscenity.

Mia finished dancing with Arthur and tapped Jake on his shoulder. "You ready to go yet?"

"You sure? We haven't been here that long," he answered.

"Long enough."

TWENTY-TWO

Three days had passed since the fundraiser. Sayid sensed a change in Gretchen. It wasn't anything obvious but her aloofness was even more pronounced than her usual deadpan responses. So it came as something of a surprise when she burst into his bedroom early in the morning and began shaking his shoulder to wake him. "How much?" she asked. Sayid rolled on his back, rubbed his eyes and grunted unintelligibly. "How much?" she repeated.

Sayid pushed himself up into a sitting position. "What?" he managed to rasp out.

"How much money do we have in the account?"

Sayid grabbed his wristwatch from the bed stand and after several seconds, managed to focus his eyes and make out the time. "It's fucking six-twenty on a Sunday. Why the hell do you need to know that at this hour?" He looked up and saw her looming over his bed, fully dressed and holding a large brown envelope in her left hand.

"Mustafa wants to know. So what do I tell him?"

"Tell him to go fu…" he paused before completing the anatomically impossible suggestion. "Tell him I'll check into it tomorrow."

"Can't you give me an estimate?"

"I suppose, but why the sudden urgency?" She didn't give a reason but simply glared icily at him. "Last time I looked, the portfolio had a market value of around five-hundred-fifty."

"Million?"

"Yes, million."

Gretchen emitted a soft sigh. "Not as much as you'd said we'd get, but it will have to do."

"What are you talking about? I never promised any amounts, and I said it would take at least a year and a half."

"Events have intervened. If it's only five hundred fifty, that will have to do. Liquidate it tomorrow."

Sayid was incredulous. "What? Why?" his voice rising as he leaned forward.

"Just do it. There is no more time."

"Jesus, I don't know if it can be done in that a short time. If I have to liquidate the holdings so fast, there'll be a premium to pay. Could be as much as ten percent."

"Whatever it is, it can't be helped. Do it tomorrow. Have the money wired into our Swiss account." She started to leave.

"What if I can't get it all sold off? I mean one or two more days shouldn't make that much difference to Mustafa, but it could mean millions."

She paused at his bedroom door. "You have until about six p.m."

"Is that when your deal for the nukes is going down?"

She took a step back in his direction. "Just to be clear, you know nothing about why the money is needed, understood? Get the money into the account tomorrow before you leave work. Then don't come back to the apartment."

"Why shouldn't I come back here? Is someone going to be waiting for me?" he said sarcastically.

"No. Tomorrow is your last day at Pilgrim." She tossed the envelope she'd been holding onto the bed. "Inside is your letter of resignation, or at least a copy of it. You can give it to Morrison yourself if you think necessary, but it will be emailed to him tomorrow at six-fifteen. You'll also find your ticket to Frankfurt. The flight leaves at ten-twenty from Kennedy. Don't be late."

He opened the envelope and inspected the ticket. "I don't want to go to Europe now."

She acted as though she hadn't heard him and left his room. Seconds later, she reappeared. "You have no choice. If you're not on that plane tomorrow night, you'll be dead by Tuesday morning."

"This makes no sense, Gretchen. I can get a lot more accomplished here than in Germany. If I suddenly up and quit for Europe, someone's going to ask questions that could lead to who knows what."

"You're identity has already been compromised, or as they say on those American TV cop shows, your cover's been blown-up."

"You mean blown, but what are you talking about? My cover hasn't been compromised."

She walked to the foot of his bed and stared straight at him. "At that fancy party the other night. Remember the Chinese girl?"

"I've known Mia for years. In fact, I've made her a good sum of money. She can be trusted. If she'd wanted to expose me, she'd have done it a long time ago."

"And her boyfriend? You trust him too?"

Sayid didn't immediately respond. "Jacob Himmelfarb doesn't know who I am, I'm sure of that."

"Well I'm not. I heard him call you Hassan, which in and of itself was enough to expose you. Your reaction only confirmed his suspicions, I'm afraid."

"I have no idea what you're talking about."

"I know what I heard and what I saw."

"If something was going to happen, it would have happened already."

"Perhaps, but it's a chance our superiors are not willing to risk any longer. Look Sayid, he's a Jew, am I not right? And you know how Jews are. They're stubborn and crafty, and their Zionist entity oppresses our Palestinian brothers. They connive and scheme, but don't underestimate them, because they aren't stupid. The Jew who recognized you won't go away, which means you must. If people like Klaus's grandfather and my grandfather had been successful, he wouldn't be here now, but he is. So you have two choices. Come with me back to Germany or stay here and find yourself the victim of a robbery gone bad." She leaned over the edge of the bed and whispered. "And I'd hate to see you end up in a pool of blood on 72nd Street." She gave him a kiss on the cheek and once again walked towards the door. "Sorry if I'm sounding like an Italian mobster. They were running a Godfather marathon on the TV this weekend. You know, that third one isn't very good. The director should have stopped at two. I guess he didn't know when it's time to quit. I'm hoping you do."

The door closed again. Sayid sat frozen in bed for several minutes before opening the envelope to read his resignation letter. It used his engagement to Gretchen and her desire to return to Europe to be closer to her family as the reason he was leaving. In addition, he had an excellent offer from a French firm in Paris that he had to act on immediately. Sayid reasoned that they'd selected Paris so no one would come looking for him in Germany, but the whole letter seemed crudely constructed and not sounding like something he'd have written. Even so, he knew his options were limited. Time had indeed run out.

He fell back on the mattress and pulled a pillow over his head. He knew it was impossible to smother oneself in this manner, and although he didn't seriously consider suicide, he would not have been terribly upset if at that moment, Jack Kevorkian walked into his bedroom and offered his services. Options ran through his head. Run away some place, but where? Tell Gretchen and Mustafa that the markets had dried up and he couldn't liquidate their holdings, but they'd find out soon enough that wasn't the case. Go to the police, but would they even believe him? If they did, it was more likely than not he'd be whisked off to Guantanamo for water boarding or be an "extraordinary rendition" candidate and end up in the hands of some foreign secret police, probably the Egyptians, and he'd already experienced that. And if the police didn't believe him, then he easily imagined himself in the place of Klaus with a bullet through his skull.

Gretchen's words kept running through his head. He'd never heard her sounding anti-Semitic before and didn't know what to make of the reference to her grandfather. Then it dawned on him that regardless of what he did, Jake and Mia were both in danger. He threw the pillow on the floor, jumped out of bed and put on jogging clothes. He slipped his cell phone into his pocket and left his bedroom. "I'm going for a run," he called out to Gretchen and didn't wait for her answer before scurrying out the door. He took the stairs down the nine flights to the street level rather than wait for the elevator. When he was four blocks away, he ducked into a Starbucks, ordered a coffee and took a seat at a table in the rear of the store. He took out his Blackberry and tried to call Mia, but the phone was dead. "I was sure I charged it last night," he muttered.

"You'll find it works better with this inside." Gretchen tossed the battery in front of him before taking a seat across the table. "You complained the other day that your battery kept dying, so I was going to get you a replacement today."

Sayid's breathing became faster. "How did..." but the rest of the sentence was trapped in his throat.

"How did I find you so fast?" She helped herself to his coffee. "Those two over by the counter eating muffins," she said tilting her head in the direction of two bearded young men. "Look, Steve, I won't say this again. You have to concern yourself with one thing and one thing only. Spend the rest of today in the apartment figuring out how you are going to get us the most money possible tomorrow." She got up to leave. "Oh and by the way, I'll be coming to work with you."

He grabbed her arm. "That will seem very strange to everyone at the office, having you there, don't you think? What's the problem? Don't trust me?"

"Tell your office mates that I just can't bear the thought of being away from my fiancé for so long." She reached down to the table and grabbed the cell phone battery. "And to answer your last question..." She held up the battery, grabbed his phone and slipped it into her pocket before walking away.

He glanced over at the two men, his babysitters, who had now taken up seats near the door. Finding time alone in the next twenty-four hours wasn't going to be easy, but neither was anything else he was going to have to do. What Gretchen didn't know was that besides his Blackberry from Pilgrim, in the pocket of his sweatpants was his old Blackberry that he'd kept from his days at PBB. He needed to call Mia, but couldn't while his babysitters were watching. The bathroom would work, but as soon as he stood up, the men started to follow. He went straight into one of the stalls in the men's room, locked the door and sat on the toilet as though he was using it. He heard the other men enter the bathroom and knew a voice call was out of the question, but he could send her a text, if the old Blackberry worked. He hadn't used it in a long time because it wasn't very reliable. He would have traded it in for a newer model, but after leaving PBB, he saw no point. He'd always kept it plugged in out of habit, but that didn't mean it would work. He held his breath and pressed the power button. Nothing happened. *Come on, come on* he mouthed as he pressed the button again, applying so much pressure that his thumb turned red. At last the unit lit up. He let out a long sigh. Now the only question was would he get cell service in the bathroom. He stared at the screen waiting for the unit to become fully functional, waiting to see how many signal-strength bars would hopefully illuminate. One did. *That should be enough, assuming PBB hadn't terminated the contract,* he thought. It was, he knew, a big assumption, but when he saw that he was still receiving email, he knew he could send a text. The message was short. "Mia – We must speak. Jake knows who I am. You may be in danger, SH." He shut off the Blackberry, pulled up his pants and flushed the toilet. As soon as he stepped out of the stall, one of his watchdogs pulled both his arms behind his back while the other searched through his pockets. They found nothing and didn't bother to search the stall. Had they, they might have found the Blackberry on the floor behind the toilet.

The next morning he arrived at work early with Gretchen in tow. His first action, after explaining to various co-workers that Gretchen was his betrothed, was to call Morrison's secretary and find out when Arthur was due in the office. When told that Morrison was out of the country until later in the week, Sayid remembered that Arthur was at a bridge tournament in Hong Kong. He was relieved. One less thing to have to deal with and confronting Morrison was never easy, although it would have been worth it to see his expression in the flesh when he learned that his financial empire was about to collapse.

Sayid had spent much of the previous night sitting in bed and planning his course of action. Around two in the morning, he realized that Gretchen's ultimatum to sell off everything might have been a blessing in disguise. For nearly six years he'd been living in America and he'd become too accustomed to the lavish lifestyle that credibility for his deception required. He thought of the corruption of Mubarak's Egypt and how people like Arthur Morrison, even if indirectly, were complicit. Just last week Arthur had bragged how he'd purchased matching red Ferraris for himself and Debbie. He went into great detail on how they could reach 125 miles per hour in less than 11 seconds, and top out at over 200, which, as Sayid sarcastically pointed out, made the cars a very practical choice for driving in Manhattan. He felt a little bad for Mia since the Morrisons, and Debbie in particular, had been great clients, but he didn't feel that bad since by his own accounting, he'd earned her millions. Morrison and his ilk had no compunction about indulging in excess even though half of the world went to bed not knowing if they'd have food to eat the next day. It didn't matter what Gretchen or Mustafa or even bin Laden himself thought, Sayid was determined to see that his vision of how to wage war to bring justice would succeed. The thought of nukes in the hands of these people was another issue altogether.

By ten o'clock, Sayid was ready to begin making trades, and he asked Gretchen one last time if she was sure that everyone knew of the potential losses because once he started, he couldn't go back. She assured him to go ahead and by ten-thirty, he had liquidated all of the holdings. "It's done," he unceremoniously announced.

Gretchen, who'd passed the time sitting on the couch in his office reading back issues of *People* and *Cosmo*, seemed startled by how fast it had gone down. "How much?"

"Five-hundred sixteen million, eight-hundred and some odd thousand. It will change slightly once all of the fees and commissions are taken out and the exchange rates confirmed."

"And you've transferred it to our Swiss account?"

"I'm just waiting for the last confirmation to come through – and there it is. Come take a look for yourself."

She walked around his desk, looked at his computer screen and saw a message confirming a deposit for fifty-six million and change. "That's only a tenth of what you said."

"That is only one of twenty-nine different transactions. This money is coming through Pilgrim's accounts. If I did a single transaction, my boss would have been called by his bankers to confirm the sale. This kept everything looking more or less normal. Arthur won't discover what I've done until after we've landed in Germany."

"Good. Then I guess we can go now. We even have time for a leisurely lunch and to get in some last minute shopping."

"You go ahead if you want to. I still have a few things to clear up."

"Right," she said sardonically and walked back to her spot on the couch and picked up another issue of *Cosmo*. "What exactly is it you have to clear up?" She didn't look up from the magazine.

"I know what you and Mustafa and the rest of the leadership think of my original plan, but if my countrymen and fellow Arabs are ever going to be liberated, it's not going to come from terrorist attacks on the West."

"And you will bring down the world economies in a few hours. How?"

"The forces are all out there like a parched forest waiting for a spark. It's surprising how few people you need to convince to start the fire. Today is Monday. By Wednesday, Thursday at the latest, Art Morrison is going to realize that his company is essentially bankrupt. When news of this hits the street, the half dozen or so men who control most of the trading in mortgage-backed derivatives are going to be clawing all over each other to try and get whatever they can for their paper holdings."

Something in Sayid's confident tone seemed to grab Gretchen's interest. She put down the magazine and walked over to his computer. "So what are you doing now?"

"Just preparing an email to send out to those half dozen men informing them that I'm leaving Pilgrim over differences with Morrison regarding the viability of those derivatives. Planting a spark in their minds which, God willing, will start the match that lights the forest fire that brings down these economies."

"You think quite a lot of yourself and your ability."

"That's not the first time I've been told that. Anyway, you can thank the U.S. government. Years ago they built the lookout towers for the rangers to spot the fires before they became conflagrations."

"And now?"

"Now? Now they've taken all the rangers off the towers. There's no one looking out for the fire." He finished drafting the emails but didn't send them. "Okay, let's go to lunch."

"You're done here?" she asked.

"Except for sending the emails. I want to come back after five to send them, and I'll take care of sending Arthur my resignation. I took the liberty of rewriting the one you prepared to make it more believable. After that, we can go to the airport and fly off to Germany."

◇◇◇◇◇◇◇

Jake heard Mia's cell phone ring. It was in the kitchen charging, as it had been since she had left for London to meet with some sculptor before heading to Paris. Without thinking, he lifted up the phone and noticed that the missed call was from Debbie Morrison. He thought of calling Debbie to let her know that Mia was out of the country but the last time he'd spoken to his ex-wife was rather bizarre and he didn't feel like experiencing that again. Then he noticed the text message symbol and without thinking, tapped the screen to view the message. "What the fuck?" he shouted. *"Mia – We must speak. Jake knows who I am..."* "Who the fuck are you? What the fuck is this "you may be in danger" supposed to mean?" Then he saw those initials again, SH. He knew it was Assanti and he was sure his real last name began with an H, but for the life of him, he couldn't think of anybody he'd ever known, Italian or otherwise, with the initials SH.

"Enough of this shit." He picked up his cell phone and hit the speed dial number for the phone Mia used when travelling out of the country. He was really angry. It was time to get to the bottom of this and her relationship with Stefano Assanti. Most men would have preferred to have such a conversation in person. Some might even resort to violence. Jake being Jake was far more comfortable doing it long distance. "Shit," he whispered when the call went to voicemail. "Mia," he shouted at the tone prompt. "It's me. Call me as soon as you get this. You got this cryptic message from Assanti, or whatever his real name is. Goddammit Mia, who the hell is he and what the fuck are you doing with him?" He hung up the phone. He didn't care that she might be offended that he'd violated her privacy by reading a message left on her phone. If she was having an affair with Stefano, he had a right to know. He had never taken that tone with her before but this time he felt justified. Jake's breathing slowly returned to normal. Perhaps it was for the best. If she wanted out of the relationship, then so be it, but he knew deep down, he was hoping she didn't.

◇◇◇◇◇◇

After landing in Frankfurt, Sayid and Gretchen took a train to Paris and checked into a small hotel off Boulevard Saint-Germain on the left bank. He still had fond memories of the city stemming back to when he lived there, although Gretchen insisted they spend most of their time closeted in their hotel room. He wasn't sure why they'd even come to Paris because he knew they'd end up in Germany. Her explanation was that it was necessary to cover their tracks by building on what had been written in his resignation letter. If, as was possible, Morrison went to the FBI to track him down, she wanted them to be looking in France, not Germany. At some point, Sayid would have to talk to Morrison, and the call would certainly come on the Blackberry given him by Pilgrim, which like all cell phones has GPS capabilities that allow the location of the phone to be fairly accurately ascertained. Three days after they'd arrived in Paris, the call finally came.

"Don't answer it," she told him.

"Isn't this is exactly what you wanted?"

"Let him call back several times first. I want to piss him off, as the Americans say."

"That makes no sense. You want me to talk to him. Let's just get this over with."

"Not yet. The angrier he gets, the more likely he is to have the call traced."

Sayid looked exasperated. "This is just stupid. If you want to create the illusion that we're going to live in Paris, then shouldn't we be seen out and about?"

"The illusion is that we are lovers. Spending all our time in this room, ignoring phone calls from the outside, isn't that what lovers would do?"

He didn't answer.

Two days later, Sayid could see that Arthur had tried more than two dozen times to reach him. When his phone rang again at one-thirty in the morning, Gretchen got up from the bed and handed it to him. "Now?" he asked, perplexed by her timing.

"Now. It's evening in New York, so he won't be able to do anything much until tomorrow."

He took the phone from her hand.

"Where the fuck have you been?" Arthur's voice was so loud that Gretchen could hear it even though Sayid had not put on the speakerphone mode. "I've been trying to call you for five days. I've left a million voicemails. I've texted. I've emailed, and you haven't had the goddamn courtesy to just once get back to me."

"I'm sort of on my honeymoon here in Paris."

"Fuck your honeymoon. Fuck Paris. Get your ass on the next plane back to New York."

"Uh, Arthur, didn't you get my letter?"

"You mean that resignation thing? I thought that was a joke. I got called out of a tournament in Hong Kong to be hounded by some damn reporter from the Wall Street Journal asking me about the liquidity of my company. The liquidity of my company? Are you fucking shitting me? Last time I looked, Pilgrim had over twenty billion in assets, that was until someone sold off half a billion while I was in China. You wouldn't know anything about that now, would you?"

Here it comes. Sayid had rehearsed this conversation in his head dozens of times in the preceding days. "I was the one who sold off that book of business."

"No shit. Who's the client?"

"I'm not at liberty to discuss that."

"Not at liberty? For all I know, you've embezzled that money for yourself. I traced the transfers to a numbered account at a Swiss bank. I swear to God, I'll have you arrested if you don't get back here and get that money back."

"Can't do that. For one thing, it's not my money. And even if I could convince the client to re-invest, I'd have a fiduciary responsibility not to do it in Pilgrim."

"You're fucking with the wrong man, Assanti. I have connections in high places. I'll have the FBI and CIA track you down wherever you are in Europe and get you extradited back. Either get me my funds or be prepared to face twenty years in federal prison."

"You're not going to do that, Arthur. Even if you could, it would not be in your own interest. If you'll take the time to follow the trades, you'll see that I was perfectly in my legal and corporate right to execute them. Look at my employment contact. You, in effect, signed off on everything I did. And if by some measure I did come back and an investigation was undertaken, they'd turn up millions in Pilgrim funds that went for your own personal use. Just take a look around your apartment or beach house at all that artwork you've collected." He could hear Morrison's breathing become somewhat labored on the other end. "Right now, you have bigger problems than tracking me down. Pilgrim is so heavily leveraged in mortgage-backed derivatives that if that market gets skittish, people are going to want to sell and you'll have a bunch of angry investors wondering why the prospectuses and financial statements they've been receiving weren't accurately reflecting the risk. But what's your alternative? You haven't got one. Think of it as a bridge hand. You've been endplayed. If you sell off your CDOs, it would cause the market to collapse sooner. If you hold on to them, the credit-crunch will in time, make them worthless. No matter how you play your cards, you've lost."

There was no reply from Morrison, and Sayid could tell that the reality of Pilgrim going bankrupt was beginning to dawn on him. "You're responsible for this," he finally said. "You little cocksucking motherfucker. If I go down, I swear I'll personally come after you and when I find you, I'll cut your fucking balls off."

"No, Arthur, you're responsible. That's what the title Chairman and CEO mean. Now, if you don't mind, I'm going back to my honeymoon." He hung up the phone and handed it to Gretchen.

"Very good," she nodded as she took it from him and put it on the nightstand. "We'll leave it here. Get dressed and pack up now. We're leaving."

"It's the middle of the night."

"That's good. Means the traffic will be light. I've a car outside."

"Where exactly are we going?"

"You'll find out when we get there."

TWENTY-THREE

J ake couldn't remember the last time he'd seen the Knicks play in person
at Madison Square Garden. Truth be told, he didn't care for professional
basketball that much, especially regular season games. He never watched
them on television. Maybe the playoffs and then probably only the champi-
onship series, and probably only if the series went to a game seven final, and
even then, only the fourth quarter... if it was a close game. As a kid, his uncle
Lenny used to take him to games at the Garden four or five times a year, back
in the days when the Knicks actually contended for titles. Lenny loved the
Knicks, which is never a good trait for a compulsive gambler, and it fell on
the teenaged Jake to protect his uncle from himself. Now the team was more
of a joke, having made the post-season just twice in the new millennium and
both times failing to advance past the first round. Still, Mia had given him two
courtside tickets that a client, probably Morrison, had given to her. She hadn't
returned his phone call and he didn't know what to make of that. He'd tried
calling her a several more times but the call always went straight to voicemail.
He stopped leaving messages. Maybe she wasn't ready to discuss this. Maybe
she'd never be, but he couldn't stand just hanging around the apartment and
waiting. He needed to get out. For sentimental reasons, he placed a hundred
bucks on the Knicks to win straight up at an Internet gambling site. When
he thought about it, he was actually looking forward to watching incredible

athletes up close, even if most were on the Boston team, with the spirit of Lenny occupying the empty seat next to him.

He had almost made it out the front door of the apartment building when he heard the doorman shout "Mr. H." Only then did it occur to him that he shared the same last initial with the mysterious SH. He turned towards the doorman and saw Debbie Morrison standing there, her hair matted from the cold drizzle that had been falling since morning. "This lady says she's here to see you."

"Actually I was hoping to see Mia," she said as she walked over to him.

"Oh, well Mia's out of town, out of the country actually, looking for paintings for you, I thought."

"I know. I was hoping she hadn't left yet." Debbie's voice was strained, her eyes looked puffy and her body was trembling slightly as she spoke.

"She did, last week. I saw where you called her usual cell, but did you try her international number?"

"I did, but she never answered."

"Yeah, I'm familiar with that problem." He glanced at his watch. "I'd love to stay and chat, but I've got to run."

She grabbed his arm. "Please Jake. Can we talk? I've got no one to talk to and I don't know what to do. Just five minutes. Please."

She was obviously distraught. Many times he had fantasized about getting back at her for all she'd put him through during their divorce. He'd imagined how great the satisfaction would be at seeing her, and Arthur too for that matter, brought down low. But now that it might be happening, the schadenfreude just wasn't there. He'd known her so long that he couldn't remember not knowing her. As much as he'd detested her he also knew that at one time he'd loved her, or at least thought he did. He took out the tickets from his coat pocket and stared at them. "Hey Al, what time do you get off duty?"

"Twenty minutes, Mr. H."

"Want two tickets to tonight's Knicks-Celtics game?"

"Sure," said the doorman and Jake handed him the tickets. "Holy crap!" the doorman exclaimed when he looked at where the seats were located. "These must cost like a hundred bucks each."

"A lot more than that. Enjoy." He turned back to Debbie and asked her if she wanted to go get a drink someplace. When she said she didn't really want to be around a lot of people, he invited her up to the apartment. "Don't take this personally," he said as the rode up in the elevator, "but you look like shit."

"Gee Jake, you really know how to compliment a girl. Why would you think I'd take that personally?" It had been his life-long penchant to always say the wrong things to women. "Don't worry, Jake. I know you, and besides, you're right. I do look like shit."

Jake unlocked the door, tossed his keys on a small table and hung up his coat in the closet. "Can I take your coat?"

"I think I'll keep it for a while. I'm freezing," she said.

"Give me your coat. It's soaking wet." Reluctantly she took off her coat and handed it to him. "You're soaking wet as well. Jesus Deb, you're a walking advertisement for pneumonia. Why don't you go and change into something of Mia's. The bedroom is over there."

She nodded and slowly walked in the direction he'd pointed to. "Would you mind terribly if I took a shower first?" she called out.

"Help yourself." He went into the kitchen and proceeded to rummage through the refrigerator for some food to put out.

She spent a long time in the shower, to the point where he began to grow concerned for her. Finally she emerged from the bedroom wearing Mia's pink terrycloth robe. Her hair was still wet but at least it was combed. "This is a really nice apartment. It kind of reminds me of our old place. It wasn't too far from here if I recall."

"No, not far," he shouted from the kitchen. "Can I get you something? Maybe hot, like tea or coffee?"

"Something a little stronger." She curled herself on the sofa and pulled a blanket up to her chin.

Jake returned clutching two glasses filled with ice in his left hand and a Diet Coke and a bottle of Jack Daniels in his right. "Jack and Coke still your drink?"

A wistful smile came to her face. "You remember. My tastes have changed some over the years. I'm not big on the Coke anymore, at least not the kind you drink."

"Sorry, it's the only kind we keep around." He filled a glass with the whisky and handed it to her still trembling hands. She downed most of it in a single gulp. "You wanted to talk."

"First, can I ask a favor?" He nodded. "Would you mind if I stayed here tonight?"

Jake's mind flashed back to their last encounter where Debbie had all but thrown herself on him. "Uh, I don't know. Mia's out of town and it might be kind of..."

"Kind of what? For God's sake Jake, believe me when I say that sleeping with you is the last thing on my mind. I don't want to go back to my apartment and have to face a horde of reporters. I just need some space to get myself together for one night. Is that too much to ask?"

"Why would you have to face a horde of reporters?"

"Can't you guess? I mean, you must have heard it on the news or seen it in the papers."

Jake took a sip of the liquor. "Apparently not."

She finished the rest of her drink and held the empty glass out to him for a refill. "Then you don't know anything. Shit, where to begin. Artie came back from some bridge tournament unexpectedly early."

"He still goes to those?"

She nodded. "He was all upset about problems at Pilgrim. Soon after he got back, we started getting calls on our home phone from reporters wanting to talk to him. How they got our private number I'll never know, but I guess that's their job. He wouldn't tell me what was going on and to be honest, I wouldn't have understood anyway, but I knew things weren't good. Then he told me that we'd need to do some belt-tightening. I thought he was just referring to maybe fewer vacations or put off remodeling the beach house."

"I wouldn't exactly describe a fifteen thousand square foot home in the Hamptons as a beach house, but go on."

"So that's when I tried calling Mia. I knew she'd been looking for new paintings and some sculpture for the gardens. I didn't want her to commit to anything just now, but I could never reach her. Anyway, Art's idea of belt-tightening wasn't to delay redecorating but to sell the damn place as well as the apartment here in the city. When I asked him where we'd live, I think he muttered Jersey, which told me just how bad things must be. He was always a bit of a heavy drinker, but I noticed that his alcohol consumption was starting earlier in the day." She took another sip of her own drink, which struck Jake as a bit hypocritical. "Two days ago, the shit really hit the fan and Artie told me that in all likelihood, Pilgrim was going to have to declare bankruptcy. When I asked what that meant for us, he said that the courts might seize most of our assets, but worse than that, his lawyers had told him that he was going to be the subject of a grand jury investigation and could be facing jail time."

"Shit. I'm sorry." As soon as he said the words, he felt like the hypocrite. Jake wasn't sorry, at least not for Arthur. He'd warned him but Arthur, being the arrogant son-of-a-bitch that he was, had brushed him off. "How did this all come about?"

"You're asking the wrong person. All I know is that when Artie told me this, he was like holding back tears, and he wasn't even drunk. I'd never seen him in such a state. He kept apologizing to me and cursing at Steve."

Jake sat forward in his chair. "Steve?"

"You know, Stefano Assanti, his boy wonder who was going to make him the richest man on Wall Street. Only now, that wasn't going to happen. Now Artie might be going to prison and I'm going to live in Hoboken. All because of that fucking wop, as he put it. Then he went into some rambling about how all the other big firms were going to be following him down the road to perdition. Those were the last words I heard from him."

"What do you mean last words?"

"Actually not his very last words. He wanted to leave the apartment. I asked him where he was going and he said out to the beach house. I said I'd go with him but he insisted that he needed some time alone, away from people and away from the city. He gave me kiss and told me not to worry, that he had some thoughts on how to get out of the situation, and that he'd make sure that I'd be taken care of, after which he drove off in his shiny red Ferrari. Somewhere past Bridgehampton, he drove off the road and wrapped his fancy sports car around a tree. Police estimated that he was going well in excess of a hundred miles per hour. Then I found a sealed envelope in my pocketbook which had a ten million dollar life insurance policy he'd taken out a few days earlier."

"Jesus. I had no idea. Well at least you can take some comfort that at the end, he was thinking of you."

"Comfort!" she snapped back. "The dumb fuck was so incompetent he couldn't even stage his own suicide successfully. I guess he didn't realize that modern cars, even small sports cars, have all sorts of safety things like air bags to increase survivability. In addition, when they found him he was wearing his seat belt. What kind of shmuck tries to kill himself in a car wreck but puts on his seatbelt? So Arthur is still very much with us, except that the accident fractured his spine, which in all likelihood will leave him a paraplegic. So it's worse than if he'd died. Maybe it will keep him out of prison but there's no guarantee of even that."

"Should it come to that, and I don't think it will, at least he'll have Mr. Assanti as company."

"Hardly. Assanti quit Pilgrim just before this all went south. He's not even in the country anymore. Moved to Europe. Paris I think Art said, and he's not sure they could extradite him even if they found him. No, if Art has company in prison, it will be from his other cronies who followed Assanti's schemes. Arthur was right about one thing, Assanti was no dumb dago."

"He may not even be Italian."

"What do you mean, of course Assanti is Italian."

"Well one thing's for sure, his real name isn't Assanti."

"Are you sure?"

"Unfortunately, yes."

Debbie shook her head. "God, how did life ever get so crazy."

"I know. I was thinking the same thing. Sometimes I wish I was back in college, back when Mia and I first met."

"I never realized you two have known each other for that long."

"We were put together in an economics class by this eccentric professor, Adam Scott Meech..." Jake stopped mid-sentence with his mouth half open. It is said that the human brain has upwards of one hundred billion neurons able to form a hundred trillion connections. With that many possibilities, moments of insight rarely come at predictable times, but when they do, they often come in blinding speed as if all the right synapses suddenly fire in sync and what were disparate pieces of information coalesce to form a clear, succinct picture.

"Is something wrong?" Debbie asked.

"What time is it in Paris?"

"Gee I don't know. Middle of the night I guess."

"Excuse me, I've got to make a call. Help yourself to more booze, and ah, feel free to stay here as long as you need to."

He went to his bedroom and tried calling Mia again on her GSM phone. He wasn't surprised when she didn't pick up. Even as he was placing the call, he was turning on his computer to look for the itinerary that she'd emailed him and find out where in Paris she was staying. What he'd forgotten was that he had left a bootable CD in the computer's drive and instead of prompting for a password, the screen asked if he wanted to install some program. He put down his phone and popped out the CD and then restarted the computer. Staring at the disc in his hand, he remembered what was lying on a shelf in a closet, below a Tupperware container of marijuana, not ten feet away. By the time he'd retrieved the disc from the closet, the computer had finished booting up. He nervously put the CD into the drive and waited as he heard it begin to spin. The computer's desktop disappeared and was replaced by a cute little slide show that David had put together for viewing the stored images of all the memorabilia his mother had saved. He clicked on the link titled "Jake – The College Years" and started scrolling through scanned images of report cards, Dean's List letters and papers. Then he came to it. He couldn't take his eyes off the first page.

```
Econ198 – Economics for Engineers and
Scientists
Adam S. Meecham, Professor


A Business Plan For
Amalgamated Equity Partners, Inc.


Presented by:
Mia Jang
Jacob Himmelfarb
Sayid Hassan
```

He slumped back in his chair. Debbie called out from the living room asking if he wanted another drink. He didn't bother to answer. Sayid Hassan. SH. The Arab kid. He sat at the computer and slowly read through the entire paper. When he reached the end, he read and re-read Meecham's comments written in the professor's own hand.

As the three of you already are aware, this business plan that you are proposing is fraught with dangers far beyond what you can imagine. Were it to actually come to fruition, it could do such harm to the credit markets in this country that they would all but dry up, and that could trigger a massive recession, even leading to another Great Depression. Fortunately, the government has enough regulatory oversight that it will never come to that. Ironically, had the Soviets been smart enough to put their efforts into attacking our economy with plans such as yours, rather than wasting all their resources on useless military expenditures, they, not us, might have won the Cold

War. Nevertheless, you have demonstrated some of the basic principles of economics, which was the purpose of the assignment. A.S. Meecham.

His comments were followed by a big "A" with a circle around it. "Jesus H. Christ," Jake whispered. "Mia, Mia, Mia. What the fuck were you thinking?" He closed off the document and opened his email looking for Mia's itinerary. As soon as he found it, he called the Hotel Luxembourg Parc who citing the time of night, it was just after three a.m., declined his request to ring her room. After ten minutes of arguing with the desk clerk that it was a matter of life and death, he was put on hold for the night manager. When the manager finally got on the line, he explained to an increasingly exasperated Jake that he couldn't connect him to Mia because she had checked out of the hotel the day before. The manager did have one piece of useful information – Mia had left behind a pair of glasses and had called the hotel to have them sent to her at the Sofitel Hotel in Munich, Germany.

Jake didn't know if this was good news or bad news. That she'd left Paris where Sayid was supposedly staying was good. That she'd gone to Germany without telling him wasn't. He tried calling the Sofitel, but the Germans were even less cooperative than the Parisians and unlike the French, the Germans were much stricter at conforming to corporate policy, refusing to even confirm that Mia was staying there. *Fucking Nazis* he muttered as he hung up the phone. A rational person could come up with any number of logical explanations for why Mia had apparently gone to Munich, but Jake's judgment was impaired by the rush of nervous adrenalin brought on by his moment of revelation. He found an Air France flight leaving later that night from JFK. If he really hurried, he thought he could make it, so he purchased a ticket online. He found his passport and threw a couple of changes of shirts, underwear and socks into a carry-on suitcase. He passed by Deb as he was heading out, gave her a spare key to the apartment and reaffirmed to her that she could stay as long as she needed to. He'd be back in a few days. On the cab ride to the airport, the driver had the Knicks post-game show on the radio. "Who won?" Jake asked.

"Believe it or not, the Knicks. I thought it'd take a miracle for them to beat the Celts."

Jake smiled. He thought of his uncle and remembered that he'd just won his bet. He was hoping that it was a sign of more good luck to follow. He feared he'd need a miracle much bigger than the one his hometown basketball team had just pulled off.

It wasn't until after six the following evening that Jake finally landed in Munich. When he'd purchased the ticket, he hadn't realized that the flight had a layover in Paris. It gave him a chance to convert some of his dollars into euros but meant that the total travel time was more than twelve hours. He tried again to reach Mia when he landed in Munich, but she still wasn't answering her phone. The taxi ride into the city was uneventful, except for the nagging feeling he couldn't shake that everyone he met since landing, from the baggage handlers to the cabbie, were descendants of concentration camp guards, sizing him up as though he had a yellow star sewn on his coat. He'd only been to Germany twice before, and each time, he had the same sensation. He knew it was irrational because in fact he'd never once experienced anything there that could be remotely construed as anti-Semitic. The same could not be said for the time he'd visited Vienna, but all those stories he'd heard relatives tell since childhood never spoke of Austrians, only Germans. Passing by traffic signs with large arrows pointing to Dachau didn't help either, and he imagined his driver following those arrows and dropping him off at a gate under a sign reading *Arbeit Macht Frei*.

But of course the driver never took that route, which would have been in the opposite direction and when the car pulled up in front of the hotel, instead of SS guards separating new arrivals into groups destined for the showers, he was greeted by two overly friendly porters asking to take his bags. He walked up to the registration counter and an attractive young lady asked him if he had a reservation, which he didn't. He told the girl that he was staying with Mia Jang and all he needed was her room number, and if she was out, could he get a spare key. The hotel clerk spent the next few minutes rapidly typing onto a computer as her expression grew increasingly taciturn. "I'm sorry, but I cannot give out information regarding our guests."

"Look, I'm her fiancé. I know she's staying here and I know she's not expecting me. It's our two-year anniversary of being a couple and I really wanted to surprise her. I'd like to have a dozen roses, maybe some strawberries, and a bottle of your best champagne sent up to the room." He was quite pleased with himself at coming up with what he thought was a great story on the spur of the moment. The clerk didn't yield. He reached into his wallet and laid out three hundred euros on the counter. "I'd really, really appreciate anything you could do."

She glanced at the money and returned to her computer screen. "If you'd like, we do have some vacancies, otherwise, there is not much else I can do for you."

"Screw it. I'll wait in the restaurant." He started to walk away, purposefully leaving the money in hopes she'd change her mind. For a moment he thought it had worked when she called out to him but it was only to hand back the cash.

He sat at the bar eating a variety of sausages, sauerkraut and potato pancakes and had just ordered his third glass of beer when he spotted Mia walking through the lobby towards the exit. He was so flummoxed that he tipped over his glass spilling beer across the bar. He quickly apologized to the bartender, threw down a hundred euros and went chasing after her. He shouted her name but she was already out the door. He ran through the lobby and saw her standing at the curb, apparently waiting for a car. He raced up behind her and tapped her shoulder.

She turned to him and gasped, "What the hell are you doing here?"

"That's the same thing I was wondering. You're supposed to be in Paris, packing to come home."

"Something came up. I can't talk about it now. Shit, Jake, why did you come here?"

"I have to talk to you. Let's go back to your room." The words were no sooner spoken than Sayid walked up behind him. Jake saw the signs of recognition in Mia's eyes and spun around. Sayid looked gaunt. His eyes glazed, his hair disheveled, his cheeks, even beneath the week-long beard growth, were sunken, all giving the signs of a man who hadn't eaten or slept well in a quite some time. "My God, I can't believe it's him."

"What's he doing here? I told you to come alone," Sayid said.

"I don't know why he's here," she answered.

"I told you to come alone," he repeated

"I didn't fucking spend the last twenty-four hours flying here from New York to go anywhere without her."

Sayid shook his head. "Let's get out of here. I have a car parked in the next block." He started walking. Mia looked at Jake with an expression that said *don't come* but he grabbed her hand and they followed Sayid. The three turned down a side street where Sayid took a key fob from his pocket and pressed it.

The lights on a Volkswagen parked across the street flashed. As they stepped off the curb, a silver van screeched to a halt in front of them. The sliding door of the van flew open and out jumped two masked men waving semi-automatic guns at them. Everyone froze. The passenger side window rolled down.

Gretchen leaned her head out of the van. "Get into the back," she ordered Sayid. Hesitantly, he stepped into the van as one of the men prodded the barrel of his gun against his back. The other masked man said something to Gretchen in Arabic that neither Jake nor Mia understood, yet each sensed he was asking for instructions.

"Let them go," Sayid shouted from inside of the van.

"Can't do that," Gretchen replied. She gave her instructions, again in Arabic, and quickly one of the men threw hoods over Jake and Mia and shoved them into the van next to Sayid. They heard the door slam shut and felt the vehicle accelerate, leading them where, they could only guess.

TWENTY-FOUR

It was the longest car ride of Jake's life, not in terms of physical time, but in psychological time. In the blackness brought on by the hood over his face, Jake kept remembering the road signs to Dachau and wondered whether that was their destination. No one spoke until the van came to a stop and Gretchen began issuing orders. Jake, Mia and Sayid were taken out of the van and had their hoods removed. They stood outside of what appeared to be an old warehouse in a grimy industrial park. It was a moonless night, but even in the dim halogen streetlights they could see that the building was surrounded by a chain link fence topped with razor-wire. It was no doubt there to keep out the unauthorized, but to Jake, it looked like the barbed-wire fences of a concentration camp, there to keep them in. Gretchen unlocked a door to the building and went in first, followed by Sayid, Jake, Mia and lastly the armed guards.

All the lights inside the building were off. Gretchen took out a small flashlight and led them down several corridors until she stopped and unlocked an interior door. She leaned inside the room, flipped on the fluorescent lights and told them to go in. It was windowless room with a rectangular metal table in the middle surrounded by five beat-up folding chairs. In one corner were stacked collapsed cardboard boxes next to packing and shipping supplies. "Wait here," Gretchen said as she closed the door and left the three of them alone. Sayid walked over to the door and turned the handle. "Locked," he said.

Mia wrapped her right arm tightly around Jake's left arm. "What the fuck is going on? Who the hell are these people and wasn't that your girlfriend?" she asked. Sayid walked over to the table and took a seat in one of the chairs without answering.

"You want to explain it to her or should I?" Jake said. "It seems that our old classmate has become a jihadist terrorist. Am I right, Sayid?"

Sayid remained silent. "What are you talking about Jake? I've been working with Sayid for years. He's no terrorist."

"For years? Funny you forgot to mention anything about him to me."

Mia released her grip on his arm, apparently realizing the implication of what she had just said. "I couldn't say anything to anybody. I'm sorry about that, but Sayid was good enough to give me access to a lot of wealthy clients, access neither he nor I would have had if they had known his real name. There's still a lot of fucking prejudice in America but as a white boy you don't see it." Jake had the impulse to argue that he was as much a minority as either she or Sayid but didn't see the point. "Why'd you come here anyway?"

"I could you ask the same question. You were supposed to be in Paris." Jake glanced at his watch. "I take that back. You were supposed to be on a plane right now flying back to New York."

"Sayid texted me that we needed to meet but he couldn't travel to Paris so he asked me to come to Munich, which reminds me, how did you know I was in Germany?"

"You left your glasses in Paris. The hotel told me where you were staying. So why did Sayid need to meet you?"

"That's a good question, Sayid. Why did you want to see me?" Sayid, who had been sitting with his forehead buried in his arms on the tabletop as though he were sleeping mumbled something unintelligible. Mia turned toward Jake. "What did he say?"

Sayid slowly lifted his head off the table. "I said, like Jake, I wanted to warn you."

"What the hell does everybody want to warn me about?"

"Your boyfriend is right. These people are part of al-Qaeda."

"I see," she said. "I guess love makes you do stupid things. Your girlfriend is one tough bitch."

Sayid laughed. "For God's sake, she's not my girlfriend. She's a psychopathic anarchist. She was my guard, sent by the higher-ups to watch over their investments."

"Then the story about your first fiancée, that was all a lie?" she asked.

"No...and yes. The story was partially true. I did have a fiancée, though she wasn't Korean. She was a Palestinian and we met in Saudi Arabia before she was falsely imprisoned and died there, or so I thought at the time."

Mia looked confused. "You thought?"

"As it turns out, she didn't die in prison because she was never put in prison. In fact, she didn't die at all, and wasn't even a Palestinian. But I didn't know any of that when I told you my story."

She closed her eyes and bowed her head. "You just changed the names to protect the guilty."

"Something doesn't sound right," Jake said to Sayid. "You knew all along what you were doing with the manipulation of mortgage-backed securities. It was straight from our days back at MIT. It was designed to fail. But there are two things I can't figure out. Why did you get Mia involved?"

"I needed seed money."

"I know Mia made some bucks from that biotech firm, but certainly not enough to start the kind of scheme that you envisioned."

"No, but she had access to the Chinese, who do have that kind of money."

Jake looked straight into her eyes. "I know why he wanted to screw the American economy, but why would you?"

"She didn't want to screw the Americans. It was the Chinese she was after," Sayid answered for her. "My little deception led her to believe that I was after the Chinese as well. She figured that if they lost huge sums of their sovereign funds, it would weaken the central government, perhaps causing its downfall."

"In hindsight, it was a bit naïve," she said quietly.

"You think?" Jake exclaimed. "The Chinese have most of their foreign investments in U.S. Treasury notes. Even if Sayid's plot succeeds, it would cause much more harm to America than China."

She couldn't look at him. "I realize that now. You said there were two things you didn't understand. What was the other?"

"Why did al-Qaeda need to have that girl watch over you? She's probably on some CIA or FBI watch list. She could have exposed you before you had time enough for the financial attack to take hold. Then all their efforts would have been for naught."

Sayid smirked and shook his head. "These people are as fooled by this scheme as everyone else. They forgot all about my plan and I doubt that they ever understood it. They just needed money fast and they used Gretchen to make sure that I'd get them their funds when the time came."

"The time came for what?" asked Mia.

"The time for buying the supply of plutonium, or uranium, or perhaps full-fledged ICBMs."

"What!" Jake shouted.

Sayid let out a slow breath. "It seems that Gretchen has connections with some Chechens who have access to some weapons-grade plutonium left over from the Soviet Union. They needed a billion dollars to buy enough for two or three bombs. I made them only half that amount but it seems the Chechens are willing to sell them enough for one bomb."

"Shit," Mia whispered, apparently realizing that she may have unwittingly aided in creating a nightmare. "But just having the nuclear material doesn't mean you can build a nuke."

"I don't know much about it. Maybe they're getting an already assembled warhead. Maybe not. I did hear that they've got some Pakistani nuclear scientist who knows how to build a bomb."

"How the hell can you live with yourself?" she asked incredulously.

"I couldn't, which is why instead of transferring the money to their Swiss account, I parked it in a different numbered account. My guess is that by now, they've come to the realization that I'm the only one who can access that account. My fear for you was that once they kill me because I won't give them the account number, they'd come after anyone who I worked with in the hope that I'd given them the access codes, and that meant that you, and maybe even you Jake, were at risk."

Jake sat down at the table. "This is all so unbelievable. I have to admit I'm impressed that you could make so many smart people buy into your scheme. I can see how some greedy bastards like Arthur Morrison would go along, but it takes a lot of people from a lot of differing organizations to rise to the level that it seems to have reached."

"Surprisingly not. In Morrison's defense, he was actually reluctant at first to get involved with derivatives. There were fewer than ten people whom I really had to convince. Then it was like a computer virus that spread out to the Bear-Sterns, the Lehmans and Goldmans, the hedge funds, the insurance companies, the Countrywides and the banks. Everybody wanted in. Adam Meecham's grand equation turns out to be true."

Mia, who had remained standing motionless against the wall as though it were a magnet and she an iron bar, spoke up. "What equation?"

Jake turned to her. "G equals F I squared. Meecham was the ultimate Einsteinphile, always quoting Uncle Albert. My favorite was *'Two things are infinite: The universe and stupidity, and I'm not sure about the universe.'"*

"Oh yeah, I'd forgotten." Mia released herself from the wall and took a seat at the table. "Greed equals fear times ignorance times…shit what was the other i?"

"Irrationality," Jake and Sayid answered in unison.

"Right. Adam Meecham. Is he still alive?"

"He died back in the nineties," answered Jake.

"It's funny how the older I get, the smarter he gets," said Sayid. "It is truly unreal the level at which greed and fear supersede intelligence and common sense. People who should know better still do stupid things if they're afraid that they're missing the boat, even if that boat is the Titanic heading for an iceberg. Of course it helps that these guys all thought they were the smartest one in the room. They'd bought into the line of thinking espoused by some right-of-center economic and social critics, who at the end of the twentieth century and beginning of the twenty-first made much the same mistake that their left-of-center counterparts made a hundred years earlier."

"Which was?" asked Jake.

"Socialist and communist theorizers could not imagine that capitalist business leaders would find it in their own best interests to see that their workers prosper. Marx could never imagine that Henry Ford would pay his workers multiple times what they could make anywhere else, but Ford recognized that he'd make more money if the people who worked from him could afford to buy his cars. Same thing eventually spread to other industries like steel and it created your great middle class. This all worked fine as long as everybody continued to prosper but when the industrial age matured and the information age began, the old models started to fail. Now it was no longer necessarily in owners' interests to make sure their workers would also be their customers. Globalization created a new playing field. Technology allowed for the trading of equity in corporations to be handled at the speed of light. Institutional investors were basically calling the shots as to what they expected from CEOs, so the bottom line became king. Hence, the great shrinking of the American middle class and as their incomes stagnated or worse, actually dropped, the incomes of the wealthiest skyrocketed. Now here's where the conservative theorists went wrong. Because companies for most of the twentieth century were, in the end, acting to better their workers' lives because they were also their customers, these economic theorists assumed that they would continue to do this. The need for governmental oversight only added cost which reduced efficiency and profits. Your government capitulated to this line of thinking by deregulating industry after industry. By the time the twenty-first century rolled around, the only large asset that most of the middle class could rely on was their homes. So you had, as the popular expression goes, a perfect storm. People cashing out on their largest, in some cases only, source of equity with a financial services industry unencumbered by governmental oversight more than happy to oblige. They were like drug dealers. They preyed on the weakness of their borrowers by giving money to anyone who asked for it, kind of like how pushers give free samples of drugs to hook their users.

"So what happens now?" asked Mia.

Sayid smirked. "These pushers are committing the cardinal sin for drug dealers. They are in essence, themselves becoming addicts, pushing their 'dope' on each other. This couldn't have happened if the police narcs, in this case government regulators, had been doing their job, but that's a whole other political discussion. In time, prices will go so out of whack as to what people can afford to pay, defaults will rise and everyone will begin to realize that the frenzied drug trip they've been enjoying is ending. Nobody will really know what their investments are worth, and like a bad drug trip, they'll crash."

"My experience with government regulations is that more often than not, they end up inhibiting growth by protecting those with political clout, who these days are those with the money, rather than letting the marketplace choose the winners and losers," said Jake. "That is no formula for economic growth."

"I'm surprised to hear those sentiments coming from you. You sound like a spokesman for the Heritage Foundation. Look, anything taken to excess can become destructive. Finding the right balance is the ideal. But given the choice between too much or too little protection from those few who would exploit the system to the detriment of the many, I'll err on the side of too much."

Mia closed her eyes and for the moment, her face seemed aglow in meditative serenity. "Balance is the ultimate goal, difficult to attain and nearly impossible to keep." Jake looked at her as though she were an extraterrestrial who had just beamed down from an alien planet. She opened her eyes and looked back at him.

"A teaching I once learned," she said.

Jake rolled his eyes before turning back to Sayid.

"Anyway, when the hell did you have time to think all of this up?"

"Uh, Jake, remember, I do have a doctorate in this crap from the London School."

"You keep saying 'your' American government. Aren't you a U.S. citizen too?" Mia asked.

"Technically, yes, as well as technically I am a citizen of Egypt. In truth, I feel as though I've no country and that's the way I prefer it. Look at all the misery that patriotism has wrought on humanity."

"The same could be said of religion," she said.

"No argument there."

Jake's face contorted before he belched, eliciting a disapproving glare from Mia. "Seems to me you're being a bit of a casuist. Did you honestly believe that a recession in America would lead to the overthrow Mubarek or the Saudis?" he asked.

"It might."

"I doubt it. And even if it did, what makes you think that whatever government replaced them would be any better? Look at what happened in Iran. The Shah was booted out and what replaced him was worse. Rarely do revolutions produce better governments, even in big countries like China and Russia, not to mention most of the Third World."

"What about South Africa or India?" Mia interjected. "They seem to have produced working democracies. Remember, America was the result of a revolution."

"And what do those places all have in common?" Jake responded. "They all had the good fortune of being part of the British Empire, which meant they had a tradition of British common law. When the overwhelming majority of the population has little experience living in a society governed by the rule of law, dictators prevail, especially when that population is made up of sectarian groups bent on killing each other. The Arabs are used to living under despots. As I said, look at Iran."

"Iranians aren't Arabs, they're Persians," Sayid corrected.

"Arabs, Persians, what's the difference."

Mia rolled her eyes. "Jake, you're living proof of stupidity being infinite. Persians are descended from Caucasians. You might as well say that there is no difference between being Burmese and Japanese."

"There is?"

"God," Mia sighed. "How did I end up living with such an idiot."

"I'm kidding."

Sayid stretched his arms over his head. "Whatever governments do come to power, they couldn't be worse than what's in the Arab world today. But not to worry Jake, because I can't see anyone replacing Mubarek other than his own son in the foreseeable future. And if by some chance it did happen..." Before Sayid could finish his thought, the door opened and in walked three armed guards followed by two other men. One sported a scraggly black and gray beard and the other was clean-shaven and looked more like a graduate student in college. Behind the men, Gretchen walked in. The bearded man ordered Jake and Mia up from their chairs.

"Where is Mustafa?" asked Sayid.

"He's occupied with more important things. My name is Rashid Aruf, and I'm in charge. Who are these others?" he asked pointing at Jake and Mia.

"They were with him when we picked him up," answered Gretchen.

"Do they know anything?"

Gretchen shook her head. "I don't know."

Aruf stroked his beard once and then took the seat where Jake had been across from Sayid. "Put your hands on the table where we can see them."

"If I had a weapon, do you think I'd be sitting here?" said Sayid. Another guard walked behind Sayid and placed the barrel of his rifle against the base of Sayid's skull. "Whatever." Sayid stretched out his arms and placed his palms down on the table. He looked closely at Aruf. "We've met before, right?"

"Once, at your apartment in New York. You ignored me back then. I strongly advise you not to repeat that mistake." Aruf spoke in a surprisingly soft tone. "Now my young friend, you were entrusted with something that belongs to us, something we need right now."

"And that is?"

"Our money."

"Oh, you need money. May I take my hands off the table?" Aruf nodded and Sayid reached into his pocket and took out a small roll of paper money, some of which were euros and some dollars and began to peel them back. "How much do you need? I think I've got maybe fifty American dollars, some Euros, and some change in my other pocket."

Aruf smiled slightly. "Very funny. You are a comedian." Aruf rocked back in his chair before suddenly bolting forward and delivering a fierce slap across Sayid's face. "I am referring to the five hundred-plus million dollars that was supposed to be put in a Swiss account."

Sayid felt a trickle of blood forming at the corner of his mouth which he wiped off on his collar. "The money is in a Swiss bank."

"Put your hands back on the table." Aruf stood and leaned forward across the table so that his face was only inches from Sayid's. "It may be, but not in our account. So I need you to take it from whatever account it is in and transfer it to the correct account."

"I can't do that."

"Can't or won't?"

"Can't, won't – what's the difference? That money is going to buy nuclear weapons. I didn't sign on for that."

Aruf stood back and began wandering around the room. He walked by Jake and looked into his eyes. Jake stared back without blinking. He did the same with Mia before walking behind Sayid. "You signed on to be a soldier for our people. There is no greater honor than serving in jihad. Your duty as a soldier is to obey the orders of those above you, not to question the tactics. I've had men shot for less insolence than you show." Aruf said nothing for the next minute, letting the tension that silence can bring fill the room, before positioning himself at Sayid's left. "What you are doing by your actions is stealing. Regardless of what you think of our plans, the money is not yours. Mustafa warned me that he had doubts about your commitment to Islam and not to trust you. But are you familiar enough with your Koran to know what the penalty is for thievery?"

Sayid turned and looked up at Aruf, who quickly drew a meat cleaver from his behind his back and hacked off the ends of the pinkie and ring finger on Sayid's left hand. Blood immediately splattered on the table and Jake felt sick to his stomach. Mia's instincts from her medical training must have taken over as she bolted from the back of the room and began applying pressure to Sayid's wound. "Somebody get me something to bandage this with, anything. Rip your shirt if you have to." Jake found a linen handkerchief in his pocket and tossed it to her. She started to wrap it around his hand.

"What do you think you're doing?" Aruf laughingly asked.

"I'm a doctor. Grab the fingertips and find some ice to wrap them in. If we get him to a hospital quickly, they may be able to re-attach them."

Aruf continued to chuckle as he picked the severed digits off the table and held them out to her. "You mean these?" She glanced down at his hand and nodded. Aruf played sadistically with the fingers before unceremoniously flinging them across the room. He then wiped the blood off his hand on Mia's shirt. "He's lucky. I really should have taken the whole hand." He turned to Gretchen. "Take her away. Women shouldn't be here in the first place."

Gretchen said something in Arabic to two of the guards before they walked up to Mia and positioned their rifles on either side of her head.

"You'd better go," Sayid told her as he grimaced. "I'll be okay."

She got to her feet. "Try and keep it elevated and keep pressure on it." Sayid nodded.

"Where are you taking her?" Jake felt the butt of a rifle slam into his midsection as soon as he spoke.

"Don't worry about her," Gretchen said. "You should worry more about yourself." Mia plaintively looked back at Jake and mouthed "I love you" before being shoved out the door by one of the guards.

"Hurt much?" Aruf asked Sayid, but he didn't answer. "Don't worry, it will soon enough. And if it doesn't, you have eight more I can take off." The door opened and Gretchen stood at the threshold. "What is it?"

"Our guests are here."

Aruf stroked his beard again, a habit that Jake was finding more and more irritating. He had an urge to run over and pull out the whiskers one by one. "Tell them I will be there shortly." Gretchen nodded and closed the door. "I am a patient man, my friend, but even I have my limits." Aruf walked to the door. "You only have eight more fingers. After that, I'll have to find other parts." The door slammed closed, leaving only Sayid, Jake and one armed guard in the room.

Mia stood in the hallway surrounded by the two guards while they waited for Gretchen. At the end of the hall, she spotted two men wearing blue jeans and black leather jackets with a silver metal brief case on the floor between them. Gretchen walked by her without speaking, went over to the men and began conversing in a language that Mia didn't recognize. In short order they were joined by Aruf and the man who looked like a college student. Mia figured that the men in the leather jackets must be the Chechens, for they didn't look like Arabs, and the college boy must be the Pakistani scientist. Gretchen returned to her. "Follow me."

She led Mia and the guards to a room nearly identical to the one where Jake and Sayid were confined, except the chairs in this room were padded and on the table were strewn some German magazines. "Have a seat. We may be here for some time." Gretchen withdrew a pistol that had been tucked into the back of her pants and laid it on the table. The two guards remained standing at the back of the room. Mia stared at the gun. "Tempted to grab it?" Gretchen asked. "You'd be shot dead by my friends over there before you could even aim." Mia acknowledged the warning by nodding. "I forgot my manners. Our two friends with the rifles are Ahmed and Akmet."

Mia glanced at the guards who, upon hearing their names, smiled back at her. "This is my brother Darrel and my other brother Darrel," she said.

"I'm sorry, what was that?"

Mia's lips curled into a slight, wistful smile. "Just something from a TV show I used to watch as a kid." She sensed Gretchen didn't understand. "It was comedy about this guy who owned this inn in Vermont, and there was this hillbilly guy who would always show up with his two brothers and would always say, 'Hi am Larry and this is my brother Darrel and this is my other brother Darrel.'"

"What kind of parent gives two of their sons the same name?"

"That was the joke."

"Seems stupid to me. Then again, what I've seen of your TV seems mostly stupid."

"I guess you had to be there."

Gretchen picked up a copy of *Der Spiegel* and began leafing through it. "Help yourself to a mag," she said without looking up. Mia shuffled a few of the magazines around but didn't pick up any. "Don't see anything of interest?"

Mia shook her head. "They're all in German, and I don't understand enough German to read them."

"I'm sorry. If I had known you were coming, I'd have had them bring some copies of People or the National Inquirer." Gretchen paused to look up. "I guess you're more of a Time or New Yorker girl."

Mia didn't take her eyes off of Gretchen. She acted and spoke like Greta Garbo in Ninotchka but with more of a Marlene Dietrich accent, although even that was slight. Mia thought back to her days as a medical student, in particular, the time spent in a psych rotation. She stared at the woman sitting five feet away, calmly reading her magazine, not seeming the least bit affected by the butchery they had just witnessed. She tried to classify exactly what personality disorder Gretchen possessed, not with the intent of treating her, but with the hope it might provide something, anything that would help her survive this predicament. Psychopath, Sayid's description, was all that came to mind. She knew Gretchen wasn't stupid though. Anyone as fluent in multiple languages as Gretchen must have a fairly high IQ. Mia remembered something about how hostages should try and befriend their captors in the hope of forming some sort of bond and thus reduce the chances of being harmed. She wasn't sure whether this was something learned from her medical training or something she'd seen in a movie but it was the only strategy that came to mind. "What are you reading?" she asked.

"Something about Madonna in England spotted at some club with Prince Harry and Johnny Depp."

"I love Johnny Depp. I think he's the best actor out there." Gretchen said nothing. "Do you like movies?"

"Sometimes."

"What about books? You have a favorite author?" Gretchen just shook her head as she flipped the page. "What kind of music do you like? Me, I love Sting and the Police. 'Roxanne...' she crooned out of key. Still no reaction from Gretchen. Mia sensed her strategy going nowhere and slumped back into her chair.

"I like The Talking Heads." Gretchen's statement, coming out of the blue, surprised Mia. "Do you know who they are?"

"The Talking Heads?" she answered excitedly. "Sure. Eighties band. David Byrne.

"Can you guess my favorite Talking Heads song?"

Mia thought for a second. She seemed to be reaching Gretchen and she didn't want to squander the opportunity. "Burning Down The House," she blurted.

Gretchen looked up from the magazine. "No," and returned to reading.

"Once In a Lifetime?" Gretchen shook her head. "Um, jeez let me think. Take Me To The River?"

"Psycho Killer" Gretchen deadpanned.

"Gee, now there's a shock," Mia responded under her breath.

"Do you know why that's my favorite song?"

"Could it be you identify with the title character?"

"Very funny. No. It is because of the lyric that goes. 'You're talking a lot, but you're not saying much. When I've got nothing to say, my lips are sealed.'"

Mia, fearing she may have pushed it too far, began to feel queasy and decided it best to drop it. "I get it. Um…"

"Say something once, why say it again."

"As I said, I get it."

"No, that's just the next line of the song."

Despite, or perhaps because of Mia's feeble attempts, Gretchen remained an enigma. Mia decided the make-her-my-friend route wasn't going to work. "Can I ask you a question?"

Gretchen tossed the magazine on the floor and picked up another. "If you must."

"Am I going to die?"

Gretchen stopped reading and looked directly at Mia. "Let me ask you a question. You are a doctor." Mia nodded. "Where did you train?"

Again Mia was surprise. "I went medical school at Hopkins in Baltimore."

"Johns Hopkins. Very impressive. Very good reputation for medicine. I would have thought that such a prestigious institution would have taught you in some class the answer to your question. Since they apparently did not, I will. Yes, you are going to die. Then again, so is everyone else, eventually."

"I mean, am I going to die in the near future, like in the next few hours."

Gretchen pinched her lips tightly and slowly nodded. "If you are very, very careful, and follow everything that I tell you to do, then you have a reasonable chance of getting out of here alive." She kept staring into Mia's eyes. "What is it?" she finally asked.

"I don't know what I was expecting. Of course you're going to say that to me, whether it's true or not."

"Then you should act on the assumption that it is the truth, because it's your only option."

"And what about Jake?"

"Jake might make it out if he also doesn't do anything stupid, and if Aruf doesn't find out about his religion."

"You know he's Jewish?"

"Don't worry, I won't tell Aruf if I don't have to."

"And Sayid?" Gretchen returned to reading the magazine. "What about Sayid?"

"Only Sayid can save himself."

"How's the hand doing?"

"It fucking hurts." Sayid tugged at the makeshift bandage Mia had applied hoping to alleviate the pain. "At least the bleeding seems to have stopped."

Despite having put himself in bed with al-Qaeda, Jake couldn't help admire Sayid's bravery in resisting Aruf. He knew he couldn't have held up as well. Jake's natural inclination was to avoid confrontation whenever possible. "What do you think they'll do to us?"

"For you and Mia, who knows? Aruf made it pretty clear what he intends on doing with me."

"How long can you hold out?"

Sayid winced as he repositioned his injured hand on the table. "I don't know, but it's my only chance of survival. If they kill me without getting access to the account, they'll never see their money. And reciprocally, if I do give them the code, then I'm of no further use to them."

"Which means they'd off you."

"Thanks for reminding me." Sayid let out a grunt as he once more tried to find a position to ease the pain.

"Hey you," Jake called to the guard who was sitting in a chair against the door. "Do you think we could get something for him? Even an aspirin would help." The guard had no reaction.

"He probably doesn't know English," Sayid explained. "Most of these foot soldiers are from Yemen or Somalia and are barely literate." Jake started to smile. "What is it?"

Jake shook his head. "Nothing. Just thinking again about Adam Meecham. I can't believe how obnoxious I was back then, and how he put up with us."

"All I know is he was the best teacher I ever had. He probably had the greatest influence on you of any teacher you ever had as well. I mean, don't you think that somewhere in the back of your head you heard Meecham's words when you gave up a big salary to try and save children in Africa?"

Jake nodded in agreement. "I still remember that time we played bridge against him for our grade. It came down to the last hand of the night."

"You under-led your doubleton king. It threw him for a loop. I can still see the shock on his face when you produced that king and he went down at six-no, doubled."

"You remember well. I wonder what the professor would say of our situation now."

"He'd probably do what he always did and quote Einstein. Something like 'The fear of death is the most unjustified of all fears, for there's no risk of accident for someone who's dead.'"

"Well that's not very comforting."

Sayid agreed. "Maybe he'd find some analogy to bridge. You defeated him by making a totally illogical play, one he didn't anticipate. One that no bridge player would have anticipated."

Jake thought about what Sayid said. "What do you think our guard over there expects us to do?"

"Huh?"

"Simple. If you were him, how would you expect us to act?"

"Not sure. I guess the only thing I'd be concerned about would be our trying to escape by overpowering him, so I'd make sure to keep my rifle ready. The surprising thing is that Aruf only left one guard here and left us unrestrained."

"So he made a mistake."

"Perhaps," said Sayid.

"Then this may be our best opportunity. But if we tried to take him on, one if not both of us would get shot."

"Most likely you since I'm the one they need."

"Again not very comforting. We have to get him to put the gun down, or at least not be in a position to use it. What wouldn't he expect? For us to get into a fight? We could fake an argument and maybe he'd come over and try and break it up."

"Maybe, but since I'm the one they need, it's likely he'd shoot you if he thought you were winning."

"Scratch that idea. It would have to be something out of the blue." Jake squirmed in his chair and stifled a burp.

"What is it?" Sayid asked.

"While I was waiting for Mia earlier at the hotel, I sat in the bar and had some of the local cooking. Some kind of sausauge."

"Wurst."

"It wasn't that bad."

"Wurst is what the Germans call their sausages. Like bratwurst."

"Whatever it was, it's doing a number on my gastrointestinal tract. I hope I can keep it down."

"As do I. Why don't you go and see if our watchdog can get you to a bathroom before you barf…though…if you barfed on him…"

Jake nodded, "That would certainly be something unexpected."

"Yes it would. The shock and disgust of it could distract him enough to allow one of us to grab the rifle. The question is, do you feel sick enough to actually do it on command?"

"There's always the two fingers down the throat. I've never done it, but as much turmoil as my stomach is in, it shouldn't take much to toss my cookies. "

"Okay then. Go over to him and explain you need to go the bathroom. He won't understand but I'll come over and explain it in Arabic and while I'm doing that, let loose. I'll grab the rifle."

"Will you be able to do that with your hand?"

"I'll have to."

Jake nodded. He took a deep breath before pushing back his chair and standing up. The guard was half asleep and for a second Jake thought of simply rushing him and wresting the rifle away. But as soon as he started towards him, the guard sat up and aimed his Kalashnikov directly at Jake. "Whoa, calm down, Osama. I just need to get to a bathroom." The guard said something in Arabic, which Jake, although not knowing the meaning, assumed was an order to get back to his seat. Jake kept walking towards him even though the guard became visibly more agitated with each step. "Help me out here, Sayid."

Sayid stood and started explaining Jake's condition to the guard. The guard remained seated while he argued with Sayid. Jake, who by this point stood just to the side of the guard, turned his back and plunged his index and middle fingers down his throat, causing an immediate gag reflex. He spun back and dumped the undigested wurst and potato pancakes over the guard. The guard let out a shriek but before he could react further, Sayid launched himself, knocking the guard off his chair as his weapon fell to the floor. "Get the damn rifle!" Sayid shouted as the two struggled.

Jake grabbed the gun but had no clue how to use it. He aimed at the two of them, but it was too dangerous to shoot. He flipped the rifle around and holding onto the barrel, swung the butt of the gun as hard as he could over the guard's head. The guard's body went limp and Jake feared he had killed him. Sayid pushed him off. "Good thinking not to fire. The noise could have given us away."

"Uh, yeah, well, I figured that. How's your hand?"

"I guess with all the adrenaline, surprisingly okay."

"Here, you take this." Jake started to hand the rifle to Sayid.

Sayid got to his feet and brushed off his clothes with his good hand. "No you keep it. I can't handle a rifle with one hand. Let's get out of here. Hopefully, the door's unlocked."

"What about him?" Jake pointed with the gun at the guard who, although stunned, was not unconscious.

"Go look over at those boxes. Maybe there's some string we can use to tie him up."

Jake rummaged through the boxes. He found some twine but it didn't look strong enough to do the job. He found a roll of duct tape and held it up. "What about this?"

"It'll do. Give me the gun. Gag him first and then tape his hands behind his back and his legs together. Don't be bashful with the tape." Jake wasn't. He used the entire roll leaving the guard looking like the Tin Man from the Wizard of Oz. "That should do it. Let's get out of here." Sayid handed the gun back to Jake and reached for the doorknob. "Moment of Truth." He turned the knob and felt the door unlatch. "So far, so good."

He cracked the door slightly ajar and peeked out into the hallway. It was dimly lit with just one fluorescent fixture on. Seeing no one around, he motioned with his head for Jake to go. "Which way?" Jake asked.

"As I recall, we came from the left so let's head that way."

"What about Mia?"

"We can help her most by getting out of here and calling the police."

"The hell with that. I didn't fly halfway round the world to leave her with these assholes. She just risked her life to help your hand, not to mention that you got her into this. So you're going to help get her out."

Sayid licked his lips. "Okay, just be quiet."

They walked down the hallway stopping at each door and listening to see if they could hear any voices from the other side. After ten minutes, they reached a door where men's voices were heard coming from the other side. "Let's burst in," Jake whispered, but Sayid held up his hand as he placed his ear against the door.

"I doubt she's in there. I recognize Aruf's voice. He's speaking with the Pakistani and there is some English being spoken, and some other language, sounds a little like German but I can't tell for sure. I think they're negotiating the nuke deal. Sounds like the Chechens brought a sample for the Pakistani to assess."

"How can he do that?"

"I don't know. Maybe they set up a lab or something."

"Should we go in?"

"I doubt that Mia would be at such a meeting. And there are probably men with more guns than we have. It sounds as though they'll be in there for some time, so let's keep looking."

Jake nodded in agreement. They eased their way past the door and continued searching. There were two more doors down that corridor, one of which was a janitor's closet. The other opened into a large empty area that must have been warehouse space. They walked quickly past rows of empty storage bins until they were convinced no one was there before leaving the space through a different door and down another corridor lined with offices. The third door down that hallway was the jackpot, for they clearly heard Mia and Gretchen's voices on the other side. "Should we knock or just burst in?" Jake whispered.

"Burst in. You ready?"

Jake nodded and clutched the rifle tightly by his chest in a position ready to fire. As quietly as he could, Sayid turned the doorknob, nodded at Jake and then flung open the door. Jake rushed in first with Sayid right on his heels. Mia and Gretchen were still sitting, clearly caught off-guard by their entrance. Gretchen lunged for the pistol she'd laid on the table, but Mia, with a sweep of her hand flung the gun against a wall. The two guards jumped to their feet and aimed their guns at Jake and Sayid.

Sayid kicked the door closed. "Tell them to drop their rifles," he shouted at Gretchen. Her eyes were transfixed on Jake's gun, less than two feet from her and aimed directly at her head. "Now, Gretchen, tell them." In Arabic she instructed the guards to lower their guns as she pushed her chair back from the table. "On the ground. Tell them to put the rifles on the ground and kick them away." She stood up and gave the order to the guards. "Shoot her, Jake."

Jake was shocked. "Huh?"

"We can't take them with us, and there's nothing here to tie them up with. So you're going to have to shoot her and the guards."

"I can't do that."

"You don't have a choice. It's them or us."

"He won't do that," Gretchen said. "He can't."

"I wouldn't be so sure of that." Jake was trying to sound as threatening as possible to mask the abject terror inside of him.

"I am quite sure." She took a step toward him. "There are at least two reasons why I know that."

"Yeah? What reasons?"

Her expression became almost serene and an assured smile appeared on her face. "I know a killer. I can see it in his eyes. You don't have the eyes of a killer. It's just not in your nature." She took another step towards him forcing him to take a step back.

"For God's sake Jake, she's a psychopath," Sayid implored. "She'd kill us without giving it a second thought."

She continued towards him. "Kill the cunt!" Mia shouted. Jake had never heard Mia use that word before and, the situation notwithstanding, it was somewhat shocking to hear it now.

"Stop or I will," he said, but she kept coming as he kept retreating until the wall would let him retreat no further. He squeezed the trigger but nothing happened. He tried again and a third time but the weapon did nothing. Bewildered, he looked down at the gun.

"See, you are not a killer." Before he could react, she delivered a blow from her knee to his midsection that caused him to double over at the waist and lose his grip on the gun. She grabbed the barrel of the rifle and the next thing he knew, she was holding it pointed at him. "As I said, it was in your eyes." One of the guards ran to pick up his rifle while the other still seemed shocked and confused and stood motionless.

"You said two reasons." He wheezed trying to catch his breath. "What's the other?"

"Oh that. You see this little lever here? This is what is known as the safety."

"What's a safety?"

"Jesus Christ, Jake," Sayid said in disgust. "Haven't you ever shot a gun in your life?"

"Only plastic ones filled with water. Look, I'm a Jew. Jews don't know about guns."

"Oh really," said Gretchen. "I guess you've never seen Israeli paratroopers in action."

"Those are Israeli Jews. I'm a diaspora Jew. You need a soldier, go get one of them. You need a dentist or accountant, I'm your man."

"Well, little Jewish man, let me show you. When the safety is in this position, the gun won't fire. It's so you don't accidentally shoot yourself. And when it's like this," she held up the gun so he could see as she flipped the lever, "it will." Gretchen whirled and fired off three shots at the guard with the rifle and two more at the other, all in a span of less than less than two seconds. They both crumpled to the floor. "See."

"Holy shit," Mia said.

"So much for Darrel and Darrel," Gretchen said and handed the gun, wisps of smoke still emanating from the barrel, back to Jake. "So be careful with it."

"Who the hell are you?" he asked.

"A friend of Ron Dougan."

"You know Dougan?" Mia asked.

Gretchen nodded.

"You know Dougan?" Jake, astounded, asked Mia.

"Who the hell is Dougan?" Sayid said.

Gretchen went over to the guards to make sure they were dead. "No time for that now. Someone may have heard the shots. We better be moving." She picked up the guards' weapons and handed one to Mia. "Do you know how to use this?" she asked her. Mia shook her head. "Well you know about the safety now. Just squeeze the trigger and please, try not to kill one of us. And here, take this as well." She handed back Mia's cell phone that had earlier been taken away. "Sayid, my pistol is over there on the floor. If you can't handle it, give it to me. Then let's get out of here." Jake remained bent at the waist still trying to get his breath back from Gretchen's blow. "Or would you rather stay here and wait for Aruf to return?"

"Did you have to knee me so hard? Why didn't you just say who you were and I'd have given you the damn gun?"

"Oh yeah, like you would have believed me. Consider yourself lucky. I was aiming for your crotch." She opened the door a crack and peeked out. Seeing the hallway empty, she proceeded. Jake looked at Mia and Sayid who, like him, both stood in disbelief. "What the hell just happened?" he asked.

Before either answered, Gretchen popped her head back in. "Care to join me?"

"Coming," Jake replied.

They moved as fast as they could, taking into account the poor lighting and the fact that at any moment, they might come under fire. When they reached the warehouse area, Gretchen paused to take out her cell phone and Mia took the opportunity to tend to Sayid. "Who are you calling?" Jake asked.

"The cavalry, as you Americans say. There's a door on the other side of this room that leads to the outside. You guys get out of here."

"What about you?" Jake asked.

"I need to go back. Aruf and the Pakistani are still here and I have to find out where Mustafa's gone."

Jake kept fidgeting with the safety on his Kalashnikov. "Who is Mustafa?"

"Sayid can tell you about Mustafa. He's the one I want." She went over to Mia. "How's he doing?"

"I'm a little worried about infection. What about those Chechens and their nukes?"

"You needn't worry about them."

"Why shouldn't we worry about them?" Sayid coughed as he spoke. He was perspiring much more profusely than any of the others.

"Because they're not Chechens."

"But I heard them speaking in Chechen," said Mia.

Gretchen laughed. "You know how to speak Chechen?" Mia shook her head. "If your boyfriend had been there, he could have told you that what you were hearing was Yiddish."

"Yiddish? Oy gevult." Jake had been listening in from behind. "So they were Jews?"

"Mossad. Fortunately Israeli Jews, not the diaspora kind. They can take care of themselves."

"And the nukes?" Jake asked.

"Just a tiny, tiny sample. Too little to do any harm, unless you swallowed it. I have been working on this for most of this decade. You and your girlfriend being here didn't help things."

"So are you an Israeli agent?"

"Do I look like an Israeli? I'm as Aryan as the Fuhrer could have wanted. My grandfather was indeed an SS officer at a concentration camp. He should have been hanged by the Allies. Instead he died comfortably in his bed in 1971 not more than fifteen kilometers from here. Officially, I'm BND, sort of our CIA, although I did live in Israel until I was nineteen and I was trained by them but that's a long story that we don't have time for now. Everyone ready to get moving?" They all nodded. "Okay. The door is at the far corner. When you get outside, you probably won't be able to get past the security fence, but there is a dumpster that you can hide in. Stay there until the police come. Got it?"

They started to move. "Be careful and try not to get shot," Gretchen said. "And Jake, remember which way that safety switch goes. Wait, Sayid, let me see you alone for a second."

"We'll wait over here," said Jake said.

"I'm so sorry about the hand."

"It's not your fault."

"Even so, I feel bad. Did you give Aruf the account number and access code?" Sayid shook his head. "Good. I'm proud of you. Listen, give me the numbers in case something happens. I'll make sure the money is safe."

He looked at her somewhat suspiciously. "Are you sure?"

"I have to be honest with you. None of us may make it out of here alive. If I have the codes, that gives us one more chance that the money will not just sit some place where only the Swiss will benefit." She pulled out a pencil and a scrap of paper. "Write down the codes and tell me where you want the money to go."

Sayid, slowly at first, wrote the numbers and named Jake's Water of Life foundation as the beneficiary. He handed her the slip. She glanced at the slip then summarily slapped Sayid's left cheek. "Idiot. You don't know for sure that this whole thing wasn't a set up. I could still have been an al-Qaeda operative and staged this escape to get you to give up this information. She crumpled the slip, tossed it into her mouth and swallowed it. "Trust no one. Now go."

Sayid scampered back to where Jake and Mia were waiting. "What was that about?" Mia asked.

"That is one crazy bitch."

"She's like Batwoman," said Jake.

"Who?"

"Ignore him," Mia said.

"For months I've detested her. I don't know who she's like, but she is beginning grow on me."

They exited the building and found themselves standing on a loading dock four feet above the street level and thirty feet from the perimeter fencing. A light fog was beginning to form making the landscape resemble a scene out of some low-budget horror movie. Sayid jumped first, followed by Mia. Jake, who always had a fear of heights, hesitated to make the leap even though the others had easily done it. "Come on already!" Mia whisper-shouted. He closed his eyes, which was not a good idea, and jumped, turning an ankle when he hit the asphalt.

"Shit," he barked.

"Quiet!" Mia scolded, then asked if he was okay. He nodded and pointed to the dumpster that Gretchen had told them to hide in. They ran across the pavement, Jake limping slightly behind the others, until they reached the container. Jake and Mia positioned two concrete blocks to stand upon enabling them to more easily open the lid. When they did, they discovered the inside was half full of refuse consisting mainly of discarded boxes and stinking of rotten food. Mia jumped back when two rats scurried out of the pile.

Jake's face contorted at the stench. "As much as it disgusts me to suggest, we should probably hide under the garbage in case someone comes looking."

"Yuk, Jake, I don't think I can. It's not the smell, but you know how I feel about mice and rats."

"Would you rather face Aruf?" asked Sayid.

"Good point," and she tossed her rifle into the dumpster and hoisted herself over the edge and into the pile. Jake put down his gun and locked his hands together forming a step to give Sayid a boost before following him into the trash. They lay silently under the garbage and waited. "This smell is disgusting," she whispered. "I think I'm going to puke."

"Already been there tonight," Jake responded. "Anybody know what time it is?"

Mia looked at her watch which glowed faintly green in the blackness of the dumpster. "Around four-thirty. How long have you been up?"

"I'm not sure, but a long time. At least twenty-four hours." Jake started shuffling through the trash. "Shit."

"What is it?" she asked.

"I put that rifle down when I helped Sayid get in here. I must have left it out there. Maybe I should go get it."

"It's too dangerous," she said. "The gun I was holding is somewhere in this crap. That will have to do." She took out her cell phone to provide some light and the three of them began rummaging through the trash.

"Here it is." Sayid picked up the rifle with his good hand. "Shine that light over here." He examined the examined the weapon closely as Mia held her phone above it. "Fuck."

"What is it?" asked Jake.

"There's a hole in the side rail just above the trigger. Gretchen must have hit it when she shot the guards."

"What does this mean?" she asked.

Sayid shook his head. "It means that the only thing this gun is good for is a paperweight. I should have taken that goddamn pistol when Gretchen offered it to me." Muffled sounds of gunshots in the distance rang out. "Turn off that phone and cover yourselves with the trash."

"Fuck. I wonder what's going on?" Mia whispered. "God, lying here under this shit and waiting. For the first time, I'm really scared."

"I'm too exhausted to be scared," said Jake. The sound of men running and shouting punctuated by the occasional burst of gunfire grew louder, which meant nearer. "Maybe not exhausted enough."

Sayid shushed the others to be quiet. They each tried to lie there as close as humanly possible to one thing they were trying to avoid becoming, corpses. The sound of squeaking metal echoed off the sides of the dumpster and it became obvious that someone was raising the lid. Through a space between two boxes, Jake could make out Aruf standing above and shining a flashlight across the top of the garbage pile.

As she willed herself to remain motionless, Mia didn't notice the rat that had managed to find its way under the cuff of her pants and up her right leg.

It appeared they were safe as Aruf started to close the lid. Then she realized the source of the sensation she felt on her inner thigh. It wasn't so much the muffled shriek she let out, for at that same moment a nearby burst of gunfire masked her scream but she couldn't control her desperate efforts to get the rodent off of her. The resulting movement of the garbage pile gave her away. Aruf flashed his light again into the dumpster. He began calling out in Arabic and fired several rounds into the garbage.

"God, I'm sorry – I'm sorry," her distraught voice cracking as she whispered.

"It's okay," Jake said, trying to calm her before pushing through the trash and springing to his feet. He held his hands above his head. "Don't shoot," he pleaded.

"Where are the others?"

"They went in a different direction."

"Really." Aruf fired off another burst from his gun, spurring Mia to jump up and raise her arms as Jake had done. "Where is Sayid? He is the one I want."

"Sayid went back to find Gretchen," Mia said. "He never gave us the account number, so we really can't help you."

Aruf glared at the both of them. "Then you are of no use." He started to raise his weapon but before he could aim it, he grabbed at his neck with both hands and dropped the rifle into the dumpster. His eyes bulged and his tongue dangled out of a corner of his mouth as he gasped for air. Sayid, who was about to follow Jake's and Mia's lead and give himself up, found Aruf's rifle lying beside him. He grabbed the gun. Athough it was difficult with only one good hand, he managed to fire a burst in Aruf's direction. Two bullets found Aruf's chest and he fell into the dumpster.

Gretchen's face appeared in the spot where seconds early Aruf had stood. "Is he dead?" she asked. Mia bent down to feel for a pulse on his neck. She looked up and simply nodded. "Shit."

"Jesus," said Jake, "you have no idea how glad I am to see you."

"I can't believe with that hand of yours, you were able to shoot straight," Gretchen said to Sayid.

"I'm a little surprised myself, but you sound disappointed."

"If I had wanted him dead, I would have used this." She held up her pistol.

"Why the fuck didn't you?" asked Jake.

"Because," she paused to help him climb out, "Aruf had information we could use, like where al-Yazid is. Uh, Jang, if you wouldn't mind, could you please retrieve my necklace from that shit-head's neck."

Mia removed the strand from Aruf and handed it to her. Gretchen put the necklace back on and started to pull Mia up. As she did, the rat fell from the bottom of Mia's pants and began scurrying over the cardboard. The sight caused Mia to lose her grip and slip back into the garbage. Gretchen fired a single shot from her Glock, killing the vermin.

"Get me out before I see another," she pleaded.

Once all three were out of the dumpster, they saw the parking area filled with dozens of cars with flashing blue lights on top. Scores of policemen, helmeted and dressed in black like combat soldiers, were milling about. Jake noticed two men lying face down with their hands cuffed behind their backs. "The Pakistani?" Mia asked.

Gretchen shook her head. "No, the little snot is in one of those bags over there."

Jake saw what he assumed to be three dead bodies being lifted into an ambulance. "Thank God you got him."

Gretchen disdainfully sneered. "As I said, he wasn't the one I wanted. I wanted al-Masri."

"Al who?"

"Saeed al-Masri, a namesake," answered Sayid as he brushed the trash off his clothes. "But his real name was Mustafa Abu al-Yazid, which is what I and people around me always referred to him by."

"Let me have another look at that hand." Mia unwrapped the makeshift bandage and tossed the bloody rag on the ground. "We should get you to a hospital." Gretchen agreed and Mia led him off to another ambulance.

"Al-Yazid is al-Qaeda's chief financial guy. I've spent most of this decade tracking him."

"The CFO, huh? I hadn't realized that these guys ran such a corporate operation. Too bad you never got the opportunity to take him out."

"It wasn't just taking him out, as you put it. We had set up this entire operation, with the fake nukes and all, so that we could trace their funds and freeze them. Unfortunately, it looks like Mustafa is back in the Middle East. And if not now, he soon will be after what went down tonight."

"And Abu al-Yazid has much higher goals than just being the money man." A new voice came from behind Jake's back. He turned to see who just joined conversation.

"Well I'll be...Ronald Dougan. I'm surprised to see you here."

"As am I to see you. You could have called me."

"You might have clued me in that Mia was working with you. It would have reduced a lot of stress."

"She didn't realize that Hassan was involved with al-Qaeda. She only came to us because she was concerned about the Chinese. I suppose she could have told you, but then again, you could just as easily have told her that you were working with us."

"The universe and stupidity. Still infinite," Jake lamented. "What about Hassan? Was he working with you also?"

"Sayid was my charge," Gretchen said. "And the simple answer is no. Sayid was deeply involved with al-Qaeda, although in the end, he rejected them."

"What will happen to him now?"

"Once he's healthy, he'll be debriefed and probably have to be detained for some period."

"Debriefed?" Jake said. "Is that your euphemism for things like water-boarding?"

"I suspect that Sayid won't need any enhanced interrogating. I know him pretty well. After all, I was engaged to him," she laughed. "Sayid has more to fear from his former comrades than he does from the BND."

"Or the CIA," said Dougan. "He may provide a wealth of intel that, who knows, may get us to bin Laden himself."

"That would be good," said Jake. "The best thing is that we ended Hassan's scheme, hopefully in time to stop it before too much damage is done."

"What scheme?" asked Dougan.

"You know, his manipulation of the credit markets in the U.S. – in the whole world really – designed to crash our economy. It could have done far more damage than these bastards ever did on 9/11. "

"That was real?" asked Gretchen.

"It's real all right. And it might have worked, but hopefully you guys can report to whoever it is that you report to, and the regulators will impose some sanity back into the markets."

"I'll see what we can do," replied Dougan.

TWENTY-FIVE

Early March 2008

The French bistro that Kat had opened on West 76th near Amsterdam had been in operation less than a month. It would not have existed were it not for Mia's financial backing. Mia had no part in running the restaurant but she liked having a place in the city that she could show up any time and be guaranteed her table, even if it was a twenty-plus dollar cab ride from her apartment in The Village. Tonight her dinner guests were a little more special and for the occasion, she had asked to Kat prepare something that wasn't on the menu. Jake, as always, was there, but so were Ron Dougan and Hannah Longworth, the FBI agent whom Jake had spent a tedious two weeks with at Pilgrim, and who now sported a modest diamond engagement ring on her left hand. Jake offered a toast to the betrothed couple over glasses of Dom Perignon, which prompted the inevitable question from Dougan as to when he'd ask for Mia's hand.

"I'm afraid she would say no. I mean, she's worth like twenty times what I am."

"But you haven't posed the question," Mia retorted. "Besides, the true number is closer to a hundred times, but isn't that why they invented pre-nups?

Dougan laughed. "I'm afraid you're trapped, Himmelfarb. But since you brought up the subject of money, let me give you this before I forget." He reached into his sport coat and handed Jake an envelope.

Inside was a cashier's check for two million dollars made out to the Water of Life Foundation. "Holy shit!" Jake exclaimed. "Where did this come from?"

"You can thank Sayid, or more to the point, the woman you knew as Gretchen Weitz."

"That's not her real name?" Jake asked.

"Maybe," answered Dougan, "but probably not. It doesn't matter since I can't imagine that you'll ever see her again. She did manage to get you a little bit of the half billion that Hassan bilked from al-Qaeda. Consider this your reward."

"I'm not sure it was worth it but I'll take it just the same. When I think back on it, I still can't believe how close Sayid came to pulling it off."

"His financial scheme?" Hannah asked. "Well you can rest assured that we've passed along what you told Ron and it will be taken care of, although I heard that apparently there are some legal hurdles. But I'm sure those will be worked out."

"You can thank our pro-business government for the hurdles," Jake commented. "Although I imagine that people in your line of work are all Republicans."

"We try and stay out of politics," Dougan said.

"Try, but we still have opinions," Hannah added. "Speaking of which, who do think the Democrats are going to choose?"

"I'm a Hillary supporter," Mia said. "Then again, I have a personal connection with the Clintons. Jake here likes Obama."

"You just want to see a woman," Jake interrupted.

"Well there hasn't been one yet, and I don't know when the next opportunity will come."

"You could say the same thing about a black man," said Jake.

Hannah groaned. "Okay, now you see why we avoid politics."

The group finished dinner and left the restaurant. "Where are you guys heading? Maybe we can share a cab?" Mia asked.

"My place," Hannah started to say. "I mean our place. It's over on the upper east side."

"It's a lot easier to get a cab on Broadway." Jake held his palms open to the sky. "Seems it has started to rain."

They had walked only a few feet before a burst of lightening followed almost instantaneously by a deafening thunderclap caused Mia to jump and clutch Jake's arm. "God, that scared me. I thought for a second it was a bomb going off."

"Just thunder," observed Dougan. "It is surprising to hear it this early in the year. You usually don't get thunderstorms until the temperature is more like April or May."

"Global warming," Jake offered.

"I thought we weren't going to discuss politics," said Mia. The group continued walking towards Broadway. A solitary figure stepped out from out of the shadows and blocked their way. He had a slight build and wore a hooded sweatshirt. Without saying a word he produced a handgun from his pocket. Everyone stopped. "Take it easy," Dougan said as he reached for his wallet. "We'll give you our money. There's no need for violence."

The man said nothing. He simply pulled back his hood and revealed his face.

Mia gasped, "Li Xuan." He fired a single shot into her chest. Hannah immediately drew her service weapon and emptied five rounds into Li. Mia, mortally wounded, collapsed in Jake's arms. "I'm so sorry," she managed to say.

"Sorry? Don't talk."

"At least we stopped Sayid's plan."

Those were her last words. Less than three weeks later, Bear-Sterns effectively went out of business when they agreed to a buy-out from JP Morgan Chase for $2 per share, more than ninety-three percent less than what the company was supposedly worth just two days before. Although the offer was later raised to $10, it was still the first large domino to fall. Within six months, Lehman Brothers went bankrupt, and AIG, America's largest insurance company, along with some of the largest financial institutions deemed "too-big-fail," needed a massive government bail-out to survive, precipitating the greatest financial crisis since the Great Depression almost seventy years earlier. $g = fi2$.